Larissa Ione is a *USA Today* and *New York Times* bestselling author. She currently resides in Williamsburg, Virginia, with her husband and young son.

Please visit Larissa Ione online:
www.larissaione.com
www.facebook.com/OfficialLarissaIone
www.twitter.com/Larissa Ione

By Larissa Ione

Lords of Deliverance series:

Eternal Rider
Immortal Rider
Lethal Rider
Rogue Rider

Apocalypse: The Lords of Deliverance Compendium

Demonica series:

Pleasure Unbound
Desire Unchained
Passion Unleashed
Ecstasy Unveiled
Sin Undone
Reaver
Revenant

Moonbound Clan series:

Bound By Night
Chained by Night

REVENANT

LARISSA IONE

piatkus

PIATKUS

First published in the US in 2014 by Grand Central Publishing,
A division of Hachette Book Group, Inc.
First published in Great Britain in 2014 by Piatkus

1 3 5 7 9 10 8 6 4 2

A CIP catalogue record for this book
is available from the British Library.

ISBN 978-0-349-40077-8

Printed and bound in Great Britain by
Clays Ltd, St Ives, plc

Papers used by Piatkus are from well-managed forests
and other responsible sources.

MIX
Paper from
responsible sources
FSC
www.fsc.org   FSC® C104740

Piatkus
An imprint of
Little, Brown Book Group
100 Victoria Embankment
London EC4Y 0DY

An Hachette UK Company
www.hachette.co.uk

www.piatkus.co.uk

For my readers. This journey has been a wild ride, and I want to thank you for sharing it with me. You are as much a part of the Demonica world as the characters who live in it. So here's to you, my friends. You've stuck with me to the end.

... Or is it?

Acknowledgments

Thank you. Sometimes those two words just aren't enough... but I have to try.

Writing the Demonica/Lords of Deliverance books has been a dream come true, and it never would have happened without Roberta Brown, who, in a stroke of genius, sent *Pleasure Unbound* to Melanie Murray at what is now Grand Central Publishing. Roberta and Melanie, thank you for taking a chance on what must have seemed like an utterly insane idea for a series.

Amy Pierpont, when you took me on as an author with *Desire Unchained*, did you have any idea that we'd end up playing with hellhounds, archangels, and the freaking Four Horsemen of the Apocalypse? Yeah, I didn't, either. Thank you for taking me to the next level and for dragging (sometimes kicking and screaming) every drop of writing talent from me. Seriously... thank you. We are a great team.

Speaking of teamwork, I need to acknowledge everyone I've worked with over the years to make this series a success... Irene Goodman, Melissa Bullock, Alex Logan,

Anna Balasi, Lauren Plude, Claire Brown, Madeleine Colavita, Jessica Bromberg, Marissa Sangiacomo, Jodi Rosoff, Leah Hultenschmidt, Kim Whalen. I know I'm forgetting someone, probably several someones, so I want to send a big thank-you to everyone at Hachette. You rock my underworld.

And finally, I'm in debt to my friends and family, all of whom have put up with the fact that I spend more time in the Demonica world than in the real one. Without your support, I couldn't have done it. But stick with me, because I promise this ride ain't over yet!

Glossary

Agimortus—A trigger for the breaking of a Horseman's Seal. An agimortus can be identified as a symbol engraved or branded upon the host person or object. Three kinds of agimorti have been identified and may take the form of a person, an object, or an event.

Council—All demon species and breeds are governed by a Council that makes laws and metes out punishment for their individual members of their kind.

Daemonica—The demon bible and basis for dozens of demon religions. It was once believed that its prophecies regarding the Apocalypse, should they come to pass, would ensure that the Horsemen fight on the side of evil. However, recent events in the three realms of Heaven, Sheoul, and Earth have rendered the *Daemonica*'s doomsday prophecies moot.

Dermoire—Located on every Seminus demon's right arm from his hand to his throat, a *dermoire* consists of glyphs that reveal the bearer's paternal history. Each individual's personal glyph is located at the top of the *dermoire*, on the throat.

Emim—The wingless offspring of two fallen angels. *Emim* possess a variety of fallen angel powers, although the powers are generally weaker and more limited in scope.

Fallen Angel—Believed to be evil by most humans, fallen angels can be grouped into two categories: True Fallen and Unfallen. Unfallen angels have been cast from Heaven and are earthbound, living a life in which they are neither truly good nor truly evil. In this state, they can, rarely, earn their way back into Heaven. Or they can choose to enter Sheoul, the demon realm, in order to complete their fall and become True Fallens, taking their places as demons at Satan's side.

Harrowgate—Vertical portals, invisible to humans, which demons use to travel between locations on Earth and Sheoul. A very few beings can summon their own personal Harrowgates.

Radiant—The most powerful class of Heavenly angel in existence, save Metatron. Unlike other angels, Radiants can wield unlimited power in all realms and can travel freely through Sheoul, with very few exceptions. The designation is awarded to only one angel at a time. Two can never exist simultaneously, and they cannot be destroyed except by God or Satan. The fallen angel equivalent is called a Shadow Angel. *See* Shadow Angel.

Shadow Angel—The most powerful class of fallen angel in existence, save Satan and Lucifer. Unlike other fallen angels, Shadow Angels can wield unlimited power in all realms, and they possess the ability to gain entrance into Heaven. The designation is awarded to only one angel at a time, and they can never exist without their equivalent, a Radiant. Shadow Angels cannot be destroyed except by God or Satan. The Heavenly angel equivalent is called a Radiant. *See* Radiant.

Sheoul—Demon realm. Located on its own plane deep in the bowels of the Earth, accessible to most only by Harrowgates and hellmouths.

Sheoul-gra—A holding tank for demon souls. A realm that exists independently of Sheoul, it is overseen by Azagoth, also known as the Grim Reaper. Within Sheoul-gra is the Inner Sanctum, where demon souls go to be kept in torturous limbo until they can be reborn.

Sheoulic—Universal demon language spoken by all, although many species also speak their own language.

Ter'taceo—Demons who can pass as human, either because their species is naturally human in appearance, or because they can shapeshift into human form.

Ufelskala—A scoring system for demons, based on their degree of evil. All supernatural creatures and evil humans can be categorized into the five Tiers, with the Fifth Tier comprising the worst of the wicked.

Vyrm—The winged offspring of an angel and a fallen angel. More powerful than *emim*, *vyrm* also possess an ability that makes their very existence a threat to angels and fallen angels alike. With a mere second of eye contact, a *vyrm* can wipe out a fallen angel or angel's entire immediate family. Considered extremely dangerous, *vyrm* are hunted ruthlessly, and so are their parents.

Watchers—Individuals assigned to keep an eye on the Four Horsemen. As part of the agreement forged during the original negotiations between angels and demons that led to Ares, Reseph, Limos, and Thanatos being cursed to spearhead the Apocalypse, one Watcher is an angel, the other is a fallen angel. Neither Watcher may directly assist any Horseman's efforts to either start or stop Armageddon, but they can lend a hand behind the scenes. Doing so, however, may have them walking a fine line that, to cross, could prove worse than fatal.

REVENANT

REVENANT

One

Revenant was one fucked-up fallen angel.

No, wait…*angel*. He'd only *believed* he was a fallen angel.

For five thousand fucking years.

But he wasn't an angel, either. Maybe technically, but how could someone born and raised in Sheoul, the demon realm some humans called hell, be considered a holy-rolling, shiny-haloed angel? He may have a halo, but the shine was long gone, tarnished since his first taste of mother's milk, mixed with demon blood, when he was only hours old.

Five thousand fucking years.

It had been two weeks since he'd learned the truth and the memories that had been taken away from him were returned. Now he remembered everything that had happened over the centuries.

He'd been a bad, bad angel. Or a very, very good *fallen* angel, depending on how you looked at it.

Toxic anger rushed through his veins as he paced the subterranean parking lot outside Underworld General Hospital. Maybe the doctors inside had some kind of magical drug that could take his memories away again. Life had been far easier when he'd believed he was pure evil, a fallen angel with no redeeming qualities.

Okay, he probably still didn't have any redeeming qualities, but now, what he did have were conflicted feelings. Questions. A twin brother who couldn't be more opposite of him.

With a vicious snarl, he strode toward the entrance to the emergency department, determined to find a certain False Angel doctor he was sure could help him forget the last five thousand years, if only for a couple of hours.

The sliding glass doors swished open, and the very female he'd come for sauntered out, her yellow-duckie-spotted blue scrubs clinging to a killer body. Instant lust fired in his loins, and fuck yeah, screw the drugs, she was exactly what the doctor ordered.

Take her twice and call me in the morning.

Since the moment he bumped into her at the hospital a few weeks ago, he'd been obsessed, and now, as Blaspheme's long legs ate up the asphalt as she walked toward him, he imagined them wrapped around his waist as he pounded into her. The closer she came, the harder his body got, and he cursed with disappointment when she dropped her keys and had to stop to pick them up. Then he decided she could drop her keychain as often as she wanted to, because he got a fucking primo view of her deep cleavage when her top gaped open as she bent over.

She straightened, looped the keychain around her

finger, and started toward him again, humming a Duran Duran song.

"Blaspheme." He stepped out from between two black ambulances, blocking her path.

She jumped, a startled gasp escaping full crimson lips made to propel a male to ecstasy. "Revenant." Her gaze darted to the hospital doors, and he got the impression she was plotting her escape route. How cute that she thought she could get away from him. "What are you doing lurking in the parking lot?"

Lurking? Well, some might call it that, he supposed. "I was on my way to see you."

She smiled sweetly. "Well, you've seen me. Buh-bye." Pivoting, her blond ponytail bouncing, she headed in the opposite direction.

Back to the hospital.

With a mental flick of his wrist, he changed into jeans, cowboy boots, and a NASCAR T-shirt, and turned his shoulder-length hair from black to brown before flashing around in front of her, once again blocking her path. "Maybe this is more to your liking?"

She gave him a flat stare. Clearly, rednecks weren't her thing.

Giving it another try, he went ginger and short with the hair, and decked himself out in a business suit. "How about this?"

More staring. He switched back to goth biker chic and stopped fucking around. "Come home with me."

"Wow." She crossed her arms over her chest, which only drew his attention to her rack. *Niiice.* "You get right to the point."

He shrugged. "Saves time."

"Were you planning to wine and dine me at least? You know, before the sex."

"No. Just sex." Lots and lots of sex.

He could already imagine her husky voice deepening in the throes of passion. Could imagine her head between his legs, her mouth on his cock, her hands on his balls. He nearly groaned at the imaginary skin flick playing in his head.

"Oh," she said, her voice dripping with sarcasm. "You're charming, aren't you?"

Not once in his five thousand years had anyone ever called him charming. But even uttered with sarcasm, it was the nicest thing anyone had ever said to him.

"Don't do that," he growled.

"Do what?" She stared at him like he was a loon.

"Never mind." Dying to touch her, he held out his hand. "You'll love my playroom."

She wheeled away like he was offering her the plague instead of his hand. "Go to hell, asshole. I don't date fallen angels."

"Good news, then, because it's not a date." And he wasn't a fallen angel.

"Right. Well, I don't fuck fallen angels, either." She made a shooing motion with her hand. "Go away."

She was rejecting him? No one rejected him. *No one.* Having been raised in a dungeon, with torture specialists and executioners as his playmates, he hadn't exactly learned the art of seduction or even polite conversation. But sex . . . he spoke that language fluently.

She started to take off again, and he blinked, confused. This wasn't right. He had his sights set on her, and she was supposed to surrender. This was something new.

Something…titillating. The confusion morphed into a sensation he welcomed and knew well; the jacked-up high of the hunt.

Instantly, his senses sharpened and focused. His sense of smell brought a whiff of her vanilla-honey scent. His sense of hearing homed in on her rapid, pounding heartbeat. And his sense of sight narrowed in on the tick of her pulse at the base of her throat.

The urge to pounce, to take her down and get carnal right here, right now, was nearly overwhelming. Instead, he moved in slowly, matching her step for step as she backed up.

"What are you doing?" She swallowed as she bumped up against a massive support beam.

"I'm going to show you why you need to come home with me." He planted both palms on the beam on either side of her head and leaned in until his lips brushed the tender skin of her ear. "You won't regret it."

"I already told you. I don't fuck fallen angels."

"So you said," he murmured. "Do you kiss them?"

"Ah…no, I—"

He didn't give her the chance to finish her sentence. Pulling back slightly, he closed his mouth over hers.

Strawberry gloss coated his lips as he kissed her, and he swore he'd never liked fruit as much as he did right now.

Her hands came up to grip his biceps, tugging him closer as she deepened the kiss. "You're good," she whispered against his mouth.

"I know," he whispered back.

Suddenly, pain tore into his arms as her nails scored his skin. "But you're not *that* good."

Before he could even blink, she shoved hard and ducked out from under the cage of his arms. With a wink, she strutted away, her fine ass swinging in her form-fitting scrub bottoms. She stopped at the door of a candy apple red Mustang and gave him a sultry look that made his cock throb.

"Give up now, buddy. I can out-stubborn anyone." She hopped into her car and peeled out of her parking stall, leaving him in the dust.

Blaspheme was practically hyperventilating as she drove through New York City's crowded streets, wishing she'd taken the Harrowgate to work today. But no, she'd chosen to drive from her Brooklyn apartment to Underworld General one last time, a sentimental stupidity that had not only taken up precious time, but had also run her straight into a fallen angel who somehow, after a short, unpleasant verbal exchange at the hospital a few weeks ago, thought they needed to date.

No, not date. Just have sex.

Her entire body heated at the thought, something it had no business doing.

But gods, he was incredible. Standing in the UG parking lot, he'd looked like a giant goth biker, wrapped in leather and chains, his massive boots sporting wicked talons at the tips. Even the backs of his fingerless gloves were adorned with metal studs at the knuckles. She'd always hated the tough-guy bullshit, but Revenant had fucking *owned* it. She got the impression that he lived his life that way; if he wanted it, he owned it.

Even when he'd changed his look, he'd still been like

something out of a magazine or movie. The cowboy boots had made her want to take up riding—not necessarily horses—and the business suit had given her some racy desk fantasies.

He wasn't going to give up on her, was he? At least not without a fight, which she was going to give him. She couldn't afford to have a fallen angel sniffing around.

Cursing, she fumbled through her purse for her cell phone and dialed her contact from the moving company. Sally answered on the second ring.

"Hi, Bonnie," Sally said, using the name Blaspheme adopted when dealing with humans. "The movers said they'll be done loading your belongings for the second shipment to London by the end of the day."

"Good," Blas said. It would be nice to go directly to UG's new London clinic directly, rather than having to use the hospital's emergency department Harrowgate to get there. "I should be there in an hour—" The Call Waiting beep interrupted. "Can I get back to you? My mother is ringing in."

Sally's cheerful, "No problem," was followed by a promise to make sure the movers would take wonderful care of Blaspheme's things and not to worry, and a moment later, Blaspheme's mother was on the other line.

"Hi, Mom." Blaspheme slammed on her brakes to avoid rear-ending a piece-of-shit truck that apparently hadn't come equipped with a turn signal *or* brake lights. She shot the driver the finger through her front windshield.

"Blas." Her mother's raspy voice came from right next to Blaspheme.

Screaming, Blas dropped the phone. "Holy shit!"

She opened her mouth again to yell at her mother for

popping into the car from out of nowhere, but when she saw the blood, her voice cut out. Deva, short for Devastation, sat in the passenger seat, every inch of her body covered in blood. The broken end of a bone punched through her left biceps, and a deep, to-the-femur burn had wrecked her right leg.

"Oh, gods," Blaspheme gasped. "What happened?"

Her mother lifted her trembling hand from her abdomen, and Blas got an eyeful of bowels poking through the laceration that stretched from just above her navel to her hip bone.

The injury itself was grave enough, but emanating from it was a vibe Blaspheme couldn't place. Whatever it was, it felt ... wrong. And very, very fatal.

"I—" Deva sucked in a rattling breath ... and slumped, unconscious, against the window.

"Mom!" The POS truck moved, allowing Blaspheme to whip the Mustang around a corner to head back to Underworld General. She automatically reached out with her mind to find a Harrowgate, and although she located one a block away, there was nowhere to park, and no way she could abandon the vehicle in the middle of the street.

Damn, it would be nice to be able to flash like the normal offspring of a fallen angel, but that wasn't an option for Blaspheme. It would never be an option.

On instinct, she gripped her mother's wrist and tried to channel healing energy into her, but that talent had been rendered useless a long time ago.

Dammit!

"Just hold on," she told her mom as she wove her car through the streets, narrowly avoiding sideswiping a cab and a messenger on a bike.

She whipped into the underground parking lot owned by the hospital but off-limits to the human public, drove through a false wall, and practically skidded to a halt in a stall in the hospital's hidden parking lot. Then, for a split second, an eternity, really, she hesitated.

Everyone at the hospital believed Blas was a False Angel. She could come up with an explanation as to why her mother wasn't the same species, but doing so could raise questions. Questions from the one person she was pretty sure was already suspicious.

A mere two weeks ago, Eidolon, Underworld General's founder and chief of staff, had been just cryptic enough in his warning to stay away from Revenant that she'd been paranoid ever since.

Her mother groaned, and suddenly, it didn't matter what Eidolon suspected. Her job…hell, her *life*… was at risk, but so was Deva's, and she couldn't let her mother die.

Quickly, she leaped out of the vehicle and ran through the sliding doors to the emergency department.

"I need help!" she barked, and in an instant, Luc, a werewolf paramedic, and Raze, a Seminus demon physician, rushed outside with a stretcher.

Moments later, Blaspheme was in an exam room, gloved up, while Luc checked vitals and Raze channeled his healing power into Deva. His scowl indicated that he was having trouble.

"Her stomach ruptured," he said. "Dammit, there's a tear in her transverse colon. I can heal the tears right now, but she needs surgery to clean out the contaminants." He looked over at Blas. "It's a huge risk, though. I know you're aware that False Angels don't respond well to anesthesia."

Shit. Blaspheme did not want to reveal the truth about her mother—and potentially, herself—but she couldn't compromise Deva's health by sending her into surgery with doctors who thought she was something other than what she was. Maybe she could play fast and loose with the facts and hope no one dug too deep.

Blas glanced up as she prepared an IV site in the back of her mother's hand. "She's not a False Angel."

Raze cocked an eyebrow. "But you said she's your mother."

"She's my *adoptive* mother," she lied. "She's a fallen angel." At least the second part was the truth.

Raze's hand jerked, and he cursed under his breath. She understood his shock; fallen angels were rare, they were mostly evil assholes, and as far as Sheoulic denizens went, they were at the top of the food chain.

Raze's ginger hair, longer in front than in the back, fell over his eyes as he leaned in for a closer look at Deva's abdominal wound. "This is strange."

Those weren't words you wanted a doctor to say. She attempted to summon her most useful FA ability, what was commonly called X-ray vision, used by False Angels to determine the health or virility of their potential victims. As a medical professional, Blas had found a better use for it.

Sadly, it barely flickered before snuffing out. Great. Another False Angel ability was failing. How long before they were all gone and her true identity was revealed?

"What's strange?" she asked.

"I can't heal her. Nothing's happening."

"What?" Blas looked up from inserting an IV catheter into Deva's vein to stare at the incubus. "Are you out of juice?"

He held up his right arm, which was covered in glowing glyphs from his throat to his fingers. "My power is at full charge. I'm telling you, it's not me. It's her."

The vibe. What if the weird vibe coming off her mother was somehow interfering with Raze's powers?

Raze glanced over at her. "Can you take a look inside her and tell me what's going on?"

"I just tried," she said. "I think I'm too emotional."

Raze nodded, apparently buying her bullshit story for the X-ray failure.

Her mother groaned, and her eyes flickered open. Her hand fumbled for Blas's. "Alone," she rasped. "I need to talk to you alone."

Blaspheme looked up at Raze. "Arrange for an OR. We'll get her into surgery right away. And page Eidolon. I want him on this." Despite Blas's fears of discovery, she needed him. As the most skilled, most experienced doctor in the entire underworld, Eidolon just might be the only one who could save her mother.

Raze and Luc took off, leaving her alone with Deva.

"Mom," she said quietly. "What's going on? What happened?"

"Angels," she said, and Blaspheme's stomach churned. "I was attacked by angels."

Which explained the vibe and Raze's difficulty healing her. Some angelic weapons caused injury that couldn't be repaired using supernatural means.

"Where were you?" Blaspheme squeezed her mother's hand when Deva's eyes closed. "Hey, stay with me. Where were you when they attacked you?"

"Home," she rasped. "They found me, Blaspheme."

A chill crawled up her spine. "They?" She had a

sickening feeling she knew who *they* were, and she prayed she was wrong.

Deva coughed, spraying blood. "I think…I think they were Eradicators. They found me." She sat up, clawing at Blaspheme's hand, desperation and terror punching through the haze of pain in her eyes. "Which means they're also looking for you."

Two

A high-intensity Satanic summons shrieked in Revenant's head as he stood atop Mount Megiddo, his lungs filling with hot, dry air.

Ignoring Satan's command, Revenant called out with his mind and voice to the highest-ranking archangel in Heaven.

"Metatron."

Nothing. A breeze whipped up a dust devil a few yards away, but other than that, nothing moved.

"Metatron!"

More nothing. Even the dust devil died a slow, agonizing death.

"Metatron!"

Fuck. He should have expected that he'd be ignored. The archangels had abandoned him thousands of years ago, so why the hell would they pay any attention to him now?

Assholes. All he wanted were some answers. Why had

they left him and his mother to rot in hell? Why didn't anyone, in five thousand years, tell him the truth before now? Before he regained his memories and got a promotion...thanks to his brother's "heroic" actions and Heaven's rule that what was done to one twin must be done to the other. And why hadn't they told him he was welcome in Heaven? After all, Reaver was allowed.

Because you aren't *welcome. You're evil. Corrupt.*

The Dark Lord's summons came again, this time blasting him so violently that pain drove him to his knees. Blood sprayed from his nose and ears, and as he gripped his head, he swore his skull was cracking.

Dammit, he was not ready to face Satan. Not that he was ever ready. No one in their right mind would happily drop everything to take a meeting with the Dark Lord. And now that Rev knew the truth about his past—or at least, about most of it—he had even less motivation to have a face-to-face with the king of all demons.

Satan had lied to Revenant for thousands of years, had even hinted that Rev was his son.

It was all bullshit, and Revenant wondered how things were going to change now that the truth had come out. One thing was certain; he wanted to be armed with as much knowledge as he could gather before he faced Satan, and only one person could give him the answers he sought.

Unfortunately, Metatron didn't seem inclined to provide any answers. Which left Revenant with only one other option.

Nursing his Satanic headache, he summoned a handful of books and flashed himself to the other side of the Earth, to the home of Thanatos, fourth Horseman of the Apocalypse.

As the Four Horsemen's Sheoulic Watcher, Revenant

was supposed to keep an eye on them. But since regaining his memories, he'd avoided them the way he'd avoided their father. Revenant's brother.

Reaver.

Every time they'd faced off since regaining their memories, they'd battled it out, and Revenant's words to Reaver during one particular encounter still echoed in his thoughts.

The very day I learned about you, I came to you as a brother. But all you saw was an enemy and a fiend. Now that is all you will ever see.

Revenant had cooled his jets a little since that moment a couple of weeks ago, but the fact remained that five thousand years ago, before their memories were wiped— the first time—Reaver had rejected Revenant, and to this day, nothing had changed.

So, no, Revenant wasn't expecting Reaver's four legendary hellspawns to welcome Uncle Rev with open arms.

And yet he was standing in front of Thanatos's Greenland castle, wondering if the Horseman known as Death would willingly open the door. More likely, Revenant would have to barge in and lay everyone out in order to get a peek at the rare books Thanatos hoarded in his library.

An electric tingle on the back of his neck alerted him to the presence of angels a split second before Harvester, the Horsemen's Heavenly Watcher, and Reaver himself materialized in front of him.

Fuck.

"Revenant." Harvester's smoky voice had always made Rev think of cat-o-nines wrapped in silk. She looked the part as well, dressed in tight black leather pants and stiletto-heeled boots, a lace corset binding her waist and plumping her perfect breasts. She looked a little paler than usual, though. Maybe getting her halo back after thousands of years of being a fallen angel wasn't sitting well with her. "Why are you here?"

"I'm the Horsemen's evil Watcher," he said, getting a kick at how his brother winced at the word *evil*. "I don't need a reason, nor do I answer to you."

"But you *will* answer to me," Reaver said.

Revenant snorted. Reaver had been sending out mental invitations to meet for weeks, but Revenant hadn't answered. He wasn't going to answer to his brother now, either.

"Bite me." He flashed himself closer to Thanatos's keep, but a heartbeat later, Harvester and Reaver were forming a wall in front of him again. How tiresome. "I was going to give Thanatos the courtesy of knocking on his door, but you're giving me no choice but to flash inside his residence with no warning. The last time I did that to a Horseman, I caught Ares and Cara in a…compromising position." He shrugged. "But whatever. Let's see what Thanatos and Regan are up to, shall we?"

He started to dematerialize, but Reaver snarled and gripped his arm, tethering him to his current position. "Just tell us why you're here."

Well, hell, maybe Reaver could give Rev the information he needed. He held up the copies of the Bible, the Quran, and the *Daemonica* in his hand. "I want to use Thanatos's library. I need to find references to Shadow Angels and Radiants, and these cryptic, contradictory tomes aren't exactly helpful."

Reaver released him and stepped back. "You want to know more about what you are. About what we both are."

"Um, yeah. Duh." Wasn't his brother a genius. "It isn't every day you get promoted to the highest-known rank of angel, and it isn't like there's a fucking manual anywhere that outlines the job description."

No, there had only ever been a handful of Shadow Angels like Revenant, and Radiants like Reaver, and since there could only be one of each in existence at any given time, there was no one to ask about it.

Reaver shrugged. "It's learn as you go."

"That's very helpful, *brother*."

Reaver made a sound of impatience and jammed his hand through his perfect mane of shiny blond hair. Revenant changed his hair color to match. Just to be a tool.

"We were given those ranks together," Reaver said. "And we can figure it out together."

Revenant laughed. "*Now* you want to play big brother? Now that I don't need you?"

"You *do* need me," Reaver said. "We need each other."

"Really," Revenant said flatly. "And why is that?"

Reaver's voice went low and ominous. "Because Lucifer is about to be reborn, and his birth is going to cause seismic shifts both on Earth and in Heaven."

This again? The Heavenly types got so worked up about reincarnated fallen angels. Okay, sure, Lucifer, as Satan's former right-hand man, wasn't your run-of-the-mill fallen angel, and the fallen angel carrying him, Gethel, had conceived him while she was still rocking wings and a halo. Oh, and in Lucifer's newest incarnation, he was also Satan's son. Which meant Lucifer was extra, *extra* special.

The asshole. In a few short years, he'd reclaim his place at Satan's side, and he'd spend his life trying to ruin Revenant's. It wouldn't matter that Rev would always outmatch him in sheer strength and ability—Lucifer would have Satan's ear and clout. When Lucifer gave a command, it would be followed as if given by Satan himself. Just the way it had been before Lucifer went and got himself killed a few months ago.

Revenant cleared his throat. "A, I don't care. B, when you cut off Gethel's wings to prevent Lucifer from being born fully grown, you reduced his powers, so stop with the 'it's the end of the world as we know it' bullshit."

Harvester shook her head, her black-as-pitch hair swinging around her slender shoulders. "It's not bullshit. We reduced Lucifer's powers, but he's still the most powerful fallen angel to ever be reincarnated. His birth will still send shock waves through the heavens."

"And," Reaver said grimly, "he's growing stronger every day. Harvester can feel him."

Ah, so maybe Lucifer's growth was the reason Harvester was looking particularly pale, and maybe a little gaunt. As Satan's daughter, she was connected to all of her siblings, born and unborn. Not that Revenant gave a shit. But it explained why Reaver did.

"It gets worse," Harvester said. "After Lucifer is born, he'll keep growing stronger, until he's reached the pinnacle of power. Once that happens, he and Satan can join forces—with you. The Trifecta of Evil, the archangels call it, because you'll be the three most powerful beings in Sheoul. Together, there would be very little that could stop you from wreaking hell on Earth. Reaver will be forced by the biblical prophecy to break all four of the Horsemen's Seals and kick off the End of Days."

The Heavenly types were as obsessed with Armageddon as they were with fallen angels. It was all getting old. "And what do you want me to do about it?"

Reaver folded his arms over his chest. "Give us Gethel before she gives birth to Lucifer."

Another rerun. Yawn. They should syndicate this shit. "Why should I?"

"Because you're an angel, Revenant. Metatron told me that we need to work together—"

"Did he now? Funny, because he won't even respond to *my* request to meet him. Has he sent me an invitation to Heaven? No? Then go rot." He flashed out of there, no longer caring about getting answers about what being a Shadow Angel meant. Besides, Satan's summons was buzzing around in his skull like an angry hornet.

Interesting how Satan had his knickers in a twist about talking to Rev, while Metatron couldn't be bothered to send even a Cherub with a message.

Fuck it. Heaven's concerns about Lucifer's birth had just made things interesting. If they were right and the Trifecta of Evil was the key to the newest round of apocalyptic threats, then Revenant was in a position of power.

And power was something he knew how to use well.

Revenant materialized inside Satan's mountainous underworld domain. He crossed the iron bridge—decorated with the hanging corpses of Satan's enemies—across a fiery moat to the gate of the king of demons' massive castle. He was given entrance immediately, an ancient fallen angel named Caim escorting him to the throne room.

The moment Revenant stepped inside the cavernous chamber, his blood chilled. Yes, the air temperature was frigid as fuck, but what turned the red stuff in his veins to gel was Satan himself, standing in the middle of what appeared to be dozens of human remains. His naked body was covered in gore, but otherwise, he could have been a male model, and the old saying that evil came in beautiful packages popped into Rev's head.

"It's good to see you, my son." Satan stepped outside the ring of carnage, and instantly, he was clean and wearing a black business suit with a clichéd silk crimson shirt and a fuck-ton of gaudy jewels.

"Don't call me that," Rev ground out. "My father was an angel."

"Sandalphon was a self-righteous jackass," Satan scoffed. "I've been a father to you in all the ways that matter."

So apparently, what mattered in a father was that they kept their sons in cages and forced them to witness their mother's abuse. Oh, and then, to be a truly good father, one should send said son to the Mines of Agony to slave for decades.

Revenant would have to remember that if he ever had a kid.

"Let's agree to disagree."

Satan smiled. The nasty smile that always came a split second before pain and death.

Oh, fuck—

Revenant didn't have time to brace himself before the Dark Lord, who had mutated into a wet, blackened, skeleton-like beast, had him pinned to the wall. Satan's claws dug deep into Revenant's rib cage, and pain rocked him hard as his blood pumped in thick spurts onto Satan's bony chest. Drool dripped out of the king of demons' mouth, which had taken on a snout-like form, his jagged sharklike teeth glistening as he gnashed them.

"Your promotion to Shadow Angel has made you the

most powerful being in Sheoul," he growled. "Except for me. It would take a thousand of you to harm me. A hundred thousand to destroy me." Indescribable pain carved out Rev's insides as Satan yanked his X-Man claws out of Revenant, ripping out his beating heart through his chest. "Keep that in mind."

Alpha demon display of power noted.

Revenant couldn't speak a word as he slid down the wall, his wobbly legs unable to support him. All he could do was watch as Satan bit into Rev's throbbing heart. Agony like he'd never known ripped him apart. He heard screaming, and through the black curtain of misery he wondered if someone else was being tortured, too. Maybe even killed; one of the surefire ways to kill an angel—of either fallen or fully haloed variety—was to eat their heart.

Then Revenant realized the screaming was coming from him.

The world spun around him in endless, miserable loops. Was he dead? Were the Grim Reaper's *griminions* even now on their way to reap his pathetic soul?

He didn't know how long he lay like a piece of meat on the cold floor before he heard the Dark Lord's voice calling his name.

Opening his eyes, he found himself lying in a pool of blood. Satan was back in his usual humanlike form, dressed in a nice suit and licking blood from his lips. Biting back a groan, Revenant shoved himself up to his knees. It took a lot more effort than he'd have liked.

"Why am I not dead?" Revenant muttered.

"You're a Shadow Angel. Only I, the entire contingent of archangels, or God himself can kill you, and it'll take a lot more effort than simply noshing on your heart."

Satan strode through the pile of remains on his way to the throne, his Italian leather shoes squeaking wetly in the gore. "And if you're entertaining any ideas of defecting to Heaven, let me just end that right now. Sandalphon might have fucked you into existence, but it's my blood that runs through your veins."

Revenant rubbed his chest, which was already mostly healed. He could even feel a new heart thumping around in there. "I don't understand."

"When you were a baby, you were fed your mother's milk, mixed with demon blood."

"I know that," he said. At least, *now* he knew that. Two weeks ago he'd been clueless.

Satan sank down on his throne made of bones. "Surely you didn't think we gave you something that came from some random demon's vein? It was my blood. I bound you to me and this realm forever. You are corrupt, and entering Heaven will corrupt the very realm. So yes, in all the ways that matter, I am your father."

Revenant's gut rolled. Being Satan's "son" didn't give him any special privileges. On the contrary, the king of demons expected more from his children, and when they let him down, he had a way of not taking it well. His daughter, Harvester, was living proof of that. If Reaver hadn't saved her from his clutches, she'd still be in Satan's dungeons, being tortured every minute of every day, in ways even Rev's sick mind couldn't comprehend.

"Is this why you summoned me, my lord? To dine on cardiac tartare and regale me with stories of my childhood?"

"Father," Satan said, his voice distilled into pure malevolence. "You will call me Father."

Fuck that. To do so would be a disgrace to his mother and his real father. "Why did you summon me?" Rev repeated.

"Why did you summon me, *Father*?" Satan snarled, and abruptly, pain squeezed Revenant's brain. "Say it."

Clutching his head, Revenant ground out, "Why did you summon me?" Another blast of pain struck him, and blood spurted from Rev's ears.

The king of demons got in his face. "*Say it*."

"*Why did you summon me?*" Revenant shouted, and then an unbelievable crush of agony drove him to his knees. Blood poured from his nose as his skull caved inward.

Satan went down on his heels in front of Revenant. "So fucking stubborn." A sly smile curved his crimson lips. "Call me Father. It's a new rule."

Damn him. Deep inside, Revenant trembled with the need to obey. The one thing that had been drilled into him almost since birth was the need to follow rules. Breaking them meant pain, and while pain was something Rev could handle, watching his mother suffer the most heinous torture because *he* broke rules was not something he'd been able to deal with.

She was long dead, but his need to follow rules was not, and Satan knew that.

Rev locked gazes with the demon in front of him. Someday he'd get revenge for everything Satan had done to Revenant's mother, but until then, he'd play Satan's game. After all, he needed to be trusted—and alive—to make the demon pay for years of suffering.

"Why did you summon me . . . *Father*?" he ground out.

Satan patted him on the head like he might do to a

child. "Very good. I brought you here for two reasons. First, Gethel needs medical attention. She's growing weaker as Lucifer grows stronger. He seems to be pulling energy from not only Gethel, but from all of my children as well. It's possible that, upon his birth, they will all die."

That definitely explained why Harvester had looked like microwaved shit. "So?"

Revenant didn't give a hellrat's ass if Gethel died. He'd hated her when she'd been an angel, and now, as a fallen angel pregnant with Satan's offspring, he hated her even more. She was a nasty piece of work who had broken a million rules while acting as the Four Horsemen's Heavenly Watcher. As for Satan's kiddos, Rev didn't like any of them, either. Reaver probably wouldn't be happy if Harvester died, though.

Satan pushed to his feet and returned to his monstrosity of a throne. "So...Gethel can't go to Underworld General."

No, probably not. The staff of UG was largely neutral to the goings-on between good and evil, but the people who ran the place, like that asshole Seminus demon, Eidolon, and his dickhead brothers and Sin, his half-breed abomination of a sister, had been personally affected by Gethel's machinations. There was no way they'd help her. Hell, she wouldn't make it out of the hospital alive.

"What do you want me to do about that?" Rev asked. "Unless I'm missing a memory of attending medical school, I'm useless."

"You will take a doctor to Gethel."

So basically, Rev would have to kidnap a doctor, because no one in their right mind would volunteer to treat a psychotic ex-angel who was carrying Satan's son... a son who also happened to be the reincarnated soul of Lucifer, the second-most-powerful fallen angel to have ever existed.

Until Revenant.

Except that Revenant wasn't truly fallen, so he supposed he didn't count.

Wiping away blood on his mouth with the back of his hand, Rev stood. "Is that all?"

"No." Satan steepled his hands in front of him and leaned forward. This wasn't going to be good. "Given all your new knowledge and memories, I question your loyalty," he said, and now the reason he'd been so insistent that Rev call him Father made sense. He was trying to reinforce ties... or *force* them, as it were.

"You have no reason to question my allegiance," Revenant assured him, even as his mind swirled with confusion about his place in the world. "I was born here. Raised here. Heaven abandoned me eons ago." He jabbed his finger into his sternum, directly over the still-raw wound from his cardiectomy. Or whatever the medical people called the violent removal of a heart from one's chest. "I did your bidding for five thousand years. Whatever you wanted done, even when your other minions wouldn't do it, *I* did it. So why in the realm of fuck would you doubt me, when you're the one who kept me and sent Reaver to Heaven when we were newborns in the first place?"

Satan studied him the way an entomologist might study an insect. "You think *I* sent Reaver to Heaven?" He laughed. The fucker actually laughed, because yeah, this subject was *hilarious*.

Revenant growled. "You gonna let me in on the joke?"

The amusement abruptly drained from Satan's expression, and Revenant suspected it was time to put his name on a heart transplant list.

"Heaven insisted on taking one twin, so I told *your mother* to choose," Satan said, and Rev's gut did a somersault. He didn't want to know this. "She refused, of course. Even after torture and two nights in my bed." He frowned. "I guess those two things are one and the same."

Nausea and impotent rage bubbled up inside Revenant, but he tamped them down, knowing full well that attacking the demon son of a bitch would only end badly. For Revenant.

"Finally, I had to threaten to torture her precious babies," Satan continued. "That's when she gave in and chose to send Reaver to Heaven. She knew, as I did, that Reaver was the good twin. The one worth saving."

A spear of pain punched through Revenant's chest, which he'd long thought was bulletproof. "No," he argued, forcing a steady, neutral tone, "she knew Reaver was the one who couldn't hack it down here."

Satan's bark of laughter sent hellrats scurrying from their hiding places. "Heaven wouldn't have taken you. Not with my blood in your veins. Why do you think no one came to rescue you? Your soul is corrupt, and it's only grown more corrupt. Tell me, since you gained your memory back and were raised to the status of Shadow Angel, has an agent of Heaven contacted you to welcome you into their loving embrace? No?" He bared his teeth. "And they never will. Mark my words."

Revenant had never known Satan to be able to read minds, but it was almost as if he'd looked into Rev's and latched onto his deepest, most secret desires. How could Revenant not want to know the place where he and Reaver should have been raised together? How could he not want to be accepted by those who had treated Reaver like family?

A silent snarl rose up in Rev's throat. Fuck it. He didn't need his angelic family. He had ... okay, so he didn't have a family. But hey, as long as he had a warm female in his bed, he didn't need one.

"I have no desire to be welcomed into Heaven's *loving embrace*." But would it kill them to offer? To at least give him the opportunity to choose for himself? He *was* an angel, after all, just like all the other haloed pukes. Just like his brother.

Satan's doubtful smile said he wasn't buying it. But then, the Prince of Lies was suspicious of everyone. Liars assumed everyone lied. "Then you'll have no problem proving it to me, right?"

"And if I do have a problem with it?"

"Then you should ask Harvester what happens when someone close to me pisses me off. Now, I'll ask you again: You'll have no problem proving your loyalty to me, right?"

Fuck. There wasn't an inch of Harvester's body, outside or inside, that Satan and his cronies hadn't peeled, smashed, cut, macerated, or defiled ... and she was his *daughter*. The only one of his offspring to be conceived while he was still an angel. He'd actually loved her, so what would he do to Revenant, whom he barely tolerated?

"Of course not," Rev ground out.

"Then here's the deal, son." His black gaze lifted to

the wall behind Revenant, where hundreds of bone rings hung from hooks.

Halos, they were called, because they'd been cut from the skulls of angels. Revenant's own mother was up there, hanging in a place of prominence and ultimate insult— from a mounted upside-down crucifix.

"You," Satan continued, "will bring me the head of an angel. And not some simpering, wimpy Cherubim or Seraphim. I want an angel from the Order of Thrones or higher."

As far as strategies went, that was brilliant. The moment Rev killed an angel in cold blood, Heaven would close all its doors to Revenant.

What Satan didn't know was that Heaven hadn't opened any doors to begin with.

Satan slammed his fist down on the arm of his chair— which, fittingly, had been fashioned from human arm bones. "Your answer."

Revenant bowed his head. He'd never liked angels anyway. "Your will is mine."

"Is it?" Satan's eyes glowed with unfathomable evil as he locked gazes with Rev. "Do not fail me, my son. You've seen how I punish traitors, but what I've done to them will be child's play compared to what I'll do to you. Understood?"

"Understood."

"Good. Because taking out a single angel is just the beginning. As a Shadow Angel, you can go places I can't and take out entire *legions* of angels. Your power will be my sword, and your primary objective will be to decimate Heaven's angel population, including my darling daughter, Harvester," Satan said, and Rev saw his relationship with Reaver go from antagonistic to full-blown Cain and Abel. "You have until Sanguinalia to bring an angel's head to me."

Sanguinalia, one of Sheoul's most important holidays, would take place in a week. Which meant Revenant had seven days to get everything he wanted from Heaven before he killed an angel and confirmed to everyone that he'd deserved to be the twin who was left behind in Sheoul after his mother gave birth.

"Go," Satan continued. "Take care of Gethel. I want Lucifer to be born healthy and powerful. I'm eager to have him at my side again."

That fucker. Lucifer had been the biggest bastard, next to Satan, Revenant had ever known. Rev had partied for a week straight after Reseph tore Lucifer apart and sent his soul to Sheoul-gra. Now the dickhead was going to be reincarnated, and in a few short years, he'd replace Revenant as the second-most-prominent being in Sheoul.

Unless...

No. Rev couldn't go there. If he destroyed Lucifer, his suffering would become legend. Generations of demons would share stories of his misery while they toasted marsh rats around the campfire.

So no, Revenant couldn't kill Lucifer. Not if he wanted to live.

But someone else...he grinned.

Because Revenant might not be in a position to prevent Lucifer's birth, but he knew someone who could.

Three

Deva's surgery, performed by Eidolon and his sister-in-law, Gem, lasted ten hours. Blaspheme had begged to scrub in, but Eidolon had relegated her to "the box," where she could do nothing but observe through a glass window. She hadn't doubted that her mother was in the best hands in the world, but she'd still hated being so helpless.

Now, as her mother was being wheeled into post-op, Blaspheme waited anxiously for Eidolon's surgery report.

He met her in the staff room outside the OR, and the moment she saw the bleak expression on his face, her heart plummeted to her feet.

"What is it?" she asked. "What's wrong?"

The stethoscope around his neck bounced against his broad chest as he walked toward her. Like all sex demons, the black-haired doctor was impossibly gorgeous, something she'd have appreciated on any other day. Something she *did* appreciate on any other day. He was mated, but Blaspheme wasn't blind.

"The surgery went well," he said, a note of compassion softening his matter-of-fact voice.

"But?"

He jammed his hands into the pockets of his lab coat. "I was able to set her broken arm, repair her lacerated stomach, colon, and liver, and treat the burn on her leg, but I couldn't use my healing ability. Something interfered with my power."

"I know." She looked down, remembering the cup of coffee in her hand, and took a drink. It was cold and stale, but it felt good going down her parched throat. "She tangled with an angel."

One dark eyebrow shot up. "That explains it."

"Will she be okay?"

Silence. It only lasted for a heartbeat, but it was enough to curdle the creamed coffee in her belly. "I don't know. I repaired what I could, but whatever weapon the angel used scrambled her insides. It actually reversed my healing ability and caused more damage, which means it was a specialty weapon, like grimlight or haloshiv."

Which meant a specialty angel had wielded the weapon. A specialty angel like an Enforcer. Or, as Deva claimed, an Eradicator, Heaven's extermination specialists. With the ability to see through enchantments and sense things other angels couldn't—like angel DNA inside someone who shouldn't have it—they were Enemy Number One to beings like Blaspheme.

"So what are you saying?" She knew, but she needed to hear it. Needed it to be real, or she'd live in a world of make-believe where everything was happy-happy and her mother would recover all by herself, the way fallen angels always did.

"She's still in danger," he said. "I'll look into some alternative treatments, but for now, it's a waiting game. I'm sorry, Blaspheme. I wish I had better news."

"Thank you," she said numbly. Her brain had shut down after the word *danger*, leaving her disoriented and reeling. "I, ah...I want to see her."

"Of course." Eidolon rested a comforting hand on her shoulder. "If you need anything, let me know. Take off all the time you want."

She gave a noncommittal nod, but she wouldn't be taking any time off. She had nothing else to do but work, and as long as her mother was in the hospital, she'd be here, too. Besides, she loved her job, had never felt as needed as she did when she was elbow-deep in someone's chest cavity. There was just something about giving life.

No number of saved lives can give back the one you took.

The nagging voice in her head was always there to keep her feet on the ground. Technically, *she* hadn't taken a life. But one had been sacrificed for her, and she was going to honor that. She had no doubt, in fact, that her guilt had been the reason she'd chosen a career in medicine.

Leaving Eidolon, she hurried to the recovery room, where her mother was hooked up to machines Blaspheme could operate blindfolded, but right now she couldn't even remember what they were called.

"Blas." Deva's voice was barely a whisper.

Blaspheme gripped her mother's pale hand and sank into the chair next to the bed. "Don't talk. You need to rest."

Ignoring her, Deva opened her eyes, the vivid aqua now hazy with pain and meds. "Where ... where am I?"

"You're at Underworld General. Don't worry, you're safe. Angels can't enter."

The problem was that Devastation couldn't stay here forever, and clearly, she couldn't return home. She could find a place to stay in Sheoul, but if Heavenly angels had located her, it wouldn't be long before fallen angels such as Destroyers, the Sheoul equivalent of Eradicators, found her as well ... and then there wouldn't be a safe spot for her in the entire universe.

Vyrm, the forbidden offspring of an angel and a fallen angel, weren't tolerated by Heaven nor hell, and neither were their parents. After nearly two hundred years of frequent moves, name changes, and close calls, Blaspheme was all too aware of that fact.

"How ... bad?"

Blaspheme couldn't lie to her mother—hell, she wasn't the best liar to begin with. "The surgery went well," she said. "But there are some complications from whatever weapon you were attacked with."

As if on cue, Deva inhaled a rattling breath, and on the exhale, blood sprayed from her nose and mouth. "The angel ... he used ... grimlight."

Shit. Grimlight, a weapon used exclusively by Eradicators, confirmed what Eidolon had said. Blas reached for a bedside tissue and gently dabbed away the blood on her mother's face as she let the reality of the situation sink in. Heaven had found her mother, which meant they couldn't be far behind Blaspheme.

"I'm going to die, Blas."

"No." She squeezed her mom's hand. "I always knew

this day could come. I've done a lot of research into grimlight—"

"The damage . . . it can't be repaired."

"I know, but you *can* survive it."

"I'll be weak." Deva coughed again. "A shell of myself."

"You could never be weak," Blaspheme murmured.

Damn, but Blas wished she could use her angelic or fallen angelic abilities to at least attempt to heal her mother, but the spell that disguised her as a False Angel was still blocking her powers even as the FA ones failed. Why her mother had chosen a False Angel as her cover, Blaspheme didn't know, but as far as wimpy demons went, False Angels were at the top of the list.

For the millionth time today, she glanced down at the barely visible scar on her wrist, the one she'd gotten just moments after her birth, when her mother performed the ceremony to conceal Blaspheme's *vyrm* identity within a False Angel aura. Practically speaking, she had been a False Angel, with all of the strengths and weaknesses inherent to the species.

But now, two hundred years later, the aura was wearing off, and when the scar was gone, so would be Blaspheme's cover. Oh, as a *vyrm* she'd be far more powerful than a False Angel, with the ability to flash wherever she wanted, summon fiery weapons, heal almost anyone of thousands of afflictions . . . but she'd also be hunted into the ground.

"Daughter," Deva rasped. "You need to perform the ritual. Before I die, I need to know you're safe." She sighed. "And I was so looking forward to Sanguinalia."

Blas patted her mom's hand and stood. "Stop being

dramatic," she said with a lightness she didn't feel. "You aren't going to die. And we already discussed this. I'm not going to sacrifice a False Angel so I can maintain my disguise. I'll find another way. Another way to save both of us."

Before her mother could argue, Blas kissed her on the forehead and got the hell out of there. She had work to do and frankly, she didn't want to dwell on the fact that between Deva's injuries and Blas's rapidly fading disguise, they could both be dead by the end of the week.

Blaspheme got a fitful night's sleep in an on-call suite close to her mother's room. After a groggy breakfast, a pot of coffee, and a quick check to verify that her sleeping mother was doing fine, she got to work.

Now she was just trying not to dwell on things out of her control as she put a series of stitches in a Huldrefox's lacerated scalp. The furry female had gotten into it with a werewolf, and from the number and severity of her wounds, it looked like the Huldrefox had been less of a worthy opponent and more of a chew toy.

"Doctor?"

Blaspheme yelped, startled by a dark-skinned lion-shifter nurse named Mbali as she pulled back the cubicle's fabric curtain just enough to poke her head inside. "My, you're jumpy today," Mbali said. "You okay, *imayama*?"

Blas had no idea what language *imayama* represented, but she knew it meant healer in Mbali's native tongue. She wondered how Mbali's native tongue would translate *No, I'm not okay. I think there's an Eradicator around every corner.*

"I'm fine, Mbali," Blas said, concentrating on leveling out her breathing and heart rate, something she'd had to learn to control during emergencies and surgery. "What do you need?"

"Dr. Morgan sent me to tell you that the staff meeting is being postponed until tomorrow. She didn't say why."

Blaspheme had a feeling she knew why. As the busy co-director of Underworld General Clinic with Blas, Gemella Morgan valued her time with her husband, Kynan, and daughter, Dawn. Her dedication to her family and to the hospital and clinic made her a hell of a doctor as well as a devoted wife and mother.

It wasn't often that Blaspheme experienced jealousy; she was thrilled to dedicate her life to medicine. But every once in a while she couldn't help but envy Gem's family life...something Blas couldn't have as long as she was forced to pretend she was something she wasn't.

"Thank you, Mbali." She snipped the suture thread and swabbed the surgical area behind the Huldrefox's ear. "Can you finish this up for me? I need to check on our fallen angel patient."

With the exception of Eidolon, Luc, and Raze, no one knew that Deva was Blaspheme's mother, or even her adoptive mother, and she planned to keep it that way. There was no sense in giving anyone the tools to put two and two together to equal *vyrm*.

Mbali happily took over while Blaspheme headed down the hall to one of Underworld General Clinic's recovery rooms, where her mother had been brought to keep her close to Blaspheme. Deva was still asleep, her short blond hair a messy mop sticking out from covers she'd pulled up to her eyeballs. Blas checked her vitals, adjusted her saline drip, and finished with a light kiss on her mom's cheek. Her mother was evil in ways Blaspheme couldn't understand, but she didn't doubt how much her mother loved her.

A three-toned beep indicated that someone had arrived through one of the two entrances to UGC, but unless her pager went off, she didn't have to—

Her pager went crazy in her pocket, bouncing around in the fabric of her lab coat. Wondering what was up, she stepped into the hall . . . and ran right into Revenant's rock-hard chest.

She leaped back with humiliating squeak number two for the day. Damn him! Did he enjoy scaring the crap out of her? She supposed she'd rather run into him than an Eradicator, but geez, he'd just taken a hundred years off her life. And was it necessary to wear all that leather and metal like some sort of armor? Inappropriately *sexy* armor?

"Are you a professional lurker, or what?" She casually but quickly closed the door behind her.

Revenant ignored her, craning his head to get a peek as the door shut. "You're treating a fallen angel?" he asked. "Must have been one hell of an injury to require medical attention."

"I can't discuss patients with you," she said, summoning her don't-screw-with-me doctor voice. "And how do you know she's a fallen angel?"

He cocked an ebony eyebrow. "I can smell fallen angel blood."

Oh, crap. She broke out in a cold sweat. Hopefully he couldn't smell *that*. Time to get rid of this too-handsome bloodhound before he caught a whiff of *her* fallen angel— or angel—blood through her fading disguise.

Clearing her throat, she queued up her doctor voice again. "What do you want?"

She scrounged her pager out of her pocket, and, somehow, the words that flashed on the screen didn't surprise her.

That big asshole fallen angel is here to see you. And then, *Is he single?*

"What do I want?" He shrugged. "I want you."

She groaned even as her body sparked to life. Her False Angel enchantment might be wearing off, but the False Angel sex drive was as fully engaged as ever. Funny how she was losing the other FA powers, but she was still horny as hell, and self-gratification was becoming less and less satisfying.

"Not this again." What was his fascination with her, anyway? Shoving him aside, she started down the hall. "I said no."

He caught up with her, matching her gait as he walked beside her. "Let me put it another way. I have a medical case for you."

Halting, she eyed him suspiciously. Damn, he was tall. He put her five feet eleven inches to shame. "What are you talking about?"

"I'm talking about a female fallen angel. She's pregnant, and she could use a checkup."

She snorted. "You knock her up?"

He recoiled so fast she considered grabbing a cervical collar in case he'd given himself whiplash. "The very idea is repulsive."

"What, the idea of being a father or screwing a fallen angel?"

"I have no problem screwing angels of any kind," he

said, his voice a low purr, and she knew he was hinting at the fact that she was, at least to outside eyes, a False Angel. "But this particular one has been…damaged."

"Is that why she needs medical help?"

"It's why she needs psychological help, but no." He waited for a male nurse pushing a cart of supplies to go past before saying, "She needs a medical doctor because her pregnancy isn't exactly routine." He cocked his head, his thick mane of blue-black hair brushing his shoulders. "May I touch you?"

Whoa. Talk about whiplash. Before she could protest, he reached out, brushing a knuckle over her cheek. Every nerve ending in her body sizzled with awareness. How did he do that so easily?

She stepped away, awkwardly enough that he had to know he'd affected her. "Why did you do that?"

"I've been told I have no impulse control or sense of social boundaries." He casually rolled one big shoulder. "At least I asked first."

"Gee, give the guy a medal." Gods, she loved the way he smelled, like musk and leather and a sinful hint of brimstone. "Tell your fallen angel friend to come by. We're open twenty-four seven." Her fingers cramped, and she realized she'd been holding her pager in a death grip. Tucking it back into her pocket, she gave him a see-ya smile. "I have work. Thanks for stopping by."

She started for the front office, but he snared her arm and swung her back around. "She can't come here. I need to take you to her."

"Sorry," she said, jerking out of his grip, "but I don't make house calls. I can recommend someone who does—"

"I need you."

Okay, now she was nearing the end of her patience. "Did you hear what I just said? I don't make house calls. No exceptions."

"You will make an exception for this patient."

Her jaw dropped, and she stared at him, dumbfounded. Who did he think he was to come barging into her place of work and demand she drop everything just because he said to? "I will do no such thing."

"I would consider this a personal favor. Which means I would owe you."

Hmm. Now that was something to think about. She didn't want to be indebted to anyone, let alone a fallen angel like Revenant, but to have *him* owe *her*...that was worth considering. She didn't know much about him, but she did know he was the evil Watcher for the Four Horsemen of the Apocalypse, which meant he was a fallen angel of high standing—and power. And with the craziness that was going on with her mother right now, Blas never knew when she'd need a favor.

"Why me?" she asked.

"Because I want you," he said simply. "And you want me."

Good Lord, he was delusional. "I don't want you."

He smiled tightly. "You will."

"You know," she sighed, "the more you say shit like that, the less likely it is that I would ever want you."

"You don't appreciate confidence?"

"I don't appreciate arrogance. There's a difference."

"And what is the difference?"

"Confidence is arrogance without an asshole."

He laughed, and holy hell, he was stunning when he

did that. "Sounds uncomfortable. I'll keep my arrogance, thank you very much."

Jamming her hands on her hips, she glared. "You still haven't said why you want me to treat your friend."

"She's not my friend. And it has to be you because you're the only doctor I know."

"If knowing a doctor was the only criteria people used for choosing one, very few people would get medical care."

He bared his teeth. "I don't give a shit about other people. I'm choosing you because I don't know anyone else."

He barely knew *her*. But she sensed...she wasn't sure. Maybe he was one of those people who bonded quickly with others. Or maybe he didn't trust easily, and she'd given him enough straightforward attitude that he thought he could put some confidence in her abilities. The latter sounded most likely.

And why was she diagnosing his mental instability, anyway? She was done arguing with him. But...something he'd said intrigued her. "Did you say the patient is a fallen angel? Is the child's father a fallen angel as well?"

"You could say that."

Since all fallen angels had once been Heavenly angels, the offspring of two fallen angels would be *emim*, neither angel nor fallen angel, wingless, but possessing a number of fallen angel powers. During her research into ways to repair the damage caused by grimlight, she'd found a necromancer's scribblings theorizing that *emim* stem cells could possibly deliver a punch of extra healing power to otherwise untreatable conditions in fallen angels like her mother.

Revenant might just have delivered the answer to Blaspheme's prayers.

"Fine," she muttered, telling herself this would all be worth it when either he repaid the favor or she healed her mother. "Give me a minute to grab an obstetrics jump bag."

"Excellent." Triumph lit his expression. "I'll meet you at the main entrance."

He took off, and as she watched his fine, leather-clad backside disappear down the corridor, she wondered about the mistake she'd just made. Because it wasn't a question of *if* she'd made a mistake. She'd crossed that particular bridge a mile back.

No, the question now was how big of a mistake it would prove to be.

Four

Blaspheme showed up at the clinic's main entrance five minutes later, still wearing bright purple scrubs and a pristine white lab coat with the Underworld General caduceus embroidered on the chest pocket. A teal stethoscope hung around her neck, and Revenant wondered how his heart would sound if she listened.

He figured it would either stop completely, or it would do a hummingbird on the back of his rib cage. That was assuming it had fully grown back after Satan made a meal of it.

No, wait…it had definitely regenerated, because as Blaspheme sauntered through the waiting room toward him, an orange duffel slung over her shoulder and her slender fingers toying with the stethoscope, he felt his pulse hammer faster with every step. Her blond hair was pulled into a high ponytail, and it swung wildly, the tip playing peek-a-boo with him from behind her waist.

Damn, he'd love to bend her over, wrap that thing around his fist, and—

"You ready to go?" she asked, getting right down to business.

He answered by shoving open the steel door. He'd discovered that there were only two ways into the clinic; via the Harrowgate from the hospital in New York, or through the door from an abandoned London tube platform. A spell prevented anyone from flashing directly into and out of the clinic, but as a Shadow Angel, he could pop in or out anytime he pleased. For now, however, he wanted to keep his status a secret. One thing he'd learned about power was that the more of it you had, the fewer people you wanted to know about it.

Some asshole out there always wanted to either take it or exploit it, as Satan had proven today when he announced his plan to use Rev as an angel exterminator.

They stepped out onto the platform and into the stale underground air. Behind them, the clinic door closed and melted into the background, concealing itself from human eyes. A few feet away, the shimmering curtain of light from the Harrowgate built into the tunnel wall ahead solidified, and a moment later, a white-skinned *blanchier* demon stumbled out, cradling his clearly dislocated arm.

Blas rushed to hold the clinic door open for him. "See Liz at the front desk. She'll get you fixed up in no time."

The demon muttered his thanks and disappeared through the doorway.

"You really do like this job, don't you?" Revenant asked, baffled by the desire to help people. Most people were assholes. They were much more likable when they were dead.

"I wouldn't do it if I didn't love it."

Folding his arms over his chest, he studied her, which, really, was no hardship. "So, when you were a baby False Angel, this was what you dreamed of doing when you grew up?"

"When you were a baby angel, did you dream of committing an offense so heinous it would get you kicked out of Heaven to become a fallen angel?" she shot back.

"Ouch," he murmured. "I didn't realize False Angels were venomous."

She rubbed her eyes, and he suddenly felt like a shit, even if he wasn't sure why. He wasn't used to having regrets.

"Sorry," she said. "I'm dealing with some family issues that are making me grumpy."

"Must be something in the air," he muttered.

"Like a virus? *That* I could deal with," she said, and he liked that she would rather deal with viral infections than people. Very cool. But odd for a False Angel. "Where are we going?"

"Can't tell you." He held out his hand, but she eyed it like what he'd offered her was a *croix viper*. "You need to take it. I'm going to flash us there."

Hefting the bag more securely on her shoulder, she glared. "If you get me killed..."

"Trust me," he said. "Nothing can harm you while you're with me. And if anyone tries, I will make them scream until their skulls explode, Humpty Dumpty style. Not even your great Eidolon and all the king's horses will be able to fix that."

"That's so...touching," she said flatly. "And graphic."

"I have mad skills when it comes to touching females."

She didn't seem to appreciate his double entendre, but then, she seemed pretty annoyed. Maybe he could get her a deadly virus to play with. With his new Shadow Angel powers, creating a plague should be a snap. "Give me your hand."

She did so, reluctantly, but he still felt a sizzling tremor of awareness shoot up his arm. Savoring the sensation, he flashed them to a region adjacent to Satan's, a region defined by its lava flows and acid lakes, an inhospitable environment in which few could survive. It was also one of the regions that was impossible for any Heavenly angel to get inside. The manor Satan had built here as his "vacation home" was so tightly guarded that only Revenant and a handful of his most trusted cronies could enter.

They materialized in the grand living room, which was little more than a giant fireplace. Four lit hearths took up four walls, and in the middle, a chaise lounge faced a torture rack.

A torture rack from which some poor shapeshifter hung, his lifeless, broken body dangling loosely from the wooden slats.

"What the hell." Blaspheme jerked her hand out of his, her horrified gaze glued to the dead guy. "Where are we?"

"Squeamish? I wouldn't have expected that of you."

She rounded on him with a snarl, and bless her little False Angel heart, she was pissed. "I'm a doctor for a reason." She threw her arm out in the dead male's direction. "That is not cool."

She started toward the stiff, no doubt to check his vitals, but Rev stopped her with a hand on her shoulder. "Trust me, he's long dead."

He released her before she shrugged away from his

touch; for some reason, the thought of her rejecting him again made his chest ache.

Idiot.

"Take me back to the clinic," she snapped, but that wasn't going to happen. He needed Lucifer to die, and he couldn't do it himself.

He was spared the ugliness of having to refuse her request when a solid gold door at the other end of the room opened with an ominous creak, and a very pregnant female entered, her tattered white gown stained with blood and who-knew-what-else. Her stringy hair fell in matted clumps around her thin shoulders, and the dark circles raccooning her eyes made her pale face appear almost ghostlike.

"Oh, my," Blaspheme whispered.

"I'm assuming this is my new obstetrician?" Gethel smiled, but even though he suspected her smile was genuine, her thin, chapped lips and sharp, blackened teeth only made it come off as creepy.

And Revenant had an extremely high threshold for what he considered to be creepy.

"I'm not an obstetrician," Blaspheme said, sounding impressively authoritative and shit, "but I'll do what I can to help you." She started toward Gethel. "What's your name?"

Gethel sank down on the chaise. "Revenant didn't tell you?" She gave him a look of mild consternation, which he blew off. "I'm Gethel. And you are?"

"I'm Blaspheme." She slowed as she approached the chaise. "Gethel . . . that sounds familiar."

Crap. This wasn't going to be good. Revenant helped Gethel ease back on the pillows, not because he gave a crap about her comfort, but because he needed Blas to not feel threatened. And if she realized who Gethel was and who the baby she was carrying would grow up to be… yeah, he needed to play this off as no big deal for a while.

"Of course it sounds familiar, you pathetic fool," Gethel snapped. She glared at Revenant. "You brought me a quack with no understanding of the earth-shattering momentousness of this situation?"

Blaspheme dropped the duffel with a thud. "Quack? I'll have you know that I've been working at Underworld General Hospital for over five decades now, and I've worked my way up from paramedic to medical doctor in charge of UG's new London clinic. As far as the rest, I'm sure the *earth-shattering momentousness* of your pregnancy is important to you, just as it is with every mother, and I'll treat you and your child with equal care."

"Bitch," Gethel hissed. "You will treat me—" Revenant clamped his hand around her throat and cut her off cold.

"You will speak to Blaspheme with respect," he growled.

"Revenant!" Blaspheme grabbed his wrist and yanked it away. "How about we set some ground rules." She jammed a finger at Gethel. "You. Call me a bitch again, and you can find a doctor elsewhere. And you"—she stabbed Rev in the chest with the same finger—"try to strangle a pregnant female again, and I'll take a scalpel to your balls. Got it?"

He grinned. Damn, her fire was awesome. Usually False Angels were more timid. He wondered if she'd be less aggressive outside of work. More pliable. Easier to get naked.

Gethel jackknifed into a sit. "You still have no idea to whom you're speaking, do you?"

"No," Blas said, "and I don't give a hellrat's ass. I'm here to do a job, so why don't you quit being a diva and tell me what's going on with this pregnancy."

Revenant really, really needed to get Blaspheme into bed.

Gethel looked to him for help, but he just shrugged. Satan had given him orders to bring a doctor to Gethel, and he'd done that. If Gethel screwed things up, he wasn't going to lose any sleep over it.

With a snarl, Gethel flopped back down on the chaise and placed her hand on her belly. "Everything was proceeding normally," she said. "I was feeding off infants to nourish the spawn, and his power grew within me every day."

There was a heartbeat of dead silence. "You were eating *babies*?"

Gethel sneered. "Of course. My son is a reincarnated fallen angel. It's required."

Blaspheme gave Rev a you-are-so-going-to-pay-for-this look. Excellent. He'd happily take anything she wanted to dish out.

Hopefully she wanted to dish out sex. False Angels were notorious for getting revenge through drawn-out, torturous sex.

Imagining the possibilities, he propped himself against a pillar and watched Blaspheme unhook her stethoscope from around her neck.

"I'm going to check your heartbeats, but first, finish telling me what's going on. How many months along are you?"

Gethel rubbed her belly almost affectionately, but Rev

had a hard time believing she actually cared about the hellspawn inside her. "Approximately six months."

Blaspheme's eyes shot wide. "You're, ah... very large for only being six months along. Have you confirmed that there's only one fetus?"

"The Dark Lord confirmed it. You can talk to him if you doubt me."

"The... Dark Lord?" Blaspheme paled. "I'll take your word for it." She shot Revenant another angry glance before looking over at the dead shifter and shuddering.

Revenant did a mental flick of the wrist, and the poor dead dude disappeared, leaving the rack as clean as if it were brand-new.

"You owe me another plaything," Gethel said, sounding genuinely sad. "That was one of Limos's servants. I could have enjoyed looking at him for a few more weeks."

Blaspheme froze with her hand on the stethoscope's bell. "Limos? As in, third Horseman of the Apocalypse, Limos?"

"Who else?" Gethel waved her hand dismissively. "Next I want one of Thanatos's vampire servants."

For a long moment, Blaspheme stood there, her face going paler by the second. "You're... *Gethel*." She took a step backward. "You... you tried to usher in the Apocalypse by killing Thanatos's newborn son."

"Duh."

Blaspheme looked over at Revenant, and he knew she was having second thoughts. Not acceptable. He had a plan, and he needed Team Good, or, at least, Team Neutral, to pull it off.

"I can't do this," she said. "The Horsemen are tight with Underworld General's staff. They're friends. I can't be treating the fallen angel who betrayed them and tried to slaughter an innocent baby—"

Gethel's barking laugh made Blaspheme back up even more, but Rev kept access to his power dancing at his fingertips, ready to blast the shit out of Gethel if she so much as thought about harming Blaspheme.

"No baby is innocent, you fool. They're reincarnated souls, all of them. They could have been serial killers in their past lives." She patted her belly. "Do you really think *this* child is in any way pure?"

Blaspheme swallowed. "The child is *emim*, yes? The offspring of two fallen angels. It doesn't have to be evil if—"

"Oh, it's evil," Rev drawled. "You kind of can't get more evil."

And technically, since Gethel had been a fully haloed angel at the time she conceived, he didn't think Lucifer would be considered *emim*, either. He'd be…*vyrm*. The only one under Satan's protection.

"I don't understand. I mean, unless the child is the spawn of Satan…" She trailed off as realization dawned. "It is, isn't it?"

"Yes," Gethel said, her voice as dark and smoky as the Mephisto char pits. "But it gets even better. The beast growing in me is the reincarnated soul of Lucifer himself." She grinned. "And the day he's born is the day Heaven and all of those asshole angels get what's coming to them."

Five

Blaspheme wanted to throw up. On the best of days hospital food didn't sit well with her, but today . . . she had a feeling she'd be losing that bologna and salami submarine sandwich. Too bad about the fries, though, because they had been pretty tasty.

"Revenant," she rasped. "Could I speak with you for a moment?" She glanced over at Gethel, who was still staring at her with crazed-out eyes. "Privately?"

"I've been looking for an excuse to get you someplace private," he said with a raunchy smile, because naturally, he had to turn everything she said into something flirty, crude, or sexual.

"Please," she ground out, hating that she had to resort to begging. "I need to talk to you."

Abruptly, he went taut, his head came up, and he went into deadly serious mode. As he stalked toward her, eyes drilling into her, she braced herself for . . . for what, she didn't know. *Violence* was the first word that came to mind, though.

To her surprise, he drew her aside and angled his big body so she couldn't see Gethel. "You have my ear," he said.

Holy...damn. That's all it took to get him to talk? He needed a *please*? She'd have to remember that.

"Um...okay." She blew out a long breath. "Look, I don't know why you care about that...that...monster on the chaise, but—"

"I don't care about her," he interrupted. "If I had my way, I'd slay her where she stands. Or sits. She broke a million rules when she was Watcher for the Horsemen and that can't go unpunished. But I have my orders."

"Orders from...?"

She had a feeling she knew, so when he said, "The Dark Lord himself," she just closed her eyes, as if doing so would block out the reality that she'd just waded, chin-deep, into the worst situation imaginable.

"I'm sorry, Revenant, but you're going to have to find someone else to treat her. I can't."

"I want you."

Gods, he was stubborn. "Even if she wasn't the mortal enemy of pretty much everyone I work with, I can't, in good conscience, treat her."

"Didn't you have to take some sort of oath to help everyone in need or some crap when you became a doctor?"

"That's a human thing, not a demon one. And trust me, even human doctors would agree with me on this."

He looked down at her, cold calculation in his eyes, and she wondered how far he'd go to convince her to treat Gethel.

"You don't have to help her," he said. "Just…give her an examination. Take some blood samples." Leaning in, so close that his warm breath fanned her ear, he lowered his voice to a conspiratorial whisper. "Wouldn't the information you gather from an exam be useful to your colleagues?"

She inhaled sharply. Was he actually suggesting that she hand over test results to people who wanted Gethel dead? Who wouldn't hesitate to use anything she told them to either locate Gethel or lethally sabotage her care? Hell, the stem cells she planned to harvest from Lucifer's amniotic fluid could potentially be manipulated into powerful weapons as well.

Revenant's suggestion was a good one, but she was pretty sure he was as evil as they came, so why would he say something like that? Maybe he was setting her up. But for what?

"I don't know," she said. "Maybe I should discuss this with Eidolon."

Revenant hissed. "I don't like him."

"I get the impression that you don't like anyone."

He ignored the jab. "I don't want anyone else involved. Do what you have to do once we return to your clinic, but for now, it's just you."

Dammit. Craning her neck, she peeked around Revenant's towering form. Gethel had gotten to her feet and was pacing around while she waited, and she appeared to be talking to herself. She was definitely one clown short of a circus. Or a massacre.

"Fine," she growled. "I'll do it." But only so she could gather information. And stem cells.

Figuring she'd probably just made the biggest mistake

of her life, she brushed past Revenant and ordered Gethel to sit. The fallen angel was surprisingly compliant, even leaning back against the cushions quietly as Blas kneeled on the floor and listened to her heart. Everything sounded normal, but the thing in her belly was a different story.

Little Lucifer's heartbeat sounded like a growl. Blaspheme's ears throbbed with pain as the sound reverberated through the stethoscope, and the longer she listened, the more painful it got. A warm trickle of blood dripped down her cheeks, but for some reason, she couldn't move. Warm, stinging liquid filled her eyes, too, and then her mouth went dry as she opened her mouth to scream—

"Blaspheme!" A voice broke through her agony, and she felt herself being shaken as she sat on the cold tiles. Her stethoscope lay next to her, covered in blood, and then Revenant's stern face filled her vision.

"What," she croaked, "what happened?"

"Your ears were bleeding and you were crying. Are you okay?"

"I...I'm not sure." Even now, her ears ached and the room spun a little, but at least she no longer felt like her head was a giant pressure cooker. "I won't be doing that again."

"My Lucifer wants to devour you," Gethel said, the glee in her singsongy voice sending a chill down Blas's spine. "As soon as he's able, he wants to fuck you dead. He wants to rip you in two and—"

Suddenly, the fires in all of the hearths whooshed out and Revenant was on Gethel, tearing her out of the chaise and slamming her against a pillar with such force that the thing cracked around the middle like a spiral bone fracture. All around them the building shook, and as swarms of demon guards rushed inside the room, they exploded. Simply snuffed out of existence in poofs of red mist.

Gods, the power Revenant wielded... she'd never seen anything like it. Didn't want to see it again.

"If I were to kill you and your wretched *vyrm* offspring," he snarled, "I would suffer at Satan's hands like no one ever has. But it would be worth it. I'm not afraid of suffering, Gethel. Remember that."

Blaspheme shuddered, unsure if Revenant or Gethel and her unholy spawn frightened her more.

And wait... *vyrm*? Gethel must not have been fallen when she'd taken a roll in the hay with Satan. Would stem cells taken from a *vyrm*'s amniotic fluid or cord blood be as helpful to her mother as *emim* stem cells?

Gethel made a futile effort to dislodge Revenant, but he might as well have been made of stone for all he budged. Finally, he released his hold and let her drop to the floor. Then, in a gesture that shocked the shit out of her after just watching him go as cold and deadly as a shark, he held out his hand to Blaspheme.

Blas hesitated, and a flicker of what she could only describe as hurt sparked in his eyes before freezing into a shard of ice. For some reason, the idea that she'd hurt him—hell, that he could be hurt at all—assailed her with guilt.

She could hear her mother's voice now. *"You're too sensitive. Compassion will get you killed. Why couldn't you have taken after me instead of your father? His angel goodness is bringing you down. You need to purge that weakness if you want to survive in Sheoul."*

Yeah, yeah, so she had a heart. When you were in the medical profession, having a heart was a good thing. Sensitivity helped you to relate to patients.

It also made you get too close and take things too hard when the worst happened.

Still, she wouldn't trade away her ability to sympathize with her patients for anything. It made her a damned good doctor, and it kept her going to work every day instead of sitting at home waiting for Eradicators to find her.

Just as she started to reach for Revenant's hand, he pivoted away to go park himself against the pillar again. He wasn't much for offering a grace period, was he? She had a feeling he wasn't generous with second chances, either.

Sighing, she pushed up onto her knees and gestured for Gethel to return to the sofa. The female shuffled over, shooting glares at Revenant, but she kept her mouth shut. Good, because everything that came out of it was unpleasant. Even when she wasn't being crude and downright scary, she sounded like she wanted to be. Like she was mentally inserting things like, "in your blood," and "while you scream," into each sentence.

Once Gethel was seated, all prim and proper in that filthy, stinking gown, Blas rummaged through the jump bag for a blood draw kit, cursing when she realized she'd left the portable ultrasound machine at the clinic. Without it to show the position of the fetus, she couldn't collect stem cells.

Unless her damned X-ray vision decided to finally come back online.

She gave it a try, her body buzzing and her eyes throbbing as she focused, but aside from a high-def flicker of Gethel's subcutaneous blood vessels, nothing happened. Not visually, anyway. The scar on Blaspheme's wrist burned as she strained, as if it were an overheating hard drive.

Dammit! Didn't it figure that the gift she used most in her profession would be one of the first to fail?

"I'm going to get some blood samples," she said, giving up before someone wondered why she was sitting there staring blankly at Gethel's belly. "While I'm doing that, why don't you finish telling me what's going on with this pregnancy."

Gethel shot a glance at Revenant, as if seeking permission to speak. At his stiff nod, she said, "Satan hired a sorcerer to cast a spell to grow Lucifer quickly. That's why he's so large now, but his growth has stopped. He was supposed to be born fully grown."

Blaspheme froze as she tied the rubber tourniquet around Gethel's biceps. "That...that would kill you."

"Worth it," she said dreamily. "But then the archangels fucked it all up. They tried to swap the child in Limos's womb with the child in mine. Limos would have been the one torn apart by Lucifer's birth, but they would have been able to slaughter him the moment he burst from her body. The only upside to that would have been that I would give birth to Limos's child." She grinned, flashing nasty sharp teeth. "It would have tasted...lovely."

Blas jabbed the needle into Gethel's vein with more force than was necessary. The fallen angel was the sickest, most twisted monster she'd ever met. And Blaspheme treated monsters every day.

As blood began to fill the vial, she glanced over at Revenant, who watched with cold detachment. Guess he was still pissed.

"Did you know about this?" she asked him.

Revenant propped his booted foot on the pillar behind him. "Do you remember when Limos was brought to the hospital a few weeks ago? When Eidolon believed her baby was dead?"

She couldn't forget. It wasn't every day a Horseman of the Apocalypse was brought into the ER. "That was the day I met you."

The tiniest smile flickered at the corner of his mouth. "Yes, it was."

Obviously, he remembered asking her to give him a blow job in the hallway. *If you answer my question, I'll let you suck my cock.*

Okay, so he hadn't so much as asked as he'd offered up his dick like it was an Oscar statue or some shit that would be an honor to hold.

He'd let her suck his cock.

Let her.

She growled as she detached the filled vial. "You're such an ass."

He waggled his brows, and so much for him being pissed. The guy changed moods like the wind changed direction during a storm.

"So anyway," he continued, as if this were an epic adventure story and he were the deep-voiced narrator, "that day, some archangels took Limos's child and tried to remotely swap it with Gethel's. They failed, but their efforts interfered with the sorcerer's spell and stopped Lucifer from being born full grown. Whatever they did also fucked up Gethel. Well, that and the fact that Reaver nearly killed her, and archangels sliced her wings off. Now she's deranged, she looks like something a hellhound dragged in, and Lucifer is twice the size he should be."

Blas suspected that Gethel had always been deranged, but she kept that to herself as she withdrew the needle from Gethel's arm. The tiny puncture sealed instantly. "So what, exactly, do you want me to do?"

"Satan wants to make sure nothing is wrong with Lucifer."

"And I want to survive the birth." Gethel bared her teeth at Blaspheme. "Fix it."

"Weren't you the one who didn't mind him being born full grown?"

"That's different. If he's born an infant, he'll need a mother."

Blaspheme blinked in surprise. She'd have pegged Gethel as the type of mother that left her kid in the car while she partied and picked up men in a bar. "Why did the archangels' efforts fail?"

Revenant chimed in. "Because I bound Limos's womb so it couldn't support any child but her own."

Gethel ran her tongue over her lips in a raunchy display. "Revenant is such a good little minion of evil."

Yes, apparently he was. He said he hated Gethel, said he could kill her, but he'd saved Lucifer's life. No matter what, she had to remember that he was working for Satan, and he wasn't a good guy.

As if you've been a model citizen. No, she hadn't been. She'd been conceived in sin, and within moments of her birth, she'd been bathed in a double evil: the blood of a demon, a False Angel taken as an unwilling sacrifice. But she'd long ago chosen a life path that would honor her father...and the female her mother used to be. Blaspheme might have been born of evil, but she refused to let it define her.

"Okay," she said, anxious to get the hell out of here, "I think I have enough. Gethel, your diet sucks. Stop eating infants and eat more leafy greens."

Gethel's head snapped up. "Lucifer needs blood."

Blaspheme jammed her hands on her hips. "Those bags under your eyes, the dark color of your blood, those nasty blue veins running across your cheeks...those are all signs of vitamin A and fiber deficiency. Do you know what vitamin A deficiency does in fallen angel pregnancies? It causes extra huge babies with birth defects." Such a huge lie. All of it. She had no idea if the female was nutritionally deficient or not, and she didn't give a shit. She did, however, want her to stop eating children. "But suit yourself. You still have three months to go and your kid is the size of a toddler already, but whatever."

She turned to Revenant and drew him aside. "You weren't completely forthcoming about Gethel and the baby." She inhaled a bracing breath, preparing herself for Revenant's reaction to the topic she was about to bring up. "I was under the assumption that the child was *emim*, not *vyrm*."

"Oh, now your precious ethics are being tested?"

"No. But knowingly associating with *vyrm* is a death sentence."

"As it should be," he said darkly, chilling her to the bone and answering any questions she'd had about how he regarded her kind. "But clearly, this case is unique. I'm not even sure Lucifer will be classified as *vyrm*, since Gethel was divested of her wings and given the boot from Heaven while she was pregnant. Lucifer could still be *emim*. Or maybe something new. Like *vemim*." He grinned. "See what I did there? Like how lunch and dinner is *linner. Vemim*."

"You can notify *Webster's* of your new term later." She gestured to Gethel, who was dragging her fingers through her stringy hair and coming away with big clumps. "I highly recommend that Gethel go to UG for an ultrasound and amniocentesis." Blas needed those damned stem cells.

"Don't you have portable machines?"

"Yes, but—"

"Good." Revenant shoved off the pillar in a graceful surge. "Then you can bring one when you come back."

"I'm not coming back." She mashed her equipment into the duffel and stood, hoping he'd cave in to her demand. She would much rather he bring Gethel to her than have to come back to this horror show. "If you want an ultrasound, you'll bring her to the clinic like a normal person. And after the procedure is done, *I'm* done. With her, with you, with…" She made an encompassing gesture with her arm. "This."

Revenant's low, pumping purr echoed around the cavernous area. "No, Blaspheme, you and I aren't done. Not by a long shot."

Six

Revenant watched Blaspheme angrily shoulder her duffel of supplies, and if glares were lasers, he'd have been reduced to ash by now. His little False Angel was PO'd.

Gods, she was hot when she was all riled up. He loved pushing those buttons, and she seemed to have a lot of them.

She strode toward him, her hips popping and her breasts bouncing with every swaying step. He was rock hard by the time she stopped in front of him.

"You can drop me off at the hospital," she said. "I need to leave the blood sample at the lab."

"I have a better idea." He took her hand before she had a chance to reject him the way she had before. Man, that had stung. He wouldn't let it happen again. "Let's get a bite to eat. I know a great place right here in Sheoul. You can get a burger made from pretty much anything."

She grimaced. "Um, no, thanks. I'm on a strict diet

of nothing gross. Just take me to Underworld General Hospital, please."

He sensed that she'd probably reached her limit with him today, which was a bit of a letdown, but Revenant had other pressing things to do anyway. Like finding out the truth behind why the fuck Heaven had left him to be raised by demons while they took his twin brother. He was dying to hear the explanation for that one.

Gripping Blaspheme's soft, warm hand, he flashed them into Underworld General's parking lot.

"Thank you," she said as she jerked her hand out of his. "I should have the test results tomorrow. You can stop by my office at the clinic."

He wondered if he'd planted a deep enough seed in her mind for it to take root with thoughts of either killing Lucifer or somehow getting Gethel to the good guys to destroy. Oh, he didn't think Dr. "Do No Harm" Blaspheme would carry out any dirty deed herself, but she could help those who would.

If he was a decent guy, he'd feel bad for using her to do what he couldn't, but he wasn't decent. He'd been raised to be a demon, and he was doing exactly what a demon would do; he was plotting to get rid of his rival before said rival was even born. And he was going to keep his own hands clean by getting others to do the wet work.

So, no, he wasn't decent.

Blaspheme, on the other hand, seemed to be suffering terribly from that affliction. Sure, he was reasonably certain she'd lied to Gethel about her diet, but doing so might have saved a lot of young lives.

"Gethel isn't really suffering from vitamin and fiber

deficiency, is she?" he asked. "You just wanted her to stop feeding on infants."

Blas shrugged. "Maybe. Are you angry?"

On the contrary, he was fascinated. False Angels were known to lure humans away from their children so other demons could snatch them. But for all Blaspheme knew, she could have been risking her life to save a few young creatures by lying to Satan's baby mama. A couple of weeks ago, he'd have been disgusted. Now he was definitely fascinated.

"Well?" she prompted. "Are you pissed?"

He shrugged. "Will saying yes get me laid?"

"Not by me," she said.

"What if I say no?"

"Same thing."

"Disappointing."

Blaspheme rolled her eyes. "Aren't you the Horsemen's evil Watcher? Don't you have things to do?" She started toward the sliding glass emergency department doors, and yes, he had shit to do, but first...

In a lightning-fast surge, he spun her and put her spine to the wall. Startled blue eyes stared up at him. Her lips parted in surprise, and he took instant advantage, lowering his mouth to hers in a fierce, demanding kiss. She inhaled harshly, and for a moment he was sure she'd push him away, but as he slid one arm around her waist and crushed her to him, she kissed him back.

Her lips were soft, tasting of vanilla and mint, and even though she kissed him tentatively, barely brushing her lips over his, his cock stirred. He wondered if the ambulances behind him ever saw any action, because he'd love to scoop her up and get hot and heavy in the back of one.

Then she was shoving against him, the heels of her palms jamming hard into his rib cage. "We're not doing this," she said. "I need to get back to work."

"What about after work?"

"Gods, you're persistent," she muttered. "And no. Not after work. I don't want to see you again until you come by my office tomorrow for Gethel's lab results." She slipped out from under him. "Good-bye, Revenant."

She practically ran inside the hospital, and this time he let her go. Tomorrow would be a new day. Right now he had a few things to do, and at the top of the list was paying a visit to Harvester. She might not have the answers he needed, but maybe she could help him get them.

He opened himself up to what he called his Watcher Awareness, allowing him to sense each of the Horsemen and Harvester, if she was in close proximity to one of them. Instantly, he felt her. She was inside a *quantamun*, a bubble-like plane of existence that allowed users to move, unseen, in the Earthly realm. Focusing on her signature, he flashed to her.

It took a moment to figure out where they were, because they weren't at any of the Horsemen's residences. Well, not exactly.

They were standing in the woods near a log cabin set a few dozen yards away from a larger cabin where one of the Horsemen, Reseph, lived with his mate, Jillian. Harvester was watching a tall, broad male sweep the porch, her attention so focused that she didn't notice Revenant materialize next to her.

She was dressed in form-fitting black jeans, knee-high leather boots, and a leather corset that emphasized her narrow waist and ample breasts he'd admired for

centuries. Too bad the former fallen angel had hated him
with a passion. They could have rocked the underworld
from his bedroom.

Now that she was an angel again, he wondered if she
was still as wild in the sack as she was rumored to have
been. Reaver would know, wouldn't he? Reaver, who had
been given everything Revenant hadn't, from a privileged
childhood with people who raised him with love, to four
extraordinary children, and a mate who adored him.

Way to feel sorry for yourself. Yeah, he knew he was
wasting brainpower dwelling on all of that shit, but he
also had five thousand years of hell to sift through, and
each new memory brought him more fucking reminders
that Heaven had screwed him over.

Shoving his baggage into the back of his head, he sauntered toward the angel. "'Sup, Verrine?"

Hissing, Harvester spun around. "Don't call me that."

"You'd rather go by your fallen angel name than your
given angel name?"

She snorted. "I could ask the same of you. Now that
you know you're an angel, why are you still going by
Revenant?"

The tiniest sliver of pain pierced his chest, but he
wasn't about to let Harvester know she'd struck a nerve.
He didn't have an angel name. The name Revenant was
all he knew.

"Because I'm a fallen angel in every way that counts,"
he said.

"Really." She cocked a dark eyebrow. "Then why not
chop off your wings and make it official?"

Falling wasn't that simple, but Harvester wasn't being
serious. She was baiting him into saying that he was

perfectly happy with his life. With having spent thousands of years in hell instead of living a life of luxury in Heaven the way Reaver had. Because yeah, he'd gotten the awesome end of the stick in that deal.

"Why not take back *your* angelic name?" he pressed her. "And tell me, *Harvester*, how hard was it to pretend to be evil for thousands of years, all the while knowing you were doing Heaven's bidding? Or *were* you pretending?"

A muscle ticked in her jaw, just barely, but enough to know he'd struck a nerve. "I struggled every day of my life to keep evil from taking over my soul."

"Because it was easier to be evil, wasn't it?" Until just weeks ago, he'd thought he was pure evil, a fallen angel with no hope of redemption. But all of that had changed, and now he found himself wrestling with who he really was. As much as he hated to admit it, he and Harvester were a lot alike.

"Evil is always easier," Harvester murmured.

"True dat." He squinted, zeroing in on the man on the porch. "Why are you spying on your werewolf slave?"

"He's not mine anymore. He belongs to Jillian now." A smile turned up one corner of her mouth. "She gave him back his birth name and granted him as much freedom as he can stand."

"That doesn't explain why you're spying on him." She didn't answer, but he realized she didn't need to.

The fact that she was here spying on the werewolf told Rev that she'd truly cared about him. She might even have set him free if he wasn't bound for life to be a slave. Nope, his slave bond, while transferable, wasn't breakable. Tough break. Revenant knew exactly how it felt to be tethered to someone by blood.

"Why are you here?" she asked tiredly. "Some diabolical plot to annoy me to death?"

"I wanted to check up on the Horsemen," he lied.

"They're fine, and unless they summon you, I'd stay out of their way."

"Aw, Uncle Revenant isn't their favorite person anymore?"

She ignored his sarcasm. He'd *never* been their favorite person. "They're a little protective of their father, and since you and Reaver aren't exactly best buds…"

"They're going to be dishing me extra large portions of asshole at the family reunion." So not a surprise.

Harvester cast a fleeting glance at him. "Can I ask you something?"

Huh. Harvester never asked permission to do anything, so this should be good. "Shoot."

This time when she looked over, she locked eyes with him. "In all the time I was rotting in my father's dungeons, why didn't you ever take the opportunity to torture me? He sent everyone else to do their best, so why not you?"

Actually, Satan *had* offered Harvester up on a platter for Rev's sadistic enjoyment. But while Revenant had no problem with killing, he couldn't torture a female. Even before he got his memories back, he'd had a particular aversion to it, even though he'd had no idea why. Now he knew. He'd seen what it had done to his mother, and he would take no part in that.

"Your pain doesn't interest me," he said.

Eyes narrowed, she studied him long enough that he damned near started squirming. "Tell me, Revenant, when he tells you to kill me, will that interest you?" He shrugged, but something in his expression must have given him away, because she murmured, "He already has, hasn't he?"

"It's against the rules for a Watcher to kill another Watcher," he said simply.

She snorted. "As if there aren't work-arounds. I've seen the archangels bend rules for their own selfish reasons. I'm sure you can, too."

Maybe, but he wouldn't. Rules were rules. "Speaking of archangels, I don't suppose you can tell me what's up with the goody-goody bastards?"

She flipped her black hair over her shoulder. "You'll have to be more specific."

"Why won't they respond to my summons?"

She gave him a flat look. "Do you really think they keep me in the loop? I haven't seen any of them since I got my halo back." She watched the werewolf prop the broom against the side of the cabin and head toward the barn and main house. "You should talk to Reaver."

"So he can tell me again that we need to work together to stop the newest threat to Heaven and Mankind? Fuck that. I don't give a shit about either."

"Is that why you've been ignoring his summons? Because you don't give a shit?"

"Pretty much."

"You need to talk to him. Stop being childish."

"Childish? We never had a chance to be childish."

She jammed her fists on her hips. "Well, you're making up for it now."

Maybe she had a point. He and Reaver *had* rolled around in the dirt during a knock-down, drag-out brawl. And he'd been ignoring his brother like a kid with his fingers in his ears doing the "nah-nah-nah, I can't hear you" thing.

Jesus. Next they'd be fighting over whose baseball team was better and who Mom liked best.

Except the latter wasn't an argument. Their mother had chosen Reaver to be sent to Heaven to be raised.

So maybe it was time for a good old-fashioned family reunion, if only to see what had made Reaver her favorite.

Blaspheme could still taste Revenant on her lips. The bastard tasted like spiced rum, and she *loved* that stuff. Why couldn't he taste like onions or garlic? And it would be awesome if he reeked, too. But no, he had to smell as good as he tasted, earthy and natural, like sex in the woods. He'd make a fantastic air freshener for some guy's man cave.

She tried not to think about him as she dodged patients and bustling staff in the emergency department, but the kiss lingered on her lips and in her mind. She shouldn't have let him near her, should have gotten away from him before he could grab her, shove her against the wall, and kiss her until her panties were damp.

Son of a bitch.

She needed to get laid.

How long had it been? She had to think back a couple of years, but she stopped herself before she went too far. He'd been a surgeon, a complete asshole, and they'd both been using each other. They'd used each other right up until the point when he'd gotten himself killed by Aegis slayers.

Yeah, she needed to just let that one go. Actually, she

should let all thoughts of sex go, because right now she didn't have the time anyway. The responsibility of running a clinic was enough stress as it was. But now her mother's life was in danger, and not just from her injuries, but from angels as well. To top it all off, Blas's own trouble with her deteriorating False Angel enchantment meant her own life and career were at risk. Her life was a mess, and she definitely didn't need to throw sex into the mix.

She dropped off Gethel's blood sample at the lab with orders to expedite the tests. She even flirted a little with the lab tech, partly to ensure that her request was honored, and partly to maintain her False Angel reputation. False Angels were the biggest flirts on the planet, and it was becoming harder and harder to act like a False Angel now that she no longer felt like one.

She used to daydream about what it would feel like to no longer need to seduce people for fun, to no longer trick humans into thinking she was a Heavenly angel sent to guide them on a life path. But now that her daydreams were becoming reality and the gifts she'd relied on, like the X-ray vision, were failing, she was a little frightened. She'd never known anything but what her fake False Angel instincts made her feel, and suddenly, she was swimming in unknown, and possibly dangerous, waters.

Speaking of dangerous waters, she gave Eidolon a quick call to see if he was available for a meeting.

"My office in five," he told her.

The Seminus demon was sitting at his desk when she got there, his short dark hair slightly flattened in the familiar shape of a surgical cap. He waved her inside, and she closed the door behind her.

"Blaspheme," he said, leaning back in his chair to peg her with shrewd black eyes. "How's your mom doing?"

He knew damned well how she was. Eidolon didn't miss anything that went on in his hospital or his clinic, but she humored him.

"She's doing as well as can be expected, thank you."

"Any word on the identity of her attacker?"

"Not so far." It wasn't as if she could go to the police, and while demons did have a justice system—which Eidolon used to be part of—it was limited in scope. Plus, as the dam of a *vyrm*, her mother was sort of an outlaw, so she couldn't seek help through normal channels such as a species Council or the Judicia.

"Are you in any danger?"

"Nothing immediate," she said, hoping it was true. When his concerned gaze lingered on her for a heartbeat too long, she sat up straight in alarm. "What is it?"

"It's probably nothing, but there have been a couple of angel sightings around the hospital."

"What?" She gripped the edge of the desk so hard she was sure she'd leave dents. "How did they get in—"

"They didn't. They've been spotted on the Manhattan streets directly above the hospital. It could be coincidence, something going on with the humans. But since your mother was attacked by an angel, I thought you should know."

"Oh. Thank you," she said with as much nonchalance as she could muster, given the fact that angels were sniffing around.

Eidolon steepled his hands together over his abs and studied her in that unnerving way he had. "I hear you had a visitor today."

Of course he had. "Revenant is why I'm here." She blew out a long breath, still rattled by the angel news. "He needed me to handle a medical issue."

Eidolon scowled. "*His* medical issue?"

Ha. She couldn't imagine Revenant ever asking for help. He struck her as the macho idiot type who wouldn't go to a doctor even if he had a battle-ax sticking out the top of his thick skull.

"Someone else's." She met Eidolon's gaze with a steady one of her own. "It was Gethel."

Gold flecks shimmered in the doctor's eyes, a twenty-four-karat sign that he was either angry or turned on, but she could guarantee it wasn't the latter. Mated Sems could only be aroused by their mates.

"Gethel," he said flatly. "You're saying you treated a female who betrayed everyone who trusted her in order to usher in the Apocalypse? An angel who tried to slaughter a newborn infant I delivered with my own hands and who is now my godson? Who helped Pestilence to torture my brother's mate, Idess? *That* Gethel?"

Shit, this was not going to go well. "It's not what you think."

Very slowly, he sat forward, propping his thickly muscled forearms on the desk as he clenched and unclenched his hands. "Then you need to explain yourself, and fast." At least he was calm, even if every guttural word dripped with menace.

"Did you know she's pregnant with Lucifer's reincarnated soul, and that his father is Satan himself?"

"I'm aware." There were red flecks mixing with the gold now, which meant he'd hit a new level of pissed. "Get to the part where your treating her isn't what I think.

Because right now I'm thinking you helped the mortal enemy of pretty much everyone I know, and I'm wondering if I made the right choice in putting you in charge of the clinic with Gem."

"Right. Okay." She swallowed dryly, wishing she'd grabbed a bottle of water from the machine outside his office. "I didn't know it was Gethel he wanted me to treat. As soon as I realized who it was, I refused."

The red in his eyes swallowed the gold and was beginning to eat up even the black of his irises. "Did he force you?" His voice rumbled like a nine-point-zero earthquake.

"No." Perspiration beaded on her brow, but whether it was because she was nervous or because she was getting hot flashes as her cover wore off, she didn't know. "But Eidolon, he gave me the opportunity to find out what's going on with her. I got a blood sample. It's in the lab right now being analyzed. I'm hoping you can use anything I learned to destroy her."

The crimson in his eyes scaled back, but only a little. "Do you know where she is?"

"No idea. Revenant flashed me directly to her lair, so I couldn't tell where we were. But something funky is going on with her. Apparently, it's the result of whatever the archangels did when they tried to swap her baby with Limos's."

Eidolon appeared to consider what she'd said. "What is this...funky? Medically speaking, *funky* isn't all that informative."

He could be a real smart-ass sometimes. "She looks like a zombie, and the hellspawn is twice the size it should be."

"What's she eating?"

"Demon younglings."

He leaned back in his chair, his eyes returned to normal. "Pregnant fallen angels need a lot of untainted, young blood," he said, and she so didn't need the reminder that her own mother had probably dined on her fair share of young blood while pregnant with Blaspheme. How many lives had ended so Blaspheme could live? "That's for a normal pregnancy. But a fallen angel carrying fucking *Lucifer* would require a shit-ton of the purest blood available."

"I told her to stop eating infants and eat more vegetables."

Eidolon blinked. And then, to her surprise, he let out a huge belly laugh. "Vegetables?"

"Leafy greens, to be exact."

Grinning, he shook his head. "Between the lack of pure blood and the introduction of greens during a purely carnivorous diet phase, she's going to be sick enough to kill a Gargantua demon."

"That's what I figured."

"I like the way you think." He sobered, but the tenseness in him was gone. Good, because she'd been afraid for her job for a minute there. "What else can you tell me about her?"

"Not much. I didn't get the chance to do more than get blood and check vitals. The baby hellspawn nearly blew my skull apart when I tried to listen to his heartbeat."

Eidolon nodded gravely. "According to Reaver, even without being fully formed, Lucifer is more powerful than most fallen angels. Once he's born . . ."

"It's going to be bad."

"That's one way to put it." Footsteps sounded out in the

hall, and he waited for them to fade before returning to the conversation. "Speaking of bad," he began, "are you sure I can't help locate your mother's attackers?"

"*Adoptive* mother," she corrected.

"Fine," he said. "Adoptive mother." Eidolon's placating smile chilled her to the bone. She'd had a feeling that he didn't believe she was a False Angel, but she hadn't realized he'd put more of the puzzle pieces together.

He might not know the truth, but he suspected.

"I'm sure," she said. "It was probably just a random thing. Angels attacking fallen angels happens all the time."

"If you need anything, I want you to come to me. You can trust me, Blaspheme."

"I know." She'd been around long enough to know that Eidolon and all of his siblings were loyal as hell, but her life was at stake, and trust didn't come easily to her. Plus, she didn't want to drag innocent people into her problems.

He nodded decisively, the matter settled in his mind. "I'm going to fill Reaver and the Horsemen in on the events with Gethel. Let me know when the lab results come back. Will Revenant want you to see her again?"

You and I aren't done. Not by a long shot. Revenant's deep voice rumbled through her memory, and she shivered at the possessiveness that had both frightened and intrigued her.

"Definitely. I think I've convinced him that she needs an ultrasound, but I'm hoping he'll bring her to me instead of wanting to take me to her."

The doctor picked up a pencil and began flipping it across his fingers. "If he comes to you, page me. This could be the key to getting rid of Gethel once and for all, but I'll handle it in your place."

"Thank you. And if you could draw some amniotic fluid, that would be great." At E's questioning look, she added, "I need Lucifer's mesenchymal stem cells. Since they can develop into multiple cell types, I think I can use them to heal my mother."

A slow smile spread across his face. "Brilliant. The potential medical applications for stem cells taken from a being as powerful as Lucifer are staggering. Getting cord blood for hematopoietic stem cells would be priceless, too, but with any luck, he won't be born at all." His pager beeped, and he quickly checked the screen. "I have to go. But Blaspheme...be careful. And don't hesitate to come to me if you need anything. *Anything*. I have resources at my disposal that you can't imagine."

Casually, habitually, she rubbed the tiny scar on her wrist. It was even smaller than it had been yesterday.

Well, Doc, got a False Angel in your pocket who doesn't mind being sacrificed to maintain my cover? No? That's what I thought.

Time was running out.

Seven

Revenant sat high above the city of Paris, perched on Notre-Dame Cathedral's towering rooftop. He'd witnessed the construction of the ancient building, and he'd always been fascinated by it. From the French Gothic architecture to the winding city streets below, he loved the sweeping size, the awe of the people milling around inside and out.

Sudden pressure inside his skull alerted him to the presence of another, and he turned to see Reaver standing a few feet away, dressed in jeans and a blue Henley.

"Hello, brother." Rev didn't bother standing. Instead, he stretched out his legs in front of him, crossed his booted feet at the ankles, and leaned back against a support rail. "I was wondering if you'd show up."

"It was hard to ignore your invitation." Reaver folded his arms over his chest. "It's impossible to concentrate on anything else when you're projecting."

"Hmm." Revenant smiled. "I guess we're even, because I can feel it when you're happy. It's nauseating. Literally."

"I'll buy you barf bags for Christmas," Reaver drawled.

"So thoughtful." He stared at his brother, wondering what would have happened if they'd been raised together. In Heaven *or* Sheoul. With a thought, he turned his black hair blond to match Reaver's. Although they weren't identical, they *were* twins; they might as well look the part.

"You've been ignoring my summons for weeks. So why are you contacting me now?" Reaver asked.

"Ah, Reaver. Or should I say Yenrieth? That *is* your given name. Your Heavenly name. Funny how I don't have one."

Reaver's blond brows climbed. "Our mother called you Revenant?"

"From the beginning." He looked up at the gray sky overhead. Rain was coming. "It didn't seem strange until now." A twinge of hurt... a feeling he'd long thought he couldn't feel but that seemed to be making the rounds lately... plucked at him. He quickly brushed it aside and filled the void with a much more user-friendly emotion. He and anger had always been intimate. "As to why I want to talk now... let's just say that my memory is back, but I still have questions."

"As do I."

"Really. And what, exactly, are your questions?"

Reaver studied Revenant for a few moments, peering at him like he was an ape. Not wanting to disappoint his big brother, Rev scratched his crotch. Sniffed his armpits. Let out an impressive belch. He was about to pass gas, when Reaver cursed.

"How about you go first," Reaver said. "Ask your questions."

Very magnanimous of him. *Must be what our mother saw in him*, Revenant thought bitterly.

"Let's start at the beginning." Rev materialized himself a lit cigar made of the finest Sheoul bloodleaf. "Who raised you? Did you know about our parents?"

Reaver wrinkled his nose at Rev's smoke. "I believed Metatron and his mate, Caila, were my parents. I didn't know the truth until you came to me on Mount Megiddo."

That had been around five thousand years ago, right after their mother's death. Right after she'd told him the truth about his origins. He'd been confused, afraid, and angry as hell about being lied to.

"I learned the truth about our birth only hours before I went to you," Revenant said. "I thought I'd been born an *emim*, that our mother was a fallen angel."

"Why did she lie to you?"

Anger bubbled up inside him, as fresh as it had been that day. "She had no choice. Satan threatened to kill us both if she ever revealed the truth." But Satan hadn't had the chance to kill his mother. No, Rev had taken that particular honor himself. Hand shaking, he took a drag on his cigar, letting the calming effects of the bloodleaf seep into his body. "So what was growing up with Metatron like?"

"I couldn't have asked for a better life."

"How sweet. I was beaten on most days." He continued before he had to see pity in his twin's eyes. "If not me, then Mother."

Reaver went taut, his teeth clenched hard. "Tell me about her."

Revenant blew out a long stream of smoke. "When you can ask nicely—"

"Please," Reaver blurted. "I don't even know what she looked like." He gazed out over the Parisian skyline, and in his profile, Revenant saw the strong line of their mother's jaw. The graceful arch of her brow. The chiseled cut of her cheekbones. In Rev's hand, the cigar shook so badly he couldn't take a drag. "I looked her up in the Akashic Library last week, but all I found was a rundown of her accomplishments."

Must be nice to have access to Heaven's largest library. Hell, the Akashic Library supposedly held the truth behind every great mystery, every forgotten scrap of history. Minus, of course, any information the archangels deemed too sensitive for commoners to gain access to.

Now should be the time when Revenant disappeared, leaving his brother in the dust to forever wonder if his questions about their mother would be answered. But their mother had always wanted Reaver to know the truth about their births and her life.

"Find Yenrieth," she rasped as she lay dying. "Find him and be the brothers you should have been."

"She was beautiful," he said, hating himself for the emotional warble in his voice. "Even with dirt on her face and hair that hadn't seen a comb since she was captured, she was beautiful." He finally managed to get the cigar to his lips. *Inhale. Exhale. Inhale. Exhale. Finish the story without breaking down like a pussy.* "We shared a cell until I was ten. Then I was taken away to work in Satan's mines, and I didn't see her again for a decade."

Not for a lack of trying, though. He'd made a million attempts to escape the mines and the demons who wielded the whips, but he always got caught.

Only later did he learn that for every infraction

he committed, every rule he broke, his mother paid the price.

"You grew up in a cell?" Reaver asked. "Like a prison cell?"

He laughed bitterly. "A prison cell would have been a luxury." He tossed the cigar to the roof and ground it to dust with his boot. "You know, like food and water was for us."

He'd always wondered why, sometimes when he was hungry or thirsty, he'd get anxious, as though if he didn't get food and water right away, he'd go crazy. Now that he had his memory back, the anxiety made sense. He and his mother had starved for years. He remembered her begging for food, not for herself, but for him. And on several occasions, she'd gotten what they needed by making trades with the only thing she had to offer.

Her body.

And not just for sex. Some demons were all about torture and blood.

As a million horrible memories bubbled up, so did the contents of Revenant's stomach. Rolling to his hands and knees, he retched. How could Heaven have left her to suffer that way? How could they have allowed one of their own to live like that? To be forced to give her body to demons in order to feed her child?

Anger struck hard and fast, scouring away the nausea and wretchedness with welcome, sterilizing flames.

Reaver watched him as he shoved to his feet. "You said you killed her."

"Glad you aren't deaf." Revenant materialized himself a pack of gum.

Reaver ground his teeth so hard Revenant heard the scrape of enamel as he unwrapped a minty stick. "Why?"

"Why am I glad you aren't deaf?" Rev asked, knowing damned well that wasn't what Reaver was asking. "Well, it would make communication more difficult—"

Suddenly, Reaver's hands fisted Rev's jacket lapels and his angelic face was in his, teeth bared, eyes glowing with Heavenly fury. *"Why did you kill our mother?"*

"Heaven killed her," Revenant spat. "When they left her to rot in hell, they signed her death warrant."

Reaver shook him. Hard. "But it was your hand that did it. Tell me about it."

"Fuck you." Rev bared his teeth right back at his brother. "I laid all those memories to rest. No way in hell I'm popping the lids off those coffins."

"I have the right to know."

"Do you?" Revenant threw Reaver off of him like a sack of potatoes. His brother tumbled through the air, striking one of the cathedral's famous stone gargoyles and breaking off one of its wings. "Because from where I'm standing, you don't have the right to know jack shit about my life. You abandoned me."

Reaver flashed himself in front of Revenant again. *"I* abandoned you? I was a newborn infant when I was taken to Heaven. How could I have done anything?"

"Not that," Rev snapped. "When I came to you at Megiddo. When I told you who I was. Do you remember that?"

"No," Reaver said, his voice dripping with sarcasm. "I have no recollection of you telling me I was your brother and that you'd murdered our mother."

Rev hadn't used the word *murder*, but hell, why not. Didn't matter that she'd begged him to do it and that he'd done it out of mercy. The guilt ate at him like acid.

"You freaked the fuck out," Rev yelled. "You didn't wait for an explanation. You got your halo all bent out of shape, and you went on a damned rampage. And because of that, because you left me to go raze some goat-herder villages and shit, we lost our memories for thousands of years. That's on you, you fucking asshole. *You.*"

Okay, sure, Rev wasn't entirely blameless, given that he'd done his own share of demolition, but most of his wrath had been focused on Sheoul, not the human realm.

Shame flickered in Reaver's sapphire eyes. "I was having a bad day—"

"Oh, right. You'd just found out that you'd sired the Four Horsemen of the Apocalypse and that your precious Verrine lied to you about it." Revenant rolled his eyes. "Waa. I grew up in hell, tortured almost every day. I watched our mother suffer unspeakable horrors. Your spoiled ass got *lied to.*" He jabbed Reaver in the sternum. "Well, fuck you, brother. It's a damned good thing Heaven took you instead of me, because your pansy ass would never have survived in Sheoul."

Maybe that was why their mother gave up Reaver. Not because she loved him best, but because she thought he was too weak to survive life in Sheoul.

Revenant was going to run with that theory. It was much easier to swallow than the alternative.

It was also less believable, but fuck it.

Reaver averted his gaze, suddenly becoming interested in his boots. "Neither one of us should have had to live like that." He lifted his lids, and his eyes glowed with regret. Or maybe it was pity. Either way, it just made Revenant angrier. "But now you're here, and it doesn't have to be like this."

"Like what? Like you being all perfect and angelic, and me being an evil bastard?" He laughed. "Sorry, Pollyanna, but it *is* that way." The broken gargoyle wing seemed to stare accusingly at him from where it had landed on the rooftop, and with a thought, Revenant repaired the stone statue. Destroying historical treasures was not cool.

"You're an angel. Let me talk to the archangels—"

"What, you really believe they're going to welcome me with open arms? They haven't done it so far. And what makes you think I'd want that? Maybe I like my life."

"I don't think you do."

"You don't know anything about me," he shot back. "You don't know what I've done in the name of evil."

"It doesn't matter. Things are different now. *You* are different."

Revenant snorted. "Tell me, brother, can you see anything at all through your rose-colored glasses?"

He looked up at the fluffy cumulus clouds meandering across a field of blue, remembering the first time he'd seen the sky when he'd emerged from the dark depths of Sheoul. He'd been endlessly fascinated, staring in wonder and trying to figure out what magic kept the clouds in the air. But that boyish wonder was gone now, and with a thought, he poofed them out of existence. He hadn't been able to manipulate the weather before, but with the Shadow Angel upgrade he could whip up nuclear-grade hurricanes if he wanted to.

He wondered how long it would be before Satan had him doing exactly that, just to kill humans and piss off Heaven.

Dammit. He needed to stop fucking around. Satan had given him a week to prove his loyalty and willingness to play for Team Sheoul, and his evil side was cool with that—as long as he didn't have to lick Lucifer's boots. But his status as an angel confused him, made him want to honor his mother.

He wouldn't be honoring her if he chose to serve the demon who had made both of their lives unbearably horrible.

Sure, she'd told him a million times that in order to survive, he'd have to do distasteful, wicked things. But he doubted that killing legions of angels and dropping natural disasters on top of humans was what she meant.

"Tell you what," he said, hoping he wasn't making a huge mistake. "I've been trying to contact Metatron. Hell, I'd settle for any archangel at this point. Take me to them, and I'll see what they have to offer."

Reaver closed his eyes, not even bothering to hide his relief that maybe his wayward brother was finally coming around. "I'll talk to them. Arrange a meeting."

"I don't have time to wait around," Revenant said. "Take me to them. Now."

Reaver shook his head. "I have strict orders to keep you out of Heaven. They don't want your taint to defile the realm. If you can—"

"My...taint?" Fury seared to ash every ounce of amity he'd been willing to extend. "*Defile?* They left me to rot in hell, erased my memories, and let me think I was something I wasn't for more than five thousand fucking years, and *now* they have the nerve to say I'll desecrate Heaven with my presence? Well, fuck you, Reaver. Fuck you and fuck them."

"Dammit, Rev!" Reaver shouted. "What do you want?"

What did he want? That was easy. He wanted to belong

somewhere. He wanted a life of his choosing, where he didn't have to fear being drawn and quartered for some minor infraction. He wanted choices. Answers. He wanted to feel comfortable in his own skin again. Because as evil and vicious as he'd been before he regained his memories, at least he'd known who he was.

But he wasn't going to tell his brother any of that. He'd only sound like a whiny imp, and besides, Reaver, with his rainbow-and-unicorn life, couldn't possibly understand.

"I want for you to fuck off, just like I said." He changed his hair back to black and flared his gold-and-silver-threaded ebony wings, reminding Reaver how very opposite they were. "Good chat, bro. We'll have to do it again sometime. As the French say, *Au revoir, mon frère.*"

Eight

Harvester waited for a long time after Revenant demateralized before she worked up the guts to step outside the *quantamun* and make herself visible to her ex-slave. This was something she should have done weeks ago, the moment she was reinstated as a Heavenly angel.

But anxiety and shame had kept her away. What if he hated her for all of those years as her servant? What if he hated her for passing his slave bond to someone else? Although she couldn't imagine that he'd hate belonging to Jillian. The human, immortal thanks to her bond with Reseph, was a gentle soul with a streak of kindness inside her a mile long.

Taking a deep, bracing breath, Harvester walked toward the barn, the cool, fresh Colorado mountain breeze bringing with it the sweet scent of wildflowers and the tang of coming rain. As she approached, the snort of a horse and the bleats of goats joined the sound of hay being moved around with a pitchfork. Did Tracker like his job?

No matter what, it had to be better than spending all his time in her old residence, where he'd cooked, cleaned, and tended to her needs...all of them.

Her stomach rolled, and she halted at the edge of the gravel drive that connected the barn to the main house. This was a bad idea. She shouldn't be here. She had other things to do, like wash her hair. And the Grim Reaper himself, Azagoth, had, just days ago, called in a debt she owed him, which meant she had an angel to hunt down. Stamtiel was also on Heaven's most-wanted list, so nailing him to the wall, literally, took priority over having a chat with her former slave.

Having talked herself into a new course of action, she ignited the spark of power she needed to flash out of there, and...let it snuff out.

Seeing Tracker again wasn't for her benefit. It was for his. No doubt he had plenty to say to her, and he deserved a chance to say it. Besides, as Jillian's mate's Watcher, Harvester was bound to run into him sooner or later. Might as well get it over with.

Then there was the fact that she seemed to be weakening as Gethel's pregnancy progressed, and she might not have many opportunities to see Tracker again. She could feel Lucifer growing stronger, and with every passing day, Harvester grew more tired and her powers were more difficult to summon. Only when she was in Heaven did she feel whole. How long would it be before she was forced to reside there permanently? She'd lose her job as Watcher, and she'd never again attend family functions with Reaver, which had, surprisingly, become one of her favorite things to do. The Horsemen and their mates had finally accepted her as part of the family, and she couldn't give that up.

But would she have to if Lucifer kept sucking her energy like a dire leech?

Was it possible that she could even die?

She hadn't told Reaver any of her fears, hadn't told him the extent of the growing weakness, but he knew something was up. She could see it in his eyes, could feel it in the way he touched her as if she were made of crystal.

She *hated* being treated like an invalid.

Decision made, she rounded the corner to the front of the barn and stepped through the open door.

Instantly, Tracker wheeled around, pitchfork poised to attack. When he saw her, he froze solid, his eyes wide with surprise.

"Hello, Tracker," she said softly.

The pitchfork began to tremble, and Harvester's heart, still hardened by thousands of years of scar tissue, managed to crack wide open.

"You don't have to say anything." She took a step closer. He didn't move, but his grip on the farm tool became white-knuckled. "I'm not here to hurt you."

"You...you're an angel now." His deep, smoky voice gave her a sense of comfort; he'd been the one constant in her life for decades.

"Who'd have thought, huh?" Certainly not her.

"Are you going to take me back?"

She couldn't tell if his question was hopeful...or fearful. "Why? Do you want me to?"

Very slowly, the pitchfork lowered, and so did his head, until he was looking at his boots, his sandy hair concealing his expression. "No," he whispered. "I like it here."

Relief sang through her. "Good. I wanted that for you."

His head came up, and the skepticism in his gaze pierced her right through the heart. "You wanted me to be happy?"

Oh, damn, this had been a mistake. He must have been so miserable with her, even though she'd tried to treat him well. As well as she could without drawing suspicions, anyway. Being nice to him would have set off alarm bells for anyone who witnessed it. She had been in hell as a spy for Heaven, and there was no way she could expose herself, not even by being nice to a slave.

"I know you don't believe me, but yes, I wanted that for you."

He looked down at his feet again. "Thank you for rescuing me from my former master. And thank you for giving me to Jillian." He shuddered. "But you should go now."

That was the first time Harvester had ever heard him be assertive, even if it was only tentative.

"Tracker? Look at me." When he didn't, that small act of resistance made her smile. But she really did need him to look at her. "Tracker! Eyes up." This time he lifted his head, and the flash of defiance in his gaze gave her hope. "Next time you tell someone to leave, look them in the eye. You have the right to your own life now. Only Jillian can take away your freedom, and somehow I doubt she's done that. In fact, I'm guessing she had to force you into your own private cabin, didn't she? And she's not making you clean the barn, either. You need something to do, so she's letting you help around the house. Am I right?"

He nodded.

"Good," she said. "Now, tell me to leave, and do it like you mean it."

His throat worked on a swallow, then two, but finally,

he met her gaze with a rock-steady one of his own. Deep inside his amber eyes, the werewolf inside him sparked to life for the first time since she'd known him.

"You need to go."

"Better." Even though her chest ached, she was proud of him. Stepping close, she took his hand and pressed a coin into his palm. "If you ever need me, this coin will allow you to summon me. I'll be there. Take care, Tracker." She started to dematerialize, but he grabbed her wrist.

"Wait." His grip was strong, sure, but his voice was gentle as he said, "I'm glad you're an angel now."

With that, he pivoted around and began tossing hay around as if she weren't still there. She lingered only a heartbeat before flashing away.

At least he didn't see the tears in her eyes.

After leaving Eidolon's office, Blaspheme took the hospital's Harrowgate to the clinic. Things were slow this afternoon, with only three people waiting to be seen in the reception area. She was still rattled by Eidolon's mention of nearby angels, but she reached up to run her fingers over her stethoscope as she walked, reminding herself that she was a professional, and right now, people needed her.

Nerves contained if not completely soothed, she spent the next six hours with patients, and then she stopped by her mother's room.

Deva was sleeping, but she cracked open her bloodshot eyes as Blaspheme studied her chart.

"Blas," she croaked. "I haven't seen you in hours. I'm glad you're okay."

"Of course I am." Never mind that there might be angelic assassins waiting to slaughter them both. She smiled reassuringly and sank down in a chair next to the bed. "How are you feeling?"

Deva closed her eyes again. "Like someone put me into an industrial-sized blender."

"That's pretty much what you looked like when I saw you yesterday." She took her mother's hand, which had healed from most of the defensive wounds she'd gotten. "What do you remember about the attack? How many angels were there? More than one?"

Eyes still closed, her mother nodded. "There were two Eradicators. They neutralized my wards and broke into my house while I was preparing for your concealment ritual."

Blaspheme ground her molars. "I said no. We're not doing it."

Deva's eyes popped open, but instead of being glazed with pain, they were sparking with fury. "You will do it, Daughter. You've known since the beginning that the spell has a shelf life of a hundred and eighty years. You've gone past the expiration date by twenty, and you're running on fumes. I didn't go through two hundred years of hell and hiding for you to be selfish now."

She was calling *Blaspheme* selfish? For not wanting to take a life to preserve her own? That was rich. Deva was the most self-centered person she knew.

"Are you losing your False Angel powers?" Deva asked.

Blaspheme white-knuckled her mother's medical chart. "Some are gone," she admitted. "My wings no longer produce aphrodisiac powder. My X-ray vision is failing. I can't charm people into not getting angry anymore." She really missed that one.

"Are you developing any *vyrm* abilities?"

"Not yet."

Deva sighed. "It won't be long. Once *vyrm* powers appear, everyone will know what you are." She squeezed Blaspheme's hand. "We have to perform the ritual. Now. Before I die."

"You're not going to die, and we've been over this." Blas slammed the chart down on the bedside table. "No sacrifices. I'll find another way."

"This *is* the only way." Deva struggled to sit up, was grateful when Blaspheme pushed a button to raise the head of the bed. "You're almost out of time. No more stalling. The Eradicators are onto us. I have a False Angel picked out for you. She's healthy, powerful, and a real slut. When you absorb her essence, you'll feel like yourself again. Maybe you'll finally get laid."

"Mom, has it occurred to you that *this* is my normal self? With the False Angel enchantment wearing off, I don't feel the need to trick anyone into sex or anything else."

"Are you saying that you'd rather let the concealment wear off so Eradicators and Destroyers can kill you? I won't let that happen. I've worked too hard to keep you safe. Your father's death can't be in vain."

Blaspheme rolled her eyes. Always the guilt trip with her father. "Do you really think my father would be happy knowing we'd sacrificed the life of an innocent to keep my true identity concealed?"

"Your father was an angel," Deva growled. "He wouldn't care if we sacrifice a demon. To angels, a dead demon is a good demon."

"But he'd want me to be happy, and I can't be happy if my existence comes at the cost of another person's life."

"You didn't know Rifion," she snapped. "You don't know what he'd want."

Tired of the same old argument, Blas stood. "We'll talk about this later. You need your rest." She glanced at her watch. She'd been off duty for hours now.

Her mother jackknifed forward and grasped her wrist. "We will *not* talk about it later. I've set a trap for the False Angel. She'll be caught at my place tonight, and by the time she bleeds out in the morning, you'll be safe. I can perform the ritual from here."

Oh…holy shit. "You are unbelievable, you know that?" Blas practically yelled.

The blood drained from Deva's face, and although Blas wished her words had caused it, she knew better and eased her mother backward on the bed. "You're woozy from sitting up so fast."

"I don't care," Deva moaned. "I need you to be safe. You're all I have. We're all each other has."

Blaspheme's anger diluted a little, but it didn't change her mind about the ritual. She had to stop Deva's False Angel from falling into whatever gruesome trap her mother had set.

"I have to go, but I'll be back soon." She handed Deva a glass of water. "Drink this and keep yourself calm or I'll order sedation. Got it?"

Swallowing sourly, Deva nodded.

Blaspheme left the head nurse with orders to sedate Deva anyway and to not allow visitors. Even though angels couldn't enter the facility—with the exception of Reaver—Blas didn't want to take any chances. An angel desperate to grab her mother could bribe, bespell, or blackmail a demon into abducting her. The clinic's Haven spell would prevent an assassination attempt, but once outside the facility, Deva would no longer be protected.

Feeling confident that her mother was in good hands, she left the clinic through the Harrowgate rather than the main exit to the tube station. If angels were watching the hospital and the clinic, they could easily nab anyone exiting into the human world, but there was no way to track people through Harrowgates.

The Harrowgate opened up a few blocks away from Deva's Key West home, in an alley behind a touristy seafood restaurant and bar. Once more, Blas wished she could use her *vyrm* powers to flash directly where she needed to be. She did *not* want to get caught out in the open, blocks away from a Harrowgate.

Cursing her mother's poor choices, she slipped out of the alley and fell in with a group of rowdy tourists enjoying the last remnants of evening twilight. Key West was one of the few places that had escaped most of the recent apocalyptic mayhem, and because of that, it had become a popular getaway for those seeking temporary asylum from the disaster that was the human realm.

Deva's pastel green and orange beach house sat at the end of a quiet drive, goofy plastic pink flamingos dotting the manicured lawn like fleas on a dog. As Blas approached, she engaged the False Angel ability to go invisible, one of the False Angel gifts Blaspheme rarely used. But as she slowly opened the front door, an uncomfortable vibration rattled her, and she looked down to see that she was flickering in and out of invisibility.

"Damn," she breathed. How much longer did she have before she was going to be exposed for what she really was?

She took a deep, bracing breath to keep panic at bay. The door swung open with a squeak, and holy shit, the place was trashed. She'd expected a scene from a battle, and sure enough, furniture was turned over and broken, dishes were shattered, and blood spatter and smears left ugly stains on the once-pristine white walls and bamboo floors.

But what she hadn't expected was the ransacking. Books had been knocked off shelves, drawers had been emptied, and papers were scattered all over the place. Someone had been looking for something, but what?

Letting go of the invisibility enchantment since it wasn't working anyway, she grabbed a butcher knife off the kitchen counter and tested the blade. The stupid knife was dull and chipped, as if Deva had been using it to chop wood. How handy it would be right now to have the *vyrm* ability to summon powerful weapons instead of relying on what amounted to a large butter knife for defense.

Dull-ass weapon in hand, she tiptoed to the bedroom, checking all of the closets to make sure she was alone—not that the angels who did this couldn't flash inside again at any moment.

As she moved to the bathroom, a crash rang out. Heart pounding, she whirled, blade poised to strike. Across the room, the blinds crashed again, blown through the open ocean-facing window.

"Damn," she muttered. She was going to have a heart attack before she got out of here.

Feeling a little foolish, she went to the den and sat down in front of the glowing computer screen on the desk. When her mother wasn't out partying and causing trouble, she was on the computer, which meant that somewhere on the hard drive there had to be information about the False Angel she planned to trap.

A hasty scan of the computer's history showed that on the day of the attack, her mother had been reading articles at theCHIVE and downloading some disturbing fetish and vampire porn that would never allow her to look her mother in the eye again. She'd also been instant messaging someone named SexySweetXOXO. A lover, maybe? Did she have a partner in crime?

She opened up the app, and right away, a message popped up.

SexySweetXOXO: Hello, darling. You left our chat so abruptly yesterday. Is everything okay?

Blas had no idea how to respond to that, and seriously, couldn't her mother have chosen any name but HornyAsHell69? Ew. Just…ew. And why in the hell was her avatar a good-looking black dude? Was she pretending to be a male?

She thought about ignoring SexySweetXOXO, but according to the time on the last conversation, chatting with SexySweetXOXO had been one of the last things her mother did before she was attacked.

Okay, so she'd play along for a few minutes, even though SexySweetXOXO's avatar was a butt with an angel tattoo on the right cheek.

HornyAsHell69: Sorry I had to go so suddenly. I had an unexpected visitor, but I'm fine.

SexySweetXOXO: Are we still on for a good time?

Well, crap. Unsure how to respond, she settled for playing dumb.

HornyAsHell69: Remind me what you consider a good time. I know what MY idea is.

SexySweetXOXO: I'm going to show you what Heaven tastes like, my sweet boy.

Boy? Okay, so her mother *was* masquerading as a male. Interesting. And weird.

SexySweetXOXO: Did you still want to meet?

Meet? What in the name of everything unholy was Deva getting herself into?

HornyAsHell69: Let me get back to you. Something may have come up.

SexySweetXOXO: Aw. :-(Let me show you a little something that might encourage you to cancel whatever it is.

A picture popped up in the IM screen of a naked blond female sitting on a bed. She was holding her breasts provocatively, her legs spread wide, her ivory stilettos digging into the mattress.

Massive gossamer wings spread out from behind her, which could have been faked...except that they weren't. Not if her sparkly, translucent pubic hair was real.

SexySweetXOXO was a False Angel. The chosen sacrifice.

Feeling sick, Blaspheme leaned back in her mother's leather desk chair. This was how Deva had planned to trap the False Angel. By pretending to be a human male, Deva was luring this female to her house, where, no doubt, a trap visible only to Deva's eyes was waiting to snap closed.

SexySweetXOXO: I'm ready for you. I have your addy, and I'll be at your place at nine o'clock to make every one of your angel fantasies come true.

Another picture popped up, this time with her bent over—still naked, of course—her perky, round ass sticking up as she spread herself with her fingers. Her wings fanned out over the bed, where dozens of assorted sex toys lay strewn about.

Aaand...that was about enough of that.

HornyAsHell69: You're gorgeous, babe. But I changed my mind. I'm not into angels anymore.

SexySweetXOXO: I can be anything you want me to be.

Blas sighed. *Thanks, Mother, for choosing a False Angel who is clearly desperate and ready to screw complete strangers.* Granted, that description fit most False Angels, but criminy, Blaspheme did not want to be absorbing that kind of personality.

Blas figured she should be grateful that her mother hadn't chosen to sacrifice a soul-eating *fugwart* or a Sensor demon, which lived to destroy half-breeds like herself. She couldn't imagine a life in which she had to kill demons who had the misfortune of being born to the wrong parents the way she had.

Okay, time to make this False Angel go away for good. Blas didn't trust her mother not to attempt to reestablish the relationship and snatch the female no matter what Blaspheme's wishes were.

HornyAsHell69: Thanks, but no. I found someone else to meet my angel fetish needs.

An image of Revenant popped into her mind, and she quickly banished it. Not only was he not an angel, there was no room in her head for him. Although she couldn't deny that picturing him naked was so much better than having the image of SexySweetXOXO's bubble butt and cotton candy cooch in her brain.

HornyAsHell69: Don't contact me again, and if for some reason I contact you in the future, ignore it. It just means I'm drunk, and I'm a mean drunk.

SexySweetXOXO: Asshole. Good luck finding a fuck as good as I am. I'm going to make sure you get kicked off every angel fetish forum on the Internet. Fuck off, punk.

Oh, good, SexySweetXOXO was a sore loser as well. Deva sure knew how to pick 'em.

Feeling like she'd dodged a bullet, Blas shut down IM and poked around the comphuter a little more, figuring that while she was here, she might as well look for anything that might have tipped off Eradicators as to her mother's identity.

Nothing. Not unless the angels who attacked were into full-moon werewolf porn and male-on-male vampire sex. Blas had to admit, though, that the vampire videos were kind of hot.

Another search of the house revealed exactly the same; nothing. Frustrated, she straightened the place up a little, and by the time the moon had climbed high overhead, she was starving.

She was about to head for the Harrowgate when her cell rang with Underworld General Clinic's "Bark at the Moon" ringtone. Rumor had it that Ozzy had recorded the song as the theme for the hospital, but Eidolon would neither confirm nor deny.

She pushed the Answer button. "Doctor Blaspheme."

"Blas." Gem's breathless voice rasped over the phone line. "It's your mom. She's in trouble."

Nine

Blaspheme hit the nearest Harrowgate at a run. The moment the gate closed behind her, the walls inside the dark space lit up with glowing maps of both Sheoul and the Earthly realm, but she didn't need either of those. Instead, she punched Underworld General Hospital's caduceus symbol, right next to the smaller clinic symbol that would have taken her to the clinic's Tube platform entrance. Instantly, the gate opened into UG's bustling emergency department.

Rushing past a Croucher demon who was holding his own bloody ear in his clawed hand, she slammed her palms down on the reception desk. "Where is Deva?"

The nurse, a new vampire recruit named Bridgette, looked up from her computer. "Your mother?"

Dammit, Blas hadn't wanted that to get out. Even though she'd stressed the *adoptive* mother thing, she knew how rumors worked. The *adoptive* part of the equation would be dropped in conversation eventually, and then the speculation as to how Blaspheme could be a False Angel if her mother was a fallen angel would start.

"My adoptive mother, yes," Blas ground out. "Where is she?"

"She's been transferred here from the clinic and taken to OR three," Bridgette said. "She—"

Blas didn't wait for the rest. She took off at a sprint, skidding around corners and crashing into equipment and carts in the halls. As the door to the operating room came into view, Gem stepped out, her blue-striped black hair tucked under a surgical cap.

"Gem!" Panting from exertion, Blas came to a grinding halt in front of the other physician. "What happened?"

"She had a cardiac incident an hour ago. A team was able to revive her, and we got her into surgery right away."

"An *hour* ago? Why didn't anyone call me?"

"There was a mix-up...I'm sorry. Your old home phone number was in the records, and when that didn't work, someone tasked someone else to call your cell...it was a fuckup. We'll address it at the next staff meeting so it doesn't happen again."

Oh, they'd sure as hell address that. But right now, she was more worried about her mother.

"Who is in there with her now?"

"Docs Soduchi and Bane," Gem said. "She's in good hands."

Yes, she was. Bane, one of several Seminus demon brothers Eidolon had hired, was extremely talented, even beyond his natural healing abilities. Soduchi had been a more recent addition to Underworld General, stolen away from the Mayo Clinic a couple of months ago. The noted cardiac surgeon was a werewolf, and when the apocalyptic shit had gone down, his true identity had nearly been exposed in all of the chaos. It had been the perfect time for Eidolon to poach him—and several other *ter'taceo* medical specialists who had been working at human hospitals and clinics.

Too bad Soduchi was an arrogant ass. But then, most surgeons were. No werewolf blood needed for that. Just a medical degree.

Gem slung her arm around Blaspheme and guided her toward the operating room's viewing area. "Let's get you settled."

Blas, exhausted and worried, allowed the other female to take her into "the box," where she watched Soduchi and the rest of his team work on her mother.

"Can I bring you anything?" Gem asked as she sank down in the seat next to Blaspheme. "Coffee? Something to eat?"

"Thank you," Blas said, "but no. Go ahead and get back to work. I'll be fine."

Gem's eyes narrowed with concern. "You sure? Because I can stay."

Blaspheme liked Gem, but right now she just needed some space. So much had happened in the last few hours, and she felt like she was going to break down at any minute.

No witnesses, her mother always told her. *False Angels' tears are an aphrodisiac to some, toxic to many. You don't want to accidentally poison someone.*

Now that the False Angel enchantment was fading, Blaspheme's tears were probably not liquid sex or toxic anymore, but she didn't want to test that theory. Not that she planned on crying, but as tired as she was, she couldn't take any chances.

Gem made promises to check in soon and left Blaspheme to observe the surgery in peace. Thankfully, everything was going well, so well that at some point, she dozed off. She woke four hours later to the sound of the door swinging open, and a boar-like Guai nurse named Chuhua entered, her hooved feet clacking on the floor.

"Gem asked me to bring you these lab results," she said in her squealing, piggy voice. "She brought you a sandwich and coffee earlier." She gestured to the tray of food with one hand and handed her a folder with the other.

Blaspheme gazed out at the surgery, which appeared to be winding down. "Thank you, Chu-hua. And please thank Gem for me."

Chu-hua smiled, her top lip catching on her tusks, and then she ducked out of there in another clack of hooved feet.

Blas looked down at the folder. Patient name: Gethel.

She scanned the contents quickly, but the intercom buzzing interrupted her. She looked out the window at the operating theater to see Soduchi giving her a thumbs-up through the glass.

Relieved, Blas shot out of the viewing area, her stiff legs protesting as she stepped into the hall and paced while she waited for Soduchi to come out of the OR.

Thirty seconds into her pace-fest, a tingle in her spine alerted her to a presence, and she knew exactly who she'd see when she turned around. Sure enough, Revenant was sauntering down the hall, his long legs eating up the distance, his black leather coat flapping around his boots, his predatory gaze fixed on her.

Geez, he was punctual. Yesterday she'd told him to

come back tomorrow, and here he was, six o'clock in the morning, all bright-eyed and bushy-tailed. She, on the other hand, must look like she'd slept on a bed of nails.

Groaning softly, she watched him approach. He might be the sexiest evil bastard in existence, but dealing with him was the last thing she needed right now.

"Revenant," she said. "Can I meet up with you in fifteen minutes? You can wait in the UG lobby or in my office at UGC—"

Naturally, Soduchi came out of the OR at the same time Revenant stopped in front of her.

"Dr. Soduchi," she said quickly, heading him off before he could start off his report with the words *Your mother.* Gods, this masquerade was turning complicated, messy, and stressful as hell. "How is the patient?"

"I couldn't do anything about the previous damage, but she's out of immediate danger. Bane is finishing up with her." Soduchi tore the green surgical cap off his head, revealing his severe blond high-and-tight that suited his hard-core personality. "I assumed she threw a clot as a result of a surgical complication, but it turns out there was a foreign blockage in the inferior vena cava that resulted in her heart attack."

"A foreign blockage? What kind?"

He opened his palm. In it was a tiny, shiny object that looked like a crystal sesame seed. "I have no idea what this is. I've never seen one before." It must have killed him to admit he didn't know something.

Revenant held out his hand. "May I?"

Soduchi looked to Blaspheme, and when she nodded, he dropped the thing into Revenant's palm. "I doubt you'll be able to determine its source—"

"It's a tracking device," Revenant said, and Blas would have been amused to see Soduchi's arrogance swatted down if she hadn't been so busy wrapping her mind around what Rev had said. "Angelic in origin."

Soduchi's expression tightened. "How do you know?"

"Does it matter?"

Blaspheme could practically smell the testosterone clashing in the air between the two males as Soduchi growled. "Who are you?"

"He's a friend." Blas jumped into the fray before things deteriorated beyond something she could control. "Well, his, ah, *friend*, is a patient of mine."

"Your friend could use a lesson in respect."

Revenant laughed, flashing fangs. Which, for some reason, made her think of the vampire porn at her mother's house. *Not* what she needed to be thinking of right now. Still, she wondered what Revenant's fangs would feel like buried in her throat.

Stop it.

"What's your name again?" Revenant asked. "So Douchey? Well, So Douchey, the day I respect a weremutt is the day my dick turns into a hot dog. So why don't you run off and find yourself a nice Milk-Bone."

Soduchi's eyes bugged out of his head. "You unimportant fuck—"

One minute, Revenant and Soduchi were there in front of her, and the next, they were several yards down the hall, with Revenant pinning the doctor against the wall with his forearm across Soduchi's throat. The writing on the gray walls, Haven spell inscriptions, began to glow and pulse as the threat of violence rose up from Revenant.

She couldn't hear what he was saying to the other male,

but whatever it was, the doctor went as white as a banshee on the night of the new moon.

A moment later, Revenant was next to her, and Soduchi was scampering away in the opposite direction. If he'd had a tail, it would have been tucked between his legs.

She stared after the surgeon in disbelief. "What did you say to him?"

Revenant snorted. "Boo."

"I don't believe you. But I don't have time to play referee." She rubbed her eyes, wondering when she'd see her bed again. "You said the object Soduchi found inside my mo—ah, my patient, is an angelic tracking device?"

He nodded. "They're implanted into the skin."

Gods, this wasn't good. "Do they burrow until they hit an organ or barrier?"

"No." He rolled the tiny device between his fingers. "They're designed to remain just under the top layer of skin, and they're only active while inside a body, whether it's alive or dead."

She frowned. "How would one get into the inferior vena cava?" At his blank look, she elaborated. "A vein that brings blood to the heart."

"Ah." He shrugged. "It might have been implanted inside an open wound. It could bore its way inside from there." He looked over at the OR door, and even though Blas was pretty sure he couldn't see through it, she started to sweat. "Who is this patient, anyway? Angels don't just go around tagging people, and only certain angels possess the ability."

"Certain angels?" She swallowed sickly. "Like?"

"Interrogators, Eradicators, Enforcers...a few more, probably." His voice went thick with contempt, while she was pretty sure hers was going to go shrill with anxiety. Why would someone track her mother...unless they were trying to get to Blaspheme? If that had been the goal, it had worked beautifully. "I'm not exactly up on angelic operations. Seems they neglected to invite me to the meetings."

Had he expected to be invited to meetings? He seemed to take the subject a little too personally.

"Well," she said, thankful that the shrill thing didn't happen, "I'll have to ask my patient when she wakes up." She held out her hand. "Can I have the tracker, please?"

A sly grin spread over his face, and she groaned. "Go to dinner with me."

"I'm not going to be blackmailed into a date, especially not over this. I won't compromise patient care. Ever." She made a come-on-and-give-it-to-me gesture with her fingers. "So hand it over. Eidolon will want to study it."

His gaze swept over her, fleeting and almost cursory, and yet she felt as though she'd been examined for hours and stripped naked. "A False Angel with principles. How...rare."

She was starting to hate the way he could find the chinks in her armor. And she *really* hated how she seemed to always be playing defense around him. If this were one of her mother's favorite sports, the Sheoul Fallen Angels would always have the ball, would always be ahead in points, and the Underworld General Vyrm would be struggling to merely get on the scoreboard.

"So you fit the fallen angel mold perfectly?" she shot back. *Field goal for the Underworld General Vyrm.*

"Hardly. But every species is defined by certain traits. All tigers are carnivores. Seminus demons have to screw or they'll die." His gaze took a slow, measuring ride down her body, and said body heated up. "False Angels need to deceive, lie, and seduce others or they'll waste away. So I'm wondering, Blaspheme, how you feed your needs if you're such a model of integrity."

Sheoul Fallen Angels score a touchdown.

She shrugged as if it were no big deal, but inside she was trembling. She couldn't afford anyone questioning what she was, especially not a fallen angel.

"I go to human clubs to fulfill my needs," she said. "At work, I'm a doctor, pure and simple."

"Good." He dropped the tiny crystal seed into her hand. "Because I despise liars and deceivers." He waggled his brows. "Seducers, on the other hand..."

Blaspheme rolled her eyes, but was spared from having to scrounge up a witty comeback when the door to the OR opened, and nurses and support staff prepared to move Deva to a recovery room.

"Why don't you come to my office," she said hastily, before someone said something about the patient being her mother. "We can discuss Gethel's lab results."

"Lead the way." The team transferring Deva pushed out of the room as they were leaving, and Revenant craned his head around. "It's that fallen angel you were treating yesterday."

Shit. "You have a good memory."

For some reason, that made him laugh. "If you only knew." He eyed her as they traversed the busy hospital halls on the way to the Harrowgate. "Blaspheme?"

"Yes?"

He hesitated. And then, "Do you feel like you belong here?"

What a strange question. "You mean here? At the hospital?"

"I mean helping people. Your species isn't known for its altruism."

She did *not* like that he kept questioning her False Angelness. "I suppose you could say that I've never really fit in with my kind. I'm a bit of a square peg."

On that, she didn't have to lie. Being born a *vyrm* made her a product of two worlds, and she didn't fit in either, which was probably why she preferred the human realm.

"Have you tried?"

"What, to fit in somewhere?" At his nod, she shrugged. "For a while, yes."

Encouraged by her mother to blend in with other Sheoulic denizens, she'd attempted to connect with her evil side, but her angel half didn't handle it well. Guilt ate at her like acid, and worse, she felt physically ill when forced into situations that required a measure of malevolence. But she'd always thought it was strange that the opposite didn't happen. Good deeds didn't disturb her sinister half.

Gods, she was messed up.

"Do you have a family?" he asked.

"My mother." They entered the Harrowgate, and she touched the symbol that corresponded to her clinic. "You?"

"A brother."

"Is he . . ." Okay, so how did one ask a fallen angel if his sibling was still in Heaven? Fortunately, Revenant spared her the awkwardness.

"He's a fully halofied Heavenly angel. Total dick."

Having no idea how to follow that up, she stepped out of the Harrowgate into the much more comfy reception area. "My office is just ahead." She waved to Judie, the Sora demon receptionist on duty. "Any messages?"

Judie's crimson tail swished behind her as she thrust a piece of paper at Blaspheme. "Just one. Eidolon wants to hear from you when you get the lab results." She hit a Hold button on the phone. "He didn't say what lab results."

"It's okay." Blas held up the folder in her hand. "I have them right here."

Once they were in her office, Revenant plopped down on the sofa across from her desk, kicking his feet up on the armrest and lying back with his hands tucked behind his head as if he belonged there.

"You have no problem making yourself at home, do you?"

His grin was a showstopper. "It's your welcoming personality and your warm bedside manner."

"My ass," she said as she sank down in her office chair. "You like challenging authority."

He winked, probably thinking he was being charming. Unfortunately for her, he was right. "You offering up your ass? Because I'll take it." Framing his hands together over his pelvis as if gripping an invisible lover's waist, he thrust those magnificent hips upward. "Right here. Right now. You can straddle me. Just. Like. This."

Oh, damn, now she was picturing exactly that, and her body reacted in a hot flush. Her False Angel libido, which she'd thought had gone dormant, spun up, making her breasts tingle and her sex ache. She hadn't experienced a reaction this strong in months, and thank gods she wasn't out in public, where she'd be driven to flirt and rub up against males like a cat in heat. No, better to be safely in her office with a desk between her and the nearest male.

She cursed her trembling hands as she threw down the folder and flipped it open. "If you're through with your imaginary porn star, we can get down to business."

"You know," he said as he sat up and swung his feet to the floor, "I'm going to start suspecting that you're anything but a False Angel if you don't start flirting even a little." Just as a panicked knot started to form in her gut, he inhaled. "But you're aroused, so maybe my little tiger really is a carnivore."

"You are *such* a pain in the ass."

He beamed as if she'd just given him the greatest compliment ever. Huffing with annoyance, she looked down at the lab report.

As usual, the lab had provided data and comparisons from past fallen angel patient lab results, but in all of Underworld General's years of operation, only one pregnant fallen angel had come through the hospital, and her blood work numbers had been substantially different. It was impossible to tell which set of numbers for each panel was more normal. She'd have to research the other pregnant fallen angel to see why she'd been admitted to the hospital.

"So," Revenant prompted, "what does the report say?"

Jack shit, that's what. "The results are basically meaningless, since we don't have much to compare them with. Pregnant fallen angels don't generally seek medical attention here, and we definitely don't have records on any prior fallen angels pregnant with the spawn of Satan."

She cursed in frustration. She'd gone with Revenant to see Gethel in hopes of learning something useful and to get stem cells, and she'd failed at both.

"All these results tell me is that if she were human, she'd be dead by tonight. Her cholesterol is off the charts, her red blood cell count is low, and she has so many tumor markers in her blood that her arteries should be clogged, but all of those things might be normal for Gethel. I'm sorry, but that's all I can tell you." She flipped the page, and handwritten notes in red caught her attention. "Hmm. Test results do indicate the presence of an unidentifiable substance in her blood, but again, that could be normal for her." Still, it was something worth looking into. She definitely needed to hand over the information to Eidolon.

"How helpful," he said flatly.

"Perhaps you can get better results with your own medical expertise," she said. "Now, if you'll excuse me, I have patients to tend to." And a cold shower to take.

Shockingly, he stood without an argument. His good behavior was only temporary, however, because in an instant, he came over the top of the desk in a fluid, graceful leap and was standing in front of her, his big body blocking everything except him.

"Thank you, Blaspheme." Lifting his hand to her face, he stroked his knuckles over the skin of her jaw. "I'll be back later."

Dipping his head with the self-confidence of a predator that had its prey in its sights, he captured her mouth in a dominating, punishing kiss. Her senses reeled as his tongue thrust past the barrier of her lips and teeth to clash with hers. Raw sex oozed from him, and despite her resolve to stay away from him, she gripped his biceps and dragged him closer.

It was what he'd expect from a False Angel.

At least, that was what she told herself as he framed

her face in his big hands and held her steady for the deep penetration of his tongue. His pelvis slammed into hers, and either that was a gun in his pocket, or he was sporting one hell of a hard-on.

Then he was across the room, standing in the doorway. She hadn't even seen him open the door. She stood there, dazed and weaving on unsteady legs.

"I would love to take you," he said roughly. "Right there on your desk. But I've got something to do, and when we finally fuck, I don't want any distractions."

"It won't happen." She cleared her throat of the embarrassing lust that made her sound a lot more wanton than she'd like. "You aren't my type."

"All males are a False Angel's type."

"As you've made clear more than once, I'm not your typical False Angel."

"And that," he said, "is why I want you."

With that, he spun around and disappeared around the corner, leaving her aching, confused, and in a whole lot of trouble.

Ten

Revenant stood atop Mount Megiddo once again, a sense of déjà vu zinging through his brain, and not because he'd tried to contact Metatron a day earlier. This was where he'd called out for his brother that first time, but the meeting hadn't gone well. Reaver hadn't known about Revenant, hadn't known the truth about anything, and he'd gone ghastbat crazy. Hurt, rejected, and drowning in the lies he'd been fed all his life, Revenant had hopped right on that crazy train, and they'd both done enough damage to all the realms that their memories had been wiped.

Good times, man. Good. Fucking. Times.

"Yo. Archangels," he shouted. "Metatron, get your holy ass down here."

Like yesterday, nothing happened. Fucking assholes. He was frustrated as shit, his mind buzzing with another of Satan's summons and his balls aching with unquenched desire for Blaspheme. Something was about to blow, and he doubted it would be his cock.

"*Metatron!*" He roared into the heavens, and all around, the earth shook as dark clouds roiled from out of nowhere, blocking out the sun and turning the land dark as night. "*Last chance. Get your holy ass down here now, or a lot of angels are going to be gracing Satan's halo wall.*"

He wasn't even sure why he was giving the archangels one last shot at giving him answers about who he was and what he was supposed to be doing with his life, not after what Reaver had said about Revenant defiling Heaven with his mere presence. Maybe Blaspheme's nobility had rubbed off a little, or maybe he owed his mother the respect of trying one more time.

Whatever it was that had him standing on this ugly hilltop, being completely ignored, it was in the past. He was done. Satan had won. Time to deliver an angel on a platter.

Flaring his wings, he started to lift into the artificial darkness. No doubt the nearby humans were freaking out, praying to their deities, sure another apocalypse was about to break loose.

Suddenly, a soft whoosh preceded a sparkling shower of lights, and a split second later, the archangel Raphael was standing there, his body emitting a soft, golden glow like something straight out of a cheesy Christmas movie. Even his blond hair shone like polished gold. Angels could contain their glow in the human realm, which meant he was intentionally being an asshat.

Well, well. Right when Revenant decides he's done with Heaven, Heaven gets a clue. Whether or not it was too little, too late, had yet to be seen.

"What is it?" Raphael asked in a glaringly bored voice.

"You aren't Metatron."

"Aren't you observant."

"Fuck off," Rev said. "I want Metatron."

"He's in a meeting. You're stuck with me."

All archangels were dickbags, but Raphael seemed to be especially dick-tastic.

"In a meeting?" Revenant grinned. Nothing got someone's attention like interrupting a meeting.

Raphael's eyes shot wide. "No—"

Too late. Revenant flashed smack into the middle of the Archangel complex. A few angels were scurrying through the halls, but none of them gave him more than a passing glance. Why would they? They had no idea who he was, and the idea that an angel from hell could simply pop into one of the most important structures in the universe was ludicrous.

He looked around, wasting no time in determining where the meeting might be. Reaver would right now be sensing his presence in Heaven, and it would probably only be a matter of seconds before his twin showed up to play bouncer.

Swiftly, he moved toward the mass of offices down a hall to the right, where the signs on the doors indicated that the rooms had been set aside for groups. He bypassed the lamely named Chamber of Eternity, the Genesis Room, and Babel Hall, and went straight for Babylon Auditorium.

Bingo.

A group of ten archangels were sitting around a giant marble table on the stage, the empty theater-style seats watching over them in silence.

"Well, well," he said as he strode down the center aisle toward them. "Looks like I'm late to the party."

Several of the angels glared at him, clearly outraged that someone had the gall to interrupt. But four of them, Gabriel, Michael, Uriel, and Haniel, knew exactly who he was, and they came to their feet so fast that their chairs tumbled backward.

"Revenant," Uriel gasped. Suddenly, the others leaped up, too, weapons in their fool hands.

A heartbeat later, Raphael popped onto the stage, his face a mask of fury. "You don't belong here," he growled, and yeah, that was exactly the problem.

He didn't belong in the exact place he *should* belong.

"And you lied to me," Revenant said. "Metatron isn't here."

"Wrong meeting, asshole," Raphael said.

Revenant frowned. "Disappointing." He threw himself down in one of the theater seats. "But since I'm here, let's chat."

A tingle spreading over his scalp indicated the arrival of his twin.

"Reaver," Raphael snapped. "It's about time. Get that piece of offal out of here."

Revenant laughed. "In a room full of stinking shit-heads, how will he know who you're talking about?"

Eleven archangels looked ready to explode. *Go ahead and paint the walls, boys. Your blood, guts, and brains could only make the gaudy decor less horrifying.*

Raphael roared. "Get. Him. Out!"

"Yes, Reaver," Rev said, "get me out before my *taint* defiles the place."

Reaver, for all his high-and-mightiness, didn't move other than to fold his arms over his chest and stare at Revenant. "Why are you here?"

"Because I'm an angel, same as you." He looked over at the horde of archangels, each of whom was charged up with power, ready to blast him. He was far stronger than any of them, save Reaver, but he wondered how he'd stack up against all eleven of them. "Same as *all* of you."

"You're nothing like us," one of the strangers spat.

He kicked his booted feet up on the back of the chair in front of him. "What's your name?"

The blond angel looked down his nose at Revenant. "I'm Khamael."

"Well, Khamael," he drawled. "Suck my balls." With a wave of his hand, he made the bastard disappear.

Instantly, Reaver was right there, hand on Revenant's throat. "Where is he?"

"Chill, bro." Rev grinned, flashing fangs. "He'll be back in a minute. As soon as he figures out how to free himself from Sheoul-gra. Of course, if he landed in an acid pool or a lava pit, he won't be looking so great when he gets back."

Reaver's fingers tightened. "What. Do. You. Want."

I want what you have, you bastard.

Revenant exploded to his feet, the shock wave sending Reaver tumbling over a dozen auditorium chairs. Rev kept his power close to the surface, ready to decimate these assholes if they tried anything.

"What do I *want*?" he asked. "What I want is answers. I want to know why you sons of bitches left me, as a *baby*, to rot in Sheoul. I want to know why *I* was left behind when you took Reaver. And I really want to know why you didn't rescue my mother."

A couple of the angels looked confused. A few others glanced away, their expressions tight with shame. But it was clear which of them had been involved in the happenings of so long ago.

Michael stepped forward. "We didn't know where she was—"

"Bullshit," Revenant roared. "Reaver, on his own, without any help from you bumbling idiots, managed to sneak into Satan's most secure prison and rescue Harvester. So don't blow smoke up my ass."

"Reaver's special." Gabriel spread his hands imploringly. "And he had prophecy and fate on his side. At the time of your birth we didn't have the capability to mount a rescue operation like that."

Oh, good, more with the *Reaver's special* shit.

"Liar," Revenant spat. "You didn't have the balls, is what you didn't have."

Raphael snarled. "Reaver, if I have to tell you one more time to get him out of here—"

"You'll what," Reaver asked. "Speak harshly to me? Glare at me? No, wait, you'll send one of my friends into a forced mating just to punish me?"

Revenant had no idea what Reaver was talking about, but he got a kick out of the way Raphael's face went the color of a baboon's ass. "Lilliana and Azagoth are a good match."

"Lucky for you," Reaver murmured. He propped his jeans-clad hip on the back of one of the chairs. "Now, since Revenant hasn't done anything other than send Khamael for a visit with Azagoth and Hades, I think we should hear him out. He wants answers, and frankly, I'd like to hear what you have to say." Before Rev could start growing a bunch of lovey-dovey warm fuzzies, Reaver pegged him with serious eyes. "But I'm warning you. One wrong move, and I'll use your blood to paint these gaudy-ass walls."

"Brother," Revenant said, "how alike we are in our thinking. Mom would be proud."

Something flashed in Reaver's eyes, gone before Revenant could tell what it was. But it looked suspiciously like anger. Because, yeah, how horrible to think that the two of them, fucking *twins*, could be alike.

Khamael flashed in, his clothing charred and in tatters, blood streaking his face and arms. His blue eyes were wild, and Rev was pretty sure the archangel's eyebrows and eyelashes had been singed off.

That was some funny shit.

"So," Revenant said as he walked slowly toward the stage. "You said that at the time of our birth you didn't have the ability to rescue us. But what about later?"

Gabriel scrubbed his hand over his face. "Look, Revenant. Our hands were tied from the beginning. Satan held all the cards. We were lucky we were able to work out a deal for *one* baby, and it was Reaver they brought to us. We had to accept that."

"Luck of the draw," Raphael said, but the way he said it conveyed his displeasure at the hand Heaven had been dealt. Clearly, he had a real burr up his ass when it came to Reaver.

Revenant knew the feeling, and he hated that he had that in common with Raphael.

"So you gave up." He was halfway to the stage now, and the archangels were starting to sweat. "Left me to grow up in hell and my mother to suffer. You just forgot us."

"We didn't forget," Michael said. "And we did try to convince your mother to leave." Several heads swiveled around to stare at him, and wasn't that interesting. They hadn't known about whatever it was Michael was blabbing about.

"What do you mean?" Revenant asked. "How could she have left?"

Gabriel swiped a pewter chalice from the table and knocked back the contents before fixing his steady gaze on Reaver.

"Are you aware that your mother could have left Sheoul with you?" Gabriel asked. "But that she chose to remain behind, even knowing that an opportunity to leave would never be presented again?"

"Metatron told me that," Reaver said, and for the first time ever, Revenant heard an emotional tremor in his brother's voice. "Most of it."

Rev could only swallow over and over as his salivary glands futilely worked to moisten his parched mouth. He didn't know any of this.

Finally, he managed a raspy "Why? Why would she stay behind?"

"To protect you," Gabriel said, his tone making clear that he thought her choice was the wrong one. "She knew that Reaver would be safe and would have a good life even if she couldn't be the one to raise him. But you were doomed to a living hell. She wanted to protect you as much as she could. She made a deal with Satan that would allow you to remain with her until you were ten mortal years old. I'm assuming the bargain was kept?"

Revenant nodded numbly. He'd assumed she'd been held against her will after his birth. Guilt turned his marrow to pudding, and he suddenly couldn't walk anymore. He halted on the crimson carpet, his knees trembling, his insides quivering. Dear...fuck. She'd sacrificed everything for him. She'd known she would suffer for all eternity, but she'd chosen to stay with him anyway. *He* was the reason she'd suffered.

"She…" He cleared his throat of the humiliating hoarseness. "She stayed with me. What did Satan get out of the deal?"

Gabriel's gaze cast downward. "We don't know. I'm sorry."

Revenant began to shake so hard he could barely stay upright. Distantly, he heard shouts and things crashing, and he realized he wasn't the one shaking. The building was. He looked down, and beneath his boot soles, black veins began to sprout in the floor, spreading through the auditorium like millions of invasive, poisonous roots.

"Get him out of here!"

"Reaver, hurry!"

"He's fouling the area!"

"We warned you! He's poison."

None of the voices made sense, even though he heard the exact words. He felt a hand on his shoulder, and as if a spell had broken, he snapped, shooting lightning from his body in a three hundred and sixty degree spread. He heard screams, more shouts, calls for Reaver to—

Arms wrapped around him in a tackle, and suddenly he was in some kind of crazy free fall through space and clouds and fire. An eternity later, the plummeting sensation came to an abrupt end as he hit something hard as shit, with Reaver on top of him. Rage and pain and shame spun up in a massive vortex of misery.

"Revenant!" Reaver's voice barely penetrated the black haze that swallowed him. "Chill out!"

A million pounds of pressure built inside him, demanding release, but all he knew how to do was scream. Scream like he had as a child, when he watched his mother suffer for his deeds.

He screamed. And screamed. And screamed. And when he was done, his voice was raw and his eyes were dry, and all around him, for miles and miles, there was nothing but blackened, scorched earth.

Even Reaver was singed, his face streaked with ash, his clothes steaming. A moment later, his brother returned to normal, and it was as if nothing had happened.

What *had* happened?

He must have asked that out loud, because Reaver kneeled next to him as he lay bleeding on the ground. "You went off like a bomb." He gestured to the surrounding landscape. "I had a feeling that's what was going to happen. We're at an old nuclear test site in New Mexico. Figured you couldn't do much damage here."

Reaver's hand came down on his shoulder, and Rev felt power channel into him, but nothing seemed to be happening. If anything, his pain grew worse. He looked down at himself, and yeah, he was pretty torn up, but it was the gash running the length of his rib cage that was hurting like a son of a bitch.

"Why am I injured?" he rasped. And shit, he was dizzy.

"Metatron told me that we heal almost instantly from any wound," Reaver replied. "Except those we cause ourselves."

"That knowledge might have come in handy before I went Hiroshima on my own ass." Except that he hadn't done it intentionally. Clearly, there were still some kinks to work out with his new Shadow Angel powers.

Reaver pumped another round of energy into Revenant, and Rev groaned, sure his organs were exploding. "Dammit," Reaver breathed. "I can't heal you. We should get you to UG."

Rev rolled out of Reaver's grip. "I'm fine." Black dots appeared in his vision. Yep, fine.

"You're not fine. I can see your ribs. Your actual ribs."

A wash of nausea made Revenant sway as he sat there, holding his hand over the wound. "I said no."

"Stubborn jackass," Reaver muttered. He jammed his hands through his hair and stared at the ruined ground. "What set you off?" When Revenant said nothing, mainly because pain had locked his jaw in place, Reaver expelled a raw curse. "Tell me what happened, Revenant. Tell me what happened to our mother."

Fuck that. No way was he telling anyone that he was the reason their mother had suffered so horribly. Yes, Reaver now knew that she'd remained behind intentionally, but he didn't need to know that every stitch of pain she'd experienced could be laid at Rev's doorstep.

"I can't."

Reaver's voice hardened. "Can't, or won't."

"Does it matter?" Agony throbbed through his torso, and he sucked in a rattling breath. He needed to get to his place. Hole up. Lick his wounds.

"Dammit," Reaver growled. "You need a doctor."

Doctor. Why yes, yes he did need a doctor. One in particular. "You're right," he said. "Guess that's what big brothers are for."

With that, he gathered his last remaining bit of strength and flashed himself out of there.

Eleven

Someone was following her.

Blaspheme wasn't sure how she knew that, but she was certain that someone was tracking her movements. Almost since the moment she left the clinic, a hinky feeling had latched on like a leech, keeping her looking over her shoulder and jumping at every loud noise.

And London had a lot of loud noises.

As she boarded a bus, she cursed her stupidity at renting a flat so far away from a Harrowgate. *The walk will be nice*, she'd told herself. *On rainy days, I can take the bus*, she'd said to her mom.

Great plan, except when there was an emergency, such as some homicidal maniac—or an angel—possibly following her.

She'd tried a repeat of the invisibility thing, but this time she couldn't fully vanish even for a minute. Some of her body parts were as visible as usual, while others were completely indiscernible, and others transparent, like a ghost.

Her False Angel aura was wearing down, and it might only be a matter of days before angels and fallen angels could detect the truth about her origins.

It was time to ask Eidolon for help.

She dug through her purse for her phone and made a quick call to check on her mother, and after Gem reassured her that everything was fine, she left a message with Eidolon's answering service. She needed to meet with him as soon as possible. She used the excuse that she had Gethel's test results, which she hadn't been able to share with him earlier. He'd been stuck in surgery all day with multiple victims of a Nightlash massacre, and she had a feeling he'd be pulling an all-nighter with that one.

The bus curbed it at her stop, and she made a speedy dash to her flat a couple of blocks away. The sensation of being spied on had gone, but the icky, oily sensation of having been watched left her feeling like she needed a shower.

Which meant that her mystery spy wasn't Revenant. If he were observing her, the shower she'd need would be an icy-cold one.

As she entered her place, she didn't think she'd ever been so exhausted. She dumped her bag on the floor of her flat and negotiated the maze of moving boxes on her way to the kitchen, wondering if she had the energy to make a sandwich. Turned out, she had the energy but not the ingredients.

She hadn't been shopping in days, and pretty much everything in her fridge had gone bad.

Cursing her stupidity at not picking up something

from the market down the street, she grabbed a cold beer and scrounged through her cabinets for microwave popcorn to munch on while she relaxed in front of the TV with her favorite show. It was *Doctor Who* night, and tonight's new episode was supposed to be a game-changer.

Her phone rang, and she was tempted to let the machine get it, until Eidolon's number popped up on the caller ID.

"Doc E," she said. "Hello."

"I'm sorry I missed your call." His deep voice rumbled over the phone line. "I got the copy of Gethel's lab results you left on my desk. But I had a question about the other item you left."

"The tracking device." Her hand shook as she took a long pull on the beer bottle. "Dr. Soduchi found it inside my mother."

"How did you know what it was?"

"Revenant told me."

"He was here?" he barked. "Again? You were supposed to call me."

She winced. "I didn't want to bother you unless he requested my participation in another house call in hell. Besides, you were busy."

"I'm still busy. I fucking hate Nightlash demons." She heard him take a sip of something she assumed was coffee. "I'm going to research this device. I'll have Wraith do some snooping as well."

Eidolon's brother Wraith had an uncanny knack for locating things no one else could. When his vampire mate, Serena, was with him, there was practically nothing they couldn't find.

"Blas," E said slowly, "is there any reason you can think of why your mother would be tagged with a tracking device?"

Even though she'd decided she needed Eidolon's help, she stood there for a long time, weighing her options and considering how much, if anything, she should tell him. Ultimately, the undeniable truth of her situation became clear. She was in trouble, and if there was anyone in the world she could trust, it was the demon on the other end of the line.

"Whoever put it there might be looking for me."

There was a moment of silence, and then, "I think we need to talk. Get a good night's sleep, and meet me in my office tomorrow. I'll text you with a time."

"You got it, boss."

"And Blaspheme?"

"Yeah?"

"Be very careful. I don't want to lose you." The line went dead, and her stomach went sour.

What had she done? For nearly a hundred years her mother had stressed that she couldn't trust anyone with her secret no matter how upstanding that person might be. Feared by angels and fallen angels alike, *vyrm* were born with a price on their heads, a price large enough that few could resist the temptation of either reporting them to authorities or killing them outright.

She doubted Eidolon would kill her for riches or fame or favors, but on the off chance that she was wrong, she was gambling with not only her life, but that of her mother as well.

She glanced at her watch and swore. Now, on top of everything else that was a shit sandwich today, she'd missed the first five minutes of *Doctor Who*.

Forgetting the popcorn, she hurried to the living room...and stopped in her tracks at the raw stench of fresh blood. A cold fist of fear squeezed her heart as she backed slowly toward the kitchen, her only thought to grab a butcher knife off the counter.

"Blaspheme." The familiar voice rasped through the room.

"Revenant?" Very cautiously, she pressed her back to the wall and inched toward the sound of labored breathing. As she peered around the corner, she caught a glimpse of Rev's giant boots on the floor on the other side of the couch. "What the hell?"

Rushing forward, she was shocked to find him sitting on the tile, propped against the wall, his clothes shredded and charred, a massive laceration extending from his right pectoral to the bottom of his left rib cage. Blood seeped between his fingers as he held pressure against the wound.

"Oh, shit," she said as she crouched next to him. "What happened?"

"Bomb...blast," he breathed. "I fucked up, Blas. Fucked up so hard."

She had a feeling he wasn't talking about the blast, but right now what mattered was getting him fixed. "I'm going to get you to UG—"

"No."

"You're in bad shape. You need—"

"What is *with* people?" He snarled, flashing fangs. "I said no."

Okeydokey, then. "Let me grab my medic kit."

As she pushed to her feet, his hand snaked out to circle her wrist. "I mean it. No hospital."

"Yeah, I got that." She peeled his fingers away. "I'll be right back."

Quickly, she grabbed her old paramedic jump kit from the cupboard beneath the bathroom sink and returned to him. His head had fallen back against the wall, and he was paler than he'd been a moment ago, his blood spilling in a pool beneath him. So much for her cleaning deposit.

"Must have been a hell of an explosion to wreck you like this," she said.

Closing his eyes, he nodded. "You don't even know."

"I'd like to."

His eyes opened. "Would you really."

The cynicism in his voice pricked at something deep inside her. Did he think that people were always bullshitting him? Maybe it was a fallen angel thing, because her mother was the same way. Blaspheme might not be the most trusting person on the planet, but Deva left her in the dust.

"Whatever it is," she said slowly, "you can tell me. Doctor-patient confidentiality."

"I thought you weren't held to human standards."

Ouch. Way to throw that back in her face. "I pick and choose." She unzipped the bag. "So spill."

He closed his eyes again. "What's your mother like?"

Whoa. Talk about a change of subject. But hey, if that was what he wanted to talk about and it would keep him calm, she'd humor him a little.

"She's extremely high-strung," she said as she fetched a pair of scissors from her bag and started to cut away his shirt. "But she'd do anything for me. She'd sacrifice ... anything." Including False Angels.

"My mother was like that." His burned hands tightened into fists, and a shudder went through him. "She was such a fool," he whispered.

Gently, she moved his hand away from his wound and pressed a blood-stopper pad against it. "She was a mother," she said. "That's what they do."

"Fuck that." He laughed, a nasty, bitter sound. "Got any alcohol?"

"Of course I have alcohol. I'm a False Angel," she reminded him. False Angels drank liquor by the gallon, their bodies converting the stuff to the powdery aphrodisiac that coated their wings. Blas didn't drink for that particular reason, especially now that she wasn't producing the powder anymore and what was left on her wings was all that remained, but her disguise did make her crave it. "But it's not a good idea to drink right now." When his upper lip curled in a silent snarl, she threw up her hands in defeat. "Fine. But when you pass out from blood loss and alcohol, don't say I didn't warn you." She replaced his hand on the pad. "Apply pressure. I'll be right back."

She fetched a bottle of Smirnoff from the liquor cabinet and handed it to him. He immediately guzzled half of it. Gods, she hoped he had a high tolerance. He was a pain in the ass when he was sober; she couldn't imagine what he'd be like under the influence. She'd bet her favorite set of scrubs that he was a mean drunk.

Settling in next to him, she laid out the supplies she'd need to sew him back together. He watched her with curiosity as she performed a rapid exam to determine the extent of his injuries, but aside from the near-evisceration wound, all she found were burns and abrasions.

She carefully cleaned the surgical area and threaded a needle with absorbable thread. "I don't have anything that will numb the area, so this is going to hurt."

He took a deep swig. "Trust me, you can't do anything to me that hasn't been done before."

Setting the needle and thread aside, she unwrapped a sterile scalpel. "Sounds like you've had a violent life."

He snorted. "Who hasn't?"

"I haven't." Thanks to her mother's paranoia, Blaspheme had, for the most part, stayed out of trouble.

"Isn't that special." Revenant held up the bottle in a salute. "Good for you."

"Yeah, good for me." She scooted in closer to Revenant and tried to ignore the heat coming off his muscular body. "I need to excise the damaged skin on the edges of your laceration. Try not to move."

He didn't move at all. He closed his eyes, put his head against the wall, and half an hour later, she was finished cleaning and prepping the wound. Next up, stitches.

"In the deepest parts of this lac, I need to put in internal sutures. It should only take a few minutes." She pierced his flesh with the needle. "Lucky for you, most of the cut is fairly shallow."

"You know you don't need to go to a lot of trouble," he said, his voice starting to slur a little. "I'm immortal. I'll heal on my own eventually."

She looked up at him. "That's why I'm not worried about infection or making this pretty." She pulled on the thread. "But you shouldn't have to be in pain until you heal."

His lids opened, just a crack, but she felt his intense gaze scorching her skin. "It's been a long time since anyone gave a shit about my pain."

She stopped breathing. She could tell him that she only cared because it was her job to care, but she sensed that when he said *a long time*, he wasn't talking about a few years, or even a few decades. Maybe not even a few centuries. Was he that awful of a person that no one could care for him? Or did he push people away so they didn't have the chance to care for him?

Either way, it was kind of heartbreaking.

"Just relax, and you'll feel better in a few minutes."

One corner of his mouth curved into a half smile. "Promise?"

"Promise."

"We'll see."

Bending over the laceration, she got back to work. "Not very trusting, are you?"

"Because people aren't very trustworthy."

She'd have argued, because she'd met a few standup humans and demons, but he'd closed his eyes again, and his breathing had settled into a deep, steady rhythm.

She spent the next forty-five minutes stitching Revenant up in silence, and as she finished, her cell buzzed with a text from Eidolon.

Meet me in my office tomorrow at 2 PM.

Doc E had never been one to mince words. She set the phone aside and turned back to Revenant.

"What was that about?" Revenant's voice was drowsy and his eyes were still closed, but he somehow managed to radiate a sense of alertness most people couldn't match after ten hours of sleep and five cups of coffee.

"Nothing."

His lids lifted as his features settled into irritation. "There is very little that pisses me off more than being lied to."

"Okay, fine," she said. "It was something, but it's none of your business. That's not a lie."

He pegged her with his black gaze. "I'm not the enemy. You know that, right?"

"Actually, no, I don't." She smoothed a bandage over his wound. "You're a fallen angel. You, more than anyone, should know that fallen angels aren't exactly honorable."

"That's where you're wrong." The bottle he seemed to have forgotten about became his best friend again, and he took a swig. "I'm not fallen. I'm a one hundred percent, full-blown, Heavenly angel." His voice lowered, became thick with liquor. "What a fucking joke."

Now he was making no sense. She reached for the bottle. "Let me just take that—"

He jerked it way. "Mine."

She huffed. "As your doctor, I'm ordering you to give that to me."

"Mine."

"Hand it over," she said between clenched teeth.

His gaze roved over her in a frank, unhurried sweep. "*Mine*," he growled, and her body flushed with heat, as if it thought he was referring to her.

"I give up," she muttered as she shoved her medical supplies back into her bag.

He gave her a lopsided grin. "I like that you give in to me so easily."

"Yeah, well, don't expect me to give in to anything else. If you want a hangover for the record books, that's your problem. Don't come asking me for aspirin."

Half-lidded eyes swept her again, and the heat intensified. "There's a pub song about how women get better looking at closing time." He held up the bottle in salute. "You're already hot as hell. But now you look like an angel."

"Aw, I'll bet you say that to all the doctors who sew you up."

"Nope. Just you." He squinted at her. Looked at the bottle. Looked back at her. "I don't know what's in this booze, but I swear it's making you look different. Like an angel is trying to break through some sort of blurry overlay."

He frowned again at the bottle, completely oblivious to the fact that she was on the verge of hyperventilating. Had the alcohol given him the ability to see through her disguise?

Do something. Fast.

"Ah, hey." She gestured to his wound. "You need to get some rest now. The wound should be healed by morning."

Standing, she held out her hand to help him up, but he popped to his feet without her. And then, as if his legs were made of rubber, he collapsed. Only the wall and her quick thinking kept him from crashing to the floor.

"Criminy, you're heavy." Holding him with one arm slung around his waist, she casually took the liquor from him and set it on the coffee table.

He leaned heavily on her as she made her way past unpacked boxes toward her bedroom. "She gave up everything for me, Blaspheme," he mumbled. "She...she... aw, fuck." His big body trembled, and his voice, which was so deep and powerful, shook as hard as the rest of him. "It's my fault. Everything that happened to her...it's on me."

"Shh." Wondering who he was talking about, she eased him toward the bed. "It's okay."

"No," he moaned. "It's not okay. It'll never be okay. She told me not to break the rules, but I did it anyway. She paid for it, over and over. And then she died at the hands of a monster." He glanced down at his own hands as if they didn't belong to him.

"Come on, Rev." She pushed him down onto the mattress. He sat heavily, remaining like that, his head hanging on his shoulders, his chest heaving as if he'd run a marathon. She lifted his feet and swung him around so he was forced to lie back, his gorgeous ebony hair spreading out over her robin's-egg blue sheets. "Get some rest."

"Lay with me." He stared up at her, his glazed eyes going in and out of focus. She'd seen enough pain and intoxication to know that those things could be the cause of his visual responses, but this went deeper than that. Behind the alcohol muddle and the haze of pain was an open wound no medicine could touch.

"I don't think that would be a good idea," she murmured.

"*Please.*" There was so much vulnerability in that one simple word that she couldn't turn away.

Wondering how the hell she'd gotten herself into this mess, she climbed onto the opposite side of the bed and stretched out next to him. Naturally, he flipped over, slung his arm around her, and tucked her against him so they were spooning. Despite his condition, she expected him to try something sexual, but within a few heartbeats, his body had stopped shaking, and he was breathing in strong, even respirations.

As she relaxed in his powerful arms, she realized he was right. She did give in to him easily.

Too easily.

Twelve

Hours after Revenant had flashed himself away, Reaver was still staring out at the charred landscape. He had no idea how to handle his brother, no idea how to get through to him. Revenant was angry, hurt, and he possessed way too much power to be so unstable.

Reaver knew firsthand how badly *that* could go, and he had a lifetime of regrets to prove it.

Reaching out with his senses to locate Harvester, he flashed himself from the New Mexico badlands to the sandy beach of a Greek island he knew well.

Harvester was wading in the crystal surf, her blue-and-white-striped sundress catching the waves as they lapped at her ankles. She wasn't one for soft, feminine styles, so the fact that she was dressed like she should be at a polo match in the Hamptons was a clue that she was having a difficult day.

That made two of them.

Silently, he sat down in the sand, prepared to simply watch her. They'd been separated for five thousand years, and sometimes, like now, he wanted nothing more than to soak up her beauty and marvel at the angel she'd become.

Sure, she was still ornery, maddening, and sometimes, downright mean, but he wouldn't have her any other way.

She slid a glance at him from underneath the wide rim of her floppy straw hat. "Hey, you."

"Hey." He leaned forward and braced his arms on his knees. "What's wrong? You don't usually hang out at Ares's place without a reason."

Ares, Reaver's son and the second Horseman of the Apocalypse, known to many as War, didn't mind anyone in the family hanging out here. But Harvester's relationship with the Horsemen was complicated, starting with the fact that she was their Heavenly Watcher...and she'd once been their Sheoulic Watcher.

She smiled sadly, and was it his imagination, or was she even paler than she'd been this morning? "I saw Whine today. He goes by Tracker now, but it seems so strange to call him that."

"Do you regret giving him up?"

"Never," she said with a brisk shake of her head. "My father would have tortured or killed him to hurt me. Besides, he has a better life with Reseph and Jillian than I ever could have given him."

"Then why are you so upset?"

She sniffed, got that muley look he knew so well. "I'm not upset. When have you ever known me to be sentimental?"

"Never."

"There you go." She started toward him, kicking through the waves. "But while I was waiting to talk to Tracker, Revenant showed up."

Reaver went on instant alert. He was trying to be patient with Revenant, to give his twin a behavioral pass because he'd truly been given the shaft, but Reaver wouldn't tolerate anyone messing with his family.

"What happened?"

"Nothing," she said quickly. "It was something he said about how it's easier to be evil than good."

"And?"

"And it reminded me how close I came a few times to giving in to evil instead of staying on the path I'd intended." She sank down in the sand beside him, the warm breeze bringing her sun-kissed scent to him. "What if I'd done it? I mean, I left Heaven with a goal, but there were times when I lost sight of that goal. When it seemed like the very side I was fighting for was fighting against me, I kept wondering why I was sacrificing myself for people who hated me."

Reaching for her, he took her hand. "But you stayed strong, and in the end you managed to do exactly what you set out to do. You saved the world, Harvester. Don't let the *what-ifs* drive you crazy."

"I'm not. But what about Revenant?"

He blinked at the sudden change of focus. "What about him?"

"He's lost. He just found out he's an angel. An angel who was forsaken by the people who should be welcoming him. And now that he knows the truth about himself, he's struggling with who he was, who he is, who he wants to be, and who he thinks he should be. He doesn't know if he's good, evil, both…I know how that feels, and I know it can send you down a road to the wrong place."

Baffled by her out-of-character compassion for someone she hated, Reaver just stared. "Why do you care?"

She laughed, but she sounded tired. "I don't. He's a jackass." Her fingers were warm as she squeezed his hand. "I care for you. He's your brother, and no matter what I think of him, I know that if you don't try to help him down the right path, you'll regret it forever."

"You're pretty amazing, you know that?"

She gave another haughty sniff. "Of course I know that."

Nope, the transformation from fallen angel to haloed angel hadn't changed Harvester a bit. He shifted, putting his face to the salty breeze. "How are you feeling?"

"You mean, is Lucifer sucking my energy?" She shook her head. "I can barely feel him at all. I'm feeling better, in fact." He thought she might be lying, but then she smiled, the sultry one that made his blood run south and his brain stop functioning. "Now, let's go home and I'll show you how much better I'm feeling."

There was nothing he'd like more, but there was something he had to do first. "Rain check? I need to speak with the archangels."

"Hurry," she said in her husky bedroom voice. "Or I'll start without you."

Erotic images flooded his brain, and he groaned. No doubt this was going to be the briefest meeting in angel history.

Thirteen

"Fuck me, Revenant."

Blaspheme's husky voice rolled through Revenant in a silken caress. Naked, she lay beneath him, thighs parted, her sex glistening with honey as she waited for him to sink his hard cock into her tight sheath.

It was about damned time. He could take her now, get her out of his system, and move on to his next conquest.

He frowned. Why didn't his usual pattern sound so easy this time?

"Fuck me, Revenant," she repeated.

Reaching down, she fingered herself, and he damned near came. He'd been with a lot of females in his life, but none of them made him feel as though he needed to be inside them or he'd die. Just fall over dead.

"Anything for you, babe." He mounted her, guiding his cock to her dripping entrance, but before he could sink into her slippery heat, she slapped her palms against his chest.

"Be careful of your wound."

His wound? He looked down, saw the bandage wrapped around his torso. How had that happened?

"That's what happens when you let emotion rule. That's what happens when you start thinking you belong in Heaven. That's what happens when you think you can be happy." She was rambling now, her words coming faster and faster. "That's what happens when you deal with archangels. That's what happens when you confide in your brother."

"No," he croaked. "That's not...that's not how it happened." How was she tapping into his thoughts and dreams he didn't even know he had?

"That's what happens when you remember your mother. That's what happens when you realize she suffered for nothing. That's what happens when you understand what a disappointment you were to her. She sent Reaver to Heaven because he was the good twin. She didn't even give you a proper name."

Rearing back, he covered his ears. "No!" His breath burned in his throat as he said it over and over. "No, no, no...*noooo*!"

Suddenly, Blaspheme was gone, and he was panting as he lay on a strange bed in a strange room. How the everliving fuck had he gotten here? And where *was* here?

Forcing himself to calm down, he inhaled slowly. Blaspheme's clean scent filled his nostrils, and things started to come back to him.

He'd been wounded...he slapped his hand on his torso, felt the very real bandages under his palm. So that part wasn't a dream. She'd sewn him up, cared for him, tucked him into bed. Reaching over onto the other side of the mattress, he felt for warmth, but if she'd been there, she was long gone.

There was a note on the nightstand.

I'm in the rooftop garden having my morning coffee. There's a carafe and mugs in the kitchen if you want some.

Cool. He loved coffee.

With a thought, he cleaned up, which was an awesome bennie of being a Shadow Angel. Instant shower and change of clothes. He went with black leather pants and a black tank top under a leather jacket today, poured himself a cup of hazelnut coffee, and flashed himself to the rooftop. Which was another bennie. As a regular fallen angel, he could only flash to places he knew. Now he could pretty much wish himself anywhere.

Yep, very awesome.

"Hey, Blas—"

A scream made his chest go cold.

Dropping his mug, he bolted around the shed he'd materialized behind, and what he saw at the front of the building turned the ice in his chest to lava-hot fury. Rage consumed him. He didn't think. Didn't so much as breathe.

He slammed into the angel who had Blas pinned to the side of the mechanicals building and was about to plunge a dagger into her heart. They both hit the rooftop, grunting as about five hundred combined pounds of angel crashed into the structure. The dagger, an ancient *aurial* forged specifically to kill angels and fallen angels, clattered to the ground.

Revenant could have demolished the fucker, incinerated him, blasted him to bits, yanked him apart like a good old medieval draw-and-quartering. But Rev had too much rage stewing inside him to use his powers. He needed a brawl. Needed to feel bone splinter and flesh pulverize under his fists.

Needed to protect his female the way males were meant to. It didn't matter that Blaspheme wasn't technically his yet. She would be, if only for a night.

One night won't be enough.

He banished that thought as he smashed his fist into the other male's jaw. The angel got a good jab in his ribs, but then they both flipped to their feet, and the battle was on.

The angel grinned as he sent a stream of liquid lightning at Revenant's torso. "Die, Fallen."

Searing heat bored into Rev. Hurt like hell, but even as smoke rose from his burning flesh, his body healed. Surprise and panic lit the other male's eyes as Revenant walked toward him, not even slowed by the angelic weapon.

"Revenant!" Blaspheme's terrified voice came from behind him. "He'll kill you!"

She was worried. How sweet.

Revenant stopped, letting the angel's lightning stream into his body, absorbing the power, memorizing the intricate pattern that composed this particular talent. All his life Revenant had been using fallen angel weapons, never knowing he had the ability to use angel weapons as well.

Now he could. All he had to do was learn them.

The other male, a bald dude with mink wings, stared in disbelief as his weapon failed. Not just failed, but backfired.

"Get used to it, fucker." Rev reversed the angel's stream of lightning and sent it back at him, a hundred times hotter.

Baldie screamed and fell back, his body sizzling and smoking. Never one to waste an opportunity, Revenant went in for the kill. Scooping up the dagger the angel had been ready to use on Blaspheme, he rushed the angel.

A whip appeared in Baldie's hand, a whip that burned like a stream of lava. Molten orange drops plopped to the rooftop, burning holes in the asphalt as he cracked the whip in an arc meant to take Revenant's head off. He ducked, the tip of the weapon glancing off his shoulder in a hiss of fire meeting flesh.

This dude was so dead.

Revenant leaped and spun, landing a kick in the other angel's throat that crushed bone, tissue, and esophagus. Baldie hit the ground in a crumpled heap, but his unconsciousness wasn't going to save him.

"Say good night, motherfucker." Straddling Baldie's unconscious form, he plunged the blade downward.

"Revenant! *Stop*."

The blade flew from his hands. Then, as if a massive fist had closed around him, his breath was squeezed out of his lungs and his body crumpled in on itself.

Reaver.

His twin stood on the rooftop, his eyes flashing blue fire. Blaspheme had palmed the blade meant to end her life and was standing against the rooftop door, her gaze flitting between Rev, Reaver, and the unconscious angel.

With a roar, Revenant broke out of his brother's magical hold and sent an invisible punch of energy back at him. Reaver grunted and flew backward, blood spraying from his mouth and nose.

"Revenant, no!" Blaspheme rushed toward him. "He's a Radiant—"

"Get back!" Reaver threw out his hand, and a tornadic blast of wind pinned her against the door.

"*Don't touch her.*" A black veil of hatred filled Revenant's vision, until all he could think about was dealing out pain to the male who was holding Blaspheme against her will.

He came at Reaver with a sword of flame and spark, and with a single mighty swing, he cut his brother in half from the shoulder to the hip. Blaspheme's horrified scream rang out, but Reaver recovered in an instant and returned the favor, slicing through Revenant's thighs with a low, spinning chop of his own blade.

Revenant hit the ground, the agony short-lived as his body regenerated.

"This fighting is pointless, brother," Reaver yelled. "We're equally matched."

"It's not pointless if you're in pain," Revenant yelled back.

But at least Blaspheme was free of Reaver's hold. In fact, before he could stop her, she yanked open the stairwell door and fled. Good, now she was off the battlefield and wouldn't become collateral damage.

Twisting around, Revenant charged his powers and prepared to fry Baldie. This was going to end.

"Do not kill that angel," Reaver roared, flashing to intercept Rev's weapon.

"Or what?" This was Revenant's ticket to security in Sheoul. The only way he could prove to Satan that he was trustworthy.

Yeah, because being the Prince of Lies's right-hand man was a dream job.

Didn't matter. He had no choice. Heaven didn't want

him, and if Satan didn't either, the king of demons would snuff him like a spent cigarette.

"Or you'll never be welcome in Heaven."

Revenant laughed. Hard. When he finally sobered, he actually felt pity for his brother. "Truly? You think the archangels would ever, in a million years, embrace me like family? You are delusional."

"I spoke with them," he said. "They're willing to make it right. Everything that happened to you as a child ... they want to fix it."

"Fix it?" Revenant practically sputtered as he got to his feet. "How in the grand realm of fuck can they fix what they put me through? What they put our mother through?"

"They said your blood is tainted by Satan, but that the taint can be removed."

Hope sparked, but he wasn't going to get too excited. Hope was for fools. "Bullshit."

"Listen to me," Reaver said, his voice almost pleading. "I don't trust Raphael, but if there's even a chance that you could be admitted into Heaven without the risk of corrupting anything, you have to take it."

Revenant didn't *have* to do anything. But he couldn't resist asking, "What's the catch?"

"You have to prove your loyalty."

Gee, that sounded familiar, didn't it? "And how do I do that?"

Reaver's hands tightened into fists. "Gethel."

Of course. "Let me guess. You want me to kill her."

"No. I want you to bring her to me so *I* can kill her."

Rev flexed his hands, enjoying the feel of Baldie's blood drying on his knuckles. "Somehow I doubt the archangels made that part of the bargain."

"They said they'll purify your blood when Gethel is in their hands. They didn't say she had to be alive." Reaver flared his brilliant gold wings—wings that made him unique among all angels. "Well? What's it to be?"

"I need to think about it."

Reaver's flat stare spoke volumes about what his twin thought of that. "You have to think about it? Seriously? You don't know if you'd rather serve good or evil?"

"You self-righteous jackass," Revenant snarled. "It's so easy for you to judge, isn't it? You, who grew up in Heaven with a family who loved you. You, who was given every opportunity to achieve greatness, and you still managed to fuck it up. If you'd just listened to me when I came to you at Mount Megiddo all those years ago, if you'd helped me instead of hating me, we could have avoided five thousand fucking years of memory loss and hell!"

"You're right," Reaver shot back. "But that was a long time ago. We need to get past that—"

"It was weeks ago!" Not technically, but it was just a couple of weeks ago that the truth had come out and memories had been restored, and Revenant was still sorting through eons of shit. "You got your memories back, along with a mate, children, grandchildren, an aunt, an uncle, and probably a couple of gilded mansions. You know what I got? Threats from both sides. I need to do their bidding or take a hike. So go screw yourself, asshole. I need time to decide which side, good or evil, is going to fuck me over harder." He started for the door Blaspheme had gone through.

"Rev—"

He whirled back to his brother and jabbed his finger into his sternum. "Don't. Don't you dare play nice

now. Take your precious angel over there and go back
to Heaven where you belong. I'll give the archangels my
decision soon."

"Revenant," Reaver said quietly, "there's an expiration
date on this offer. If Gethel gives birth before you deliver
her to us, the deal is off."

Of course it was. Heaven couldn't possibly offer him
sanctuary simply because he was an angel. Nope. There
had to be strings attached to something that should have
been his by birth.

"Why were you here with Blaspheme, anyway?"
Reaver asked.

"What's it to you?"

"I worked with her for years at Underworld General
when I was Unfallen, and I consider her a friend. Don't
hurt her, Revenant, or you'll answer to me."

Revenant made a theatrical, sarcastic gesture with his
hands. "Ooh, scary."

"I mean it."

Whatever. He was sick of this shit. He should just kill
the angel who attacked Blaspheme and be done with it.
Except that when he looked over at where the bastard had
been, he was gone.

Instant, sharp alarm rang through him. Blaspheme
could be in trouble.

And God help Baldie if he had her, because this time,
Rev wasn't going to give the fucker the courtesy of dying
in the human realm.

Revenant was going to drag that haloed bastard to
Sheoul and kill him there.

Where his soul could languish in misery for all
eternity.

Fourteen

They were brothers. *Brothers*. As if it wasn't shocking enough that Reaver and Revenant were twins, the other revelation had blown Blaspheme away.

Reaver said that he and Revenant were evenly matched. Reaver was a Radiant... which meant that Revenant was a Shadow Angel.

A fucking *Shadow Angel*, the most powerful being in Sheoul, save Satan. If she'd thought Revenant was trouble as a fallen angel, that was nothing compared to what he really was.

Her breath came in terrified, spastic bursts as she ran down the fire escape stairs, past her apartment floor and down, until she tore through the door at the base of the building and sprinted up the sidewalk. She had no idea where she was going, just that she had to get away from two of the most dangerous individuals to have ever existed.

Gods, her mother was going to kill her.

Hey, Mom, guess what? You know how we've been keeping a low profile and staying away from angels and fallen angels? Yeah, well, I managed to attract the attention of both. Oh, and the best part? One is a Radiant and the other is a Shadow Angel. Awesome, right?

Stopping to catch her breath, she leaned against a light pole and buried her face in her hands. How could her life have gotten out of control so fast? Her False Angel enchantment was rapidly wearing off, both she and her mother had been attacked, she'd become obstetrician to Satan's baby mama, and now she'd landed in the center of some sort of family squabble between two extremely lethal individuals. All she needed now was to get fired from her job or hit by a truck.

She didn't know how long she stayed there like that, trying to gather her thoughts and corral her anxiety, but eventually an elderly man with a cane stopped to ask if she was okay. She thanked him, grateful for the dropkick back into reality.

A reality in which she'd neglected to grab her purse as she made her getaway, which meant she had no cell phone, no transit pass, and no money. She could hear her mother's voice now.

Didn't I teach you anything about bugging out in an emergency?

Wondering how much worse things could get, she reached out with her senses and located a Harrowgate about half a mile away. If she could just get to UG without anyone attacking her, she'd be safe. But it really sucked that her new apartment had been compromised. She'd only just moved in, and she couldn't afford to break the lease, lose her deposits, and pay new ones somewhere else.

Plus, finding a place in an area that hadn't been ravaged by the apocalyptic events of last year wasn't easy.

She hoofed it as fast as she could past fish-and-chips shops, pubs, and a bustling corner grocer, the tug of the Harrowgate growing more intense with each step. Finally, as she darted between a bookstore and a butcher shop, she saw the gate shimmering against the bookstore's brick wall. With no humans about, it opened up, beckoning to her with the promise of safety.

From out of nowhere, she heard the flap of giant wings. Terror squeezed her heart, cutting off her scream as she dove for the gate. Arms came around her, and a heartbeat later, she was standing in the middle of what looked like a log cabin—if log cabins were built from charred wood and brimstone.

The furry skin of some sort of demonic animal lay on the packed-earth floor, and a few pieces of stick furniture were scattered randomly around, as if whoever lived here didn't do much actual *living* here.

The arms released her, and she whirled, prepared to fight for her life with teeth and nails, if that's what it came down to. But when she saw Revenant standing there in his usual leathers and chains, she wasn't sure if she should be relieved ... or more terrified than ever.

"What the hell are you doing?" The adrenaline dump made her question come out as a shout, but at this point, she didn't give a crap. "Why did you snatch me like that? Where are we?"

"This is my place."

This windowless, barren hovel was his home? The idea

that she was standing in a Shadow Angel's lair, no doubt deep inside Sheoul, with no way to tell anyone where she was, drove a spike of fear straight through her heart.

It also pissed her off. If he was going to kill her, she wasn't going to temper her thoughts or her words. "You need a new Realtor."

His dark brows pulled together in irritation. "Yeah, well, when you're a fallen angel under Satan's thumb, you don't have a lot of options."

"Really?" she snapped. "Because I'm betting that Shadow Angels can pretty much have what they want."

He ran a hand through his hair with a frustrated shove. "The Shadow Angel thing is fairly recent."

Rubbing her arms because it was freezing in here, she relaxed a little, figuring that if he hadn't killed her or at least chained her to a wall by now, he wasn't going to. Hopefully.

"Recent is a matter of perspective," she said. "For an immortal, recent can mean something that happened in the last thousand years."

"It's been a little over two weeks."

"Oh." That took a little of the wind out of her indignant sails. "Well, thanks for showing me your digs, but I really have to get going."

He glanced over at the fireplace, which lit with a *whoosh*. "Not until you tell me why that angel was trying to kill you."

There were so many ways she could play this, but she went for the obvious. "Because I'm a demon. Angels kill demons for sport. Was that a serious question?"

"Yes." His leather jacket creaked as he crossed his arms over his chest. "They don't just pop onto random rooftops hoping to get lucky and find demons to kill. He was hunting you. Why?"

Closing her eyes, she replayed the scene in her head... a scene that had started out with blue skies, bright sunlight, and the trill of pigeons walking the roof's ledges.

"Vyrm."

The angel's hatred dripped from his voice as he materialized in front of Blaspheme. She let out a scream, dropping her coffee cup as she scrambled out of her chair. Glass shattered and coffee splattered, but she barely noticed. The only thing she could see right now was the huge warrior standing on the roof in military combat gear, his body laden with weapons.

"H-how did you find me?"

An aurial, *a blade specifically designed to kill angels and fallen angels, appeared in his hand.*

"I don't answer vyrmin questions."

Cute, how he'd turned vyrm *into* vermin. *She wished she was going to live to appreciate the wordplay.*

"Blaspheme?"

Revenant's voice broke into her not-so-fond memory. What had he asked her? Why the angel was hunting her?

She shrugged, hoping he'd buy her false indifference. "I have no idea. Maybe there's extra incentive this week to slaughter False Angels. And you know, maybe you could explain how you found me? You'd better not be tracking me, or—"

He held up her Coach bag, which, apparently, he'd pulled out of his ass, because she swore he hadn't been holding it a moment ago. "I saw you didn't take your purse with you, so I guessed that you'd have to use a Harrowgate for transportation. I checked the Harrowgate closest to your apartment." His black eyes glittered. "That was stupid. Anyone with half a brain would have known to waylay you at that Harrowgate."

She gaped in indignation. "So now I'm stupid?"

He tossed the bag onto one of his rickety chairs. "Now you're *safe*."

Somehow she doubted that. Oh, she was certain no one was going to get past Revenant to get to her. But could someone get past him to *save* her?

"I would have been safe if I'd gotten to Underworld General."

Revenant reached up to rub the back of his neck, causing his shirt to rise up on his hard-cut abs. "The hospital has been breached before."

He had a point. Sort of. And man, that sliver of flesh between the hem of his shirt and the top of his leather pants was distracting. Leave it to False Angel instincts to make her horny in any inappropriate situation.

"Not by Heavenly forces," she ground out, irritated by her reaction to him. "Angels can't get in."

"Reaver can."

As a Radiant, Reaver was the exception, but she hadn't worried about that, since Reaver rarely came to the hospital. But now that Eradicators knew what she was, how long would it be before Reaver found out and popped into the hospital to confront her?

Panic frayed the edges of her control, and she started to look around for an escape. It wasn't logical, but her mother's training had instilled in her a need to locate all exits wherever she went, especially if she felt trapped or afraid.

"Hey." Revenant softened his voice and moved toward her. "I promise you're safe."

"Safe from the angel, maybe, but what about from you?"

"You think I'll hurt you?" He cupped his hand around her nape, his touch surprisingly gentle. "I want you in my bed, not in a grave."

Oh, gods ... yes.

No!

She shrank away from him, even though the mention of his bed made her heart beat a little faster. "I don't think so." He only wanted her because he thought she was someone she wasn't. She didn't want to be within a thousand miles when and if he learned the truth. He'd already admitted that he thought death sentences were reasonable for people who associated with *vyrm*. How would he feel about *actual vyrm*?

"Why not?" he asked. "You haven't fucked a male since Yuri."

Her jaw dropped. "E-excuse me?"

His smirk managed to be both amused and mocking. "Yuri. I'm sure you remember his name. By all accounts, you were pretty into him."

She gasped in outrage. First of all, she hadn't been into the arrogant surgeon. At the time, she'd believed he was beginning to suspect the truth about her, so she'd gotten intimate with him. Pretended to love the thorny flails and shit.

Second of all ... "You've been checking up on me? How dare you! I told you I go to clubs to fulfill my needs."

"Really?" More amusement. More mocking. "Which ones?"

"Just last week I partied my ass off at Thirst." In truth, she'd gone to the vampire club with some nurses from the clinic for the sole purpose of playing False Angel slut, and she'd done a lot of flirting, but she'd gone home alone. "And how do you know about Yuri anyway?"

"I'm resourceful, Blaspheme. I can find out anything I want. It's just easier to ask. So why don't you tell me what you're hiding."

"Why are you so certain I'm hiding something?"

He looked over at the massive sword on the wall, its magnificent, double-edged blade dulled by age and the smoky light in Revenant's lair. The ebony hilt, its cross-guard decorated with sharp teeth, flowed fluidly to the skull-shaped pommel. The thing suited Revenant well, beautiful, wicked... and somehow tarnished.

"For thousands of years, my job was to hunt down anyone Satan or Lucifer deemed to be undesirable or an enemy. That included half-breeds, angels, *vyrm*, traitors." He trailed his finger along the edge of the blade, and for a brief moment, she pictured him thrusting the sword through her *vyrm* heart. "I learned to recognize deception."

Shit. Just... shit. In an effort to keep from sounding terrified, she smiled glibly. "And how do you do that?"

A trickle of blood ran down the sword's edge, but before it reached the tip, the metal soaked up every drop.

"Usually I can smell it. See it. Sense it." He swung away from the sword and nailed her with black eyes so intense that she took an unbidden step back. "But you... it's like I should be picking up on a secret, but something is blocking it. I'll find out what it is, Blaspheme, so why don't you just tell me now."

"Why don't you go fuck yourself?"

"I'd rather fuck you."

His crude words became images in her mind, and damn her False Angel desires, because now all she wanted was to turn the images and words into action. Sweaty, naked, throbbing action.

Besides, she'd be fooling herself if she thought he was going to give up trying to bed her, and he clearly was a hellhound with a bone when it came to what he believed she was hiding. Trying to stay away from him wasn't working, and she had no doubt that he wasn't going to just go away.

It was time to opt for preventive surgery and cut him out of her life like a suspicious tumor. And like any good doctor, she'd use every method she had at her disposal, including what little aphrodisiac she had remaining on her wings if necessary.

"Okay, then." Her mouth actually watered in anticipation of what she was about to say. "I have a proposition for you."

One black eyebrow shot up. "I'm listening."

Summoning every ounce of False Angel magic she had left, she sauntered over to him. Slowly. Seductively. He thought she was different, so she'd show him exactly how identical she was to the species she was pretending to be.

The crazy thing was that this all felt so natural. Crazy, because the FA enchantment should be wearing off, not intensifying her desires.

"Sex," she said, lowering her voice to a husky, deep False Angel drawl that drew males like a magnet. "I'll fuck you if you'll take me to Underworld General." His gaze darkened dangerously. "But only once. Just enough for you to get me out of your system."

Male triumph lit his expression. "Agreed," he rumbled. "I'm sure once will be enough. It always is."

She should have been happy to hear those words. At best, sex had never been anything but a pleasant diversion from real life, and at worst, it had been a necessary cover for her False Angel persona. But for some reason, Revenant's casual acquiescence stung. It made no sense, was completely illogical.

And yet, as she stepped into his hard body and his erection pressed into her belly, all she could think was that his interest in her had never been about *her*.

It had always been about his dick.

"One more thing," she said.

His hands closed on her hips, gripping them possessively. "What's that?"

Very deliberately, she grasped his arms and shoved them away from her body. "You don't touch me unless I tell you to. Not with your hands, not with your mouth, and not with your fangs."

He looked like he'd been slapped. "Say again?"

"Those are the rules. During sex, you don't touch me. After the sex, you take me to UG."

"Why the fuck can't I touch you?" he growled.

"Because I don't trust you. Show me that you can keep your word. Show me you can keep yourself under control."

A vein in his temple throbbed. "This is a... rule?"

"Yes."

For a long time he stood there, so motionless she couldn't even see the rise and fall of his chest. And then he inclined his head, his black-as-midnight hair falling forward in a sexy curtain she wanted to wrap around her body.

"If that's the only way I can have you, then so be it."

Casting him a sultry False Angel smile, she slid her fingers beneath his waistband and tugged him toward what she hoped was his bedroom. If not, her take-charge attitude was going to fizzle like a rain-drenched campfire and she'd look like a fool.

But, she supposed, looking like a fool was better than being dead.

Fifteen

Revenant's body was on fire.

As he let Blaspheme lead him to his bedroom, he marveled at how easily his little False Angel had gotten him to concede to her demands. He'd always been the one to control sexual encounters, to say when, where, and how it all went down. Hell, when a female *went down*, it was because *he* wanted her to.

And now this gorgeous, mysterious False Angel was leading him around by his cock, literally, and he was allowing it.

But then, at the end of the day, he was male, and he'd do pretty much anything for sex. Truly, if more females understood the power they held over males, they'd rule all the realms.

He willed the candles in the wall sconces to light up as they entered the bedroom.

"Dungeon chic," Blaspheme said, taking in the shackles anchored to the stone walls. "Nice. And a little cliché, don't you think?"

"Clichés exist for a reason." He started to reach for her, cursed, and yanked his hands away. Rules were rules. Even if they were infuriating.

She stopped at the foot of the bed and turned to him, her hand still gripping his waistband. The tips of her fingers brushed the head of his erection as she shifted her hold, and his body responded instantly, spiking his heart rate, his blood pressure, his breathing... Shit, he was going to stroke out the first time she *really* touched him.

"Take your clothes off," she demanded.

"You aren't going to take them off for me?"

She graced him with a flirty smile that was so feminine and sexy that he didn't wait for her answer. He wished his clothes away, and *poof*, they were gone.

Instantly, her teasing playfulness shifted into something hotter. More intense. If he'd known that getting naked was all it took, he'd have pulled a Magic Mike the first time he met her.

Her eyes took him in, his muscles flexing where her gaze landed. By the time she reached his rock-hard cock, his entire body was just as hard, primed for whatever she wanted.

"What do you think a False Angel would do now?" she asked.

He had no idea what a False Angel would do, but he knew what he'd suggest. "She'd lick my balls."

She cocked a blond eyebrow. "Really." She might be playing it cool, but the delicate aroma of her arousal rose up, heightening his own.

"Really."

He didn't think she'd do it, so he let out a strangled moan when she dropped to her knees and pressed those soft, silky lips against his sac. Holy hell, she was doing it, she was licking and sucking, nibbling and—

"Damn," he breathed as she sucked a testicle into her mouth and hummed around it. He caught himself before he palmed her head and guided her mouth to catch the release that would be coming at any second.

But before he hit mission critical status, she was up on her feet, her teasing smile making it clear that she knew exactly how close he'd been.

And how much agony he was now in.

False Angels were evil.

"On the bed," she commanded, and as much as he detested being told what to do, he hit that mattress in record time, lying on his back while he watched her strip.

She didn't tease him out on this. With the same crisp efficiency he'd seen her use when he'd been tending to his wounds, she shed her clothes, leaving them in a neat pile at the foot of the bed. Then she stood there, looking both tentative and eager, though how she managed that, he had no idea.

Nor did he care. Not when she was standing at his feet, her elegant, supple body a work of goddamned art. Her breasts were full and heavy, the dusky nipples peaked with arousal. Her slim waist was made for a male to circle his hands around as he lifted her up and down on his cock.

And between her legs, she was smooth, her plump nether lips parted slightly, just enough to show a hint of glistening pink flesh.

Holy hell, his dick hurt.

"I thought False Angels were proud of their...special ornamentation."

"As we've established, I'm not your normal False Angel." She climbed onto the bed, the mattress sinking under her weight. "I wax."

He groaned. "I like."

She crawled up his body, her palms sliding up his shins to his thighs, her eyes bright with hunger. "Do you want to touch me?" Her husky voice vibrated all the way to the balls she'd just sucked so skillfully.

"Fuck, yes."

Her grin was downright sinister. "Too bad."

Lowering her head, she brushed her lips over the head of his cock. The thing jerked, slapping her across the mouth. As punishment, she nipped him on the sensitive seam just under the crown.

His bark of pain and pleasure made the chains on the wall rattle.

"Well, well," she murmured. "Someone likes that."

"Someone has never had that done to him before." In five thousand years, no female had ever done that. And he'd had some rough-as-fuck partners. "Do it again."

"I have a better idea."

Better than that? No way—

Oh, fuck, yes. Straddling him, she scooted forward, that sweet cleft coming closer and closer to his face. His mouth began to water and his fangs began to pulse, and even his dick was leaking.

He'd never been so desperate to get intimate with a female in that way. It was as if he'd starve if she didn't lower herself against his lips in the next ten seconds.

As she gripped the headboard and positioned herself

above him, he fisted his hands at his sides, praying for control. The rules…he couldn't break the rules. But damn, his fingers itched to touch her. To spread her. To penetrate her.

"False Angels are supposed to taste like apples." Licking his lips, he lifted his head to meet her as she tilted her hips, putting her sex in contact with his mouth. She moaned as he slipped his tongue between her plump folds. Her slick honey flooded his mouth with the crisp tang of red apples, milder than he'd expected, mixed with her own feminine spice he'd take over fruit any day.

Pain shot up his wrists, and he realized he was clenching his fists so hard his nails were digging into his palms. Willing his hands to relax, he pierced her with his tongue.

"Yes," she breathed. "Like that."

Oh, so she liked when he pushed his tongue deep inside her? Too bad. She was torturing him, so he'd do the same.

He'd always been about the what-goes-around-comes-around.

Shifting his head for a better angle, he dragged the flat of his tongue through her valley, flicking the tip over her clit at the end of the upstroke. She cursed darkly, her body quivering as he did it again. And again. On the fourth pass, he lingered on her swollen knot of nerves, circling it as her hips rolled to match his rhythm.

Her orgasm was close, so close that the air became charged with her need. His cock and balls throbbed, and he hoped like hell the no-touching gag order didn't apply to him, because he palmed himself and squeezed, holding back what was no doubt going to be a climax for the record books.

"I'm going to come…Rev…oh, Rev…*yes*." She cried out, going taut as shudder after shudder racked her body.

Now would be the time when he should flip the sitch, throw her on her back and dive into her. Or slip out from under her, shove her head into the pillow and lift her hips, and drive into her from behind, his balls slapping her wet sex with every hard thrust.

But he couldn't touch her. He nearly howled with frustration as her gasps of pleasure ebbed. Her legs trembled as she scooted back and sank heavily onto his abdomen. Gods, she was beautiful as she looked down at him, hair wild, her face flushed and glistening with a fine sheen of sweat, her eyes glazed with pleasure, her swollen lips parted as she panted.

"Let me touch you now," he growled.

Leaning forward, her hair falling like a curtain around them, she brushed her mouth over his. "No."

"Sweetheart, you have one hell of a cruel streak."

She smiled and started a slow slide down his body, her mouth kissing a red-hot trail as she went. Closing his eyes, he let her body caress him, the skin on skin turning his body into a hypersensitive sex toy he wished she'd hurry up and ride.

As she inched lower, her warmth engulfed his erection as it slid between her plump folds. The sudden sensation rocked him hard, jacking his entire body off the bed as he tried to penetrate her. But she would have none of that, and even as he arched his hips upward, she eased backward, breaking contact.

"Blaspheme." His voice was a combination of snarly and needy. "You're playing with fire."

"Good," she said with a naughty wink. "Because it's cold in here."

"Fuck." He threw his head back on the pillow, pressing his palms into his thighs, willing himself to stay in control. To not circle that waist with his hands, hold her steady, and impale her with his painfully hard cock.

"Hmm." Rolling her bottom lip between her teeth, she teased him by tracing the veins in his shaft with her finger. "Was that an invitation?"

"Yes," he ground out. "An invitation. An order. A motherfucking plea. Call it what you want, just fuck me."

"Show me your fangs."

Instant fangage. He'd show her his freaking liver if she'd just make him come. Reaching out, she touched the tip of a canine.

"Vampire fangs are erogenous zones," she purred. "They can even come if you stroke their fangs long enough."

"So?" The idea of her fang-jerking some bloodsucker made him want to slaughter the next vampire he saw. Another finger joined the first, and Revenant found himself getting his first FJ.

"So…is it the same with fallen angels?"

As if his erection was the one getting stroked, he felt the orgasm building in his balls.

"Apparently," he gasped, gripping his cock again and squeezing until the pain overrode the pleasure. Holy shit, when he finally came, he was going to make a fire hose look like a squirt gun.

"Interesting."

"Interesting?" he croaked. "You know what would be interesting? If you'd let me touch you."

"And why's that?"

His control was slipping. He felt it in the way his heart was beating against his rib cage and his hands were clenched to the point of bleeding. He heard it in the guttural tone of his voice. Tasted it in the blood from his bitten tongue. Smelled it in the arousal that mingled with hers.

"Because I would have you up against that wall, my hands pinning yours so you'd know how this feels, and I would rail you so hard you'd feel me for a month. And after we both came, I'd have you on the floor, pulling a sixty-nine that wouldn't end until I tasted a dozen of your orgasms. Before you could even *think* about recovering, I'd fuck you in every way a male can fuck a female. And I wouldn't stop. Not until you begged." He slammed his fists into the mattress. "Damn it, Blaspheme, I need to be inside you." He sucked in a harsh breath. "Let me... inside you."

Her eyes flared, and for the first time, he understood how False Angels truly lured males. Not with seduction, but with innocence. She was wide-eyed but breathing hard, quivering delicately but coating his shaft in her arousal. Every male instinct inside him screamed to take her, and to do it hard and fast, and then again, slowly, thoroughly. He wanted to learn every inch of her body and how each inch responded to him. He wanted to teach her what made him crazy, and then he wanted to wipe every other male from her memory.

And what the hell was he thinking? This was the False Angel magic at work, because it sure as fuck wasn't his own brain throwing out all that crazy shit. He'd never wanted to claim a female for himself. Sure, he'd had casual lovers, more than he could count. But the moment he started looking forward to seeing a lover was the moment he checked out of the relationship.

Hell, if he'd been in this position with Blaspheme just a month ago, he doubted he'd be so infatuated. No, he didn't doubt. He knew. Her ethics and goodness would have repelled him like DEET repelled mosquitoes. But with his returned memories had come new emotions, regrets, and pain, and somehow Blaspheme was tapping into that, making him want more than just sex... when it was clear she *only* wanted sex.

Blaspheme's breath heaved in and out, her breasts rising and falling as if beckoning his touch. He reached for her—

No!

His entire body shook with the force it took to stop his hands. Holy hell, his control had slipped to nothing. She'd set down a rule, and he had been about to break it. He trembled harder, but then warm, soft hands gripped his cock and stroked up and down, working together to massage him into compliance.

"There you go," she was saying in a soothing voice. "Fastest way to ease out an adrenaline overload is sex."

Adrenaline overload? Maybe the False Angel ability jacked into the adrenal glands and rendered their partners unable to follow orders. It was as good an explanation as any, and he was happy to lay the blame for his slipup on her.

Feeling better now, he arched into her hands and fucked her fists as they pumped him.

"Hurry," he growled. "I need to be inside you."

"For once I agree with you."

Shifting, she stood his cock up and positioned herself over the tip. Then she paused, and he ground his teeth at the agonizing delay.

"Wait." She bit down on one kiss-swollen lip. "Protection."

"False Angels can only breed with False Angels," he said, and shouldn't she know that?

"Yes, I know. But you're some kind of super fallen angel. What if—"

"I'm an *angel*," he pointed out. "Angels aren't fertile in Sheoul. Prevents demons from capturing them and using them to breed hybrid abominations."

"How *is* it possible that you're an angel anyway?" She frowned, losing the saucy, aroused edge, and shit, he had to get back on the sex track.

"I never fell from Heaven. Long story. I'll tell you after." He arched up, reminding her that now wasn't the time for talking. It was time for fucking.

"Should be a good story." She stroked his cock in her fist, giving it a couple of good pumps before replacing it at her opening.

He held his breath as she lowered herself, head thrown back, lips parted, her sex swallowing his erection in slow, torturous increments. The erotic sight made him groan, his sex kicking hard inside her as if urging her to hurry.

"That's it. Fuck, that's so it," he breathed. "You're so damned wet."

A low, hungry moan broke from her lips as she took him to the hilt. She swiveled her hips and rose up until he nearly came free of her tight heat, and then she sat down again, faster this time, but still way too slow for his tastes.

He hoped she was done with the control-freak trip she was on, because it was his turn.

On the next upstroke, he dug his heels into the mattress and arched his hips to buck her, lifting her knees off the bed and forcing her to fall forward. As her palms shot out to brace her body on his chest, he rolled his hips, penetrating her deep.

Her gasp of pleasure joined his as the pace picked up, breathing became frantic, and the sound of slapping bodies dropped them into a maelstrom of ecstasy. Her breasts, flushed and heavy with arousal, bounced as she rode him, and when she cupped one, tweaking the nipple between her fingers, he nearly came undone.

"Show me your wings, Blaspheme," he murmured breathlessly. "I want to see all of you."

He thought he saw a flicker of alarm in her eyes, but a heartbeat later, delicate wings spread from her back, extending high into the air. Unlike true angel or fallen angel wings, they were neither leathery nor layered with feathers, were instead shimmery and translucent, like a bride's veil sprinkled with glitter.

They were so transparent, in fact, that they seemed to flicker in and out of existence until finally, she folded them neatly behind her back and let them fade completely away.

"Beautiful," he whispered.

She met his gaze, catching her bottom lip between her teeth. The intensity in her expression, the sultry cast of her eyes and lips...damn, he was ready to spill into her, to make her moan his name from that sexy mouth.

"So are you." She arched in pleasure, the graceful curve of her body the epitome of False Angel perfection. "You're a bastard, Revenant, but a beautiful one."

Never had anyone given him such a precious compliment, and for a few stuttering heartbeats, he froze, committing her words to memory.

Rolling her hips, she clenched her internal muscles and took him so deep he swore he felt the beat of her heart at the tip of his cock. His sac pulled taut with impending release as it met the hot flesh between her legs with every erotic move she made.

Given the intensity of her torture, he lasted longer than he thought he would, but he couldn't have predicted that when his climax came, he'd hit another damned plane of existence.

As his balls throbbed, his entire body seized up, racked with pleasure so intense he could only roar in exquisite agony. Distantly he heard Blaspheme's soft cries, felt her clamp down around him in rippling waves. Another orgasm rear-ended the first one, and he was launched into the stratosphere again as his body blew apart.

Holy ... *damn.*

When the world came into focus again, he couldn't move. He felt disembodied, could only lie there, dizzy, boneless, Blas's warm weight something he would gladly bear all night.

She lay on top of him, breathing heavily, her sweaty skin plastered to his. He wondered if his half of the deal they'd struck was over yet, so he could finally run his hands through her silky hair that fanned over his shoulders. But then he decided he couldn't lift his arms anyway, so the no-touching thing was irrelevant.

"I can't move," Blaspheme muttered, her breath whispering across his throat.

Move? Revenant couldn't even speak. He managed a

grunt he hoped sounded like agreement, and he felt her lips curve into a smile against his skin. That one tiny intimacy, a secret, satisfied smile while they were still connected, wrapped around him like a warm embrace.

The sensation was as intense as it was unfamiliar. He loved females and he loved sex, and he'd had a lot of both. But this was the first time he'd felt like this, as if he couldn't get enough. Not of just sex, but of a female. Of Blaspheme.

He could lie like this forever. Maybe the Earth would stop spinning, the realms would stop fighting, and everyone would leave him and Blaspheme the hell alone. Revenant had never been one to dream . . . any dreams he might have had were destroyed on that Megiddo hilltop all those years ago, when Reaver had made it clear that brothers or not, they weren't family, and Rev didn't belong in Heaven.

But here he was, dreaming. Which was insane, considering his life was in the worst possible place it could be right now, with both Heaven and hell screwing with him. Neither side was known for being especially forgiving when it came to battles between good and evil, which meant that no matter what he did, someone was going to rain a whole lot of hell down on his head. Literally, if Satan was the one he pissed off.

So yeah, lying in bed and dreaming of a future where he was in any way happy was stupid.

But as Blaspheme let out a contented sigh, he realized he was happy at this very moment. He was going to embrace it. Savor it.

Because something told him it wasn't going to last.

Sixteen

Revenant woke to the tap of Blaspheme's fingers on his sternum. He'd fallen asleep? Seriously? He never crashed after sex.

Opening his eyes, he glanced at the clock on the wall, and yep, he'd lost a couple of hours. He canted his head to the side, smiling when he saw Blaspheme facing him, her body stretched against his as he lay on his back, her hand running up and down his chest.

"Hi." She returned his smile with a shy one of her own.

"Hi." His voice was shot to hell, but in a good post-coital way.

"So," she said, not wasting any time, "how is it that you and Reaver are brothers? And why didn't Reaver ever mention it before?"

Groaning, Rev threw his forearm over his eyes. "You got something against coffee before conversation?"

"Nope. But while you were sleeping I rummaged

through your kitchen, and I couldn't find any." She jabbed him in the ribs. "So? Spill."

Figuring he couldn't avoid getting back to real life, Revenant tucked his arm behind his head and stared at the ceiling. "Reaver didn't mention having a brother because he didn't know until a couple of weeks ago. Neither did I."

"How can that be?"

"Our memories were erased. Twice."

Sitting up, she snared a blanket from the foot of the bed and covered herself. Too bad. He could look at her creamy breasts all day. "I'm lost."

He was lost, too. "Yeah, well, I'm still trying to work out thousands of years of memories myself." Reaching over, he fingered a tendril of her silky hair while he considered how much to tell her. He didn't trust anyone, but False Angels, with their lying, seductive ways, were even less trustworthy. And Blaspheme, while she wasn't like any False Angel he'd ever met, was undoubtedly hiding something from him. He might have been drunk when he saw some sort of crumpling aura around her last night at her apartment, but he was perfectly sober now, and he still sensed that there was something not right with her.

That said, he didn't know how she could possibly use anything he told her against him.

"Our mother was a battle angel," he said finally. "She was pregnant with a potential Radiant, and she was betrayed by an angel to Satan's forces. Our father was killed in the battle, and she was taken to Sheoul. She gave birth to twins. Heaven worked out a deal to take one of the infants, and Sheoul would take the other."

"Oh, wow," she whispered. "So that's how you're an

angel, not a fallen angel. Heaven took Reaver, didn't they?"

"Yes. I was left behind, raised in a ten-by-ten cell in a dungeon." The memories came at him like blows, but he quickly blocked them and got away from that messy part of the story. "Years later, after I learned the truth, I went to Reaver, and it didn't go well. He'd just discovered that the female he loved had betrayed him and that he had four grown children. He was pissed, I was pissed... let's just say that between the two of us, we caused a whole lot of destruction."

"What's a whole lot?"

"The kind that requires thousands of angels to rewrite history in the minds of humans."

She swallowed. "They can do that?"

"Apparently they've done it several times."

"Holy shit," she breathed.

"Yeah." He scrubbed his hand over his face. "So I lost my memory. Satan told me that I was a fallen angel, and that I didn't remember my time in Heaven because sometimes fallen angels lose their memories when they fall from grace. I bought it. I believed it when he told me that I was kicked out of Heaven for assassinating fellow angels." He snorted. "I toed the evil line like a champ. Fuck, I need a drink. You?"

She shook her head.

"You sure?" He swung out of bed and strode, naked, to the portable bar in the corner. "Don't think I've ever met a False Angel who wasn't a lush."

"I have to work later. For some reason, Eidolon frowns on his staff showing up drunk."

He poured himself a shot of Sheoul's finest absinthe,

made the old-fashioned way, with wormwood grown in the corpses of imps. "Ah, that's right. You're a False Angel with ethics."

"Yeah. Ethics." She rubbed her temples as if fending off a headache. "So how long did you go around thinking you were a fallen angel? Also," she grumbled, "you should put on some clothes. You're a menace to society when you're naked."

Ah, his ego loved the stroking. He definitely wasn't getting dressed now. "I believed I was fallen for five thousand years, give or take a century or ten." He knocked back the neon-green liquor, relishing the stinging burn down his throat. "Then, a little over three decades ago, Reaver did something bad again. He broke a huge rule and was punished. Want to guess how?"

"Ah...memory loss?"

"Yep. Well, that and he lost his wings. Went to work at your hospital. And here's the kicker. The agreement Heaven made with Sheoul when we were born said that whatever was done to one of us had to be done to the other. So my memory was wiped. Again."

The alcohol sting in his throat turned bitter. Breaking rules resulted in chaos and pain and all kinds of shit, and Reaver's reckless disregard for the rules had done exactly that.

"Jesus," she whispered. "So you lost five thousand years of memories in an instant?"

He nodded. "Reaver at least knew that he was being punished. Me? One minute I was...ah...doing fallen angel stuff, and the next I was wondering why the hell I was standing in Sheoul's Horun region, covered in blood, and standing over the body of some *vyrm*."

The color faded from Blaspheme's cheeks. Her physician self must be appalled by the killing Revenant had done.

He poured another drink. "Like I told you earlier, hunting *vyrm* and other undesirables was my job. I was Satan's little assassin helper. I didn't know that at the time. I only remember now."

He'd been a straight-up badass hell-bent on destruction, and he'd been proud of it. Now, knowing he had Satan's blood running through his veins, corroding his body and soul like Drano, the memories left him confused. He was evil—how could he not be? But he was also an angel whose mother had loved him.

His fingers curled around the shot glass so hard his hand shook. Fuck, he was lost.

"I wandered around for a year after the second memory wipe, scrounging out a living in Sheoul, turning myself into a hired hand. And then Satan's minions came for me. He told me the *vyrm* must have erased my memory before I killed him, and that I had been a fallen angel for thousands of years, blah fucking yadda."

Blaspheme's skin was still pale, but some of the color had started to return. Good. He didn't like seeing her upset.

"And then your memory came back a couple of weeks ago?" she prompted. "How did that happen?"

"Reaver again. You sensing a pattern?" Revenant was struck by an urge to seek out his brother and start another brawl. "He rescued Harvester from Sheoul and saved the realms or some crap. For his actions he was raised to Radiant and given his memory back. And because whatever is done to one of us has to be done to the other—"

"You were turned into a Shadow Angel."

"You got it." He raised his glass in a begrudging toast. "To my heroic twin brother and his shiny halo."

"But why wouldn't you be a Radiant? I mean, you're an angel, right?"

The liquor went down smoother this time. "Because there can only be one at any given time. There has to be a Shadow Angel for balance, and Reaver won the hero lottery while I was fed Satan's blood as an infant. It corrupted me, gave me all of the qualities and abilities of a fallen angel." He tongued a fang. "Including these."

"So your inner angel is masked," Blaspheme mused. "Interesting." She climbed out of bed and started dressing. What a shame. "You said your mother was imprisoned when she was pregnant. What happened to her after you were born?"

He should have expected the question, but it still stabbed him in the heart. "She died after a couple of decades of torture."

"I'm sorry," she said as she fastened her bra. "Did you know her at all?"

"Yeah." The alcohol in his belly turned sour, and all he wanted now was to vomit. "Can we not talk about this?"

"I should be going anyway." She tugged on her pants. "We had a deal, remember?"

Yeah, he remembered. And he was kicking himself in the nuts for making it. He wasn't ready to let her go. He should be; he'd never had a problem letting a female go in the past. But suddenly, he was aching at the thought of parting from her.

It's that damned False Angel magic.

Of course. Hopefully it would wear off once she was out of his sight. But what if it didn't? What if she was intentionally enchanting him? That was one of a False Angel's many methods of finding sustenance. They used their pheromones and seductive skills to enchant, their aphrodisiac powder to seduce, and then they severed ties and gorged on the emotional agony they caused. The more heartbroken the male was, the more energy she took from him. If she was lucky and he died, she feasted.

That wasn't going to happen to Revenant. He was stronger than that. If Blaspheme thought she could play him, she was going to be brutally disappointed.

He clothed himself in an instant, going with jeans and a black Four Little Ponies of the Apocalypse T-shirt, and then he watched her finish dressing, wondering if she'd make some sort of flirty play to draw him in even further. Sure enough, as she slipped on her shoes, she shot him a teasing smile.

"That was fun." Slinging her purse over her shoulder, she strutted over to him and drew her finger down his chest, halting at his waistband. "Interesting T-shirt choice."

"It annoys the Horsemen's stallions."

"I have a feeling you like poking dangerous things with sticks, don't you?"

"If the stick is sharp enough, no thing is dangerous."

She cocked a blond eyebrow. "Really? Because I don't think I could find a stick sharp enough to make you less dangerous."

"I'm not a danger to you, Blaspheme." Putting his fingers to her throat, he stroked the silky skin right over her jugular vein. "Not if you've been honest with me."

In an instant, her demeanor changed, intensified, almost as if she had a split personality, and the other one had come out to play. Gone was the easygoing, flirty doctor, and in her place was a temptress with pouty lips and half-lidded eyes. Her delicate wings flared out and tucked away again, and in the smoky light from the wall sconces, he could see glittery particles floating in the air.

Aphrodisiac powder. She was attempting to enchant him with it. And okay, he suddenly felt a little amorous, but it didn't overshadow the disappointment rolling through him that she'd so blatantly use a False Angel trick on him. Did she really think he'd fall madly in love with her and then collapse in a sad little puddle of grief when she left him high and dry?

"I am what I am," she said in a low, smoky voice that filled his brain with fantasies of doing her in front of a roaring fire. A campfire, a forest fire, a freaking fire in the Pits of Pain, he didn't care. "Thank you for the distraction. Now I need to get back to the clinic."

Dropping his arm, he snared her hand. He wasn't going to let her screw with him more than she already had. "I'd say it would be even better next time, but there won't be a next time."

"Then we're in agreement."

The hard-to-get angle wasn't going to work with him now that he knew what she was up to. Anger bubbled up, but he tamped it down, figuring he had the upper hand now, and once he had it, he didn't give it up.

Still gripping her, he flashed to Underworld General's parking lot.

"Well," she said crisply, whipping her hair over her shoulder, "I guess this is it. Nice knowing you, Revenant."

"No," he said, "this isn't it. I still need you for Gethel."

Now that Heaven had made him an offer, he needed Lucifer to die more than ever. His death would mean Rev wouldn't lose his status in Sheoul, but it could also get him a welcome into Heaven. Either way, *he* would have the power to choose his destiny. Win-win all around.

Of course, that was assuming Blaspheme and her doctor buddies were devising a way to rid the realms of Lucifer. They had to be. Eidolon's family was too tied together with Reaver and the Horsemen, and there was no way they couldn't be plotting to destroy Gethel, and with her, Satan's brat.

She started toward the sliding glass door that led to the emergency department. "I told you to bring her here."

"I can't do that."

"Then I'll find you another doctor," she called from over her shoulder.

"Unacceptable."

She spun around, and a sudden chill infused her voice. "Yeah, well, here's the thing. You might be a Shadow Angel with powers and influence I can't even comprehend. But here, in this medical facility, I lay down the law. So let's part ways without a scene, shall we?"

Revenant banked his frustration. He was used to getting what he wanted, but in this case, he was going to back off. For now. But he'd be back, and he wasn't going to settle for any other doctor.

No, he wasn't as through with Blaspheme as she'd like to think.

From now on, he'd run the Revenant/Blaspheme show, and any plot twists that came up would be orchestrated by him, and him alone.

Blaspheme was shaking so hard by the time she entered UG's emergency department that her head hurt from her brain rattling around inside her skull.

She'd had sex with Revenant. Good sex. *Really* good sex.

And he hadn't even laid a finger on her.

As she strode through the halls on the way to Eidolon's office, her body flushed hot from the memories.

And then it flushed cold as she remembered the story Revenant had told her as they lay in the aftermath of their passion. He was an angel born and raised in hell, forced to become something he wasn't.

Sounded familiar.

She hated that she could relate to him, especially since he admitted to killing *vyrm* like they were nothing more than flies that needed to be swatted. If he learned the truth about her, would he destroy her as nonchalantly?

He'd terrified her when he'd said he wasn't a danger to her...as long she was being honest with him. So what had she done? She'd tried to use her seductive powers on him, aphrodisiac and all, in hopes of distracting him. Making him feel something for her so he wouldn't kill her.

Clearly, it hadn't worked, since he'd said there wouldn't be a next time for them.

She should have been happy about that, but for some reason, his rejection had stung. Gods, she was an idiot. She wanted him out of her life, and yet, when he agreed, she got upset.

How could he be such a danger to her but at the same time, make her feel...safe? Because she *had* felt safe with him. He'd saved her from an angel assassin and then took her someplace where only someone harboring a death wish would try to get to her.

Then there was the simple chemistry of their relationship. She was flat-out attracted to him. His power and darkness drew her, but beneath all of that, behind the arrogant wall of defense mechanisms, was a male no one had loved for a very long time.

The physician in her wanted to heal him. The False Angel in her wanted to seduce him. The female in her wanted to comfort him.

The *vyrm* in her wanted to run.

Instead of running, she walked calmly through the hospital halls and made a quick call to Gem, who assured her that her mother was stable, but that she was raising hell with the staff. Throwing things was bad enough, but Deva had also tried to bite a nurse, earning a Gargantua-sized headache when the Haven spell kicked in.

"I'm sorry, Gem," Blas sighed. "I'll talk to her."

Great. This was the last thing she needed.

Wondering what else could possibly go wrong today, Blas hung up as E's office came into view, and she found him inside, a half-eaten ham sandwich and a cup of fruit in front of him on the desk. Her stomach growled, reminding her that she hadn't eaten anything since a half of a bran muffin with her coffee this morning.

"Blaspheme," he said, looking up from the stack of papers he was going through. "You're early."

"Figured I'd get a head start on my day." She gestured to the chair across from his desk. "May I?" At his nod, she sat and got right to it. "Did you know Revenant is Reaver's brother?"

One dark eyebrow arched. "Yes."

Yes. Like it was no big deal. "And you didn't think to tell me?"

"It didn't come up."

"Really? And I suppose the fact that he's a Shadow Angel slipped your mind as well?"

Eidolon sat back in his chair, his coal-black eyes flat and cold. "I understand that you're under a lot of pressure right now, but be careful, Blaspheme."

She cringed inwardly at the realization that she was mouthing off to her boss. Not only that, but she'd never known Eidolon to be unfair. Still, this was her life, and she was in trouble. If she had to ruffle a few feathers, so be it.

Well, she probably shouldn't ruffle *his*.

"I'm sorry, Eidolon. I'm just...I'm in a bad place right now." She closed her eyes and tried to put her thoughts in order. When she opened them again, his expression had softened. "I was attacked at my new apartment today."

He jolted straight up in his chair. "By what?"

She hesitated, even though she knew it was past time to come clean. "By an angel."

"How did you get away?"

"Revenant saved me." He'd been like an avenging angel, dark and horrifying, and yet she'd never been happier to see anyone.

"Why was he there?"

She shook her head. "Long story. Then Reaver showed up, and they fought...it was a disaster."

Eidolon swore. "You can't go back to your place."

"I know." She looked down at her lap and fidgeted with the gold clasp on her Coach bag. She never fidgeted. "I can get a hotel room, maybe move every couple of days—"

"You'll stay here. That's what the on-call rooms are for." He reached for his cell phone. "I'll have someone fetch whatever you need from your apartment."

"I don't think that's necessary," she said, hating to be a charity case.

"You and your mother have angels after you," he pointed out, as if she wasn't aware. "Now is not the time to take unnecessary risks. Which means you need to stay away from Revenant and Reaver as well. Unfortunately, thanks to their power upgrades, they can *both* enter the hospital."

Obviously, her own thoughts had gone down that path, but why would Eidolon's? Unless he knew the truth about her. She played dumb, wanting to test the waters before she laid it all out. "Why do you think Revenant and Reaver would be after me?"

His dark gaze pinned her down. Hard. "I think it's time we stopped with the games, don't you?"

Busted, all she could do was utter a raspy "Yes."

"Good. Now, I'm going to ask you some questions, and I want some straight answers." At her nod, he continued. "Deva isn't your adoptive mother, is she? She's your birth mother."

Her heart kicked so hard in her chest that she thought it might be bruised. "Yes," she whispered.

"But you aren't *emim*, are you? Your father wasn't fallen. He was an angel."

This time, she didn't have enough saliva to answer, so she just nodded.

"How much time before your False Angel enchantment fails?"

"How . . ." She cleared her throat. "How did you know?"

"Do you recall a few years ago, when Yuri went a little far during one of your . . . sessions?"

How could she forget? A total, utter sadist, Yuri had harbored a love for sexual torture, and he apparently had no idea what "safe words" were.

"Yes."

"I offered to heal you, but you refused."

"I refused because if you used your healing powers on me, you'd have known I wasn't a False Angel."

"I suspected you were hiding something, but I didn't know what. Then, a few months ago, you assisted me during surgery. The eviscerated Slogthu demon, remember? You were massaging his heart as I sent a wave of power into him. At that moment, I sensed angel inside him. Since purebred angels can't enter the hospital, it meant you were a half-breed. But False Angels can't breed with other species, so I put two and two together."

She felt sick to her stomach. Making it worse was the fact that she just now understood that this was about more than her and her mother. Eidolon's knowledge of her situation could get him put to death.

"Have there been any more angel sightings?"

He inclined his head. "Bane confronted one in the parking lot this morning. I just got done healing his broken jaw."

Ah, gods. "I'm so sorry, Eidolon. I've put your hospital and clinic at risk," she said. "I'll go as soon as I can pack my desk up—"

"The hell you will. We need you."

"But my presence is causing trouble, and it's only going to get worse."

He laughed. "It's almost like you haven't worked here

for decades. This place is practically fueled by trouble. Or
have you never met my siblings? And mate. And in-laws.
I could go on." He shoved the sandwich aside and rested
his forearms on the desk, clasping his hands as he leaned
toward her. "Look, Blaspheme, we take care of our own
here. If I truly think the hospital or clinic is at risk, we'll
make other arrangements. But one thing we don't do is
abandon our own. You're family, and I won't let anything
happen to you."

For all of Blaspheme's life, her mother had stressed
that the two of them were the only family each other had.
Blas had believed it. But at some point, the staff at Underworld General had become her family as well, and hearing Eidolon say that made the outside world seem a little
less scary.

"But what about Reaver?" she asked, speaking of
scary. "He's your family, too, and if he finds out what I
am, he'll kill me."

"We don't know that. He has a tendency to not follow
the herd when it comes to protocol. But when and if he
learns what you are, let me worry about that. I'll handle
Reaver. Now," he said, "how long until your enchantment
wears off?"

"Could be any day," she said miserably. "My mother
said that once my *vyrm* powers start appearing, my False
Angel aura will disappear completely, and my true identity will be visible to every angel and fallen angel who
sees me." She looked up at him. "You're aware that if you
turn me in, you will be awarded more riches than you can
count."

"I know."

"And if you don't turn me in and it can be proven that

you were harboring a known *vyrm*, you will face more tortures than you can count before your own species Council kills you."

"Are you trying to talk me out of helping you? Because it won't work."

"I'm just making sure you understand the risks."

"I was a Justice Dealer before I became a physician. I'm well aware of the consequences of my actions. So let's not talk about it again, shall we?" At her reluctant nod, he continued. "So what have you got planned to renew your cover? Another Fallen Angel sacrifice?"

Ugh. The very idea made her want to scream. "My mother is planning on it, but I won't do it."

"Why not?" He gestured to the fruit, but she shook her head.

"I won't sacrifice an innocent."

He plucked a grape from the container of fruit. "There's no such thing as an innocent False Angel."

"So you're saying you think I should do it?" she asked, incredulous.

"No." He popped the grape into his mouth and chewed slowly before continuing. "I'm saying I'd understand if you did. Do you have another plan?"

She blew out a long breath. "I've spent decades researching an alternative, but haven't found anything."

"I've done a little research myself," he said, stunning her. He'd been trying to help already? "I haven't found much information on *vyrm*, probably because they're usually killed before they reach adulthood. But I did find this." He slid a piece of paper at her.

She frowned as she studied the writing. "It's a ritual of permanent alteration."

"It supposedly works only on fallen angels, but maybe since you're half fallen angel, it'll work for you, too. Apparently, the spell will turn a fallen angel into any species of demon as long as they have the right ingredients."

She kept reading, her hope growing... and then crashing. "What it requires... it doesn't make sense. The essence of death? What the hell does that mean?"

"I don't know." He ran a frustrated hand through his short hair, leaving unruly tufts behind. If there was anything Eidolon hated more than not knowing something, she couldn't say what. "But I don't think what I found was the complete ritual."

"Where did you find this? The hospital's library? One of your Justice Dealer contacts?" She lowered her voice, realizing the ridiculousness of doing so, given they were in a private office. But better safe than sorry. "An evil sorcerer?"

He shrugged. "Demonic Spells dot com."

She stared. "Seriously?"

"Yep." He popped another grape, and she heard the seeds crack as he chewed. "But it's just an excerpt from a larger tome. I couldn't find the title, but it appears to be a necromancer spellbook. I have Wraith working on it. He can locate almost anything, but until he knows what, exactly, he's looking for, he's sort of chasing ghosts."

Necromancer magic wasn't something to be trifled with, but at this point, she was running out of options. And actually, she knew a certain Seminus demon doctor whose background in necromancy and fetish for False Angels might pay off. *Bane, buddy, you might just become my best friend today.* She made a mental note to give him a call as soon as she was finished here.

"Thank you, Eidolon. What you've done…it means the world to me. I don't know how I can pay you back."

"Don't get killed. That's payment enough." He stood, a clear sign that this convo was done. "As far as your mother, she can stay here, too, for as long as you both need to after she's healed."

Her eyes stung at his kindness. Oh, she knew a large part of his motivation was keeping her as a doctor, but he was also loyal to a fault.

"Thank you again," she said. "You almost make me believe I can get out of this alive."

Almost.

Seventeen

"Well, well, if it isn't my favorite fallen angel."

Revenant sat in the underworld pub known as the Four Horsemen, working on his ... tenth? ... mug of Pestilence porter as he lounged in the corner booth and watched the curvy succubus saunter toward him. She was carrying her own mug of Horseman-themed brew, Famine ale, if he wasn't mistaken.

"'Sup, Laylach."

Her ruby lips curved into a seductive smile he'd seen wrapped around his dick once or twice. He waited for his cock to remember and get all excited, but it didn't seem to want to come out to play.

Lay, as she fittingly liked to be called, sank down in the booth and scooted next to him. Her short skirt hiked up, revealing her lack of panties and a whole lot more. The scent of her arousal engulfed him, but still he felt dead below the waist.

Her hand came down on his thigh. "Wanna hit the back room?" She slid her palm up to cup his crotch. "Or I could do you right here."

Across the room, another succubus was doing exactly that to a Bathag demon, his moans carrying through the air as she blew him from under the table.

"Not now," he said, keeping his eye on the front entrance. "You can fondle me all you want, but that's not what I'm here for."

"Yeah? Why are you here, then?"

He grasped her wrist and shoved it into her lap. "Nunya."

She frowned. "Nunya?"

"Yeah. Nunya business." In the other booth a portly Oni male had joined in, lifting the succubus onto the bench so he could fuck her while she sucked the Bathag. The patrons at the bar were cheering and making ribald comments, and he had a feeling an orgy was about to start.

It would be the second one tonight.

He should be worked up into a sexual frenzy by now, but dammit, all he could think about was Blaspheme and how she'd tasted. How she'd felt. How she'd sounded when she came.

Now his cock joined the party, and Lay, not one to miss a cue, had him unzipped and was stroking him in a heartbeat. For a moment, he closed his eyes and let her work him, her expert touch something that should have gotten him revved in an instant.

But she made the mistake of whispering in his ear, telling him how badly she wanted to suck him off. But her offer wasn't the mistake. Her mistake was that she wasn't a False Angel named Blaspheme.

Fuck, he had it bad. Yes, she was sexy and mouthy and drop-dead gorgeous. And she had a streak of decency in her that drew him, made him want to be decent, too.

But she was also of a species that used deception to fulfill their needs, and by all accounts, no False Angel had ever settled down with a single male. Even when they hooked up with a male False Angel for breeding purposes, they only stayed until they conceived.

And why in the hell was he even thinking about this?

Snarling, he shoved Laylach away, zipped up, and scooted over before she realized he was going to deflate in about two seconds.

"Sorry," he said gruffly. "I told you. I'm not here for that."

She pouted prettily. "Maybe next time?"

"Sure, babe," he said vaguely. "Next time."

She grinned, satisfied with his answer, grabbed her beer, and headed for her next mark. As she sidled up to a Ramreel at the end of the bar, the front door opened, and the demon he'd been waiting for walked in.

The Orphmage, a Neethul demon powerful enough to earn the status of Satan's personal mage, caught sight of Revenant instantly and came over. "I'm surprised you wanted to meet here," Gormesh said. "It's very public."

Which was precisely why he'd chosen this location. Word of this meeting would get back to Satan, and he wanted to make sure it didn't look like he was trying to hide anything.

A twinge of pain shot through his head, and wouldn't you know it, Satan was sending a summons. It wasn't urgent; the pain would increase as the urgency grew, and right now it was merely an annoyance. But still, the timing was curious.

Gormesh took a seat across the booth from Rev and

flashed a mouthful of sharp, white teeth. "You know I don't meet with anyone outside my residence. I almost didn't come."

Revenant slammed his fist on the table, startling the cocky bastard. "Don't fuck with me," he growled. "You were salivating over the opportunity to meet with a Shadow Angel to see what I want. So let's cut the shit."

Gormesh's sleazy smile made Rev want to rip it off his face. "Let's do that, then. What is it you want from me?"

"Information. I want to know what you did to Gethel to speed up Lucifer's birth." Actually, he didn't give a shit. But the only way he was going to get the information he needed was to pretend this was about the pregnant fallen angel.

"Ah." Laylach caught Gormesh's attention, and he watched her lead the Ramreel into the back room as he leaned back in his seat. "It was a blood spell. But it didn't work, thanks to the archangels' interference."

"Your spell did something," Rev said. The orgy across the way had gained two more participants. Someone was going to have to disinfect that table. "Lucifer is twice the size he should be."

Gormesh shrugged. "What do you want me to do about it?"

"I want to know if it means he'll be born soon, or if there's still three months to go."

"I have no idea. Have Gethel see a physician."

"Gee," Rev drawled. "I hadn't thought of that."

"No need to get pissy." The air became charged with sex, tangible enough that Rev felt it skate across his skin in an electric tingle. Gormesh felt it, too, and began to rub himself through his muslin breeches. "I'm just saying that I can't tell you when Gethel will drop the little bastard."

Shit. Revenant wasn't ready to make any rash decisions regarding handing her over to Reaver, but he definitely didn't want to procrastinate and risk her giving birth before he could decide if, when, or how he'd surrender her to Heaven.

At this point, the only thing he was sure about was that *if* he chose to hand over Gethel, he wanted into Heaven on his own terms, not because a bunch of archangel pricks said they'd purify his blood in exchange for her.

"She had a prenatal checkup a couple of days ago," Revenant said as Gormesh got more serious with the fondling. "Tests revealed an unknown substance in her blood. Know what it might be? And put your cock back in your pants before I slice it off and feed it to the hell stallion outside."

Cursing under his breath, Gormesh shoved his pencil dick back inside his breeches. "Fuck if I know. Does her physician think it's harming her?"

Just the word, *physician*, gave Rev a hard-on. Blaspheme had gotten way too deep under his skin.

Revenant shifted into a more relaxed pose, giving Gormesh the impression that the next question meant nothing to him, when the exact opposite was true.

"The doctors are stumped. If it *is* harming her, do you know if it can be removed? If her blood can be purified?"

Revenant didn't give a shit if Gethel's blood could be purified. This was all about him. If Revenant could purify his own blood of Satan's taint, then he wouldn't need the fucking archangels to do it. Which meant they couldn't blackmail him into shit, and he could hang out in Heaven as much as he wanted to.

Yeah, it'll be great to hang out with people who don't want you there.

So what? He didn't need to be wanted. He needed to take what was his, whether or not the archangels approved.

Gormesh cast a longing glance at the orgy in the other booth. "Purification depends on what the substance is."

Revenant looked at the Orphmage over the rim of his beer mug. "What if it's blood?"

"She has blood in her blood?"

The dense idiot. "What if she drank Satan's blood?"

Gormesh's gaze narrowed, and Revenant started to sweat. "Of course she ingested his blood. It was part of the ritual required to prepare her body to host Lucifer."

"How do you know?"

"Because I was there," Gormesh said, the faintest hint of a smile turning up his blue-tinged lips.

"When Lucifer was conceived?"

Gormesh reached for his crotch again, but wisely jerked his hand away. "Yes."

Okay, now they were getting somewhere. "Can she be cleansed of Satan's blood?"

Say yes. Please say yes.

"No."

Disappointment soured Rev's porter. Shit might as well be vinegar. "Are you sure?"

Gormesh growled. "I am the most powerful mage to ever exist. And when I say that, I don't mean in Sheoul. I mean in all three realms." He leaned forward, slapping his hands on the table. Dude was worked up. "Not even Heaven has an angel who can wield magic as well as I can. So question me again at your own peril."

Revenant laughed softly, his body languid from the alcohol, but his mind was razor sharp. "You do remember who I am."

The Orphmage, drunk on a power trip fueled by the sex magic in the air, sneered. "Even you can't match my ability to control the environment. Your power is limited in scope, while mine is—" He cut off in a strangled wheeze as Revenant's *limited* power garroted the moron.

Revenant hadn't even moved a muscle. Didn't think he could, given the Pestilence porter's relaxing effect.

"Just yesterday, I stood in Archangel Hall and sent an archangel to Sheoul-gra. An *archangel*. Do you know what an archangel is, fuckhead? Sending him to the demon graveyard guarded by Hades *and* the Grim Reaper took less effort than getting an erection." He squeezed Gormesh's throat harder. "Now, do you really want to see whose dick is bigger?"

Gormesh's gray eyes were bulging and wild. "No," he wheezed.

"Good. You're smarter than you look." Revenant released the Orphmage, who grabbed his neck and sucked in huge lungfuls of air. "Let's try this again. Are you sure Gethel's blood can't be purified of Satan's blood?"

Gormesh coughed, still holding his neck tenderly. "Yes."

"How do you know?"

The Orphmage hesitated for a heartbeat. "Because I tried it on your father."

"You...what?" Rev shook his head, unable to process that. Finally, he croaked, "Sandalphon died in the battle that got my mother captured."

"Technically...no, he didn't." Gormesh signaled the barmaid for a War Lager. "Your father was badly injured. Dying. He was taken to Satan, who decided to try an experiment. He force-fed your father his blood. Sandalphon healed, was subjected to gruesome torture and experiments, and then I was brought in to try to remove the taint of Satan's blood from his own." Before Rev could ask why, Gormesh held up his hand to stop him. "The Prince of Lies's blood turned your father dark. Satan wanted to send him to Heaven as a spy, but he needed to be sure the taint couldn't be removed. The angel who betrayed your parents to Satan joined me in my efforts to remove the taint, but we couldn't do it. The attempt killed him. We tried again with a captured Seraphim, this time letting the angel return to Heaven, but later we learned that whatever purification process the archangels used killed her, too. I assure you, removing Satan's blood is impossible."

Revenant couldn't believe what he was hearing. His father had been forcibly turned evil, and then he'd died in Sheoul, just like Rev's mother... which meant that his soul was suffering eternal torment in hell, unable to get out and join all the other angelic souls in Heaven's Hall of Heroes. And all because he had been betrayed by someone he should have been able to trust.

"Who is this angel who betrayed my mother to Satan?" he ground out. The skin covering his wing anchors itched as the desire to spread his wings and rain down hell on the bastard filled him.

He'd just chosen his angelic sacrifice to Satan.

Gormesh scratched his chin thoughtfully. "Ba'addon. Raphael's father."

Raphael's father was about to die a horrible death. Raphael would be next. *All* of the archangels would be next. They'd lied to him about cleansing his blood so he could reside in Heaven. They'd fucking *lied*.

His blood started to boil—literally, causing his skin to

steam and crack. He had to force himself to calm down. Raging out would only raise suspicions about why he was so angry, and it certainly wouldn't help him get any answers from Gormesh if he blew up the pub and everyone in it.

"Why would Ba'addon betray Heaven like that?" he growled. "Does Heaven know? Where is he?"

Gormesh ticked off his dirt-stained fingers as he spoke. One finger. "He's dead. Satan killed him." Two fingers. "I doubt Heaven knows what he did." Three fingers. "I'm certain he didn't see what he'd done as a betrayal. He wanted power. Prestige. He believed that his name, Ba'addon, was a form of Abaddon, the angel prophesied to do battle with Satan. By turning your parents over to the Dark Lord, Ba'addon thought he could get close enough to do that. His bones now make up the seat of Satan's throne."

Fitting, Rev supposed, that the angel who betrayed his parents now had to support Satan's ass.

Shaken to the core, he could barely string together coherent words for his next question. "But . . . why would everyone think my father died in battle?"

"Because we returned his body to the battle site with a message that we had your mother." Gormesh cast another hungry look at the orgy, and Revenant decided he'd had enough. Of Gormesh. Of Sheoul. Of half-truths and total lies.

No one but his mother had ever been honest with him, and suddenly, he needed that comfort as much as he'd needed it as a child.

And he knew exactly where to get it.

Eighteen

Eidolon had just put down his son for a nap when Reaver arrived. And good thing for him that he knocked lightly instead of using the doorbell. After an hour of the toddler's explosive, exhausted screaming, Eidolon was thankful to have gotten the boy to fall asleep. He'd kill whoever woke him.

"Hey, man," Eidolon said as he led Reaver to the kitchen. "Thanks for coming by."

Reaver took a seat on a counter bar stool. "You said it was important. And I always like to hang out with Sabre." He looked around. "Where is the little tyke?"

"Napping. And if you wake him up, you get to deal with him."

Reaver grinned. "Fair enough. Where's Tayla?"

"She should be home in a couple of hours. She's out with Kynan and Decker investigating a suspected Soulshredder attack in Missouri."

"So she's still with DART, huh? Not back with The Aegis?"

Eidolon shook his head. "Even with the key Aegis players dead, the organization has still been going down a dark path. Kill demons first, don't bother asking questions later. Tay says The Aegis is lost to corruption and extremism. But the good news is that the Demon Activity Response Team is growing as Aegis defectors find their way to DART."

In Eidolon's opinion, The Aegis had always been a lost cause, so secretive and full of hatred that they couldn't see that not all demons were evil. DART, started by Aegis defectors and working in conjunction with human law enforcement authorities, operated like a demon CSI unit, investigating suspected demonic activity and eliminating verifiable threats to humanity. Demons deemed harmless were left alone.

"Good." Reaver watched Tayla's ferret, Mickey, dash through the kitchen and slide under the china cabinet in the dining room. "I heard some gossip today. About Idess and Lore."

It was Eidolon's turn to grin. "We got her pregnant."

"We?"

"Well, we don't know who the father is yet, but yeah, we did the procedure last week."

Lore, Eidolon's half-breed brother, was sterile, but he'd desperately wanted children with his mate, Idess. So Eidolon and his other two brothers, Wraith and Shade, had donated sperm, and Eidolon had implanted it deep inside Idess's womb. They'd all agreed that no matter who the biological father was, the child would be raised by Idess and Lore.

Reaver cocked a blond brow. "I know a Seminus demon can't orgasm without being, ah, inside his female, so how..."

Eidolon laughed at the angel's discomfort. "Our mates had to help. There are work-arounds." The memory of Tay's hot mouth working him made his loins stir, and dammit, now he hoped she'd get home a lot sooner than a couple of hours.

"You know," Reaver said, "ten years ago I would never have predicted that your lives would turn out the way they have."

"Trust me," Eidolon muttered. "I'm as shocked as you are."

Eidolon's dog, Mange, trotted into the kitchen and nosed around the china cabinet for his friend. Sometimes, like now, he couldn't believe he had a dog, a ferret, a son, and a mate, and he could only thank the Powers That Be that he'd been fortunate enough to have been given such a gift.

Reaver's smile faded, and he braced his forearms on the countertop. "So why did you ask me here?"

Eidolon sighed. Time to get back to the real world. "What do you know about *vyrm*?"

Reaver blinked. "Do you have a *vyrm* patient?"

"No." Eidolon left it at that. He trusted Reaver with his life, but he wasn't sure he trusted Reaver with the life of someone whose species was hunted ruthlessly. "But as you know, this is a sensitive subject."

Reaver nodded. "*Vrym* have been known to look into the eyes of an angel or fallen angel, and a moment later, everyone in his family falls dead. You can see why they're hunted." He shifted, hooking one booted foot on a stool rung. "But I've never hunted one, let alone killed one.

Vyrm are the product of both good and evil, which means they have a higher than average shot at not becoming evil scumbags. Because of that, they shouldn't be killed because of abilities they *might* use."

"Glad we agree on that." Eidolon took a bracing breath and got down to it. "Can you tell me how they might disguise themselves? *Without* a sacrifice."

"Without a sacrifice?" Reaver blew out a soft whistle. "They'd need a damned potent spell, and no matter what, they'd need blood or a body part from someone incredibly powerful. Someone with either angel or fallen angel in his or her genetic makeup. I'll see what I can find out."

"Thank you." Eidolon felt Mickey's tiny feet skitter over his shoes. "So...what's going on with your brother?"

Reaver cursed softly. "Hell if I know. He's hurt and bitter and frankly, I don't know how much I can trust him." His voice dropped low with anger. "I think he might hand over Gethel to me, but then...I don't know. It shouldn't be a question. He should just do it. After everything Satan did to him and our mother, why the fuck would he even entertain the idea of playing for Team Evil?"

"Maybe because Team Good isn't always...good. I hate to say it, buddy, but at least you always know never to trust evil. But you know better than anyone that Heaven has an agenda, and if yours doesn't match up with theirs, you're fucked."

Reaver slammed his fist on the counter, his eyes flashing with blue lightning. "It doesn't matter. The archangels gave him a way out. Heaven has its problems, but it's still infinitely better than Sheoul."

Eidolon loved Reaver like a brother, but the angel sometimes got lost inside his own tunnel vision.

"You're aware that Wraith grew up in a situation similar to Revenant's, and for a long time after he escaped, he didn't know his place in the world. The people who should have cared for him hurt him." Eidolon chucked an empty box of toddler crackers into the trash. "For almost a hundred years, he kept everyone at a distance and always took the road of least resistance. It sounds like Revenant is doing the same, looking for the least painful path to survival."

Reaver snorted. "Why are you defending him?"

"Because I wish someone had done that for Wraith."

Cursing, Reaver rubbed the Underworld General caduceus tattoo he'd recently had inked onto his biceps to settle a lost bet with Eidolon. "How did you deal with Wraith for as long as you did?"

Mange nudged Eidolon's hand, demanding a good scratch behind the ears. "Wraith . . . was a challenge."

"I know. I was there. I still can't believe he's even alive, let alone settled down with a mate and a kid."

"No one is more surprised about that than I am." Eidolon snagged a bottle of his favorite Belgian ale from out of the fridge and tossed it to Reaver. "The key was finding something he cared enough about to change his life."

"Serena."

"Yeah." He shrugged. "Look, I don't have a lot of advice when it comes to insane brothers. I didn't do so well with either Wraith or Roag. At least Wraith is still alive. But I *can* say that Revenant's anger is probably coming from a place of fear. Fear of rejection, fear of being hurt, fear of the unknown. If you can identify the fear, you can get past it."

"Abandonment."

"What?"

"I'm pretty sure Revenant has abandonment issues. And he's obsessed with rules. No idea why." He took a swig of his beer. "But fuck, E, I don't know if I can ever trust him. Satan's blood runs in his veins. He was raised in Sheoul and has five thousand years of bad history behind him."

"Can't you say almost the same about Harvester?"

"Yes, but she was always working for the greater good."

"And yet she was a fallen angel, where Revenant is an angel."

"So is Raphael," Reaver growled. "And he's a bastard. *Angel* isn't code for good."

"All I'm saying is that I nearly gave up on Wraith a time or two. It would have been a mistake. Until you know for sure that Revenant is beyond saving, you can't give up." Eidolon let Reaver chew on that for a few minutes before saying, "That said, I'm a little concerned about his relationship with Blaspheme."

"Yeah, I already got a peek into that disturbing development." Reaver jammed his hand through his hair, which fell back into place in perfect gold waves. "I didn't have a chance to warn her not to fuck with him. The last thing he needs is to get run through the emotional False Angel wringer. He might kill her."

"That's not what's going on," Eidolon said softly.

"Are you sure?"

"Yeah." Eidolon bent down to pet Mange again, but Mickey chose that moment to streak around the cabinet and nip the dog's tail. The two of them took off like a shot, and now it was only a matter of time before he heard the crash of furniture. "He's obsessed with her, and she's the only one he'll allow to treat Gethel."

Reaver's hand froze with the beer bottle halfway to his mouth. "Tell me you didn't just say that a doctor from Underworld General is giving medical assistance to the evil monster who tried to murder my grandson." The bottle in Reaver's hand shattered, spraying beer and angel blood all over the counter.

"Take it easy, man." Eidolon grabbed for the roll of paper towels. "You know I wouldn't authorize that without a good reason."

"I'm waiting."

Eidolon sopped up the mess as he spoke, hoping the angel didn't break something worse, like Eidolon's head.

"Blaspheme performed a brief exam and got a blood sample. She didn't actually treat Gethel, and if anything, she made things medically worse for the bitch instead of better." He met Reaver's steady sapphire gaze. "This has given us an opportunity to get to her. We can't pass it up, so if you have any brilliant ideas, now is the time to share."

Silence stretched as Reaver rubbed his chin. "A few centuries ago," he said slowly, "Heaven experimented with something called solarum. They hoped to use it to wipe out evil on a massive scale. Unfortunately, solarum is impossible to produce quickly or in large quantities, so they gave up. But for something like this..." He nodded, as if talking to himself. "You're saying you can get close to Gethel?"

"If Revenant will take me."

"And if he won't? If he insists on Blaspheme being Gethel's physician?"

"It would be her choice whether or not she wants to help destroy Lucifer."

Reaver gave a reluctant nod. "Agreed. But you understand that anyone who *helps* Gethel and her unholy spawn will be considered my enemy."

"Understood," Eidolon said.

Reaver made the slightest gesture with his hand, and the blood, beer, and broken glass disappeared. "I—" He broke off with a curse. "Speaking of enemies, I gotta go. Revenant's in Heaven again."

Nineteen

Heaven was huge. Vast beyond even Revenant's comprehension. It was also beautiful. Rev felt almost sad as he strolled through a verdant meadow dotted with blossoming trees and framed by snowcapped mountains, his footprints leaving behind dying grass and rotting flowers. As he watched, the decay spread, and he wondered if it would continue unchecked after he left. Would the damage he was causing with his presence be repaired when he was gone, or would Heaven be permanently scarred by his evil?

As he gazed up at a soaring eagle, he felt a tingle on the back of his neck, knew Reaver had arrived to expel him. On the upside, Reaver's tingle was far better than Satan's drilling headache, which seemed to be cut off by the Heavenly barrier. Cool.

"What are you doing here, Revenant?" Reaver's voice came from behind him.

Revenant didn't turn around. "Walking."

Reaver appeared several yards in front of him, looking obnoxiously angelic in dark gray slacks, a blue shirt, and his twenty-four-karat wings arched imperiously behind his shoulders. "And you couldn't have done that on Earth or in Sheoul?"

Rev flared his own wings, figuring they might as well get the cockfight started. "Why should I? All of this belongs to me, too, does it not? I *am* an angel, after all, same as you." He stopped a few feet away from Reaver and waited for the inevitable, *You aren't the same as I am.*

So he was surprised when his twin turned away to gaze at the mountains. "Have you made a decision regarding Gethel?"

"Yes."

"And?"

Revenant waited until Reaver turned back to him. He wanted to make sure his brother knew this wasn't some bullshit ploy to wring more promises out of the archangels. That this wasn't a game. Rev had always been a straight shooter, and he wasn't going to change now that he knew he was an angel.

"I'm not going to hand her over to the archangels."

Reaver closed his eyes. "Then we aren't the same," he murmured.

"No shit. One of us isn't tainted by Satan's blood."

Reaver's eyes shot open, their jeweled depths sparking. "It doesn't have to be like that! The archangels—"

"Lied!" Revenant shouted. "They lied to me about purging his blood from my system in exchange for Gethel."

Surprise flashed in Reaver's expression, but it was gone

a moment later. Guess he wasn't all that shocked that archangels would lie.

"They gave me their word. I won't let them go back on it," he said. "Neither will Metatron."

"Metatron," Rev hissed. "Does our loving uncle know about this bargain?"

Reaver frowned. "I don't know. Why do you think they're lying?"

"Because the archangels' deal was bullshit," he snapped. "They brought the offer to the table knowing all along that they couldn't honor their side of the bargain. Purifying my blood can't be done."

Reaver scowled. "Are you sure?"

"Do you think I'd be this pissed if I wasn't?" He crushed the delicate petals of a yellow-winged rose under his boot, hoping to get some satisfaction out of destroying something, but all it did was make him feel like crap. "They set me up. If I'd brought Gethel to you—or to them—there is no place in the universe where I could hide from Satan. And you know damned well the archangels won't give me sanctuary in Heaven if my presence kills everything around me."

Reaver glanced sadly at the destroyed flower as if Rev had slaughtered a lamb. "There's got to be something we can do."

Revenant let out a bitter laugh. "I'm open to suggestions."

"We'll work together on this."

"Work together? Why?"

"Because we're brothers."

"Really? That's it? We're separated by birth and five thousand years. We're no more brothers than Genghis Khan and Elvis are brothers."

"That's crap, and you know it." Reaver's voice was a near shout now. "We *are* brothers, and we can overcome anything. I watched the Sem brothers' relationship nearly destroyed by their own infighting once, but they managed to pull their shit together and now they're tighter than ever. The sibling bond isn't something to be taken lightly. You saw what happened with Reseph."

That had been some crazy shit. At the time when Reseph's Seal had broken, Revenant wasn't yet the Horsemen's Watcher, and he'd still believed he was a fallen angel, so he'd been rooting for Team Evil when Reseph became Pestilence. Team Evil had lost, but the price of victory for the Horsemen had been high. They were still mending fences, but Rev wasn't sure he and Reaver could do the same.

"You say we can overcome anything," he said. "But how am I supposed to get over the fact that we wouldn't be in this situation if not for you. It was *your* actions, both times, that caused our memory loss. And then, for five thousand fucking years, I did things that would melt your halo. So tell me, dear brother, how we overcome that."

"We can't overcome anything until we talk," Reaver said, sounding like a damned relationship counselor. "We've both done things we regret. We were both given the shaft by archangels. We both lost our parents. We have more things in common than not."

Reaver's pretty words didn't move Revenant at all. "And yet, only one of us can stand in this lovely meadow and not kill everything he touches."

Reaver jammed his hand through his perfect, flaxen mane. Just to be an ass, Rev changed his hair color to match.

"Why here?" Reaver asked softly. "Why did you choose this place, specifically?"

"Because our mother used to talk about it." He closed his eyes as if it would shut out the memory, but it seemed that the question had unlocked a door Rev would rather not be opened. "Sometimes, after I was beaten for whatever grave infraction a small boy could commit, she'd try to distract me from my pain with stories of Heaven's beauty. This, the Meadow of Azna, was one of her favorite places to walk when she was pregnant with us."

Reaver swallowed. Looked out over the landscape with renewed brightness in his eyes. "Did she talk about our father?"

"Right before she died, she said Sandalphon was a great warrior, and that he would have been an even greater father. She said they used to sit in this meadow and plan for our futures. He made cribs for both of us, and he swore to protect us from all harm." Revenant snarled. "He was a liar. Same as the archangels."

"Sometimes it's impossible to protect those you love." The regret in Reaver's voice diluted Rev's anger a little. Reaver's own children had been raised without him, and with the exception of Thanatos, their lives had been less than ideal, and in Reseph's and Limos's cases, horrific.

In the distance, Singing Lilies started up a lullaby, their song a buzzing tinkle in the fresh air. Revenant's memories crashed into him so hard he stumbled. His mother had put words to the lilies' tune as she'd rocked him to sleep.

"Revenant?"

Reaver's voice droned in the background as Revenant drowned in memories so powerful he couldn't breathe.

Their mother's voice had been magical, so pure that when she sang, even the demons in the cells next to them would weep and the guards would halt in their tracks to listen.

Moonbeams and sunshine, the clouds and the seas, all part of the many worlds I want you to see. Fear not the unknown, nor the depths of the night, for nothing can harm you when I hold you tight.

Revenant's breath burst from him in an agonizing rush. Just as his mother had sung those words to him, he'd sung them to her as she lay dying in his arms.

He looked out at the beautiful meadow, now pock-marked by the decay left by his footsteps. He'd come here to find something of his mother... and he had.

But his presence had poisoned her beloved meadow. He couldn't stop hurting her, could he? She'd been imprisoned because of him. Tortured because of him. Killed because of him.

And now, her favorite place in the universe had been ruined. Because of him.

It was time to face the facts. He didn't belong in Heaven, and he never would.

Blinking to clear his watery vision, he collected himself, digging deep into his bottomless well of hatred.

"Tell the archangels I've made my decision."

"Rev, don't—"

"I'm not handing over Gethel." Nope, he'd make sure Lucifer died in the womb, and then he'd rule Sheoul at Satan's side. "They can go fuck themselves."

With that, he flashed out of Heaven.

Forever.

Twenty

Blaspheme had just spent the most miserable night in a cot next to her mother in the on-call room. Then the shower water had been only lukewarm. Now the blow-dryer didn't work. She was going to scream.

The one positive was that her mother was getting stronger. Eidolon had personally given her a checkup last night, and while he was concerned that the internal damage caused by the grimlight weapon could still cause problems, he figured that if she continued to improve, she'd be ready for discharge in a week or so.

"Blaspheme," her mother called through the bathroom door. "Your pager thingie is beeping."

"Thanks, Mom," she muttered.

"What did you say?"

Blas raised her voice. "I said, thanks, Mom!"

"You don't have to yell."

Blaspheme conked her head on the mirror. How were

they going to occupy not only the same space, but the same *tiny* space for who-knew-how-long?

Screw the hair; she had to get to work. So what if she was an hour early? She should see if she could work an extra shift tonight, too.

She grabbed a green scrunchie that matched her scrubs and tied her wet hair up in a high ponytail. After brushing her teeth, she scooted out into the bread-box-sized on-call residence room, where her mother was kicking back on the bed and watching *The Today Show*.

"Take it easy today, Mom," she said. "You're still healing. No more harassing the staff."

"Then you shouldn't have ruined my plans to trap the False Angel."

Blas clamped her jaws shut so tight her teeth throbbed. "I have to work with these people, Mother," she ground out. "So behave. I'll come get you for lunch."

Deva muted Al Roker with an impatient click of the remote. "I can't stay here forever."

"And you can't go home," Blaspheme pointed out.

Her mother rolled her eyes. "I have plenty of friends I can stay with."

"And you're really willing to risk your friends' lives like that?"

Her mother snorted. "Yes. They'd risk my life, too. It's what evil people do, Blaspheme." She reached over to the bedside table for a cup of lime Jell-O. "I'm damned impressed that you're doing the same thing."

"This is different."

"Really? How? You're putting your friends and this hospital at risk, don't you think?"

"Yes, but..." Blaspheme trailed off. But what? But

nothing. Oh, gods, she was as bad as her mother, wasn't she? Eidolon had assured her that staying here would be fine, and she'd been so eager to save her own skin that she hadn't even argued beyond a token protest. "You're right," she said. "We can't stay here. But we aren't putting any-one else at risk, either."

Deva shook her head. "How did I manage to raise you to be so scrupulous? You're half fallen angel, love. Act like it."

"You used to be an angel once," Blas pointed out. "Don't you remember that at all?"

"I remember it being very boring. There's a reason I tried to shake things up amongst the archangel ranks."

"Tried to shake things up? You got yourself kicked out of Heaven!"

Deva hurled the remote across the room, shattering the thing in a fit of temper. "You don't know what it's like there," she said, lisping a little as her fangs elongated with her growing anger. "The angelic hierarchy is all-important, and heaven forbid someone try to rise above their station. Some of us wanted more power, and Raphael was going to give us that. If not for his buddy, Stamtiel, giving me a suicide mission that got me caught, we'd have brought about a revolution."

This was the first Blaspheme had heard of an archangel's involvement in the plot her mother and father had been mixed up in. Leave it to Deva to crash spectacularly.

"Boy, when you do something, you do it big, don't you?"

Deva shrugged and settled back against the pillows now that her fit was over. "What is it humans say? Go big or go home?" She gestured to the destroyed remote. "Be a good little imp and get me a new one."

Blaspheme threw her hands up in defeat. "I give up. I have to go to work. Don't leave the hospital, and please try to stay in the room." The last thing Blas needed was her mother wandering around the clinic and causing trouble. "I'll be back later."

"And then what?"

"I don't know," Blas admitted. Gods, she hated the wait-and-see approach, which was funny, since that was what ninety percent of being a doctor was about. Wait and see how a patient would respond to treatment. Wait and see if surgery was a success. Wait and see if your patient died because you couldn't do enough for them.

"I think I should go crash with friends, and you should stay here. I can't be here, Blas. This place is too . . . sterile. And smelly. And it's full of annoying sick people. How can you stand it?"

Maybe her mother staying with friends wasn't such a bad idea. "Look, Mom," she said as she shrugged into her lab coat, "we'll talk about it later. I have to go."

She snatched up her stethoscope, cell phone, pager, and purse and darted into the hall, closing the door firmly behind her. She really could take only so much of her mother. A little Deva went a long, *long* way.

Taking a deep, relaxing breath, she started toward the clinic's Harrowgate. Since she had almost an hour before her shift started, she wanted to do some research into the information Eidolon had given her yesterday. UG's library was extensive and eclectic, filled with not only medical texts, but also mystical texts and non-fiction books related to the demon realm. Eidolon especially liked to collect books specific to individual demon breeds and species. The smallest detail could mean the difference between life and death during an emergency.

Her pager beeped again, and she nearly fumbled it as she juggled her stethoscope and the little device. When she saw the screen, she stopped dead in her tracks.

Revenant is here. Again. He wouldn't wait and we couldn't stop him. He's loose in the clinic.

Loose. Like a wild animal. Only far worse.

"Blaspheme!"

Her heart skipped a beat at the too-familiar voice from behind her. Dread and excitement dueled within her as she turned around to see him at the far end of the hall, dressed from head to toe in black leather. Goth boots with thick soles added another couple of inches to his already towering form, and the weapons strapped to his body sent a message that if you weren't intimidated enough already, it was time to roll over.

His lustrous ebony hair flared out behind him as he walked, and she self-consciously reached back to her own heavy, wet rope hanging down her back.

Her heart thumped harder with every step closer he came. How could she be happy to see him but at the same time be nervous as hell? As for him, she had no idea what he was thinking. His expression could have been carved from stone, and the wraparound sunglasses hid his eyes behind a shield of black.

Clearing her throat, she prepared to say hi, but just as she opened her mouth, a door down the hall opened and her mother stepped out. A thousand scenarios played out in her head in an instant.

Not one of them ended well.

Almost as if in slow motion, Deva looked left at

Revenant. Then right at Blaspheme. There was a smile when Deva saw her. And then her brain caught up with her eyes and she whipped her head back around to Revenant.

Suddenly, Deva stumbled over her own feet as she wheeled toward Blaspheme.

"Run," she mouthed.

Before Blaspheme could stop her, Deva bolted toward the clinic's tube station exit.

"Wait!" Blas yelled. She started off after her, but as she and Revenant met at the junction in the hallway, her mom disappeared around a corner.

"What was up with that?" Revenant asked.

Blas could only stand there like an idiot. Showing too much interest would arouse suspicion. "I guess she wanted to go home."

"It was that fallen angel I saw before." His luscious lips dipped in a deep frown. "She looked familiar. What's her name?"

Her mother had changed her name every few years, but if she truly looked familiar to Revenant, Blaspheme didn't want to offer up any of her names.

"I can't tell you that. Doctor-patient confidentiality," she said, happy to invoke human standards of care when the situation called for it. "But I don't know why she'd look familiar to you. Maybe it's part of your memory thing?"

"Maybe." He didn't look convinced. "Maybe I banged her before."

Oh, Christ. Blaspheme so did not want to go there. The idea that she and her mother had screwed the same guy was too disgusting to entertain.

"Gosh, I can't wait until you start talking about me like that. Some nameless chick you banged."

His head whipped around, and although she couldn't see his eyes, she felt their intensity as he stared at her. "I would never speak of you like that," he vowed darkly. "And I will never forget your name."

Okay, then. Talk about knocking someone breathless. Blaspheme struggled to inhale without sounding like she'd run a marathon. No male had ever spoken to her like that before, as if she mattered. False Angels were what most demons considered a "great to date but not to mate" species, so males were rarely in it for the long run. Unless, of course, they'd been seduced and enchanted. When that happened, all their pretty words meant nothing.

She got the feeling that what Revenant had just said meant the world.

"Good to know," she said with a casualness she didn't feel. Needing to do something—anything—other than stand awkwardly in the hallway, she started toward her office. Hopefully her mother would call soon to let Blas know she was all right. "Why are you here, anyway?"

"Gethel is bleeding," he said as he fell into step next to her. "It's not bad, but you should see her. And don't tell me to bring her here, because it's not happening."

"I'm sorry, but I'm busy. Eidolon volunteered to go in my place. Let me just give him a buzz——"

Revenant grabbed her wrist as she reached into her lab coat for her phone. "No one but you."

She sighed. "Revenant, we've been over this. We're done."

"This isn't about you and me. It's about the fact that I don't trust anyone else."

She gave him a skeptical glance, but his hard, uncompromising expression told her nothing. "But you trust me?"

"I don't trust anyone. But I trust you more than anyone here."

"Why?" She lowered her voice so a passing vampire nurse didn't get a load of gossip fodder. "Because we had sex?"

"No. Because you helped me when you didn't have to."

"You were in pain," she said. "I'm a doctor. I don't like to see people suffer. Besides, I couldn't exactly kick you out of my apartment. You're kind of ... big."

He was big *everywhere*. The thought made her flush inappropriately hot.

One lip curled in amusement, flashing a bit of fang. "But you didn't have to be as nice as you were, either."

Okay, she'd give him that. "Revenant," she sighed. "I really can't do what you're asking. I was just on my way to the library to do some research—"

"What kind of research? I can help."

She slowed, seriously considering his offer. With his thousands of years of accumulated knowledge, not to mention the fact that he was uber-powerful, maybe he could help. She was at the point of desperation, and while she couldn't tell him the complete truth, she supposed she could share her problem with a little rearranging of the facts.

"I'm looking for an enchantment that will disguise me from angels. Make me look like another species or something."

His lip curled again, but this time, there was no hint

of amusement. "Does this have something to do with the attack?"

"Yes. Obviously, I'm being hunted for some reason. Could have something to do with a patient I treated or maybe I'm being confused for someone else. Either way, it's clear I'm not safe, and I can't stay at UG anymore. I can't put anyone else at risk."

He came to an abrupt halt. "Put me at risk."

She wheeled around to face him. "Excuse me?"

"You can stay with me. Think about it," he said as he stroked his hand down the hilt of a blade at his hip. "No one in their right minds would come after you with me around."

True, but how long would it be before *he* was the one she had to run from? Her pager went off in an urgent tone. "Hold on." She glanced at the message, and her heart stopped.

Your gallbladder blanchier *patient from yesterday is code 12. Hurry.*

"I gotta go!" She ran toward the Harrowgate leading to the hospital, and wouldn't you know it, Rev was right on her heels. She didn't bother taking the time to tell him to go away. He wouldn't listen, and her mind was racing anyway.

The *blanchier*'s operation had been routine and unremarkable, so what the hell? She hit the Harrowgate at a run, with Rev sliding in after her. There was only one flashing light inside, and that was the symbol for Underworld General. She touched it, and instantly the gate opened into the hospital's bustling ER.

She jogged to the surgical wing and the bank of rooms set aside for post-op patients, and the insane activity outside the second door on the right told her that was the *blanchier*'s room.

Several staff members were frantically trying to revive the pale, elflike demon. Slash, another of several Seminus brothers Eidolon had hired recently, was gripping the *blanchier*'s ankle, his *dermoire* glowing madly as he channeled healing power into him. Unfortunately, the *blanchier* was a species that didn't respond well to a Seminus demon's healing power.

"Fuck," he barked. "Something is shutting down all his systems."

Bane, his brother, snatched the IV bag off the pole. "This is saline. It's fucking *saline*."

Oh, shit. *Blanchiers* were highly allergic to saline. Who would have ordered a saline drip? Or had someone accidentally spiked a bag of saline instead of glucose? Blas grabbed the demon's chart and scanned it for physician orders.

Eidolon had ordered labs. Bane had given an injection of hydrogen peroxide. Blaspheme had ordered...saline.

All around her, the alarmed beeps from hospital equipment and the raised voices of the people trying to save the demon faded into a distant buzz. Blaspheme's pulse fluttered in spastic bursts as guilt stabbed her in the chest like a dull blade. She'd marked the wrong damned box.

"No," she whispered.

Revenant appeared at her side and peered at the chart in her hand. "What is it?"

Nausea racked her, stealing her voice, and when she could finally talk, her voice was barely a whisper. "It's my fault. I meant to mark D5W. I remember now. I was distracted and...fuck. I didn't even sign my name on the chart." Shoving the clipboard onto its hook at the foot of the bed, she leaped into action. "Someone give him a glucose injection. Hurry!"

"We already did that. He's dying," Slash said.

"Did you try adrenaline? Cefazolin?" She scrambled for the open drawers and cabinets, knocking stuff out of the way as she desperately sought every drug known to help *blanchiers*. "Acetazolamide?"

"We've tried everything!" Doctor Shakvhan's shrill voice rang out, but Blaspheme didn't stop tearing through supplies, knocking wrapped syringes, bandages, and who-knew-what-else to the floor.

Behind her, she heard Revenant's low curse. She stopped her frantic search to watch him shove his way through the crowd of doctors and nurses.

"Hey!"

"What are you doing, asshole?"

"You can't be in here—"

Revenant ignored everyone to lay his hand on the demon's forehead. For a moment, everyone went silent as the room filled with a strange, electric energy. A heartbeat later, the patient inhaled a great, gasping breath, and all the machines that had been beeping in alarm suddenly went back to normal.

Shocked expressions quickly yielded to relief, and then the scramble to stabilize the guy began.

"You saved him," Blas croaked, her mouth dry from the adrenaline overload. "Oh, damn. You did it." Her hand shook as she swiped a paper cup from the dispenser, splashed water into it, and downed it to relieve her parched mouth. When she could speak without sounding like a three-pack-a-day smoker, she asked, "How did you do that?"

He shrugged. "I'm powerful as shit."

"If you ever get tired of your other job, I'm sure Eidolon would hire you," she said, only half kidding.

Revenant went taut. "I don't heal, Blaspheme. I kill."

His words struck her oddly, as if he'd gone dead inside when he spoke them, as if he had no choice but to kill. But he'd saved her life. He'd just saved the *blanchier*. Yes, she was terrified that he'd turn on her if he learned the truth, but for some reason, she was even starting to question that. He'd been too good to her, his touch gentle, his gratitude genuine.

"If all you do is kill," she said, "then why did you heal the *blanchier*?"

Revenant glanced over at the flurry of activity around the demon. "So you'll owe me."

That, she didn't doubt, but she didn't give a shit what his motivation was. He'd saved the patient, and he might very well have saved her job.

Leaving the patient in capable hands, she slipped out of the room, followed by Revenant and both Slash and Shakvhan. Shakvhan immediately lit into her.

"You stupid twat," she snapped. "You could have killed that patient. If not for your friend here, the *blanchier* would be dead."

"I know," Blas said.

"I told Eidolon he was making a mistake when he put you in charge of the clinic with Gem. I'm reporting you."

Revenant peeled off his sunglasses, and Blas shivered at the ice in his dark eyes. "Do that, and you'll be dead the moment you step outside this hospital," Revenant said, the stark emotionlessness of his statement much more frightening than if he'd been angry.

"Easy," Blas said, laying a restraining hand on his shoulder. "Doctor Shakvhan is doing her job." She was being an asshole about it, but Blaspheme would be just as pissed if the situation had been reversed. "Go ahead and report me to Eidolon. I'm going to talk to him when he gets here for his shift anyway."

Shakvhan sniffed. Then she eyed Revenant in a new light now that she'd calmed down a little. As a succubus, the doctor was hypertuned to all males, especially those who were especially...virile.

"Who are you?" she asked.

"He's Reaver's brother," Blaspheme said. "Revenant."

Shakvhan's eyes flared. "I thought you looked familiar." She glanced at her watch. "I have some time before my next surgery...want to see the inside of a supply closet?"

Supply closet was code for sex, and Blaspheme bristled. Didn't matter that she had no claim to Revenant. Hell, she didn't even want him. But for some reason, she didn't want anyone else to have him, either. Especially not the bitchy succubus.

Blas didn't give him a chance to reply. "Sorry, Shakvhan, but we're on our way to a house call."

"I don't know," Revenant said as he looked the curvy female up and down. "There's no hurry."

You bastard. Then she saw it, the impish glint in his eyes. He was trying to make her jealous. And the bitch of it was that it worked.

"Fine," she said. "Take your time. But I start shift in about forty-five minutes now, so the clock is ticking."

She didn't wait to see if her bluff worked or not. She started toward the administrative offices, hoping Eidolon had come in early like he usually did. If not, she'd wait outside his office door.

Revenant caught up with her before she made it ten feet. She was strangely relieved that he hadn't gone with Shakvhan.

"Blaspheme?"

"What?"

"Why did you admit to your mistake? You could have lied and escaped punishment."

"*Someone* would have been punished. Major mistakes like that don't go ignored. Eidolon and his brothers don't let shit slide, and they shouldn't. I can't let someone else pay for my incompetence."

He gazed at her for so long that heat flushed her face and she started walking faster, as if she could escape his stare. "What? Why are you looking at me like that?"

"Because," he said quietly, "I've decided that I'm not through with you. Not any time soon."

"Oh, come *on*," she groaned.

He suddenly went taut, and she followed his gaze down the hall, where Eidolon was striding toward them, his expression stern, his eyes burning gold. Looked like Shakvhan had already called him.

"You want to tell me what the hell happened with the *blanchier* demon?"

"I fucked up." She cursed the tremor in her voice. "I take full responsibility for what happened."

Eidolon scowled at Revenant before turning back to her. "Can I talk to you in private?"

"Of course."

A shadow passed over Revenant's face, but he managed a forced smile of all teeth and fangs and no amusement. "I'll wait here."

Eidolon led her a few paces down the hall. "What's going on, Blaspheme? That was a serious mistake, and it's unlike you."

"I know. I don't know what I was thinking. I was distracted by everything going on with my mother and my ... you know. I'm not excusing what I did," she added quickly. "I'll make it up. Take extra shifts. Take janitor duty. Whatever you need."

"What I need is for you to get your head on straight." Eidolon's words were harsh, but his eyes had lost the angry gold glow. "Between work, your mother, and your ... other issue, your attention is too divided. Starting right now, I don't want you to treat patients. Administrative duty only until we find a way to repair your disguise."

"What? Wait, no—"

"My decision is final," he interrupted in a tone that discouraged argument.

Tears stung her eyes. Her work was all she had, especially now that her apartment had been compromised and her mother was in the wind.

"Look," he said, his voice losing the stern edge. "This won't affect your status here. You're still in charge of the clinic. But you're off your game. We need you at your best."

He was right, but she couldn't help feeling as if she'd let him down. She'd let everyone at UG down. All she'd wanted her entire life, even during the years when she and her mother had moved from town to town so they'd never be pinned down, was to be a doctor. The desire to help others had always been strong inside her, and equally strong had been the desire to belong in a tight-knit community.

Now she couldn't help people, and that tight-knit community would surely see her as a screwup no one could trust. Hot tears burned her eyes, but she dashed them before they could fall. Gods, she felt like a fool.

"We've all been where you are, Blaspheme," Eidolon said gently. "Sometimes personal issues interfere with our professional lives, and one of them has to be resolved before we can move on with the other." He glanced over at Rev, who was watching them like a hawk, and lowered his voice. "I spoke with Reaver about the Gethel situation. He had an idea that might or might not work, but we don't have a choice. Given Lucifer's size, Gethel could give birth at any moment. Let me know when Revenant is ready to take someone on a house call."

"That's why he's here now. He wants to take me to her."

Eidolon gave a curt nod. "I'll go."

She gripped his arm, and she swore she heard a soft growl coming from Revenant's direction. To be safe, she released the doctor. "He won't deal with anyone else, and I can't put anyone else at risk. I'll go."

"This isn't your fight, Blaspheme."

"Eidolon, you've risked your life a million times for this hospital. But you have a family now that needs you. I don't. And Revenant...I don't trust him with you, and he won't take you anyway. If anyone is safe with him, it's me."

"Blaspheme—"

"Please don't argue. You know I'm right."

Eidolon closed his eyes and blew out a long breath.

"Take the blue obstetrics bag in my office. There's a specially marked syringe in it. It'll have a thirty-minute delay. You'll know what to do."

"What's in the syringe?"

"Something called solarum. It was Reaver's idea."

She'd heard rumors of an angel-produced evil-eradication substance created by liquefying sunbeams. Was solarum that product?

A page came over the intercom for Eidolon, and the rotating red lights on the walls began to flash, indicating an incoming emergency via ambulance.

"I have to go," he said. "But Blaspheme, your suspension doesn't change anything. You're still a vital part of the hospital and clinic, and both Wraith and I are looking for anything that will help you with your issue. And be careful. Your safety is the most important thing right now. Understood?"

She nodded, mainly because she couldn't speak around the knot in her throat.

"Good. Come straight here after you see Gethel. Got it?"

She nodded again. Eidolon took off, and Revenant was there instantly, so fast he must have flashed to her.

"What happened?" he demanded. "He made you cry. Do you want me to kill him?"

"No," she croaked. "And please don't mess with Shakvhan, either. To kill her or ... otherwise."

She couldn't believe she'd just asked him not to have sex with the succubus, but then, she couldn't believe she'd almost killed a patient, either.

"Then what? I don't like to see you ..." He trailed off, cursing, as if he was beating himself up about admitting to having feelings like normal people. "You're upset. I need to do something, Blaspheme."

She turned to him, desperate for anything he could do to take her mind off what she'd done. She'd made a nearly fatal mistake, and now she'd lost her job. Even if the suspension was only temporary, probably a matter of days given how fast her False Angel enchantment was failing, it felt like she'd been fired. People were staring at her already, looking at her like she was a murderer.

"My office," she said. "I need to get away from here—"

Suddenly, they were standing next to her desk. "What else?" His hand snapped out and caught her by the chin. She inhaled sharply at the possessiveness in his gaze, the way it heated her skin like an erotic sunburn. "Please, Blaspheme. Let me help you."

"Why?" she rasped. "Why do you want to help me? Why are you so fucking obsessed with me?"

"I don't know." He smoothed his thumb along her jawline, and she leaned into it, more starved for contact than she'd like to admit. "Something about you draws me. False Angels are always dark, but there's a light in you that seeps out and warms me."

She should be terrified that he had noticed yet another frayed thread in her disguise, but it occurred to her that every time he pointed out something that made her different, it was a compliment. He *liked* that she wasn't a standard-issue False Angel.

Dipping his head, he brushed his lips over hers. "I haven't been warm in a very long time, Blaspheme."

His words were like a balm, a caress that both soothed her and aroused her. She suddenly knew what she wanted,

and although she knew it was wrong, she couldn't bring
herself to care. Regrets were for later.

"Fuck me," she said. "Make me forget about all of
this."

Instantly, his arms came around her. "You sure?"

"I'm sure." At this very moment, crazy as it was, she'd
never been more sure of anything.

Twenty-One

If Revenant could lock this moment away in a time capsule, he would. If he could stretch this moment out and make it last forever, he would.

Not since his mother had been alive had a female needed him. Truly *needed* him, and something inside him shattered.

This was why he'd truly saved the *blanchier* demon. Not because he wanted Blaspheme to owe him, but because she'd needed him, even if she hadn't known it at the time. And something about her made him want to do good, even if all he did was save the life of a demon who probably wouldn't have lifted a finger to save anyone else.

He looked down at the beautiful female standing before him, her eyes liquid with the pain that was so clearly tearing her apart, and he knew he'd do anything she asked. He was an idiot—an idiot who was still ignoring Satan's damned summons—but right now he didn't care.

This was a noble female he didn't deserve, and he knew that for sure after watching her admit to a major error that she could easily have covered up. Instead, she'd faced her boss like a warrior and accepted her punishment.

She was unique, not only among False Angels, but among most demons.

In that moment, she'd become the person he trusted most in the world.

He felt the impact of that knowledge all the way to his soul, damaged as it was, and he had the strangest urge to fold his wings around her in the most intimate of angelic embraces. He'd never done it before, but what made the desire truly odd was that angels only experienced the impulse when their partner was another angel. He hadn't thought False Angels counted.

"Revenant, hurry."

His heart pounded at the sight of the desperation tangling with desire in her liquid gaze.

"No rules, right?" His hands made quick work of her scrub top and pants. "No stupid no-touching rules."

"No," she moaned as he lowered his mouth to her breast and licked a nipple through the delicate lace of her bra. "No rules."

"Fuck, yeah." He pushed her back against her desk and dropped to his knees to kiss the smooth, bare expanse of her belly. "Spread your legs."

Bracing her palms on the edge of the desk, she obeyed, arching against him as he kissed his way down her abdomen, admiring the honed, rippling muscles that flexed as he worked his way to the elastic of her low-slung beige panties. His cock pushed painfully hard against his leathers, but he ignored the needy son of a bitch as he used a fang to rip her underwear down the front.

"I liked those," she muttered.

"I like them better in the garbage." She was bare to him now, and unlike when they were at his place and his hands were fisted at his sides, he now had no idiotic rules to restrain him. He dragged his palms down her hips to her sex and used his thumbs to spread her wide.

She was ready for him, glistening with arousal already. His blood caught fire, burning with the intensity of the sun's surface. He'd been desperate to taste her before, but now he knew how she tasted, and his mouth watered.

He didn't waste another second. He buried his face between her legs, pressing the flat of his tongue hard against her core, using his own pulse to thud against her with a steady but gentle beat. The pressure made her squirm and pant as she gripped his head and held him as if afraid he'd suddenly stop.

Not gonna happen.

Adrenaline surged through him, hot and potent as he dragged his tongue through her valley in a lazy sweep and slid one finger inside her dripping core. Her deep moan vibrated his mouth as he began to lick her in earnest now, relishing her unabashed noises and pleading whispers.

"I love this," she breathed. "You're so … good."

Maybe, but he knew for a fact that he'd never been this into it, this hungry for female flesh. He kissed her deeply, drawing her pulsing bud between her lips, flicking his tongue over the tip, and then he sucked. Hard.

"Holy … shit … Rev … I'm going to—" She broke off with a cry. Her fingernails scored his scalp, and her channel clenched around his fingers as she rode his hand and tongue.

She looked down at him, catching his gaze as he finished her off, easing his finger out of her as he continued to stroke her lightly with his tongue. Her mouth was parted with panting breaths, and her cheeks were flushed with passion. The sight of her like that made his cock strain inside his pants, demanding release.

Then, as the sexual glow waned, the sadness in her eyes reappeared.

Fuck that. He wasn't going to give her one more second to think about anything but him.

He stood, gripped her hips, and tugged her hard against him. Her heat scorched him even through his layers of leather.

"Now," he growled into her ear, "we do this *my* way."

Blaspheme really hoped Revenant's way was rough and raw, because right now, that was what she needed. Wanted. Craved.

The room spun as Revenant wheeled her around so her spine was against his chest. "Your wings," he growled into her ear. "Show them to me."

It didn't occur to her to refuse, even though the last time she'd summoned her False Angel wings during sex with him, they'd flickered in and out of existence.

Careful to not release any remaining aphrodisiac powder, she let her gossamer wings flare out, filling the narrow space between their bodies. Revenant groaned, and she closed her eyes as his hands drifted from the base of the wings all the way to the tips. His warmth surrounded her as they stood like that, plastered against each other, with him caressing what no one else had ever touched.

She never took her wings out during sex. They were a tool abused by False Angels to seduce and deceive, but right now, *she* was the one being seduced.

And she reveled in it.

Too soon, she felt the telltale weakening of her aura, knew the wings would disappear. Reluctantly, she made them fade away, and Rev's hiss of displeasure vibrated her spine.

"I didn't tell you to put them away."

She reached back and dug her nails into his thigh. "You don't get to tell me to put them away."

His breath was hot against her cheek as he took her earlobe between his teeth and bit down hard enough to make her gasp. "This is *my* show, angel."

There was no warning. All at once, he stepped back and bent her over the desk with a hand on the back of her neck. Her palms and cheek slapped the wood at the same time, enough to sting, but not hurt. Holding her down with one strong hand, he drove the other between her legs, cupping her swollen sex. She was still throbbing from her climax, and when he slipped a finger between her folds and rubbed her, the first stirrings of a second one began.

Just as she pushed back against him, desperate for more pressure, he tightened his grip on her neck and withdrew his talented fingers. She moaned at the loss of sensation, felt his knuckles brush her rear as the sound of a zipper rang out.

Anticipation made her pant so hard she saw her breath form condensation on the desk's surface.

The blunt tip of his penis pushed into her, lingered, and then he slammed home. She cried out in exquisite pleasure. He pulled back and thrust again, harder, and her desk slid on the floor. He didn't seem to notice, kept up the delicious onslaught.

He knew exactly what she needed. No downtime. No talk. No emotion.

The squeak of her bare skin on the wood joined the erotic sounds of Rev's panting breaths and the slap of his thighs on the back of hers. Her hip bones banged on the desk, and she knew she'd have the bruises to show for it, but oh, what beautiful bruises they'd be.

"Is this what you wanted?" His guttural voice sent tingles across her skin. "Do you want more?"

"Yes," she rasped. "More."

"That's my angel," he whispered.

Abruptly, he yanked her upright, and a piercing, searing pain tore into her neck, followed immediately by an ecstasy so intense that she screamed. She'd never been bitten before, had never wanted to be that vulnerable. She hadn't known what she was missing, but she wouldn't make that mistake again.

Pleasure spiked as his arm came around her waist to hold her while he fucked her, lifting her off the floor with each powerful thrust. The smooth rub of his leather against her skin was like an erotic caress, and the thought that he was fully clothed was the last straw. Her orgasm crashed over her like an ocean wave, tumbling her endlessly in ecstasy and drowning her in bliss.

Nothing had ever felt like this before. She'd had a lot of sex and a lot of orgasms, but this was more than a physical release. It was emotional as well, and as Revenant stiffened and his hot seed splashed inside her, pressure filled her chest cavity.

The sex had been amazing and exactly what she needed, but it had only delayed the inevitable, the realization that her life had gone to hell in a handbasket, and hope was all she had left.

Twenty-Two

That, Revenant thought, had been some of the best sex of his life. He'd always liked to fuck the way he fought; messy, with no holds barred, and this definitely counted. Blaspheme's desk had skidded across the room, shoved into a now-dented file cabinet, and her neck was streaked with blood. When he pulled out, his seed would spill out of her, marking her with his scent.

Normally, now would be the time when he would zip up and leave the female sated and sleepy, and he'd go find another.

But he didn't want another. And he didn't want to leave. He didn't want empty sex with females whose names he didn't know or wouldn't remember ten minutes later.

It made no sense. Well, it did if Blas had used her False Angel powers on him, but he'd watched, waiting for her to engage her charm or aphrodisiac, and nothing had happened. She'd asked him for sex, but not to seduce him

or even to have a good time with the closest dick. She'd
needed him, had laid herself bare, giving him access to
her body and soul.

In thousands of years, no one had done that, and his
heart fluttered with a foreign sensation that made him
feel like he'd guzzled a dozen bottles of the best French
champagne.

Shit. He had genuine feelings for her, didn't he? And
wasn't that some damned inconvenient timing? Even if he
didn't have both Heaven and Sheoul breathing down his
neck, he didn't want the kind of complications emotional
attachments brought. No, those strings got knotted real
fast, as his relationship with Reaver proved.

Retracting his fangs, he licked the punctures in Blaspheme's throat, lingering a little longer than was necessary as he lapped up every drop of her sweet blood. She
shuddered as he pulled out and carefully released her so
she wouldn't fall.

She immediately gripped the desk to support her shaky
legs. He knew the feeling. His own legs were liquid with
spent passion. Sure, he'd fucked harder and longer in the
past, but somehow, in this brief, intense encounter with
Blaspheme, his mind and body had given over more than
they ever had.

Stepping back, he mentally cleaned himself up, tucked
his semihard cock back in his pants, and zipped. With
another mental tweak, he tidied Blaspheme as well, and
then bent to gather her clothes.

"We should go see Gethel now," he said, fully engag-
ing business mode in an effort to leave the emotional shit
behind.

He tossed her scrubs, lab coat, and stethoscope onto

the desk…and casually slipped her destroyed underwear into his pocket. He'd never been a sicko who kept souvenirs of his conquests, but for some reason, he hadn't been able to let go of Blaspheme, and he thought that maybe keeping something of hers would help.

Yeah, that's some loaded rationale. Keep something that belongs to the female you need to let go. That'll help you forget.

Irritation at his own stupidity made his voice harsher than he intended as he barked, "Come on. Gethel's not getting any less pregnant."

Blaspheme's shoulders heaved, and she made a sound that froze him in place.

"Blaspheme?" She made the sound again, and alarm shot through him. "Are you okay?"

"Yes," she croaked. And then, "No."

Suddenly, sobs racked her body and she slid to the floor in a crouch, her face buried in her hands as she cried.

Raw emotion seized him, scrambling his insides and setting him on the edge of hyperventilation. He couldn't handle seeing a female cry. Memories of his mother huddled in the back of her cell as she rocked back and forth and wept brought him to his knees in front of Blaspheme.

Very gently, he pulled her against him and used his body to buffer her violent sobs. He didn't say anything; what was there to say? He wasn't even entirely sure what was wrong. All he knew was that she was in pain, and he was fucking helpless to do anything about it.

After what seemed like hours, her crying let up enough for him to reach onto her desk and fumble around for the tissue box. He found a slip of paper with some sort of cryptic writing on it, and then his fingers found what he was looking for.

He pressed a tissue into her hand. "Hold on for a second, okay?"

She nodded, turning away to blow her nose as he stood and gathered her clothes. He tucked the piece of paper and her cell phone inside her purse, and then he lifted her into his arms and flashed them both to his bedroom.

He expected her to argue as he carefully tucked her into bed, but she went as limp as a cooked noodle, which was a measure of her exhaustion.

"I'm sorry." Her voice was a muffled whisper into the pillow. "I don't usually have breakdowns like this."

"It's okay." He climbed into bed and drew her against him as her sobs became sniffles, and finally, she didn't make any noise except soft snores.

Closing his eyes, he relaxed. Truly relaxed for the first time in...he couldn't remember. But what he did know was that this felt right, no matter how hard he tried to tell himself that it didn't. And when the wing anchors on his back began to itch, he once again had the most bizarre desire—

That's when it happened. His wings sprouted from the slits near his shoulder blades. The left one, blocked by the mattress, lay useless against his back. But the right one spread out in ebony, gold, and silver glory, and he didn't fight instinct as it lowered over Blaspheme's body, covering her in a protective cocoon of feathers.

He'd given her the Angel's Embrace, an act of affection, promise...or love.

Gods, he was a fool.

Blaspheme woke to the mouthwatering aroma of grilled meat. She opened her swollen eyes, wincing at the dry, gritty aftermath of a crying jag. It had always seemed strange that an excess of tears could produce such a parched sensation.

Wait…she'd been crying in her office. In front of Revenant. She groaned and covered her head with the blankets.

Blankets that smelled like Revenant.

God, how could she have fallen apart like that? She wasn't even sure what, exactly, had caused her to break down, but what she did know was that it couldn't happen again. She was stronger than that. She'd had to be, to survive this long.

"Hey." His voice, smoky and resonant, broke into her thoughts, but she wasn't sure if that was a good or a bad thing. "I have food."

She poked her head out of the covers and peeked at him as he entered the bedroom with a brown paper sack. "Food?"

He held up the grease-stained bag. "Fresh delivered from my favorite underworld pub."

Hunger beat out embarrassment, and she sat up, realizing at the last second that she was naked. Hastily, she tucked the blankets between her arms and ribs to keep herself covered.

Not that Revenant hadn't seen every inch of her by now. Still, naked during sex was different than naked and emotionally exposed. She felt like he'd seen not only her body uncovered, but her mind as well.

Something glittery caught her eye, and she reached across the pale blue comforter, her fingers finding the most exquisite feather. Roughly the size of a bald eagle's tail feather, it was a luxurious blue-black satin shot through with gold and tipped with silver.

"Wow," she said. "Yours?"

Revenant turned about ten shades of red. Why, she had no idea. If her feathers looked like this, she'd be showing them off all the time. Sadly, hers were the translucent with a pinkish shimmer that all False Angels had, and while they looked exotic from a distance, up close they were crepe paper–thin and meant only for show.

Not that she was complaining. She had no idea what her real wings looked like, and she didn't want to know. Knowing meant her False Angel enchantment was gone, and she'd likely be dead before she could get intimate with her feathers.

"Ah...yeah. It's mine." Revenant sank down on the bed and pulled four foam boxes out of the bag, plus napkins and plastic utensils. "There's smoked ribs, saucy meatballs, and chops."

"Not one for vegetables, huh?"

He opened the last box to reveal crisp, golden fries. "Voilà. Vegetables."

"As a physician, I'm going to throw down a bullshit flag on that one." Carefully setting aside the feather, she reached for the box full of charred ribs, but pulled her hand back at the last second. "Dare I ask what kind of meat this is?"

He rolled one broad shoulder in a lazy shrug. "Dunno. How strong is your stomach?"

She had a feeling he was teasing, but she wasn't going

to test that theory. She poked a meatball with a plastic fork and gobbled the thing down in two bites. Next, she put a hurting on the ribs, not caring that Revenant was watching her with a self-satisfied smirk on his face.

"What?" she mumbled through a mouthful of fries. "Never seen anyone eat before?"

"I like watching you eat. I'd have liked to cook the food myself, but I didn't want to leave you alone while I went hunting."

"That's very thoughtful of you," she said, even as she wondered how often he cooked for females. "But I'm definitely not going to ask what you would have gone hunting for."

"That's probably wise."

They finished eating in surprisingly comfortable silence, and when she was done, Revenant disappeared into the bathroom. He returned with a wet washcloth and stunned her into silence when he very tenderly wiped her face, dabbing beneath her eyes with the greatest of care. Then he moved on to her mouth and hands, catching every bit of sticky sauce and fry grease.

She had a feeling he'd tended to someone like this before. It was hard to imagine that this big, bad Shadow Angel could be so gentle and caring.

As he finished up, she covered his hand in hers. "Who was she?"

He knew what she meant, and shadows flitted in his eyes. "My mother," he said quietly.

And then, as if he'd gotten a shock stick rammed up his ass, he shoved to his feet and tossed the washcloth in a corner pile of clothes. He yanked a black Guns N' Roses T-shirt out of his drawer and handed it to her.

"I don't have any underwear that'll fit you, but I think I have a pair of sweats that'll work if you cinch up the waist. You know, a lot."

"It's okay. I can wear my scrubs. I should be going anyway."

"Where? Back to the hospital where you just got suspended?"

His words stung...because he was right. Her life was spiraling out of control, and the suspension had been the last straw. Angels were after her, her False Angel enchantment was wearing off, her mother was missing, and she'd lost her job. Then she'd had amazing sex with Revenant that had felt anything but casual.

Her emotions were frayed, but for some reason, here in Revenant's lair, it was easy to let all of that go.

"Revenant? Why did you bring me here?"

"You were upset." He gathered up the boxes and trash and shoved it all into the bag it had come in. "You needed to be safe. This is the safest place for you to be."

"But why? I was safe at the hospital, too."

"It's a...rule."

She climbed out of bed and started to dress. "A rule?"

He nodded. "When a female is in distress, you tend to her." He appeared to consider what he'd just said. "Unless she tries to kill you. At that point, she's fair game."

Blaspheme slipped into her scrub pants. What *was* it with him and rules? He'd gotten himself worked up about her no-touching directive the first time they'd had sex. At the time, she'd thought it was weird, but she'd written it off as Revenant not wanting to give up control. But it seemed that this was something very, very different.

"So...you follow every rule?"

"Rules exist for a reason," he said gruffly, as if she shouldn't question it.

"What if they're stupid?"

"It doesn't matter. If it's a law, it's law."

She rolled her eyes as she shrugged into her scrub top. "I read once that there's a law somewhere in California that says you can't dust furniture with dirty underwear. Are you telling me that you think people should be arrested for dusting their furniture with worn skivvies?"

"No. That's a moronic law, and people shouldn't go to jail for that." At her triumphant grin, he held up his hand. "But if it is, in fact, a law, people shouldn't get pissed for being arrested because they broke it. Stupid or not, it's the law." He pressed on the wall, and a hidden panel slid out of the way, opening up his bedroom to an outdoor forest of gnarled trees and funky bushes with thorns as large as her hand. "But straight up, I'd kill anyone who rubbed their skanky underwear on my furniture. Fucking nasty."

He tossed the bag of garbage and leftovers outside, and almost instantly, a dozen furry things she could only describe as raccoon-spiders scurried over and demolished the bag and its contents. The panel slid closed again, and she could just shake her head at the weirdness that was so normal to him.

She was so lucky her mother had chosen to raise her in the human world where, comparatively, very little was creepy.

"Revenant?"

He swung back around to her. "Yeah?"

"Why are you such a stickler for rules? I mean, I know you're technically an angel, but you live and work in

Sheoul. You were raised here. Sheoul is all about chaos and lawlessness. So why are rules so important to you?"

He swallowed hard, his Adam's apple bobbing up and down, and she suddenly knew this was related to his hellish childhood.

"It's okay," she said. "You don't have to tell me."

"No." He swallowed again. "I ... want to. I don't know why, but I do." He made a beeline for the little portable bar in the corner, but before he reached it, he halted, head hung low, as if he couldn't bear to take another step. "Is your False Angel magic acting on me? Is that why I suddenly have this burning desire to confide in you?"

"What? No. Of course not. This is *me*. Not some kind of enchantment."

"But you *are* a False Angel. It's in your nature to enchant and deceive."

He had a point about a False Angel's nature, but she had no idea how to convince him that she wasn't using any False Angel abilities on him. Hell, she didn't know if she even could anymore.

"As a False Angel," she said, feeling strangely uncomfortable about saying that, "I can choose when to use my gifts and when not to. I swear to you, I'm not using them."

He eyed her, and she found herself desperately wanting him to believe her. To trust her. And at the same time, shame was a weight in the center of her chest, because she wanted him to believe a lie.

How messed up was that?

And then the truth of the situation hit her so hard she almost took a step back. She was falling for him. Falling for a male who admitted to killing *vyrm*. And wasn't that the perfect cap on this epically crappy day.

"I'll take you at your word, Blaspheme," Revenant said. "And I never do that, so don't make me regret it." Before her brain could process a response, he continued. "The rules," he said, thankfully getting back to the topic at hand, "are important because breaking them always has serious consequences. My mother taught me that."

"How well did you know her?" Blas had assumed he'd been raised alone in the cell he'd mentioned the other day.

"She...chose to stay behind with me after Reaver was taken," he said. "She used to tell me that laws should be created sparingly, because the breaking of a law, even one that seems insignificant or stupid, has consequences. But I didn't listen. I was a rebellious kid with Satan's blood winging around inside me. My playground was a torture chamber, and my best friends were the same cell guards who tortured me."

Blaspheme could only stare in horror. She'd thought her childhood on the run was bad, but she'd never complain again. Ever.

"Revenant, I'm so s—"

He cut her off with a *please don't* gesture. She got it— she hated pity, too.

"So my mother tried to warn me. Pleaded with me to follow the demons' orders and never disobey their laws. Of course I did everything I could to get into trouble. I didn't give a shit that they beat me." He jammed his hands into his pockets and looked down, his head hanging loosely from his hunched shoulders. "It didn't occur to me that my mother had to watch it. And because it didn't occur to me, I kept breaking rules. Then, one day, while I watched, they beat her instead. I didn't mean to break rules after that, but sometimes...fuck."

He scrubbed his hand over his face, and when he was done, he looked tired. Defeated.

Blaspheme's heart bled for him. She couldn't even begin to imagine the kind of terror he must have felt watching his mother be abused for something he'd done. His guilt must eat at him like acid. Dying to comfort him in any way she could, she moved forward, but he backed up, clearly not wanting to be touched right now.

"How long did you have to live like that?" Gods, her voice was as unsteady as her emotions were right now. She wanted to cry for him. To scream in outrage. To kill the bastards who had done that to him and his mother.

"They took me away from her when I was ten," he said. "Sent me to a mine to dig for magma crystals."

Magma crystals, found only in Sheoul, were rare and precious, coveted by necromancers to use in powerful spells. By all accounts, the mining of them was so dangerous that no one volunteered to do it. Slave labor was the only way the things could be acquired.

"I tried to escape," he continued in a raspy, tormented voice. "For ten years I tried to find a way to get back to my mother. What I didn't know until later was that every time I made a break for it, she was hurt. Raped. All the usual stuff they do to females. So, yeah. You follow the fucking rules no matter what, because if you don't, bad shit happens."

Blaspheme's throat felt raw, as if she were the one to have shared that horrible story. To have shared the screams that had no doubt been wrenched from him.

"Revenant," she whispered.

His head came up with a snarl. "Don't."

Ignoring him, she moved forward, and again, he backed up. But this time, she didn't stop until he hit the bedroom wall. He snarled again, baring his fangs. Like a wounded animal, his behavior was defensive, not aggressive, and she knew instinctively he wouldn't hurt her.

"Easy." Very slowly, she cupped his face between her hands and met his haunted gaze. "Thank you for telling me. You don't have to say anything more. But if you want to, I'm here for you."

His dark eyes roamed her face, searching, she assumed, for sincerity. Little by little, the last traces of resistance vanished, and he hauled her against him. His strong arms surrounded her, but she got the feeling it was she who was holding him up as he hugged her tight, burying his face in her hair, his body as stiff as a backboard.

They stood like that for a long time, until he finally murmured, "Are you for real, Blaspheme?"

She pulled back, found herself looking up into those fathomless black eyes. "What do you mean?"

"I mean that I've got shit coming at me from all sides... from my brother, from Heaven, from Sheoul. You're the only thing that makes sense right now. I can't get fucked over by you, too."

How bizarre it was that they were both in very similar situations, and that only made her feel extra guilty for lying to him.

Maybe she should tell him the truth. Or at least tiptoe around the truth to see how he'd feel about... about what? Screwing a *vyrm*? Confessing his sins to someone who had been lying about who they were?

Even if he didn't want to slaughter her for being a *vyrm*, he'd probably do it for lying to him.

Finally, she settled for a response that was one hundred percent truthful. "I would never intentionally hurt you. Please believe me when I say that."

Revenant opened his mouth to say something, but a muffled buzz drew both of their focuses to her purse on the floor.

"I wouldn't have thought I'd get cell service down here."

He shrugged. "Demon technicians can do pretty much anything." He gestured to the purse. "Go ahead and get it. We should get going anyway. Gethel's waiting."

The reminder made her groan. A groan that was cut short by the distinct buzz tone of her mother's instant message handle.

She fished the phone out of her bag as Revenant left her alone in the bedroom. The screen blinked, and Deva's kitten avatar popped up. Her mother loved cats. Practically lived for Cat Saturday on theCHIVE.

Honey, r u there?

Blaspheme typed out her response with one finger. *I'm here, Mom. Where are you? Are you safe? How are you feeling?*

I feel ok. I'm safe. R u?

Damn, Blas hated the shortcut crap. She made it a point to type out everything properly, even if it took a million times longer. *I'm fine. Why did you run?*

The male in the clinic. He's the 1 I told u about.

Blaspheme frowned. *What one you told me about?*

There was a pause that took way too long. Long enough that Blas managed four laps around the bedroom before her phone finally vibrated in her hand. When she looked down, what she saw stopped her heart dead in her chest.

The male called The Destroyer. Blaspheme, the fallen angel in the clinic... he's The Destroyer. He's the bastard who killed your father.

Twenty-Three

Revenant waited for Blaspheme on his front porch, looking out into the bottomless chasm that circled his house and the ten acres of land surrounding it like a waterless moat. He'd lived in this impenetrable fortress for three decades, basking in the privacy that was broken only when he brought someone here or made the stone bridge visible to those he invited.

Like the food delivery dude.

He'd liked it here, he supposed, but now he wanted something different. Better. More befitting of someone like Blaspheme.

She didn't belong in a place like this. Hell, she didn't belong in Sheoul at all.

As he gazed across the dark depths of the canyon to the vast, craggy Mountains of Eternal Suffering, he felt shame that he'd brought her here. And how strange it was to feel shame when, for nearly five thousand years he'd felt nothing of the sort.

But Blaspheme had left him off balance, awash in unexpected new feelings and dusting off emotions he hadn't used since his mother died.

I'm here for you, she'd said. *I'm here for you*.

Warmth blanketed his heart, replacing the frost that had deadened the muscle. It felt as if the organ was truly beating for the first time, and the lightness, the energy he felt, was amazing.

Overcome with an urge to kiss the ever-living hell out of her, he went back inside, found her sitting stiffly on his couch, her purse over her shoulder, her hands folded in her lap.

Something wasn't right.

"Hey," he said. "What's wrong?"

"Nothing." She stood, but she avoided his gaze. "We should go. We can stop by UG so I can pick up an obstetrics bag and the portable ultrasound machine."

Maybe she'd gotten some bad news while she'd been in the bedroom. He wanted to ask, and yesterday he would have. But something had changed between them since then, and he'd entered into a strange dynamic he wasn't familiar with.

He wasn't exactly the most patient person on the planet, but he'd give it a shot for once. Maybe she'd tell him on her own when she was ready.

He just hoped she was ready soon. His newfound interest in trying to be more patient probably wouldn't last.

Her hand felt stiff and cold in his as he grasped it and flashed them directly to her office.

"Wait here," she said, still not meeting his gaze.

She took off, and he wasted time by checking out all the knickknacks on her desk and on her shelves. She seemed to be a fan of butterflies. Little crystal figurines in bright, cheery colors decorated the office, and on her walls, two huge watercolor paintings of blue and yellow butterflies bracketed her medical degrees and award certificates.

All he had on his walls were racks of weapons and a couple of enemy skulls.

Blaspheme returned, two large bags slung over her shoulders. To be gentlemanly, something completely new, he took both bags.

"You like butterflies," he said, stating the freaking obvious. "Why?" To him, they were nothing but winged worms.

"Because," she said, snaring her purse. "They spend the first part of their lives in disguise, ugly, not knowing their full potential. But when they can finally be themselves, they can fly and be the beautiful creatures they were born to be." A thread of sadness infused her voice. Guess she really had a thing for winged worms.

And she *still* wouldn't look at him.

"Blaspheme?"

"What?" she snapped.

Whoa. "Did I do something to piss you off?"

The thick blond lashes that framed her intense blue eyes flipped up. "No," she said quickly. Too quickly. "I just have a lot on my mind, and frankly, I'm not looking forward to treating that evil skank."

He sensed there was more to it than that, and while he might be dense about female moods, he had a feeling she would only get angrier if he pushed more.

"We won't be there for long," he said. "And if you're

worried about your safety, know that I will kill anyone who tries to harm you."

"Yes," she said in a nasty tone, "because that's what you do, isn't it? You kill. How easy is it for you? How many butterflies have you crushed under your boots, Revenant?"

Taken aback by her sudden anger, he fought to stay calm when he really wanted to lash out. Which was a first.

"I am, for all intents and purposes, a fallen angel," he said flatly. "Killing is in my nature. *Enjoying* it is in my nature. You knew this when you fucked me the first time. And the second. And *now* you're taking issue with it? That's like being angry at a shark for killing a seal. It's in his nature."

"And that's the problem," she whispered. "That's the problem in a nutshell."

Revenant flashed Blaspheme to Gethel's residence without another word. The moment they materialized, Gethel lit into Revenant with ear-shattering shrieks about taking his damned time bringing a doctor.

"Chill out," he said as he sank into a chair near one of the hearths. "It's not like you're going to die from a little bleeding."

Blaspheme held up a hand. "Enough. Gethel, I need you to lie down on the sofa. I'm going to perform an ultrasound and get a sample of amniotic fluid."

"Will it hurt?"

"Yes."

Gethel grinned. "Good."

Blaspheme just shook her head as she squatted down

on the floor and rummaged through the duffel for the supplies needed for the amniocentesis. Her fingers closed around something strange... Frowning, she drew out a small, filled syringe with a piece of paper secured around it with a rubber band.

As Gethel positioned herself on the sofa and lifted her tattered maternity blouse to expose her belly, Blaspheme checked out the paper.

One word, written in Eidolon's neat script: *AMNIO-INFUSION*.

She stared at the letters, trying to make sense of them. Then it hit her. The syringe was filled with the solarum Eidolon had mentioned. Instead of injecting saline into the amniotic sac during a normal amnioinfusion treatment, she was supposed to inject the solarum—

She jerked, nearly dropping the syringe. Poison. The pale yellow liquid inside the syringe's barrel was poison to evil beings, and the more evil, the more poisonous it was. And Lucifer, being the son of Satan...

Oh, damn.

She looked over at Revenant, who had just shoved to his feet to pace back and forth between pillars. He didn't seem to be interested in what was going on, but Gethel huffed.

"Are you just going to sit there, you stupid cow?"

"No," Blas said absently. "Of course not." It was a measure of how flustered she was that she didn't snap back at the evil mother-to-be, and when Revenant shot a look in their direction, she knew she had to get her shit together.

First things first, she needed to gather amniotic fluid. It only took a few minutes to set up the ultrasound machine, which she'd use to determine the position of the fetus and the best location to insert the needle. As the unit warmed up, she made an attempt to engage her False Angel X-Ray vision...and was shocked when it flickered to life.

Warmth infused her body as the gift took hold with an almost orgasmic sensation. It was as if the False Angel enchantment were taking its last dying breath, and she intended to use it for all it was worth.

Quickly, she focused on Gethel's swollen belly, and instantly, the form inside took shape. She expected to see the outline of a monster, but instead, she saw what appeared to be a run-of-the-mill baby, no different from what she'd see in a human hospital.

It's not a baby. It's not human. It's not even a demon. It's Satan's son. Evil incarnate.

Keeping that thought firmly in mind, she chose a spot to place the needle she'd use to withdraw amniotic fluid.

"You're going to feel a pinch..." She inserted the needle, using her special vision to ensure that she hit a pocket of fluid and not the infant. A moment later, she withdrew the full syringe, capped it, and tucked it into the duffel. Stem cell collection successful.

The solarum-filled syringe sat next to the ultrasound machine, its contents glinting in the chamber's smoky light.

Do it.

Blas closed her eyes. She'd taken on the mission to do this, to destroy Lucifer in the womb. She'd done it to keep Eidolon out of harm's way. She could go through with it. She had to.

Taking a deep, bracing breath, she palmed the syringe and oriented the needle so she could jab it straight down, into the back of Lucifer's skull.

Her False Angel vision snuffed out, but it didn't matter. The needle was positioned, and even if she somehow missed, just injecting the stuff into the amniotic fluid should do the trick.

It would destroy Lucifer.

Do it.

But she was a doctor. How could she take a life, even if that life was evil? It was still a life, and she was born to heal, not destroy.

Do it!

Her hand shook and her eyes stung, and in the pit of her stomach, the food she'd eaten with Revenant churned. Why was this happening to her? If Lucifer were to strike out at her, she could fight back. She could kill. But this was different. This would sit on her soul like a bruise for the rest of her life.

But by killing him, you'll be saving thousands of lives.

Hundreds of thousands. Millions, maybe. Come time for the biblical Apocalypse, Lucifer would fight at Satan's side, orchestrating the suffering of every living thing on the planet.

"What the fuck are you doing?" Gethel snapped. "I don't have all day. I have a basketful of kittens to eat."

Blaspheme's hand jerked. "Kittens? I told you, *leafy greens.*"

"You said not to eat infants."

"No meat. At all. Doctor's orders."

Gethel hissed. "I don't believe you." She pointed at the syringe poised over her belly. "And what is that?"

"Contrast solution," Blas lied. "It'll help with the ultrasound."

The sound of Rev's heavy boots striking the floor came

close, and Blaspheme's pulse spiked. Had he seen through the lie?

"Hurry." Gethel dropped her head back against the sofa armrest. "When you're done I'm going to eat the kittens and have someone rustle me up a human infant or two."

Rev was almost on top of her. Blaspheme gripped the syringe tight. No more waffling. This bitch and her monster child were going down. If guilt plagued Blas for the rest of her life, so be it.

Her hand shook even harder and nausea bubbled up, but she ignored both and started to shove the needle home.

Suddenly, something crashed into her, knocking her over and sending the syringe flying out of her grip. Revenant tumbled to the ground, and as he shoved to his feet, his boot came down on the syringe, smashing it and splattering its contents all over the floor.

"Oh, hey, sorry." He gave her a sheepish grin. "I tripped over the ultrasound machine. Hope I didn't mess anything up."

He'd tripped? Mr. Uber-agile had *tripped*?

"Fool!" Gethel barked. "Lucifer is going to skin you alive the moment he learns to wield a blade."

"He's welcome to try." Revenant kicked aside the bits of syringe. "But until then, you need to keep him healthy, so listen to the doctor and eat your damned green shit." He glanced at Blas. "Finish up. I'm ready to get the fuck out of here."

Twenty-Four

Revenant strode away from Blaspheme, cursing himself over and over as he walked. Contrast solution. She'd claimed the syringe had contained *contrast solution*.

He might have believed her had he not watched the drama playing out in her expression as she positioned the needle over Gethel's belly. Whatever substance she'd been about to inject into Gethel had been poisonous, and Blaspheme had been tormented by the murder she'd been about to commit.

At first, Revenant had mentally cheered her on. *Do it! Destroy the bastard!* But when Blaspheme's hand began to shake and her eyes became haunted, his enthusiasm had taken a hard hit. Suddenly, he couldn't bear the idea that the female who had dedicated her life to saving others was going to stain her soul with murder.

Granted, he didn't consider killing Lucifer to be

murder, and he figured that ninety-nine percent of the population of Heaven, Earth, and Sheoul wouldn't, either. But Blas was the one percent, and she'd never recover.

He couldn't put her through that, and like the self-destructive fool that he was, he'd pretended to be a clumsy oaf so he could sabotage her attempt.

And the worst part of it was that he'd done it even after Blaspheme had insulted him.

How dare she judge him for what he was? Had he judged her for being a False Angel? Okay, maybe. But he'd gotten past that. He'd seen beyond *what* she was to *who* she was. At least, he liked to think so.

No, he knew so. He'd seen her own up to her mistakes. He'd seen bravery when she'd stood up to him. When she'd called him out on his arrogance. He'd been on the receiving end of her generosity and caring. And he'd felt her vulnerability when she believed her world was crumbling down around her.

So why couldn't she see *him*? Was all of that *I'm here for you* bullshit just that? Bullshit?

Dammit! Without thinking, he slammed his fist into one of the support pillars in Gethel's massive great hall, putting a new framework of cracks from floor to ceiling.

Gethel and Blaspheme both glared at him, but he didn't give a shit.

Finally, after what seemed like hours, Blaspheme packed up her gear and came over to him.

"She's fine for the time being," she said in a low voice. "I need to have an obstetrics specialist look over the ultrasound, but I'll tell you right now, I doubt she'll survive the birth."

He shrugged. "Satan doesn't care about her. He's concerned about Lucifer."

Blaspheme's expression was sour. "The little abomination looks healthy."

Healthy. Something that could be laid at Revenant's feet. Thanks to his impulsive act of compassion for Blaspheme, Rev was going to lose his status as the second-most-powerful being in Sheoul. Rev could *not* lose that status, not now that he'd given up on his pathetic dream of being welcomed in Heaven. Once he killed his first angel, he'd burn all those bridges but good.

So, no, he wasn't going to give up his position at Satan's side, especially not to Lucifer, who had spent his fair share of his first incarnation making Revenant's life miserable. Yes, if Revenant could, he'd destroy the mother-fucker in the womb right now. But with no place to hide from Satan, doing so would be a death sentence.

"Can we go now?" Blaspheme asked.

Revenant started to say yes, but a door on the far end of the hall opened up, and two Ramreel guards dragged a beaten, bloody vampire inside.

Gethel gestured to the rack across from the chaise where she was lounging. "Put Thanatos's minion there. I want to watch him die slowly."

Fuck. As the Horseman's Watcher, he couldn't let this go.

"Come on," he said as he took Blaspheme's hand. "Let's get you back to the clinic." He'd deal with Gethel and her bloodsucker toy once Blaspheme was safely back at Underworld General.

He flashed them to UG's parking lot, and the second they materialized, Blaspheme yanked away from him.

"You're just going to let that vampire die? Take me back. Let me help him."

"You're not going back. The vampire is none of your concern."

"He was injured," she said, incredulous. "Of course he's my concern!"

Sudden anger rolled him like a rogue wave. Why couldn't she be selfish, petty, and immoral like a proper False Angel should be?

"Toughen up," he snapped. "You can't save all the kittens, vampires, and butterflies. And sometimes you have to crush something under your boot to get what you want. Deal with it."

She slapped him. Hard enough to make his cheek sting. "You bastard." Raw, burning hatred rolled off her in a wave that scorched his skin. "Is it so easy for you to ignore suffering?"

She really did want to see the worst in him, didn't she? "What changed, Blaspheme? What kind of message did you get on your phone that made you suddenly hate me so much?"

"Hate you?" Her voice lashed at him, striking as viciously as the demons had done when he was slaving in the mines. "It's me I hate. I knew I shouldn't let you in. I knew I shouldn't allow myself to care about you. But I was a fool, and now I have to live with myself."

She cared about him? Was that caring now past tense? "I hate to tell you this, angel, but we all have to live with ourselves."

He didn't wait for a response. She was too worked up, and he had a situation to handle. Not to mention the drill of a summons in his head that was getting worse the longer he ignored the sender. Satan did not like to be kept waiting, and if Revenant didn't obey soon, he'd be in for a nice flogging or another organ-ectomy.

Funny how he used to respond to Satan's demands right away, but now that he had his memory back, screw it. Revenant was going to take tardiness to the limit. Probably not the brightest thing to do, but it seemed that the rebellious streak he'd had while working in Satan's mines as a child was making a comeback.

Revenant flashed back to Gethel's place, where the Ramreels were securing the vampire to the rack. "That, boys, is a no-no."

He flicked his wrist, and the horned demons flew across the room to land in unconscious heaps on the tile floor.

Gethel shoved to her feet, sickly black, scaled wings spread, blue veins snaking across her skin. Her eyes had gone oily, and an aura of power pulsed around her.

"You will not ruin my playtime," she growled.

He ignored her as he strode over to the barely conscious bloodsucker. He willed the metal cuffs to open and caught the vamp as he slumped over. A blast of power slammed into Revenant's skull, knocking him into the rack and sending it crashing to the floor.

"You bitch." He swung around, readying his own power, but Gethel nailed him again, this time hard enough to break his jaw. It healed almost instantly, but now he was pissed.

He dropped the vampire and caught Gethel by the arm. She cursed at him, lashed out with nonstop blasts of power that snapped his bones and crushed his organs. Every step he took was pure agony, but he didn't slow down, didn't stop until he had her slammed against the fallen rack and strapped to it.

"What are you doing?" she screamed.

Guards rushed in from every door, armed and ready to take down the threat to their Dark Mother, but when they saw that Revenant was the threat, they skidded to a halt as one unit and stood there, unsure what to do.

"Leave her like that," Revenant commanded them. "Leave her until morning. If I come back and she's free, whoever let her go will answer to me."

Ignoring her curses and shouts, he gathered the vampire and then, with a dozen raunchy curses in a dozen languages, he went to the pantry and grabbed the basket of fucking kittens and flashed to Thanatos's Greenland castle. Thanatos and his wife, Regan, were seated at their dining room table with their son, Logan, who had mashed peas all over his face. The boy's pet hellhound, Cujo, made an immediate run at Revenant, fangs bared, drool dripping from gaping jaws that could swallow a lamb whole.

"Cujo, halt!" Than barked, and the steer-sized beast, not yet fully grown, skidded to a stop. But that didn't mean he suddenly got friendly. No, the mutt crouched, still snarling, still thinking it could kick Revenant's ass.

Damn, Rev hated those things.

With a glare that promised the hellhound a swat with a rolled newspaper the size of an oil tanker, Rev dumped the vampire onto the floor and set the basket of mewling cats next to him.

Thanatos, the blond braids at his temple swinging, jogged over. "Ewan, shit." He crouched next to the bloody vamp on the floor. "He missed roll call this morning.

We figured he'd stayed out too late and had to hole up at daybreak. Did you do this to him?" He scowled at the jiggling basket. "And what's up with *that*?"

"Present for Logan. And no, I didn't fuck up your vampire, but thanks for thinking the worst of me," Revenant drawled. "I saved him from Gethel. You're welcome."

Figuring he wasn't going to get a round of applause or anything, Revenant prepared to flash out of there, but before he made it, Thanatos introduced Revenant's spine to the wall and was in his face, teeth bared as fully as the hellhound's.

"Where is she?" he snarled. "You had better tell me she's dead."

"She's alive and kicking and due to give birth any moment," Revenant said, enjoying the fury that built in Thanatos's expression with every word. It wasn't that he didn't like Thanatos...he just didn't like being attacked for no fucking reason.

"You piece of shit." Thanatos gripped Revenant's jacket lapels and slammed him against the wall again. "*She tried to murder my son.* And you can casually talk about her like she's a happy housewife with a pregnancy glow?"

It was really tempting to lay the Horseman out, but the sight of Regan, standing in the dining room with Logan held protectively close to her chest, made something tumble inside his own chest. How many times had *his* mother held him like that when demons opened the door to the cell? How many times had she endured watching her son ripped away from her so either he or she could be beaten?

So as much as he'd like to shred Thanatos for being a

dick, he wasn't going to do it in front of a mother and her child. Instead, he used a tiny thread of his power to throw the Horseman backward, right into the stupid hellhound. The mutt yelped, and Thanatos hit the ground, only to pop back to his feet, fully armed and armored.

"Don't do it, Horseman," Revenant warned. "I have a raging Satanic headache and little patience. And keep in mind that I didn't have to bring back your vampire."

"What, you want an award for doing the right thing?" Thanatos signaled for Cujo to stop inching toward Revenant. "You want kudos? Bring me Gethel."

"No can do."

Thanatos sheathed his sword but remained armored. "You know, when we found out you were our uncle, that you're an angel like our father, we hoped you'd at least try to become part of the family. But you don't know what family is, do you?" Thanatos's diatribe shouldn't have bothered Revenant, but like earlier, when Blaspheme laid into him, the words cut deep, because no, he didn't know what a family was. And he didn't realize until this moment that he *wanted* to know. "Family doesn't protect the monster under the bed. Only monsters protect other monsters." He threw his hand out at the door. "Get out, *Uncle.* Go to hell where you belong."

Revenant got out, but as he dematerialized, he realized Thanatos was right. He did belong in hell, and he always had.

Twenty-Five

Despite a crazy childhood that involved a lot of moves and name changes, Blaspheme had always felt like she was on the right side of luck. But lately, it seemed as if her luck had run out, and maybe it was a coincidence, but it all seemed to have started the moment Revenant came into her life.

She'd known better, but he'd wormed his way past her defenses with his oddball charm and heart-wrenching vulnerability when he told her about his childhood. And then he'd gone and saved a patient she'd nearly killed, earning her eternal gratitude.

Then it turned out that Revenant was exactly who she'd thought he was from the beginning.

A cold killer with no conscience.

Gods, what an idiot she'd been. And really, she had no one to blame but herself. She couldn't even blame Revenant. He was a meat-eating shark, like he'd said, and she'd expected him to become a vegetarian. Tiger sharks couldn't change their stripes, and neither could a Shadow Angel.

Of course, *vyrm* could change their stripes, couldn't they? All they needed was a blood sacrifice and a few magical chants. Maybe she should have done the ritual her mother wanted her to do. If she had, she'd have mustered up the stones to destroy Lucifer today. Instead, her *vyrm* was showing, her angel half rising like a phoenix from the ashes of her False Angel aura to give her a conscience.

As a result, she was now standing in Underworld General's staff lounge telling Eidolon that she'd failed to inject the solarum into Lucifer. Reaver was there, too, listening intently to her every word.

It didn't matter that no one was angry; their disappointment was even worse.

"I tried," she said. "I just... couldn't."

She couldn't even lay the blame for her failure on Revenant, no matter how much she wanted to. She'd hesitated from the beginning, and ultimately, it was her fault that Gethel was going to give birth to the evilest of evils.

"We can try again," Eidolon said. "Reaver can get another dose of solarum—"

"No," he said roughly, "I can't. It took hundreds of years to distill just that amount. It was all we had." He cursed. "There's got to be another way. Harvester is getting sicker, and I can't sit by and let it happen."

"Harvester?" Blas frowned. "What does she have to do with this?"

Eidolon shoved a paper cup under the coffee machine nozzle and mashed a button with his thumb. "Lucifer is drawing energy from his siblings. It's weakening her.

I paid her a house call earlier today...she lost twenty pounds overnight."

Reaver clenched his fists, and the blue of his eyes turned stormy, like lightning striking the ocean's surface. "Wraith located two of Satan's sons and one daughter, and they're all wasting away. Another reportedly died this morning."

Oh...oh, gods. If Harvester died, it would be Blaspheme's fault. Harvester's, and all fallen angel deaths, would sit squarely on her shoulders, and why? Because she'd been too self-righteous to put an end to a great evil, simply because it couldn't yet defend itself?

No, that wasn't entirely true. Lucifer had nearly crushed her skull when she tried to listen to his heartbeat, so what if she *had* managed to inject him? Would he have been able to lash out? To kill her, even?

No matter what, she should have tried.

"I'm so sorry, Reaver. I didn't—"

He silenced her with a gesture. "We don't have time for regrets. We need action. I'm going to scour Sheoul from top to bottom to find Gethel, and I don't care if I have to battle Satan himself to do it."

"Reaver, think about—" Eidolon broke off as Reaver vanished. "Son of a bitch. That maniac is going to get himself killed." He swiped his cup of coffee off the machine platform. "Did you at least get a sample of amniotic fluid?" Wordlessly, she handed him the syringe. "Good. I'll get an injection prepared for your mother. Can you get her in here this afternoon? I heard she sort of checked herself out."

"I'll send her a text right now."

The door burst open, and Bane stuck his blond head inside the room. "Blas, do you have a minute?"

At Eidolon's go-ahead nod, she slipped out into the hall with the other Seminus demon. Last night she'd asked him for a favor, and she hoped he was here to tell her he'd done what she'd asked. If so, she owed him ten weekends off.

"Tell me you got the book," she said, resisting the temptation to cross her fingers like a superstitious twit.

He grinned. "Yep. Come on."

She followed the towering Sem to the hospital's Harrowgate. The wall lit up with multicolored map outlines, which he tapped until the door opened into a featureless, dark, cavernous area.

"Um...I thought you said you had it."

He shrugged, his thick shoulders rolling beneath his blue scrub top. "My moms have it. They wouldn't give it to me until they met you." A sheepish grin added a boyish cast to his handsome face. As incubi, all Seminus demons were impossibly hot, but somehow Bane and his brothers took *hot* to a scorching new level. "Okay, that's a lie. You have to get it from them." He patted her on the back as they stepped out of the gate. "Good luck."

"Wait...your moms?" Despite the lack of light fixtures, a hazy luminosity from above allowed her to see Bane...but nothing else. "As in, more than one?"

He nodded. "With very few exceptions, Pruosi demons are born female, and the sisters stay together for life. They mate at the same time with the same male, and the resulting young are taken care of by all the females. None of my brothers or I know which female gave birth to us. They're all our moms."

Huh. She'd known that Pruosi, a species of necromancer succubi, were generally born female and purebred no matter what species of male had sired them, but she hadn't known they lived in sister-communities.

Blas looked him up and down. "I would love to study the way Pruosi and Seminus DNA battle it out to determine the resulting offspring's species. Did your mothers know that Seminus demons are always born purebred male when they bred with your father?"

"They knew." He shrugged. "Change of pace to have sons, I guess." He gestured to a new soft green glow emanating from an opening in the dark wall ahead. "They're in there. I'll wait here. Oh, and Blas? No matter what you do, don't lie to them."

"I wouldn't dream of it," she said.

His hand, covered in the same type of glyphs that every Seminus demon bore, snapped out to catch her wrist in a firm grip.

"I mean it," he said, his voice dripping with warning. "They don't respond well to lies, and I promise you, they'll know. These are demons who work in black magic and death. They're a motherfucking four-point-five on the *Ufelskala* scale. Don't screw with them."

She swallowed dryly and pulled away. "Understood."

Blas rubbed the scar on her wrist as she walked through the doorway. Beyond it, in a featureless dark room that didn't even seem to have walls, ten females who could have passed as albino humans sat in a circle, their bodies wrapped in sheer fabric that hid precisely nothing. In the center of the Pruosi circle, black candles formed another circle around a wooden bowl that held what appeared to be blood.

"Blaspheme," they all intoned at once, and her hair stood on end. So very creepy. "What do you seek?"

"I seek a necromancy spellbook."

The females had yet to look at her. "Why?"

No matter what you do, don't lie to them. "I'm looking for a spell to disguise myself." Not a lie, but not very detailed, either.

"For what purpose?"

Why did they keep speaking in unison? "To hide from people who want to kill me."

"Who wants to kill you?"

"I don't know." Surely that didn't count as a lie. It wasn't as if she knew specifics.

The females leaned into their circle, and a buzz of whispers vibrated the air like a million angry bees. Shit. Had Blas screwed up?

She waited, sweating bullets and fighting stomach cramps. Finally, just as she started to think she couldn't take the suspense anymore, they straightened again. And still they didn't meet her gaze.

"The book you seek is behind you," they droned. "But we do suggest you hurry to use it."

Hurry? Did they need it back right away? "Of course," she breathed. "And thank you. Thank you so much."

"We do this not out of the goodness of our hearts, healer. We do it for payment."

Oh. Of course. "I don't have much money, but I can borrow some, or I can offer services—"

"Not payment from *you*." Every head came up or swiveled completely around, and glowing red eyes focused on her like lasers. "Payment from those who hunt *vyrm*." They smiled, their pale lips stretching gruesomely over sharp, stained teeth, and Blaspheme's heart stuttered. "So hurry, healer. Hurry."

Terror made Blaspheme clumsy as she wheeled around, grabbed the tattered book off a wooden stand she knew hadn't been there before, and darted to the Harrowgate, where Bane was waiting.

"You could have told me they wanted payment," she yelled as she practically dove inside the gate.

"I thought you knew." Joining her, he hit the Underworld General symbol with a thump of his fist. "They're Pruosi. They don't do anything for free. Hell, they expect their own children to pay them back for being born."

In the darkness lit only by the brightness of the maps inside the Harrowgate, she stared at the demon. Seminus demons were considered purebred, but they always inherited gifts and abilities unique to their mothers' species. Blaspheme hadn't really considered what would happen if a Sem had been born to a truly malevolent mother.

"So how does your Pruosi breeding affect you?"

He shrugged. "My brothers and I can all reanimate corpses."

Ew. "You guys must be the life of the party on Halloween."

"I remember this one time—" The temperature inside the small space plummeted, and Bane's skin flushed white as his eyes went red, just like all the females in the Pruosi circle. "I can see death coming," he said, his deep voice utterly devoid of tone. "It's all around you, Blaspheme. It's coming, and it can't be stopped."

Revenant's head was pounding by the time he reached Satan's residence, only for Revenant to be told that the Dark Lord was waiting for him in the dungeon.

That couldn't be good.

Revenant trudged down the claustrophobic circular stone staircase, his flesh crawling as the sights, smells, and sounds of his childhood came back to him. Inside, his organs jangled, as if they remembered as well and didn't want to be spilled all over the floor.

Again.

His boot hit the filthy dungeon floor with a thud that echoed through the massive torture chamber. It was apparently a slow day today, with none of the apparatuses in use and only two demons hanging from chains on the far wall. Two halls broke off from the main chamber, leading to what had been his childhood recreational area: cell blocks, kitchens, and rooms set aside for storage, equipment repair, and specialty torture.

Ah, memories.

Instinctively knowing where he'd find the king of demons, Revenant took the hallway on the right. The hallway that led to the cell where his mother had been kept.

Sure enough, sitting on a wood bench inside the cell was the Prince of Lies himself. He was leaning back against the stone wall, dressed like he was in for a day of work at a law firm. Only the massive black horns sprouting out of his head kept him from looking the part of a lawyer.

Or maybe the horns completed the look.

"Interesting choice of meeting sites," Revenant said casually, although he felt anything but.

"I thought you'd appreciate it." Satan ran his hand almost lovingly over the bench. The bastard knew Rev's weakness, and he was using it well. "Your mother's blood still stains the wood."

Revenant had had a lot of practice controlling his emotions, and the rage that welled up now was no exception. Inside, he was burning with it, but outside, he kept his expression blank, his mouth shut. But someday, he swore, he *would* make Satan pay for what he'd done to Mariel. How, he had no idea, especially given that he didn't have Heaven's backing.

Satan looked up. "How is Gethel?"

"As hideous as ever. The doctor doesn't think she'll survive Lucifer's birth."

"Shame," Satan said, but he didn't sound all that broken up. "This doctor…her name is Blaspheme, yes?"

Mother. Fuck. Revenant quickly tamped down the sudden, searing panic that winged its way through him. He didn't like that Satan knew about Blaspheme. At all.

"Yes."

Satan nodded. "Bring her to me."

Oh, hell no. "My Lord, I don't think—"

"*Bring her to me!*" Satan's shout shut down every sound in the dungeon. "Since you've failed to deliver an angel, I want your female."

"You gave me until Sanguinalia to hand over an angel," Revenant pointed out. "But I'll go get one now."

"Oh," Satan said silkily, "you *will* bring me an angel. But right now I want your female."

The demon was taking way too much interest in Blaspheme, which meant he suspected she meant something to Revenant. Somehow, he had to convince Satan otherwise.

"She's not *my* female," Rev said. "I barely know her."

"Really." The demon's gaze narrowed dangerously. "Have you not taken her to your home? Twice? Do you not hang out at that demon medical facility like a pathetic stalker?"

Rev's pulse kicked up a few notches. "You're spying on me?"

"I told you I question your loyalty now that you know you're an angel. In fact, I've even had Gethel tethered to her residence. No one can remove her but me." He stroked the bench again, his fingers tracing the faded outline of a pool of blood. "I would think you would question your own loyalty, given what was done to you and your mother."

What was done. He said it as if he himself hadn't ordered every horrible thing that had happened to Rev and his mother.

Revenant shrugged, but holy hell, his heart was racing. "Shit happens. I'm not welcome in Heaven. I've made my peace with serving you."

As if. Revenant had decided not to turn over Gethel to the lying archangel bastards, but that didn't mean he was going to kiss Satan's clawed feet, either.

"Then you'll bring me the female. Alive."

Revenant frowned. "Why would I bring her to you dead?"

"You truly don't know, do you?" Satan murmured.

"Know what," Rev gritted out. Gods, he hated games.

"Your little False Angel is exactly that. False."

This time Rev didn't give the demon the satisfaction of a response. He was done with swatting at a toy he'd never reach.

Finally, realizing Rev was going to stand there silently, Satan shoved to his feet, his grin defining the word *malevolent.*

"A little Pruosi bird visited me today. Told me the False Angel is a *vyrm*. The very *vyrm* you were hunting when your memory was taken from you by the archangels the second time," he said slowly, and Revenant's heart froze into a solid block of ice.

No. Satan was lying. He had to be.

And yet, as Revenant's mind spun with reasons the demon would lie, things started to make sense. Like why Blaspheme had seemed so different from other False Angels. And why he'd believed she was keeping a secret from the beginning.

She'd lied to him. She'd made him swear to keep his hands off of her while she fucked him because she didn't trust him. And the whole time, it was *she* who was steeping in deception. She'd fucked him, all right. In more ways than one.

Anger and hurt twisted inside him, knotting into a huge tangle of fury. He'd opened himself up to her. He'd helped her. Protected her. He'd trusted her when he hadn't trusted anyone in thousands of years.

He'd *trusted* her. Son of a bitch! He should hand her over to Satan like he'd commanded.

"So bring her to me. I don't care what condition she's in when you do, as long as she's breathing." Satan glanced around the cell as if it were an old friend. "She'll look good in here, don't you think? Just like your mother."

Twenty-Six

Six hours after returning to the safety of Underworld General, Blaspheme had made some progress on the cryptic information Eidolon had given her regarding a solution to her False Angel problem. The Pruosi book of necromancy was definitely the source of Eidolon's information. Bane, after recovering, with no memory, from the trance-like state he'd entered in the Harrowgate, had been able to translate some of it, but Blaspheme had done most of the translation work herself, and she thought she had a pretty good handle on it.

She needed the DNA of whatever species she was going to disguise herself as, plus...the blood of some powerful immortal being she couldn't yet pin down. The DNA would be the easy part. Getting blood from some immortal stranger was going to be the challenge.

The sensation of being watched came over her, and she looked up from her table in the clinic cafeteria to see Gem walking toward her. The bright blue streaks in Gem's black hair matched her scrubs, but she wore ghastly orange rubber clogs that matched precisely nothing. In the universe.

"Interesting place to work," Gem said, eyeing Blaspheme's layout of papers and books all over the round table.

"I didn't feel like being alone in my office or the library," she said, sweeping aside a pile of crap to make room for Gem. Even with the sideways glances she got from staff members who must have heard the gossip about her fuckup with the *blanchier* demon, she preferred being here over being by herself. The activity in the cafeteria made her feel safe. And kept her from losing her mind. Or thinking about Revenant.

Gem didn't sit, instead remained standing across the table from Blas. "There's something…different about you today."

"I don't know what," Blas said lightly. "Nothing's changed."

Everything had changed. She just wished she didn't have to lie about it.

"No, something's definitely different." Gem cocked her head, studying Blaspheme so intently that she squirmed. "I couldn't see any scars on you until today."

Blaspheme broke out in a cold sweat. Gem was half Soulshredder, a demon that could see physical and emotional scars that were invisible to everyone else. The breed, one of the most evil on the *Ufelskala* scale, exploited those scars, fed on the pain and misery of the victim. As far as Blaspheme knew, Gem kept that side of herself under control, but that didn't mean she didn't still possess the desire to use the abilities and instincts unique to the species.

"Don't worry," Gem said quietly. "I won't tell anyone what I see."

Blaspheme was afraid to ask, but she might as well know. "What do you see?"

"I see a strange overlay, like a second skin that's peeling off of you." Gem's hands flexed at her sides. "It makes me want to rip into it and expose whatever is beneath." Gem's green eyes sparked with an eerie glow, and the tattoo around her neck, the one that she'd had inked to contain her inner demon, began to pulse. "Blaspheme, whatever is going on with you, you need to fix it, because it's not looking...right." She took off like her feet were on fire.

Shit. Seriously, could things get any worse?

As if she'd cursed herself, the lights in the cafeteria began to flicker. And then, out of nowhere, Revenant appeared in a maelstrom of lightning and swirling black clouds. His wings were spread high, nearly touching the ceiling, and his eyes, dear Lord, his eyes...the black irises had swallowed the whites, leaving him with oily pools of hate framed by thick, inky lashes. He was horrible and beautiful, terrifying and magnetic, and fear clawed at her.

People in the cafeteria screamed as the force of the storm surrounding Revenant lifted them off their feet and slammed them into the walls.

The writing on the gray walls, the spells and incantations that prevented violence, glowed with an intensity she'd never seen. And they clearly weren't working.

"You lied to me." Revenant's rumbling voice could have been dredged from the deepest, darkest depths of hell, and sheer terror gripped her heart.

She stood up so fast her chair tumbled to the floor. "Revenant, I don't know what you're—"

"I trusted you. I cared about you. I fucking saved your soul, and you *lied*!" Tables and chairs overturned, and trays with food and dishes crashed to the floor. Anyone who was still conscious scrambled for the exits.

Oh, bloody hell. He knew. Panic frayed her thought processes, and the only thing she could do was play dumb. And wait...he'd saved her soul? She wasn't even going to ask.

She paused, giving the last conscious person in the room time to scramble out of the cafeteria. This wasn't a safe place for *her*, let alone anyone else.

"I'm still not sure what you're talking about," she said as the metal door clanged shut.

Thunder shook the building. "Are you honestly going to deny that you're...*vyrmin*?"

A shiver of fear crawled up her spine, and Bane's earlier words screeched through her brain. *I can see death coming. It's all around you, Blaspheme. It's coming, and it can't be stopped.*

She was dead. The only question was whether Revenant would make her death happen quickly or slowly. Merciful or painful. Either way, she supposed she had nothing to lose.

"Do you blame me?" she asked, cursing the unsteadiness in her voice. "You're an angel. You kill my kind for sport." Sudden rage overshadowed her fear, making her reckless as she moved toward him. "You murdered my father, you son of a bitch."

"Your father? Who the fuck was your father?"

"An angel named Rifion," she snarled. "You slaughtered him."

"Rifion?" Revenant laughed. The bastard actually laughed. "Did you even know him?"

"I never met him," she spat. "Because you killed him before I was born."

"Who told you he died before you were born?"

She stopped in front of him, fists clenched. Maybe she'd get in a blow before he squashed her. "My mother."

"Then your mother is a liar." He bared his fangs, which looked twice as large as she'd ever seen them. "I shouldn't be surprised. Like mother like daughter, right?"

"You don't know anything about my mother."

"No? She's the fallen angel you've been treating here, isn't she? She's the one who freaked out when she saw me in the hall the other day. It all makes sense now. She knew who I was. And she's the one who texted you at my house. She's the reason you suddenly hated me."

There was no point in denying it. All she could do was make an idle threat or plead for her mother's life.

"Leave her alone," she begged. "Please. She hasn't done anything—"

"She lied to you." He seemed to relish saying that.

Blas clenched her teeth and ground out, "No, she didn't. She loved my father, and she wanted me to know him, but I never got the chance because *you slaughtered him*!"

"Yes," he drawled. "I did. And I enjoyed every second of it." He flared his wings, and the storm surrounding him died down. "You're lucky you didn't know him." He got right up in her face, practically foaming at the mouth. "When I caught him, he begged for his life."

"So?" She shoved him hard in the chest, but she might as well have been trying to move a boulder. "Who wouldn't?"

"*I* wouldn't."

"Yeah, well, good for you. But not everyone is a great and powerful Shadow Angel with a black heart."

He snarled. "He didn't just beg for his life. He bartered. And do you want to know what he bartered with?" He didn't give her the chance to ask. "Your life, and that of your mother."

"I don't believe you."

"No? Well believe this. He cried like a baby. Said he could tell me where his mate and *vyrmin* daughter were if I would just spare his life." Revenant spat the words like bullets, each striking a vital organ and making her stumble backward. His massive shoulders rolled as he prowled after her, pressing, stalking, never letting up. "Said he could tell me all about the machinations your mother fell into with an angel named Stamtiel. Now, how would I know that if your father hadn't blabbed like a frightened child? He was ready to give you up to save his own skin. *That* is who I killed. A pathetic coward who didn't deserve a family. Not an angel who fathered a *vyrm*."

"No," she whispered.

The backs of her knees bumped into a chair, and she nearly fell. Rev's hand shot out to catch her, and wasn't it gentlemanly of him to prevent her from being hurt before he killed her? But, she supposed, even death-row prisoners got a last meal before they faced the executioner.

"Yes," Revenant whispered back as he released her arm. "He was scum, and he doesn't deserve your denial."

She wanted to deny it. Needed to deny it. But even as she shook her head in stubborn refusal, things started making sense. Something about the way her mother had talked about her father had been off. And that was on the rare occasions in which Blas had been able to get her to discuss him.

Deep down inside, Revenant's version of Blaspheme's father's life and death resonated with her.

But if Revenant was telling the truth, it meant that her father had been alive longer than what her mother had claimed. Blaspheme could have met him. Known him. Maybe she could have saved him.

"Even if I believed you, you still killed him. You said yourself you used to hunt *vyrm*. Did you really expect me to assume you wouldn't kill me if I told you the truth? You know damned well that *vyrm* aren't safe from angels or fallen angels. That there's a standing order on both sides to kill us. It's a rule, Revenant. A fucking *rule*. So tell me, *Destroyer*, if you were me, what would you have done?"

A brittle silence fell, interrupted only by the voice on the intercom warning of a disturbance in the cafeteria. She hoped no security forces would try to get inside, because she didn't doubt Revenant's ability to slaughter every one of them with a mere thought.

Finally, the oily black pools in his eyes receded, and he gave a slow, shallow nod. "I'd have done the same thing," he said gruffly.

She blew out a relieved breath she hadn't even known she was holding. She'd gotten him to chill on the lie, which, admittedly, she'd started to feel guilty about. Until she learned he'd killed her father. But just because he was no longer spinning up hurricane-force winds didn't mean he wasn't going to slaughter her where she stood.

"So where do we go from here?" She eyed the exit, as if she had any chance at all of escaping. "Are you going to kill me?"

His spectacular wings folded against his back and disappeared. "For deceiving me or for being a *vyrm*?"

"Either, I suppose." How nice that they could so civilly discuss her demise.

"Three weeks ago I'd have killed you for either," he said, his voice as cold and sharp as a frozen blade. "I thought I was a fallen angel with a directive to kill *vyrm* . . . and all beings considered to be abominations. Satan hates half-breeds."

"And now?" A shiver racked her body, and she hated herself for it, because fear wasn't the only thing running the show. Just standing near Revenant made her heart flutter and her sex ache, and how crazy was that? Talk about your mixed messages. *Please don't kill me. But if you do, can you give me an orgasm first?*

And she couldn't even blame her False Angel enchantment, because if Gem was right, there was very little left of it. A glance at the scar on her wrist confirmed her worst fear. It was all but gone; only a pinprick of faded white flesh was visible above a blue vein at the base of her palm.

"Now . . . I don't know." He clenched his fists as if doing so would keep him from wrapping his hands around her throat.

Closing her eyes, she rubbed her temples in hopes that she could massage her brain into thinking more clearly.

"What did you mean when you said you saved my soul?" She opened her eyes and met his gaze, which flickered with some unidentifiable emotion.

"I stopped you from killing Lucifer."

Her heart plummeted to her feet. Oh, gods. He knew? How? She opened her mouth to deny it, but that would just be another lie. Instead, indignant anger gave her a voice.

"Bullshit," she snapped. "You didn't stop me because you care about the state of my soul. You stopped me because Lucifer is evil and he plays on your team."

The air, which smelled like someone had left fish sticks baking in the oven when they fled the cafeteria, went eerily still.

"No, Blaspheme," he said, his voice as dark and hollow as the inside of a body bag, "I wanted him dead. He tormented me and my mother every day for years. He defiled..." Averting his gaze, he inhaled raggedly, and Blaspheme's heart squeezed painfully tight. "He defiled us both. Then he spent thousands of years screwing me over, framing me for shit just to watch Satan torture me...fucking asshole. The day he died was the best day of my life. Now he's coming back, and it means jack shit that I'm more powerful than he is. Satan will favor him. Heaven doesn't want me, so all I have is hell. And trust me, if you have to do Satan's bidding, you either want to be his right-hand man, or you want to fly under the radar. I'm not under the radar anymore." His eyes snapped up, and in their shadowy depths Blaspheme saw unimaginable pain. "I can't be second to Lucifer again. I...can't. But I couldn't watch you do something that would haunt you forever. You're a healer, not a killer."

Oh, sweet hell. She couldn't even begin to understand what he'd gone through, but she now understood how much of a sacrifice he'd made for her.

"And," he said with a roll of his eyes, "I went back to Gethel's and got the vampire." He lowered his voice to a mumble, even though there was no one around to hear him, and she swore the faintest blush spread over his cheeks. "And the kittens."

Blaspheme stared, and for a moment, she almost believed that she must be part Soulshredder, because the big, dangerous Shadow Angel radiating death like a malevolent power plant had morphed into something else before her very eyes. Something more relatable. Something admirable. And yet, something no less dangerous.

"I'm sorry," she croaked. "I should have injected Lucifer. I should have been stronger. I screwed up—"

In an instant, she was in his arms, held tight against him, his mouth crushing hers in a punishing kiss. Her senses reeled as he thrust his tongue between her lips before speaking. "No. Killing isn't in your nature. Never apologize for things that aren't in your control."

His words sapped the energy from her muscles, and she sagged against him, clinging to his leather-clad biceps with a white-knuckled grip. "We'll destroy him. Somehow, we'll find a way to rid the world of him for good."

He tucked her head against his broad chest and stroked her hair with a tenderness that left her floored. "My priority is to get you out of danger."

"I'm afraid," she whispered, relieved to finally confide in him. "My False Angel enchantment is failing—"

He pulled back so suddenly she swayed. "Then we fix it." The determination in his expression would have terrified her if he hadn't just sworn he wouldn't hurt her. "Now."

"I'm trying, but I'm not going to sacrifice anyone to do it." She gestured to the papers and books. "I've found a way . . . I think. I just can't figure out all of it."

He released her carefully, as if he was fully aware that

her legs felt like rubber. "You have a Pruosi book of necromancy. How did you get it? The Pruosi don't just give those up."

"I have a friend."

"Some friend," he murmured as he braced his fists on the table and leaned over to look at her notes. "Essence of death?"

"Yes. That's what I'm having trouble with." It occurred to her that she was discussing how to save her life with the male who killed her father, but if Revenant could help her, she had to try. "Essence of death or the tears of the hungry. I need one of those ingredients. And the blood of a legend or something." She rubbed her temples. "I don't know. The translations are kicking my ass, and I'm running out of time."

Revenant's gaze turned inward. "My mother used to speak of the essence of death. I have no idea what she was talking about, but she claimed that the essence of death was also an elixir of life for those who can't die."

Blaspheme blinked. "That makes no sense."

"Try hearing that as a five-year-old boy," he said dryly.

Her cell phone rang, and as Revenant went through the mess of paperwork on the table, she grabbed it, somehow not surprised that Eidolon was on the other end of the line. "*What the fuck is going on in the cafeteria? Are you okay?*"

"I'm fine," she said, doing her best to stay calm…to keep *him* calm. "Revenant is level. But please, E, keep everyone away."

"I can't do that, Blaspheme."

"You have to." She gripped the phone so hard she expected the screen to shatter. "He knows the truth about me, and he's cool with it. But let's not antagonize the situation. I'll be out in a few minutes."

"You have ten." The line went dead.

Revenant didn't ask about the call. He stared at the notes for several minutes, and then he flipped through the book, studying several pages before groaning.

"What?" She peered at the pages, but she saw only the same meaningless script she'd been poring over all day. "What is it?"

"The blood of a legend is the same as the essence of death. You need the blood of Death. Thanatos. Or tears of the hungry, or of Famine."

Realization dawned. "Limos. So I need Thanatos's blood or Limos's tears?"

Revenant's glossy ebony hair swept over his shoulders as he shook his head. "Forget Limos's tears. You want Thanatos's blood. Trust me, the last thing anyone wants to do is make Limos cry. Her brothers and mate are psychotically protective." He lowered his voice to a husky murmur. "Not that I don't get that."

Warmth spiraled through her at the possessive tone and at the memories of how protective he'd been over the last few days, battling an angel who tried to kill her, threatening Shakvhan, caring for her after her meltdown. Looking at him, all dark and covered in leather and weapons, no one would guess that he could be as gentle as he was lethal.

"I'll ask Reaver to get the blood," she said. "Maybe if I talk to him, explain all of this—"

"Fuck, no," Revenant broke in. "You can't trust anyone, Blaspheme. He's an angel, and they're more single-minded when it comes to killing *vyrm* than fallen angels are."

How well she knew that. "But he's Reaver. I know him. He wouldn't kill me." She hoped.

"Are you willing to bet your life on that?"

"I don't have a choice."

"Yes," he said, "you do. I'm going to get the blood for you."

Blas exhaled on a sigh of relief and gratitude, but it was cut short as a potential problem popped into her head. "Wait . . . surely a Watcher taking blood from a Horseman to use in a spell is forbidden."

"Let me worry about that."

Her gut twisted. "I'm right, aren't I? It's against the rules."

At the stony expression that fell over his face, she felt the blood drain from hers. Obeying rules wasn't just a code for him; it was his life, tied irrevocably to his traumatic youth and his mother's death. Blaspheme would never again put him in a position that might tempt him to break a rule, let alone ask him to willingly break one.

Except she was already doing that by asking him to not kill her.

"No." She grabbed his arm, desperate to make him understand that he couldn't do this. "I won't let you. I'll find another way."

"There is no other way." Very gently, he peeled her hand away and stepped back. "I'll be back soon."

"No!" But by the time her scream faded in the air, he was gone.

Twenty-Seven

Blaspheme blasted through the cafeteria exit and skidded into the clinic hallway, where dozens of people had gathered, including Eidolon and his brothers, Shade, Wraith, and Lore. Every one of them was geared up and poised for a fight, danger and fury radiating from them in scorching waves that stung her skin.

"He's gone," she said, but Shade, Wraith, and Lore shoved past her anyway.

Eidolon took her arm and pulled her aside. "What happened? Are you sure you're okay?"

"Yes." She caught a glimpse of her mother jogging toward them, because yeah, this was just what she needed right now. "Eidolon," she said hastily. "Can you contact Reaver? Revenant is going to do something stupid. I need to stop it. Fast."

"I can try."

"Send him to Thanatos's place. Please hurry." Eidolon

took off, and she met her mother halfway down the hall. "We need to talk."

Deva frowned. "What happened in there? I came to get that injection you texted about, but all hell was breaking loose—"

"It's not important." She gestured for her mother to duck into an empty exam room. Once inside, she closed the door. "I need to ask you something, and I need you to be honest."

Deva blinked with wide-eyed innocence. "Of course."

Blaspheme snagged a paper cup from the dispenser on the wall and stuck it under the faucet. "You always said you fell from Heaven because you were helping an angel to locate an object that Heaven didn't want to be found, and that The Destroyer killed my father before I was born. But all of that was a lie, wasn't it? Please, Mom, I need the truth. It's important."

Deva bit down on her bottom lip hard enough to draw blood. "If I tell you, you could be in danger—"

"I'm already in danger! I need to know the truth about your fall and Father's death. The whole story."

Deva sighed, and Blas's heart sank. As much as she wanted to believe Revenant, she'd wanted to know her mother was being honest, too.

"It wasn't all a lie," Deva said. "Not the part about the object, anyway. Your father got involved with a rebel group in Heaven that wanted to replace Metatron with Raphael. Raphael worked out a deal with his friend, Stamtiel, to retrieve a mystical item that would allow Raphael to destroy Metatron. Stamtiel would take Raphael's place as an archangel, and Raphael would fill Metatron's shoes."

Oh, dear . . . God. Rebellion in Heaven was bad enough. But plotting against not only an archangel, but *the* archangel was beyond the pale.

"I was afraid your father was going to be caught. He was so reckless and too open about his feelings toward Metatron, and people were starting to talk. So I agreed to help Stamtiel while your father kept the peace in Heaven." Deva kicked aside a length of chain meant to hold down combative patients and sat down on the exam table. Tucking her hands between her knees, she closed in on herself, and for the first time, Blaspheme saw vulnerability in a female she'd always viewed as a rock-hard pillar of strength. "I was caught, relieved of my wings, and booted out of Heaven. But becoming a fallen angel didn't change anything between me and your father. We stole secret moments together until I learned I was pregnant. At that point, I went into hiding until after you were born."

"And then what?" Blaspheme offered her mother a cup of water, but she refused.

"He was still plotting with Raphael and Stamtiel, and he couldn't afford to be connected to us." Her mother took a deep, shuddering breath. "He hooked up with another female and disappeared from our lives. I only saw him once after that."

Blaspheme could hardly believe this new version of events. Her entire life was more of a lie than she'd thought. "What happened when you saw him?"

"He attacked me. He didn't want anything to do with me or you, and I didn't know it, but Raphael put a price on my head. He can't afford for anyone outside his close circle to know he was plotting against Metatron. Maybe Raphael still *is* plotting against him."

Blaspheme sank down on a rolling stool before her legs gave out. "So do you think the attack on you was about Raphael tying up loose ends? Or was it because I'm a *vyrm*?"

Deva shrugged. "Could be either. Or both. It doesn't matter. I should have told you all of this sooner, but I was trying to protect you. That's why I told you your father died before you were born. I didn't want you to waste your time trying to find him, only to face the same rejection I did." She looked up, her gaze liquid with unshed tears. "I loved him. I *fell from grace* for him, and he abandoned us."

Deva didn't know the half of it, and she wasn't going to. Blas was going to keep Revenant's tale of her father's willingness to hand over his ex-mate and daughter to herself.

"I'm so sorry, Mother," she whispered.

Deva exploded to her feet. "Do not dare pity me. I wasn't completely innocent. I deserved to fall, and I've accepted what happened afterward." She jabbed her finger into Blaspheme's breastbone. "So do *not* feel sorry for me. Why are you wasting time with this, anyway? You should be getting ready for the False Angel ceremony—"

"How many times do I have to tell you that I'm not doing it?" Blaspheme hurled her cup into the garbage without having taken a single drink. "I'm working on something else. Something you won't be happy about, but it's my choice."

Deva's eyes darkened dangerously. "Daughter," she growled. "What have you done?"

This wasn't going to go well. "The Destroyer," she said. "His name is Revenant. He's a Shadow Angel. And he knows the truth about me."

"He what?" Deva's shout rattled the pictures and anatomical models hanging on the walls. "How? And why the fuck are you standing here like it's no big deal when you should be hiding?"

"Because," Blas said, "I'm the one who told him. And...I'm kind of sleeping with him."

Her mother, the rock-solid pillar of strength, lost all the color in her face...and passed out.

Twenty-Eight

After swiping a vial from one of Underworld General's supply cabinets, Revenant materialized outside of Thanatos's keep, figuring that if he was going to be asking for a huge favor, he might as well get off to a good start and not pop in out of the blue. Steeling himself for the confrontation, he knocked on the door. A minute later, Thanatos was standing there, his expression shuttered, but the 3-D scorpion tattoo on his throat was writhing.

"What do you want?" Thanatos scowled. "And since when do you knock?"

"Would you rather I didn't?"

"No. Never mind." Than stepped outside and closed the door behind him. "Well?"

This wasn't going to be easy. Dealing with the Horsemen never was. "I need a favor."

Thanatos crossed his arms over his chest. "Do tell."

Yeah...not easy. But he had to protect Blaspheme. If

she could disguise herself as another species of demon, Satan would never be able to find her, and Revenant would do anything to keep that from happening.

Even if this went against Watcher rules.

"I need some blood."

One tawny eyebrow shot up. "Ever heard of a blood bank?"

"I need your blood."

The other eyebrow joined the first. "I'm going to say no, but for shits and grins, tell me why."

Revenant clenched his teeth to keep from lashing out. He was here to be nice, after all. "It's for someone else. She'll die without it."

"Huh." Thanatos turned to the door. "Too bad. Bye, Uncle Rev."

Revenant grabbed him by the shoulder and spun him back around. He was prepared to beg, but he'd fight if he had to.

So against the rules.

"You said I don't know what family is," Revenant said, "and you were right. I've never really known until now. This female *is* family."

Thanatos's pale yellow eyes narrowed as he considered what Revenant said. But when his mouth flattened into a grim line, Revenant knew he'd lost him.

"Please, Thanatos." Fuck, it hurt to beg. He hadn't done it since his mother was alive, when he'd begged the demons not to hurt her. The day Satan had granted him authority, he'd slaughtered every demon who'd hurt her. Every demon but Lucifer, who had been far more powerful than Revenant.

"She's all I have," he added, because damn the Horseman, he wasn't budging.

Except that he wouldn't have her for long. Once she was disguised, he could never see her again. There was no way he'd risk leading the king of demons to her doorstep. The reality settled over him like a death shroud, cold and claustrophobic, and he struggled to keep from breaking down right here in front of the one Horseman of the Apocalypse who would enjoy it the most.

"Bring Gethel to me," Thanatos said, his voice softer than it was before, "and we'll talk."

"I can't do that." He would have, if it meant Blaspheme would be safe, but now that Gethel had been tethered in place, Revenant couldn't do a damned thing.

Thanatos shrugged. "Then I can't give you my blood."

Panic pierced the bubble of Revenant's control. The Horseman wasn't going to play nice, and Revenant needed this as much as he needed air.

"Dammit, Thanatos!" Revenant's shout brought Cujo from out of nowhere. The beast slammed into Revenant from behind, knocking him into Thanatos, and suddenly, the courtyard became a blur of steel, teeth, and claws.

Pain lashed at him from every side as the hound ripped into him and Thanatos sliced and hacked with a scythe meant to separate limbs from even the most powerful beings. Rev healed almost instantly, but that didn't mean that every bite, gouge, and slice didn't hurt like fuck and piss him off.

He threw a bolt of lightning at the damned mutt, reining in the intensity at the last moment to keep from killing the beast. As bad as his relationship with Than and his family was now, if he slaughtered Logan's pet and guardian, there would be no coming back from that. Ever.

Cujo yelped and tumbled several yards before landing

in a heap near a stone wall. Cursing, Thanatos swung his scythe in an arc that would have severed the top of Revenant's skull from his head if he hadn't ducked at the last second. As Thanatos recovered from the swing, Revenant slammed his fist into the Horseman's face. Than's nose exploded in a pink mist of blood, and that was all Rev needed.

He whipped the pilfered vial from his pocket, tackled the Horseman, and pinned him to the ground with his hand around Than's throat. While the big male cursed and bucked, Rev scooped blood into the vial and capped it with one hand before leaping away.

He'd just broken a major rule. The knowledge left him dizzy, panting as if he'd run a marathon, which was probably why he didn't sense the danger.

He barely felt the warning tingle before he was lifted off his feet by an unseen force and hurled into the same wall the hellhound had hit. But Revenant's body plowed through it, his bones shattering along with the stones. He fell heavily to the ground, the agony of his bones knitting back together knocking him off balance as Reaver and Harvester strode toward him, their expressions matching masks of rage.

They both hit him with blasts of power—Harvester's loaded with fire, Reaver's a concussion wave that blew out his eardrums and turned his organs to jelly as his skin burned. He screamed with the pain of it, his vision going dark as his eyes melted.

"I warned you, Revenant," Reaver growled. "I warned you that if you harmed my family in any way, I'd come at you in every way I know how."

As his body healed, they hit him with another blast,

and another, keeping the injuries and pain constant so he couldn't recover fast enough to strike back. With every drop of concentration he could muster, he thought about Blaspheme, pictured her heart-shaped face and brilliant blue eyes, and flashed to her.

"Oh, bloody hell."

"What the fuck?"

"Shit, not again!"

At the cacophony of voices, Blaspheme looked up from the pile of garbage she was sweeping off the cafeteria floor. Gasping, she dropped the broom, and stood there, stunned.

Revenant was on one knee in the center of the room, his singed wings out but not extended, blood dripping down his face and body. Wisps of smoke curled in thin tendrils from his clothes as he unfurled to his full, impressive height.

"Revenant!" She ran to him. "What happened? Are you okay?"

He opened his palm to reveal a small vial containing a few drops of what she assumed was blood.

"Thanatos was . . . uncooperative."

"Oh, Gods, Revenant," she said. "I'm so sorry—"

"It's okay. Nothing I can't handle. I'm nearly healed already."

"I wasn't talking about the injuries."

His black, bloodshot eyes locked onto hers, and for the next thirty seconds, all she could do was think that of all the females he could look at like that, he'd chosen her.

"Don't be sorry, Blaspheme." His voice was throaty, as smoky as his clothing. "Whatever consequences my actions have earned, I'll be glad to pay them."

Her eyes burned and she didn't know what to say... and it turned out she didn't need to say anything, because abruptly, Revenant shifted into battle mode. Expression stony and body taut, he went for the Pruosi spellbook and slapped the vial of blood down on the table.

"You sure this will work?" he asked.

She flipped to the page that went into the details of the procedure. "It should. All I need is DNA from whatever species I'm going to disguise myself as. We've got False Angel DNA samples in storage, so I can maintain my cover—"

"You've got to disguise yourself as something else. And you'll need to get a new job."

She stared at him. "Are you high? I'm not leaving UG."

"You have to." He jammed his hand through his lush hair. "Satan is onto you."

"Funny, Rev." When he didn't smile, her heart seized. "Wait... you aren't kidding, are you?" Satan was onto her? *Satan?*

Revenant inhaled a shaky breath, held it, then exhaled softly. "It's my fault. I led him to you, and now he wants to use you to ensure my loyalty. The only way you'll be safe is if you get a new identity and a new life."

There had been a time when getting a new identity and a new life was a regular event, but she'd put down roots here, and she couldn't give that up. "I can't do that. I've put everything into this job. This place. These people. This is my life, Revenant."

"And it'll be your death if you stay."

She sank numbly into a chair. "This is unbelievable. I'm always going to be the worm, aren't I?"

"The worm?"

"The one that doesn't turn into a butterfly. I knew that re-disguising myself as a False Angel again wouldn't be me, exactly, but at least I know what to expect. I've felt like an angel...of sorts. Now I'm going to be trapped again, inside a body I don't want."

"You won't be trapped. You'll be—" He broke off as Eidolon entered the cafeteria and jogged over, his expression calm, but she knew the look in his eyes.

Trouble was brewing.

"We have a situation," he said, lowering his voice so no one but Blaspheme and Rev would hear. "Angels have surrounded the hospital and the clinic, and somehow, they've managed to shut down the Harrowgate. No one can get in or out without going through the angels."

"I can," Revenant said.

Eidolon inclined his head. "You and Reaver are probably the only ones who can still flash in and out."

"What do they want?" Blaspheme asked, even though she knew.

"They want you. And your mother. And they said they won't leave until we hand you both over."

Revenant watched the Seminus demon who ran the hospital, hoping that the next words out of his mouth weren't *Come on, Blaspheme, let's hand you over.*

Because the doctor would have to die.

"Blaspheme," Eidolon said, "don't worry. We'll figure this out."

"I can flash Blaspheme and her mother out of here," Revenant said. "I'll get them to safety. And then I'll deal with the angels. Wipe out the lot of them."

And he'd relish every second of it. When he was finished, it would look like giant ogres had a pillow fight in the hospital's parking lot.

A bloody pillow fight.

"That'll be a temporary measure at best." Blaspheme tucked her hands into her lab coat pockets. "They know who I am. Where I work. And I don't think—"

A flash of light filled the cafeteria, and on its heels was the warning tingle unique to Reaver. A heartbeat later, the angel materialized, still looking as pissed as he had been at Thanatos's place. His murderous gaze zeroed in on Revenant.

Here we go again.

"This sibling rivalry is becoming tiresome," Revenant drawled.

Reaver, having no sense of humor that Rev could see, hissed. "I'll deal with you later." He looked over at Eidolon. "What's happening outside? There's an entire legion of angels barricading the hospital."

"You think I didn't notice that?" Eidolon turned away to order a nurse to test Harrowgate operation between the hospital and the clinic.

Reaver rounded on Revenant. "Is this your doing? Does this have something to do with why you attacked Thanatos for his blood?"

"He has nothing to do with the angels," Blaspheme said, putting herself between Rev and Reaver. Which was adorable. "As for what happened with Thanatos, that's my fault. Revenant got the blood for me."

Reaver scowled. "For you? Why?"

"Don't," Revenant warned, but the muley glare Blaspheme gave him said she was determined to spill the beans.

Revenant primed his power, just in case Reaver reacted badly. And then his brother would see just how far Rev would go to protect those he cared about.

"Because I'm a *vyrm*," Blaspheme blurted. "And I needed the blood to complete a spell that will conceal my true nature."

Reaver's brow climbed up his forehead as he glanced over at Eidolon. "It was Blaspheme you were talking about the other day?" At the doctor's nod, Reaver exhaled a curse. "You could have told me why you needed Thanatos's blood, Revenant."

"Yeah, because it was so easy to talk while engulfed in fire. Oh, and the crushed lungs didn't help with that, either."

"*You* did that to him?" Blaspheme's hands clenched as if she wanted to take a swing at Reaver. Revenant was tempted to nullify the hospital's antiviolence spell so she could. "He's your brother! How could you?"

Eidolon held up his hand. "We can deal with family matters later. Right now we have to do something about the angels. Injured patients can't get in, and there are at least two mated Sems, including myself, who can't get to their mates. The situation will go critical in a few hours unless we can hitch rides with Reaver and Revenant."

Ah, right. As incubi, Seminus demons needed sex to survive, and while the unmated ones could get it from anywhere, mated Sems were limited to sex with their females.

"So all these angels are here for Blaspheme?" Reaver asked. "Seems a little drastic, even for extremists like Eradicators."

Blaspheme swore softly. "I don't think this is entirely about my being a *vyrm*. They wouldn't send an entire legion of angels for that. This is bigger, and I'd be willing to bet that if you dig deep, you'll find that an archangel named Raphael is responsible for this."

Revenant thought Reaver's head was going to blow off. "Tell me," Reaver growled. "And don't leave anything out."

Blaspheme shared the information she'd apparently gotten from her mother earlier, and the longer Reaver listened, the more Rev could feel the fury building in him. His brother was a bomb with a lit fuse, just waiting for someone to throw it. Revenant had a feeling that Raphael was, very soon, going to experience an explosion.

Good. If Reaver could take care of the angels' UG embargo, Revenant could concentrate on what to do about getting Satan off Blaspheme's back. Unfortunately, there was no easy solution to that.

Blaspheme definitely had to perform the Pruosi spell, but as long as Raphael was alive and Satan was still looking for her or her mother, she was in danger. What if one of them caught Deva and tortured her into revealing her daughter's location and new identity? Revenant didn't trust the fallen angel's ability to stand up to the kind of torture either of the assholes could dish out.

Frustrated, he thumbed through the Pruosi book, hoping a miracle would jump out at him. Something that would save Blaspheme without her having to lose everything. Maybe there was a spell that would trick Raphael out of Heaven. Or bind Satan's ability to spy on Revenant. Hell, at this point, he'd be happy tossing the Dark Lord into a bottomless pit and—

He broke off as a thought occurred to him. Could it be so simple?

"Revenant?" Blaspheme rested her palm on his shoulder. "What is it?"

Turning his head, he kissed her hand before flipping to the page he'd merely glanced at before. And there it was. The crazy ramblings of a Pruosi demon whose words had been made immortal between the pages of the *Daemonica* itself.

They try, one after another, to send the beast into the abyss. Failure to them all, but the one who holds the key.

It was a long shot, completely insane, but at this point, that was all he had.

Twenty-Nine

As Revenant contemplated the logistics involved in his long shot of a plan, Blaspheme put her head together with Eidolon and Reaver over the angel situation outside UG. A few minutes later, Eidolon's blond brother, Wraith, sauntered into the cafeteria.

"Yo, Blaspheme. Your mother is standing just inside the ER doors and taunting the angels in the parking lot. I like telling angels how douchey they are as much as anyone, and she's got some righteous zingers, but they're going to start throwing vehicles at the building if you don't stop her."

Blaspheme groaned. "I'm on it."

With Blaspheme gone, Rev figured it was a good time to have a chat with his brother. Naturally, Reaver gave him the evil eye as he approached.

"I think I've found a way to eliminate a few of our problems," Revenant said. "Namely, Satan, Gethel, and Lucifer."

"I'm listening."

Revenant glanced around the cafeteria, which had filled to capacity with patients and staff who were freaked out by the angel presence outside the hospital and clinic.

Rev didn't trust any of them, except, maybe, Eidolon. Revenant didn't like the guy, but he had to admit that the doctor ran a tight ship and seemed to value his family, friends, and employees. No wonder Blaspheme liked working here.

"Meet me at Megiddo." He flashed away, materializing at the same time as Reaver on the Israeli hilltop.

"Why here?" Reaver asked.

Revenant looked out over lands that had seen battle after battle over the course of thousands of years. Fitting, perhaps, that Revenant and Reaver, who had done nothing *but* battle each other, were here now for what Rev hoped would be the last time.

"Because it's time I answered your question," Rev said, "and this was where you first asked it."

"And what question is that?"

"You asked what happened to our mother."

"And you said you killed her." Reaver rubbed his chest, and Revenant wondered if he felt the same ache Rev did when he discussed her. "But you never said why or how it went down."

Revenant closed his eyes, mentally preparing himself to go back to that awful time and place. To his credit, Reaver didn't rush him, merely waited in silence. Finally, Rev opened his eyes and looked his brother in the eye. He deserved that, at least.

"I told you I was separated from our mother and taken to slave in magma crystal mines, yes?" At Reaver's curt nod, Rev continued. "Ten years later, I was taken to Satan. Filled with lies and half-truths. Promised power and influence. Once he felt I was loyal to his cause, he sent me to fetch our mother from the dungeon where she'd been kept for two decades. I didn't know what he was going to do to her, but I knew it wouldn't be good. She knew it, too."

Gods, he could still feel her frail frame hanging on to his when they'd been reunited in that filthy cell where he'd spent the bulk of his childhood. The years had not been kind to her, and she was but a shell of the beautiful angel he'd remembered.

And yet, in the depths of her dull, sunken eyes, there had been a spark of life that burned bright when she'd seen him. The breath that shuddered from her lungs had reeked of despair, but her strength shone through even the wear and tear on her body.

"I escorted her out of the dungeon, but I couldn't take her to Satan. I tried to run with her, to get her out of Sheoul, but we were surrounded and trapped by Satan's forces. She had no power left in her, and I wasn't powerful enough to flash with someone else, so we holed up in a cave and waited to die. That's when she told me the truth about who I was."

"Who did you think you were before that?"

"I grew up thinking I was *vyrm*. Our mother told me what Satan told her to say, that she was an angel imprisoned for mating with a fallen angel. But while we were holed up, she told me about our father. About you. She was desperate for me to find you and for us to be a family. It was her greatest hope that somehow you could help me rid my blood of Satan's taint." He took in a deep, shuddering breath. "And then she begged me to kill her."

Reaver closed his eyes. "Aw, damn."

The air around them went still and cold. Rev didn't know who was responsible for that, himself or Reaver, but the damp chill settled deep in his bones, making them ache as much as his soul.

"I couldn't do it," Revenant said. "Not at first. I refused, argued, was prepared to fight Satan's forces to the death. But as they closed in, they shouted out their orders...what they intended to do to us before they took us in chains to their master. I didn't care about myself, but I knew her suffering would be beyond measure." He held out his palm. "Give me your hand."

Reaver hesitated, the distrust between them thickening like an invisible wall.

"I'm going to show you," Revenant said. "You need to know." And he didn't think his voice would make it through the entire tale.

Finally, Reaver pressed his palm flat against Revenant's, and Rev queued up the memory he'd tried so hard to forget.

"Please, Revenant." Lying limp in his arms, Mariel gazed up at him with eyes that were once brilliant sapphire blue, but were now pale and cloudy. "I'm so far gone that you don't need a special weapon." She cupped his cheek in one trembling hand. "Feed from me. Drain me as far as you can. My blood will strengthen you and weaken me so your blade can finish it."

"Mother, no. I can't do what you're asking. Your soul will be trapped down here—"

"You must. Hurry. They're coming." A tear slid from her eye and plopped to his arm, and all he could think was if she had her way, the next thing dripping from her would be blood.

"*Please, no,*" *he whispered.*

"*Do it!*" *She lowered her voice to a gentle murmur, barely audible over the pounding footsteps and coarse laughter of the approaching demons. "I love you, Son. Tell Yenrieth that I love him, too. I hope he can forgive me for abandoning him.*"

Revenant's tears joined hers as he bent and pressed a tender kiss to her forehead. "I love you," he rasped.

"*Hurry.*"

Against every instinct that screamed for him not to do this, he bared his fangs and bit into her throat as tenderly as he could. In his arms, she went taut, but gradually her body relaxed, until her strong pulse became stronger as her body tried to compensate for the blood lost.

He wept as he fed, and eventually, her heart couldn't keep up. The tap of her heartbeat against his teeth grew weaker and slower, until he couldn't feel it at all.

She wasn't dead, but she was close. The rumble of Satan's advancing army made the ground shake outside the cavern they'd hidden inside. He had a minute. Maybe two.

"*Forgive me, Mother,*" *he whispered as he palmed the dagger at his hip. With the greatest of care, he brushed her hair back from her pale face and sang the lullaby she'd sung to him when he was little.*

"*Moonbeams and sunshine, the clouds and the seas, all part of the many worlds I want you to see. Fear not the unknown, nor the depths of the night, for nothing can harm you when I hold you tight.*"

He could barely see through his tears as he shoved the blade between her ribs and pierced her heart. In his arms, her body went limp, and in an instant, she was gone.

At some point during the instant replay, Revenant and Reaver had gone to their knees in the dirt, were both panting and shaking.

"I killed her," Revenant choked out, feeling as if he'd slammed that blade into his own chest. "I killed her and tried to flash out with her body, but she was right. I couldn't take her with me. And since the flashing ability only allowed for me to flash to somewhere I'd already been, I was screwed. I materialized at one of the places on our escape route, and from there I ran like hell. I was on the run for...fuck, I don't know how long. I eventually found a Harrowgate and used it to get to the human realm, where I contacted you."

"And I fucked that up." Reaver's gaze was tormented. Just days ago, hell, hours ago, Rev would have savored his brother's pain like the most decadent dessert. Now it turned his stomach. "I'm sorry, Revenant. Damn, I am so sorry. I didn't know what you'd gone through—"

"Would it have mattered?" He exploded to his feet, the agony of losing his mother and then being rejected by his brother washing over him as fresh and vivid as if it had happened yesterday. "You hated me on sight."

"No, Revenant." Reaver came to his feet slowly, as if he was concerned about a sudden move setting Rev off. He looked down at his boots, his perfect hair falling forward to conceal his face, and Rev realized that, for the first time, he hadn't changed his own hair color to match his brother's. "I hated *myself*. We might not be identical twins, but in you I saw myself. I saw someone who had been lied to, and I made it about me, when it should have been about us." Suddenly, he tugged Revenant against him, and it was a relief to find that Reaver was trembling as forcefully as

Rev was. "I can't pretend to understand what you went through with our mother, but you need to know that nothing that happened to her was your fault. It was her choice to stay with you, and it was her choice to die."

They remained like that for a long time, until Reaver pulled back and said the words Revenant had wanted to hear for so long, but couldn't admit even to himself.

"I won't abandon you again," Reaver swore. "We're brothers, and it's past time we acted like it."

Revenant had no idea how to do that. For that matter, he didn't know if they'd even have the chance.

"I wish we had time," Rev said, his voice still beat to hell from the trip down memory lane. "But I have to protect Blaspheme, and the longer I wait, the worse it could be for her."

"You mentioned something about Satan, Gethel, and Lucifer?"

Rev nodded. "I have a plan, but I'm going to need an angel."

Reaver cocked an eyebrow. "An angel?"

"Satan wants me to prove my loyalty. Which means he wants both Blaspheme and an angel. I'm not giving him Blaspheme. Don't suppose you know of an angel who deserves a fate worse than death."

Reaver smiled grimly. "As a matter of fact, I do."

"If you're thinking of the same asshole I'm thinking of, this plan might work."

"What plan?"

"One that could get us both killed."

Reaver snorted. "Should have led with that. I'm in."

Clearly, recklessness ran in the family. "You haven't heard the plan."

"Then lay it on me," Reaver said. "We're going to do this thing, and we're going to do it together, the way we were born."

And the way they were probably going to die.

"Hello, Raphael."

The archangel nearly jumped out of his skin, which Reaver thought was pretty damned funny. Raphael liked to pretend he was cool and collected, often emulating Metatron—poorly. Now Reaver knew why he did that.

He wanted Metatron's job.

"What the fuck are you doing in my house?" Raphael eyed Reaver's gold wings, which Reaver had taken out to remind the archangel that he was about a thousand times more powerful than Raphael.

"I came to ask how long you'd been plotting to take down Metatron."

Raphael laughed, sounding genuinely amused. "I have no idea what you're talking about."

"Yeah, well, I don't have time to toy with you, so I'm just going to put it all out there. I know you've been working with Stamtiel for at least two hundred years. So I'm going to give you a choice. Either I take you to Metatron for your execution, or I give you a fighting chance at survival."

"Go ahead." Raphael crossed his arms over his chest. "Take me to Metatron. You have no evidence—"

"I have Stamtiel."

Every drop of blood drained from Raphael's face. "You're lying."

Reaver used his mind to display a live feed on the far

wall. A live feed showing Harvester standing next to a gagged and bound male angel. She grinned and waved. Reaver waved back, and she blew him a kiss, followed by a naughty wink.

"As you can see, he's alive and willing to squeal in exchange for his life." His life, however, was already forfeit. Harvester was just waiting for the go-ahead.

"How?" Raphael rasped. "How did you find him?"

"I wish I could take credit, but Azagoth did all the footwork. We'll handle the wet work." Reaver shook his head. "You should have known better than to mess with the Grim Reaper's mate."

"It wasn't me! It was Stamtiel—"

Reaver punched the archangel in his lying mouth, relishing the sound of knuckles striking flesh. Too bad Raphael healed instantly, the blood from his split lip vanishing almost before it formed full droplets.

"You gave the order," Reaver snarled. "It's time. It's time you paid for every heinous act you've committed. But do you want to know what act truly secured your place at the top of my revenge list?"

Reaver moved toward the archangel slowly, using every step to ratchet up the fear in the bastard's eyes. Raphael tried to flash out of there, but Reaver had already placed a restrictive shield over the residence. Raphael wasn't going anywhere.

"Please," Raphael begged. "Everything I've done was for the good of the realm—"

"The realm? Seriously? Was it good for the realm when you stole my daughter's unborn baby and tried to implant it in Gethel's womb?"

"I gave the baby back," Raphael protested, his voice

degenerating into a pathetic whine that only pissed Reaver off more.

"Only because Harvester agreed to sleep with you in exchange." Reaver caught the archangel by the throat and lifted him into the air. "I'd kill you now, but I have other plans."

"Please—"

"Shut up. It's time that you paid for your evil deeds. You, Raphael, are going to reap what you have sown."

Thirty

Blaspheme paced around the cafeteria table that had become her temporary office, her mind spitting out a million different ideas to end the hospital siege, get Satan and Raphael off her back, and still be able to keep Revenant. Most of her ideas could solve one of the issues, a few could solve two, but not one touched on all three.

There had to be a way. She couldn't give up Revenant. She didn't care if she had to be on the run for the rest of her life. But she couldn't put him at risk for Satan's wrath, either.

Revenant materialized a few feet away, and she immediately ran to him. "What happened? Where's Reaver?"

Revenant drew her into his arms and held her tight, but the sensation of rightness and comfort shifted to tension when she felt the taut lines of his body. Something was wrong.

"Everything's going to be okay," he whispered into her hair.

His chest muffled her voice. "Revenant, you're scaring me."

"Listen to me," he said, pulling back so he could look her in the eye. "Raphael is no longer going to be a problem for you or your mother, and the angels outside are already dispersing. But I need you to go through with the Pruosi spell."

"Dammit, what's going on?"

He framed her face in his warm hands with such care that she could hardly believe this was once the infamous male known as The Destroyer. "I'm going to make sure that Satan never bothers you again."

Her stomach churned, and she wondered if her lunch was going to be making a second appearance. "I really don't like the sound of this."

"This is important," he said gravely, which did nothing to ease the nauseated tumble in her belly. "If I don't return, Reaver will make sure you're safe. Just promise me you'll perform the spell."

Her pulse went all erratic, as if it were tapping out Morse code for *Oh, shit* against the walls of her arteries.

"If you don't return?" She gripped his biceps, digging her nails into his jacket as if trying to muscle him into staying. "Revenant, no. Whatever it is you have planned, you can't do it."

"I have to. I need you to be safe." He stroked his knuckles along her jaw so gently she wanted to weep. "And it's been a long time coming. I've never believed in fate before, but this feels...right."

"Please don't," she begged, not caring that her pride

was in the toilet. "You can't. You can't come into my life, make me fall for you, and then leave me!"

"You fell for me?" One side of his mouth ruffled in a cocky smile.

"How can you not know that," she whispered.

Dipping his head, he lowered his mouth to hers and kissed her sweetly. Reverently. "Thank you. I've lived more in the last week than I lived in my entire life. You *are* a butterfly, Blaspheme. Your beauty transforms everything around you."

He stepped back, and panic seized her. "No." She reached for him, but he sidestepped and nodded to someone behind her. Too late she realized what was happening. Eidolon's strong arms folded around her, caging her against his broad chest and rendering her unable to get to Revenant no matter how hard she struggled. "No!" she screamed. "Don't do this."

For a torturous, fleeting second, she swore she saw tears in Revenant's eyes. And then he was gone. She stared at the empty air where Revenant had once stood, and when her brain caught up with her eyes, she collapsed against Eidolon and sobbed.

Sobbed until there was nothing left.

Revenant was still reeling from his good-bye with Blaspheme when he flashed to Gethel's residence. By some miracle, Blaspheme had fallen for him, which made leaving her even worse. Especially because he'd fallen for her, too, and the very real possibility that he might not ever see her again made his heart clench.

It also made him angry. He'd lived five thousand years

alone, and he'd finally found the female who brought out the angel inside him he hadn't known existed ... and Satan was going to take that away from him.

Anger fueled every step he took in search of Satan's vile baby mama. He found her in her lush bedroom, wrapped in furs and studying herself in front of the mirror.

"Do you think I'm fat?" Gethel asked, peering at her side profile.

"As a cow."

"Asshole." She wheeled around with impressive speed, given that she *was* as big as a cow. A pregnant cow. "Did you bring that doctor bitch again?"

Gods, he was going to love taking her down. "I brought something better."

Her pale eyes lit up. "What is it?"

"An archangel."

With the way she flushed and began to pant, he thought she was going to orgasm right then and there. "Who?"

"Raphael. Do you know him?"

Her lips curled back from sharp, pointy teeth. "I despise him." She looked past him, as if Raphael were standing in the doorway. "Where is he?"

"I had to leave him in the Temple of Gog. See?" In the center of the room, he cast a 3-D image of Raphael, bound and unconscious, next to the statue of Gog that sat along the temple's back wall. Proof was always a good thing when you were going for deception. "Live angels can't enter Satan's territories. I figured I'd let you have a shot at him before I slaughter him and hand his head over to the Dark Lord."

"Take me," she said. "I want to feed on his haughty archangel blood."

So predictable. "I can't do that. Satan cast a spell on this place so no one can kidnap you."

"I can leave of my own free will," she said. "I'll go myself. You'll accompany me as protection."

Her command made him grind his teeth, but accompanying her had been the plan all along. "Take my hand," he said. "Temple of Gog."

Grinning, she flashed them to the temple, fashioned from ancient Roman buildings to worship some of the earliest and most powerful demons to exist in Sheoul. As they materialized, Reaver lunged from where he'd been concealed behind a pillar and clamped a Tal around her throat. The glass cuff, made by angels to render fallen angels helpless, shaped itself into an invisible collar, squeezing hard enough to allow only wisps of air to pass through her windpipe.

Best of all, as her eyes bulged and she grasped at the Tal, she couldn't speak.

"Where's Raphael?" Rev asked, and Reaver gestured to a shadowed corner, where the archangel lay, unconscious, on his back. "Did you have any trouble?"

Reaver yanked Gethel toward Raphael. "Nope."

Suddenly, Gethel's face went exorcist, morphing into something horrible, and the thing in her belly began to push against her skin as if it wanted out.

"Shit," Reaver snapped. "We need to hurry. Lucifer is strong even in her womb. If he were to be born now ..."

He didn't have to finish. The coming battle was going to be impossible to win as it was. Throwing in Lucifer, whose power was predicted to eclipse the power he'd wielded in his past life, was going to ensure that neither Revenant nor Reaver survived this. And Revenant had no

doubt that once Lucifer was grown, he'd make everyone
Reaver and Rev loved pay as well.

"I'm out of here. Get ready, Bro, because all hell is
going to break loose."

Literally.

Thirty-One

Revenant stood outside the entrance to Satan's private baths, inhaling deeply. Again. And again. This was it. He was either going to do the impossible...or he was going to die.

He entered without knocking. Steam that reeked of sulphur swirled around him as he walked toward the bubbling pit in the center of the black-tiled room. Satan was in the pool with three females and a male, all different species.

Revenant didn't wait for Satan to show surprise that he'd entered without an invitation. He blasted the four demons in the pit with a sweet Shadow Angel weapon that disintegrated the fuckers into nonexistence. Not even their souls survived.

"Revenant," Satan hissed. "What the fuck are you do—"

Revenant attacked, tackling the demon as he rose from the water. They crashed onto the stone deck with a wet thud. Before Satan could even blink, Revenant slammed his fist into his throat.

It was like hitting a steel pipe.

Satan struck back with an uppercut into Rev's gut, knocking him into the sacrificial table used to drain the blood of victims into the pool. The stone tabletop smashed into a dozen pieces, showering Rev with dust and pebbles.

"What *the fuck* is going on?" Satan's roar of fury sent the ghastbats in the rafters into an explosion of squeaks and flapping wings.

Revenant pitched to his feet. "I got your damned angel. I've proved my loyalty, so you're going to leave Blaspheme alone."

Satan laughed. "You stupid bastard. I will have Blaspheme. No angel could be worth what I plan to do to her."

The smug son of a bitch. "Not even an archangel?"

Instant mood shift. Satan wiped blood from his chin and stood a little straighter. "An archangel, you say." A smile twitched at the corners of his mouth, and Revenant swore he saw a little drool. The bastard was taking the bait, just as Gethel had. "Is this archangel dead?"

Revenant shook his head. "I figured you'd want him alive, so I didn't bring him here." No living angel could enter this region of Sheoul, and if Revenant—or anyone—tried to flash a Heavenly being inside, he or she would materialize dead.

Yeah, Satan was drooling. "Where is he?"

"The Temple of Gog."

The Prince of Lies nodded in approval. "Nice. His power will be limited there. Not that it matters, of course. I can kill him with my pinky."

"I'd like to see that, my lord," Revenant said. He'd *pay* to see that.

Satan narrowed his eyes. "Then why did you attack me?"

"Because," Revenant said. "You questioned my loyalty. Don't fucking do that again."

Now Rev waited. The demon would either respect what Revenant had done... or he'd fry him. Probably literally, given that one of Satan's favorite torture methods involved a giant iron skillet and rendered Gargantua lard.

Finally, just as Revenant was contemplating the spices that would go best with Shadow Angel stir-fry, Satan's black eyes locked onto him.

"You have balls made of brimstone, Revenant." He bared fangs as sharp as blades. "But do it again and I'll cut those balls off and feed them to Blaspheme. Understood?"

Rev inclined his head in the shallowest nod he could get away with and still appear respectful.

"Good. Now who is this archangel?"

"His name is Raphael."

A slow, malevolent smile spread across Satan's face, and his eyes glowed with unholy excitement. "I can't wait to break him," he said almost breathlessly. "Let's go."

Revenant and Satan materialized inside the Temple of Gog at the same time. In the next heartbeat, Reaver was there, snapping a Tal around the demon's throat. Revenant leaped away as Satan roared in fury, his body contorting and expanding, growing taller and wider and fuck, this wasn't going to be good. Rev hadn't expected the Tal to work, and sure enough, they might as well have collared the demon with a silk ribbon.

"Now!" he shouted. "Hurry!"

Reaver didn't have a chance to carry out the next phase of their plan. Satan's snarl became a physical thing, a wall of hellfire that shot from him in a 360-degree shock wave of pain.

Revenant heard Reaver's scream of agony even over his own hoarse cry. His skin blistered and peeled, layer upon layer, until he could see his own bones peeking out from charred muscle.

The Dark Lord's giant fist, now the size of a Volkswagen, swiped Revenant aside as if he were a mere fly. He sailed through the air, striking the Gog statue with a crash of broken bones and marble.

Reaver must have gotten the same treatment, his muffled grunt joining the sound of stone collapsing around them.

Revenant's body felt as if it were caving in on itself, but somehow he managed to draw in power, taking it from the very air around him. His wounds began to knit together as he sought a bigger, more powerful form.

"You traitor!" Satan's voice, deep, guttural, was a weapon in itself, shattering Revenant's eardrums.

The surge of pain triggered a chain reaction inside him. Anger seared him more intensely than Satan's fire had. This bastard had been the source of all of his pain. All his mother's pain. He had to pay.

Leaping to his feet, which were now clawed, huge to match the monstrous form he'd shifted into, he blasted Satan with every weapon in his arsenal. All of them. At once.

The demon screamed and fell back, blood, limbs, teeth, horns…it all burst into the air in a gory mist as Satan's body exploded. The temple, painted in dripping crimson and internal organs, shuddered, as if it knew something terrible had just happened.

And was going to happen again.

"Reaver!"

Revenant's twin was a mangled, twisted mess, but with Satan out of commission, he could—

"*You fucking cunt!*" Satan materialized in front of Rev with a giant sword of lava in his clawed hand. Oh, fuck—

Revenant dove, rolling as he hit the ground. The edge of the blade caught him in the ribs, opening his chest down to the bone and turning his blood to ash. Pain blurred his vision, but out of the corner of his eye, he saw Reaver, nearly regenerated, limping toward the pentagram he'd drawn with Gethel's blood in the center of the room.

Satan's head swiveled toward Reaver.

Keep his attention!

"Fucker." Revenant staggered to his feet, resisting the urge to wrap his arm around his rib cage. The bleeding, charred flesh wasn't healing like it should. "You twisted son of a bitch. Did you really think I'd sit by and let Lucifer take what should be mine?" Throwing out his hand, he sent a focused beam of angelic radiation at the demon, severing the bastard's left arm at the elbow. The sword clattered to the ground, a hand still wrapped around the hilt.

He paid for that with a fist to the gut. No, *through* the gut. Revenant's jaw locked in agony as Satan's fist did a through-and-through, punching out of his back.

"I should have ripped your wings off and shoved them

up your ass a long time ago." Steam bellowed from Satan's nostrils, and hate glowed in his crimson eyes as he jerked his bloody hand free of Rev's body. His mouth stretched into a hideous, sharp-toothed smile as he leaned in close enough for Rev to smell his fetid breath. "But no time like the present. Bend over, you stinking piece of offal."

In a blur of motion, the demon clamped his hand down on Revenant's skull and spun him, face-first, into the ground. Revenant screamed as he felt one wing rip away from his shoulders. Fuck, this was going to hurt—

The glint of metal flashed in the torchlit temple. Still pinned to the ground, Revenant caught a glimpse of Reaver slashing his palm with a dagger. The pentagram flared to life, pulsing and glowing as if hungry for the blood that ran down Reaver's arm in a thick rivulet. Even as Satan roared a curse, Reaver dropped to one knee and slapped his hand in the center of the pentagram.

Suddenly, a screaming vortex of lightning stretched from the ceiling to the floor, coming down on top of the Dark Lord, swallowing him whole.

"Hurry," Reaver yelled, and yeah, duh. Nothing was going to hold Satan for long. They had thirty seconds at best before the king of demons burst out of the lightning storm and squashed them like flies.

Clenching his teeth against the pain of his wounds, Revenant shoved to his feet to face Raphael and Gethel, both of whom had come free of their bonds during the battle. Raphael was armed with an elemental sword, which harvested nearby elements to form the blade. Lightning made his blade pretty badass, and as he hacked into Gethel's shoulder, a blast of power knocked her into the electrical tornado. Cool. Two down, one to go.

Raphael turned on Revenant. "Bastard! You and your whore of a mother should have died down here—"

Revenant's bellow of rage knocked the archangel off his feet. Rev was there before Raphael hit the ground, and in a single, fluid sweep, he hurled the motherfucker into the vortex to join Satan and Gethel.

"I can't hold it!" Reaver's shout was barely audible, eaten by thunder and electric snaps and the furious screams of the three assholes inside the funnel.

Rev limped to Reaver, the hole in his midsection and the deep laceration in his chest running with rivers of blood. He wasn't healing, and Reaver wasn't in much better shape. The room spun in sickly crimson and gray blurs as he swung around beside Reaver so they were shoulder to shoulder. Reaching deep, all the way to his soul, he drew power from the realm around him, so much power that he buzzed with it, burned with it, *became* it.

In his mind, he chanted, visualizing a giant magma crystal box reinforced with Heavenly currents of power. As the crystal trap formed around the three beings, Reaver transferred his energy into it, infusing the thing with another layer of angelic power to create a prison of good and evil unlike anything ever created. Hastily, he looped a thick length of chain around the cube and anchored one end to Heaven and the other to Sheoul. He wasn't even sure where the ability or idea to create such a thing came from...instinct, the Pruosi book...he didn't know. All he knew was that he and Reaver had one shot at this, and Revenant would spare no effort.

The lightning died down, but the wind picked up and began to suck in the malevolent atmosphere that permeated the temple. Inky shadows shrieked as they were pulled into the vortex and sent spinning into oblivion.

The building shook and trembled, the floor bucking beneath their feet. Revenant could barely see through the hair that whipped in his face from the wind that would put an EF5 tornado to shame. Furniture, stones, and who the hell knew what else battered him and Reaver as they tried to hold on to the trap and keep it solid.

"I can feel Satan and Lucifer pushing back from inside the box," Reaver shouted. "We can't hold it much longer!"

"I know!" Revenant dug deep for every last drop of strength. "Ready?"

"Go!"

Closing his eyes, Rev attempted to repeat the gathering of energy inside him that took place when he'd lost his shit at the archangel meeting. But instead of blowing himself up, he needed to redirect that same power at the trap.

His body buzzed with energy, filling him with drug-like ecstasy until once more it burned. Threatened to sear him to ash.

Time to let loose.

In a whoosh of fiery agony, power exploded from him, engulfing the whirling trap in a nuclear blast. But as the shock wave blew back and Revenant prepared for another wave of pain, it fizzled. A light breeze caressed his face, all that remained of the detonation.

A light. Fucking. Breeze.

"Revenant! Watch out!"

The energy he'd sent at the trap suddenly rebounded, striking him like a speeding train as it reentered his body. He felt his bones snap like toothpicks, his organs liquefy, and his teeth get torn from his gums. He screamed as the power tore him apart...and then put him back together.

Holy shit. Wielding that kind of power was both heavenly and hellish, wonderful and terrible.

And it hadn't worked to seal the trap. The box was too strong. Ironically, its strength was protecting those inside it, allowing them to reinforce its walls with their own powers.

This was going to fail, and then Revenant and Reaver were going to die.

"Reaver," he gasped.

"Why the hell are you waiting? Do it again!"

"It's not going to work!" Revenant's eyes stung as grit and dust ground into them. Yeah, it was the grit. He wasn't tearing up. "I've got to do it from the inside."

"The fuck you do!" Reaver's hair was plastered to his sweat-drenched skin and he was bleeding from dozens of wounds, but his gaze was fierce as he looked at Rev. "Do it like we planned!"

It wouldn't work, and he knew it. In order to seal the box, he had to damage its occupants and interrupt their flow of power.

"Reaver..." His voice was raw from yelling, and he wasn't sure his twin could even hear him. "I'm glad we got to be brothers."

"What? No! Rev, don't—"

"Keep Blaspheme safe. Tell her...I wish I could have seen her butterfly wings."

"*No!*"

Revenant reversed his powers, sucking them back into his body. Every cell vibrated at a level so intense that he saw himself glow with searing heat as he dove into the cage. He had a brief glimpse of Satan and Raphael throwing themselves against the walls, their roars of rage rolling through the air in a constant thunder.

Satan lunged at him with clawed hands and T. rex–sized teeth made to shred flesh from bone.

Revenant let the explosion go.

The world went crimson.

Reaver felt his brother die.

Unbearable pain ripped through him as a fissure broke his soul wide open. "No," he whispered, even as his legs gave out and he hit the floor in a crack of kneecaps. "No."

This wasn't supposed to happen. They were supposed to get a chance at being brothers. They might not have ever been let's-toss-a-ball-together brothers, but they could have worked out their own thing.

Reaver struggled to breathe. Revenant had sacrificed his life for him. For everyone. He'd also just taken out the top three assholes in the universe. Four, counting Lucifer.

The screaming vortex dialed down, and the cage's spinning slowed. In a moment it would stop and melt into oblivion. For how long, Reaver didn't know. This kind of magic had a shelf life, and he just hoped they got at least a few decades out of it.

"Revenant," he rasped. "You son of a bitch."

He looked over at the cube as it slowed to a lazy, wobbly spin. The crystal had gone opaque, the surface dulled, except for—

Reaver shot to his feet. The trap's door hadn't closed. Something was jamming it open, and blood was streaming like a river from out of the foot-wide gap. Inside, something stirred.

Fuck!

Extending his tattered wings, he shot into the air and banked hard to the right, grabbing the edge of the door as the cage spun. He clawed for purchase, gritting his teeth as he reached for the shredded arm that was jamming the door. If he could just shove it back inside—

Shit, wait! He recognized that arm. Hoping it was attached to Revenant's body, he swung his legs up and wedged himself into the doorway as he yanked on his brother's wrist. Revenant's broken body, mangled and slippery with blood, slid out of the trap and flung to the floor.

As Reaver launched away from the cube, he caught one last glimpse of Raphael, his body regenerating from the dozens of pieces it was in. Satan, already mostly re-formed, lunged as the door closed. His gaping maw and sharklike teeth were the last things Reaver saw before the cube became a solid chunk of angel-reinforced crystal.

Reaver hit the ground next to Revenant's shattered body as the trap began to vibrate, faster and faster, until it winked out of existence.

Everything went dead silent.

The trap was gone, launched into an abyss of nothingness.

A vision flashed before his eyes, words on a page he'd read a million times.

"And I saw a dark angel come down from heaven, having the key of the bottomless pit and a great chain in his hand. And he laid hold on the dragon, that old serpent which is the devil, and Satan, and bound him a thousand years."

It was that moment in which Reaver understood what

had just happened. The biblical prophecy had been there for eons, running alongside the one that said Reaver would ultimately break the Horsemen's Seals and kick off Armageddon.

Revenant was part of that prophecy, and he'd just fulfilled it.

The momentousness of what had just happened combined with relief and grief, but he pushed through it to gather what was left of his brother in his arms.

"I'm sorry, Revenant," he whispered.

And just then, he felt a spark of life. It was weak and flickering like a dying lightbulb, but it was there.

Hastily, Reaver channeled a stream of healing power into his twin, but nothing happened. If anything, the thread of life inside became even more brittle and unstable, and shit, Reaver had to get him help.

"Hold on, Brother. Please... hold on."

Thirty-Two

"*Eidolon!*" Reaver's voice boomed through the hospital...and it wasn't coming through the speaker system. "*ER STAT.*"

Blaspheme's heart jumped into her throat. Leaving behind the DNA samples and all the supplies she'd gathered to alter her identity, she sprinted from her office to the clinic's Harrowgate, shouldered past UGC's new dentist, and leaped inside the gate. The second she stepped into Underworld General's Emergency Department, the metallic tang of blood assaulted her nostrils and she knew it was Revenant.

Across the room, in the closest trauma cubicle, Eidolon, Shade, and Raze were channeling power into his unresponsive body.

Crying out, she ran over, shoving her way between Reaver and Eidolon's brother-in-law, a dhampire paramedic named Con who was doing his best to start an IV.

"What happened?" She took in Rev's broken form, the splintered bones punching through mangled flesh, the hemorrhaging gashes, the exposed body parts that shouldn't be on the outside of his body.

Reaver's voice was hoarse. "I think he's dying."

"No." She shook her head so hard her hair stung her cheeks. "He can't. He's a Shadow Angel. Nothing can kill him!" She was screeching now, as if yelling would make her words true.

"Satan can," Reaver said. "But he did most of this to himself."

"Eidolon," she cried. "Please. Save him."

She knew the doctor and the others were doing their best, but the grim expression on Eidolon's face said it all.

Revenant wasn't going to make it.

After all of this, he was going to die in front of her. After everything they'd been through, after he'd broken a sacred rule for her, now he was going to die. Was this the kind of consequence he talked about when he discussed his reluctance to break rules? Steal blood from a Horseman and pay with your life?

She jammed her hand into her pocket and clutched the vial of blood. She was going to smash it, destroy the damned thing. In the back of her mind, she knew she was being illogical, that destroying the vial wouldn't bring him back, but she had to do something.

The essence of fucking death was going to—

The essence of death was also an elixir of life for those who can't die.

Revenant's words rang through her ears as if funneled through a blow horn.

"Reaver." She held out the vial. "What about this?

Thanatos's blood. Revenant said it was also an elixir of life."

Reaver frowned. "He did?"

"Your mother told him that."

He lifted the vial from her hand. "It can't hurt." He popped the rubber stopper, but she grabbed his wrist.

"No." Oh, gods, was she really doing this? She glanced at Revenant, his lifeless eyes staring blindly at the chains hanging from the ceiling, and she knew it was the right thing. "You need to ask Thanatos."

"But we have the blood right here."

"Listen to me." She clung to Reaver, her knuckles going white with the force of her grip. "Revenant broke a Watcher rule by taking it, and Thanatos clearly wasn't willing to give it up. To use it without his permission to save Revenant's life would be a huge violation. Revenant wouldn't want that, I promise you. This goes all the way back to his childhood. All the way to your mother. Please, ask Thanatos."

"Fuck," Reaver muttered, but in an instant, he was gone.

"We don't have time for this," Eidolon growled at Blaspheme. "Our powers are the only thing keeping him alive. Once they fade..."

His *dermoire* was glowing brighter than she'd ever seen it, same with Shade and Raze. But their power was limited, and already she was seeing a flicker in the intensity of the glimmer shooting down Raze's skin glyphs.

"I know," she whispered. "Believe me, I know."

While she waited, she held Rev's cold, limp hand, sticky with his blood.

"Don't you die, you bastard. Don't you dare die."

She repeated the words over and over, as if they were some sort of protective mantra that would keep him going. And fuck, how long did it take for Reaver to convince his son to save his brother?

"I'm fading," Raze croaked, and Blaspheme bit back a sob at the sight of Raze's *dermoire* losing its reddish-golden glow, its black lines swallowing the light.

Sweat dripped off Shade's brow as he gripped Revenant's ankle tight. "I'm running on fumes."

"Hold…on," Eidolon ground out, his own *dermoire* starting to flicker as well. "Where the fuck is Reaver?"

On the other side of the emergency department, the Harrowgate flashed, and Reaver burst out, followed by Thanatos and Ares, the Horseman known as War. Both Horsemen were fully armored, as if they suspected that this was some sort of trick.

"Let's do it!" Reaver had the vial open before he skidded into the trauma room. Wasting no time, he dumped the contents between Revenant's shredded lips. "Stand back," he said. "Everyone but Shade and E."

Blaspheme stayed. He gave her an I-warned-you-look, but wisely, he didn't argue.

The Harrowgate flashed again, and Limos, her mate Arik, and the last Horseman, Reseph, entered. Great. More people who would witness her breakdown if this failed.

Closing his eyes, Reaver laid his hand on Revenant's forehead. A low-level hum started up, startling Blas when she realized it was coming from Reaver. A golden glow surrounded him, and she watched in fascination as it seeped into Revenant's body.

"Thanatos," Reaver gritted out, "more."

Instantly, Thanatos was there, a dagger in his hand. In a motion so fast she saw only a blur, he sliced into his wrist and placed the laceration against Revenant's mouth. Limos appeared next to her brother, her pregnant belly bumping up against Revenant as she touched her fingers to a single teardrop in the corner of her eye.

"I don't know why I feel the need to do this," she whispered, "but..." She pressed the tips of her wet fingers to Revenant's forehead.

Tears of the hungry. Of Famine.

Reaver's glow intensified, blinding Blaspheme with painful stabs of light. Eidolon and Shade shouted in agony, and then they were blown backward, and the stench of charred flesh filled the room. She heard a commotion, people calling for help, but she was frozen in place, unable to move, let alone see.

She must have blacked out, because a moment later, she felt hands lifting her off the ground.

"Wha... what happened?"

Reaver's blurry face appeared in front of hers. "I warned you."

"Revenant," she gasped. "Is he—"

"I'm... here." Revenant's throaty voice rumbled through her like a long-overdue caress.

She wheeled around, nearly knocking herself over again as her wobbly legs tried to reorient themselves to the new vertical position. Revenant was lying on the table, his body covered only in a sheet up to his waist, and although he was bruised and looked exhausted, he was whole.

"Thank you, oh, gods, thank you." Blaspheme threw herself on him, hugging him hard, as if he hadn't just been pretty dead.

He threw an arm around her, holding her tight against his chest. "What...what happened?"

Reaver gripped Revenant's hand and squeezed. "We won."

"Awesome."

Blaspheme straightened, afraid of hurting the ribs that only moments before had looked like a jigsaw puzzle. "You died. That's not awesome."

"But we imprisoned Satan for a thousand years," Revenant said, his voice as torn up as his body had been.

Shade, his right arm wrapped in bandages, snorted. "Seriously. What did you guys do?"

Reaver frowned down at Revenant. "How did you know they'd be gone for that long? Prophecy?"

Everyone who had gathered outside the room filtered in, and suddenly the tiny space was packed with Horsemen, Seminus demons, and a couple of mates.

"The Pruosi tome." Revenant swallowed. Winced as if his throat was sore. Blas had a feeling he'd be feeling the aches and pains of this battle for a while. "It's kind of a recipe book. I combined a recipe for a brig and an abyss, and both have a shelf life of a thousand years."

"So wait," Eidolon said, wearing bandages that matched Shade's. "You're serious. You're saying you locked Satan in a magical brig and tossed him into an abyss? Satan. *For a thousand years?*"

"And we locked him up with Raphael, Gethel, and Lucifer."

Wraith, lounging against the doorjamb, whistled. "Dude, he's gonna be *pissed* when he gets out."

"We'll worry about that in nine hundred and ninety-nine years," Revenant said. He took Blaspheme's hand

and tugged her down onto the bed. "You didn't perform your ceremony."

"The blood went toward a better use," she said. "And you'll be happy to know that Thanatos willingly gave it to you. And more." She smiled over at the pregnant Horseman. "And Limos gave you her tears."

From near the doorway, Thanatos dipped his head in a slow, respectful nod. Limos rolled her eyes.

"What ceremony?" Wraith asked, and Eidolon used that opportunity to usher everyone out to give them some privacy.

When everyone was gone and Blaspheme was alone with Revenant, she allowed herself to relax. The tautness in his body melted away as well, and for a moment, they lay there in silence, reveling in the relief that the nightmare was over.

"I wish you'd told me what you had planned," she finally said.

"You only would have worried more."

"That's not your call to make," she said sternly. "Next time, you tell me. Got it?"

He chuckled. "The next time I imprison Satan inside a mystical box?"

"You know what I mean," she ground out.

His arms closed even more tightly around her. "I know."

Another comfortable silence wrapped around them, and she almost wished they could remain like this, with no immediate worries, no dealing with anything except recovering from wounds, physical and mental. But at some point they needed to discuss the future, and Blaspheme had spent too much time facing uncertainty to want to delay the talk they had to have.

"So," she said softly. "What now?"

His hand sifted through her hair as she snuggled against his chest. "That depends, I guess."

Her stomach clenched. "On what?"

"On if you can get past what I did to your father."

She pushed up onto her elbow so she could look at him while she spoke. "My mother told me everything. You were right. He was a bastard. And even if he wasn't, you weren't... you. Your past doesn't matter to me, Revenant."

He grinned. "That settles it, then."

"Settles what?"

"We're getting mated."

She nearly swallowed her tongue. "Ah... what?"

"You don't have to say yes right away." His expression turned serious. "But never doubt what I feel for you. I lost everything the day my mother died, including my soul. And when no one else saw the good in me, not even my brother, you did. You brought me back to life in more ways than one, Blaspheme, and I never want to be without that lifeline again." His hand came up to cup her cheek. "I love you, and whether you say yes or no, that will never change."

Tears stung her eyes. "I love you, too," she said, her voice breaking with the force of her emotion. "You let me in when no one else could. Yes, I'll mate you. I'll *so* mate you."

Sliding his hand around the nape of her neck, he drew her down for a kiss so full of promise that the tears let loose. "I want you. Here. Now."

Through her tear-blurred vision, she saw the evidence of that pushing the sheet into a tent. "As your doctor, I would be remiss if I didn't say you should rest and avoid sex."

His eyes shot wide in horror. "For how long?"

With a sly smile, she burrowed her hand under the sheet. "Until I say otherwise." Her palm found him, thick and hard. "For now, I promise you're in good hands."

He groaned. "Who am I to go against doctor's orders?"

Smart male. And as his doctor, she was prepared to give him a lot of orders.

Thirty-Three

An hour after being released from the hospital, Revenant strolled along a deserted tropical beach, face raised to the heavens as he watched seabirds sail across the blue sky. He'd sent out a mental summons to Metatron, and while he hoped the archangel would show up, he'd learned to temper his hopes.

"Hello, Revenant."

Rev almost smiled. Almost. He turned. "You finally deigned to see me, huh?"

Metatron's silver-blue eyes flashed, matching the seizure-inducing, color-shifting robe that reached all the way to the leather sandals on his feet. "I would have responded to your other summons, but—"

"But you were busy," Revenant said with a dismissive wave.

"But you weren't ready," Metatron corrected.

Revenant scowled. "Ready for what?"

"Everything that's happened." Metatron gazed out at the sunset, his face glowing as the sun's golden rays kissed it.

Fucking archangels and their shimmery shit.

"What you and Reaver did...it was something no one else could have done. All of the angels in Heaven combined couldn't have done that."

Revenant snorted. "Yeah, well, it was dumb luck. Reaver and I shouldn't have been able to do what we did. We both should have died."

Metatron turned back to him. "Did you ever wonder why your mother named you Revenant?"

Well, technically she'd named him the Sheoulic equivalent, which was unpronounceable to almost anyone with a tongue.

"I guess." He'd wondered a lot. Mainly because she hadn't given him an angel name.

"Mariel sometimes had clairvoyant episodes," Metatron said softly. "I believe she foresaw your return from the dead, and she gave you a prophetic name to subconsciously guide you. To keep your soul on track to that destiny."

As much as Rev would like to believe Uncle Met, he couldn't see his mother putting that much thought into a fallen angel name when she hadn't put any at all into an angelic one.

"Whatever, Obi-Wan," he muttered. "What does my name have to do with Reaver and I locking Satan away?"

"It has a lot to do with it." Metatron's eerily intense gaze seemed to penetrate all the way to Rev's brain, and he had to wonder if the mighty archangel could tap into all of Revenant's shameful deeds. "You see, your mother was just as clairvoyant with your other name."

For being an archangel, his uncle was kind of clueless. "I don't have another name."

"Of course you do. She smuggled it out of Sheoul, written in blood on the inside of Reaver's swaddling cloth," he said. "And I find it interesting that during your time in Sheoul you were often called The Destroyer, because that's what your angelic name means."

Revenant shook his head to clear it of whatever was affecting his hearing, because Metatron couldn't have just said what he thought he'd said. But the archangel was looking at him expectantly, so maybe Rev *had* heard right.

"What name?" he croaked.

"Abaddon." Metatron's voice sang with resonance so powerful Rev felt it all the way to his marrow. "The dark angel destined to lock Satan away for a thousand years. You were the key, Revenant. When Satan finally breaks out of his prison, Reaver will break the Horsemen's Seals, and the End of Days will kick off. But until then, you and Reaver have given the realms ten hundred years of peace, just as you were prophesied to do."

"What?" He sounded like he was being strangled. "Prophesied? By who?"

Metatron stared. "Haven't you ever read the Bible in any of its forms and translations? You and Reaver have been central to the Apocalypse since the first waters streamed into the Nile. The signs were there from the beginning. You two thick-skulled dopes just kept missing them. Honestly, there were many times I didn't think either one of you would find your path."

"That makes two of us," Revenant muttered. "Wait... if this prophecy is biblical, Satan knew about it, right?"

"No doubt. He had a prophecy written into the *Daemonica* that countered it. That's why your mother hid your name. The prophecy hadn't been written at the time you were born, but again, she saw it coming. She couldn't let your real name be leaked or Satan would have destroyed you. No one, not even the other archangels, knew. My mate and I were alone in that."

Mind. Blown. But now so much made sense. All the hell he, his mother, and Reaver had gone through had been for a purpose.

Which didn't make it any less sucky.

"Did you know my blood can't be cleansed of Satan's taint? Were you in on the bullshit deal Raphael and his cronies offered me?"

"I'm sorry about that, Revenant," Metatron said. "I am aware that there's no way to remove the taint while Satan is still alive, but I didn't know about the deal. I didn't know until after all of this was over that Raphael lied to you. The other archangels who tried to double-cross you will be dealt with. And screw it, you *are* welcome in Heaven whenever you want. On my word, you won't be harassed by any archangel, and we'll repair the damage you cause, even if it takes centuries."

"Thanks," Rev said, even though he didn't intend to step foot in Heaven as long as his presence destroyed everything around him. His mother's memory deserved better than that.

Metatron inclined his head in acknowledgment. "And Revenant, you do realize that Sheoul is yours."

He snorted. "Uncle Met has a sense of humor." He paused. "Oh, hold on...no you don't. You're serious?"

Metatron shrugged. "Satan is gone, and Lucifer's

soul is trapped with him. You are now the most powerful being in Sheoul. You can rule it as you see fit until the time comes when the trap containing Satan fails and Reaver breaks the Horsemen's Seals."

Revenant's lungs seized up. He was hell's new overlord? "I don't...how..."

"It's prophecy, straight from the Book of Revelation," Metatron said. *"And they had a king over them, which is the angel of the bottomless pit, whose name in the Hebrew tongue is Abaddon."* Metatron's expression turned grave. "You can't turn Sheoul into a haven for the good and holy, and you can't eradicate demons. There must be a balance of good and evil in the universe, so Sheoul must continue on as a bastion of malevolence. But that doesn't mean you can't...temper it. You can alter existing laws, even if you can't completely disavow them."

Revenant's mind, already blown from the earlier revelations, couldn't fully comprehend what the archangel was saying. "Like?"

"Like the fact that when humans...or angels...die in Sheoul, their souls must remain in Sheoul for all eternity, to be tortured by any demon who wishes to do so."

"I can release the souls?"

"If you desire."

Revenant practically trembled with that desire. How many tormented souls could he free? Including his mother's and father's. Reseph's baby sister's. So many souls could finally find peace.

"Being Sheoul's big boss is going to take a lot of time," Revenant pointed out. "And I already have a job."

And why in the hell was he arguing, when all along

he'd been scheming to take a position of power in Sheoul? Metatron was offering *the* position of power, and here Revenant was waffling like an idiot.

"With the *Daemonica*'s apocalyptic prophecy completely out of play, the Horsemen no longer need Watchers. Only Reaver can break their Seals now. You're released from your duty, as is Harvester."

Holy shit. "What about Blaspheme? She's a *vyrm*—"

Metatron laughed. "She's not a *vyrm*. She's an angel." While Rev stood there in stunned silence, the archangel continued. "Her mother... what name is she going by now?"

"Deva. Ah... Devastation."

"Huh." Metatron nodded in approval. "Good name. Anyway, she maintained the relationship with Blaspheme's father after Devastation fell, which is why they believed Blaspheme was *vyrm*. But Blaspheme was conceived the day before her mother lost her wings."

Revenant inhaled sharply. "So she was conceived by two angels, not one angel and a fallen."

"Exactly. And your children will also be full angels. They will be welcomed... nay, *embraced*... in Heaven."

Children. By all that was holy and unholy, Revenant never thought he'd go there. When he'd believed he was a fallen angel, some bone-deep instinct warned him to be careful, to not bring a child into the world. But now... now he had a future, and his children would grow up safe and with parents that loved them.

Still... "*Vyrm* persecution has to stop," he said. "I saw the hell Blaspheme went through. All *vyrm* will be welcome in Sheoul."

"Then we'll honor that," Metatron swore. "From this

day forth, no *vyrm* will be hunted. But if any show signs of angelicidal tendencies, we *will* act."

That was fair. "Agreed." Revenant stuck out his hand, but Metatron merely stared. And then, in a move that shocked the shit out of Revenant, Metatron engulfed him in an embrace.

"My nephew," he murmured. "How I've longed for this day. I saw it coming since the day the heavens were formed, but there were times when my vision grew so murky I feared the prophecies had changed." He drew back, and Rev reeled at the emotion flashing in his uncle's eyes. "Welcome home, Revenant. Welcome home."

It was nothing less than an ambush.

Revenant and Reaver, working as a team, flanked Reseph as the Horseman reined his white stallion, Conquest, to a halt on the Oregon beach. The steed snorted and snapped at both Rev and Reaver, who stood just out of the beast's reach.

"'Sup?" Reseph swung down from the saddle, clad in only a pair of swim trunks. The guy wore as few clothes as possible, and Rev swore he was naked more often than not. "I was just exercising the big guy before the barbecue."

The barbecue at Reseph and Jillian's Colorado hideaway was already in full swing, but Reseph knew that. According to Reaver, sometimes when the entire family was together, the Horseman needed to get away for a little while, to try to outrun the memories of what he'd done to his siblings when his Seal had broken and he'd become the evil demon known as Pestilence.

"I have something for you," Revenant said.

"For me?" The blond Horseman eyed Revenant suspiciously. "What would that be?"

"Open a gate to your sister's grave."

Reseph's eyes flared before narrowing. "Ariya? Why?"

"Trust me." It was a bold thing to ask, given their history, but Revenant had always been a risk taker.

Reseph hesitated, the tense silence broken only by the sound of crashing waves and a few seagulls calling out from overhead. Finally, he looked to Reaver, who nodded. "Okay, but if this is a trick, I swear I'll find a way to destroy you."

"Noted."

The Horseman called out to his stallion. "Conquest, to me."

The beast whinnied before dissolving into a spiral of smoke. The tendril of vapor writhed as it fused with Reseph's forearm until it settled into his skin as a tattoo-like glyph in the shape of a horse. No doubt not wanting to take any chances, Reseph armored up with a flick of his finger over the crescent scar on his throat. Instantly, shiny metal plates folded over him from out of nowhere like a damned Transformer.

Revenant had always thought that the Horsemen had been given some really cool gifts.

When the Horseman was fully outfitted, he opened a personal Harrowgate, and one by one, he, Reaver, and Revenant stepped through, coming out on the small island of Steara in Sheoul. The little piece of land was an oasis of greens, reds, and purples, a rare gem in the typical dark ugliness of hell.

Near the beach, in a protected alcove, was a small grave, its hand-carved marble headstone eclipsing the tiny mound that lay in its shadow.

"What's this about, Uncle?" Reseph's voice was rough, edged with more suspicion.

Rev stepped up next to his nephew. "Your baby sister was human. Her soul has been trapped here for thousands of years."

"Thanks for the recap."

Closing his eyes, Revenant opened his mind to his wishes, and a moment later, a blond child, her hair and eyes so similar to Reseph's, was standing before her brother, as tangible as the headstone.

"Say good-bye, Reseph," Revenant said softly. "I've released her soul from Sheoul. In a moment, she'll be carried away to Heaven."

The Horseman fell to his knees in front of her, and both Revenant and Reaver turned away.

"You surprise me, brother." The emotional hitch in Reaver's voice resonated deep inside Revenant. To care so much for someone else was a curse. And a gift.

"Surprised that I'm capable of being nice?"

"No." Reaver's blue eyes sparked. "Surprised that you're aware of Reseph's pain."

"A few weeks ago, I'd have used his pain against him," Rev admitted gruffly. "But since getting my memory back, I know how it feels to know a loved one is suffering." He smirked. "Some people deserve all the suffering they get, and I'm happy to dish it out. But it seems that I've inherited some sort of protective gene from our parents, and I won't let anyone in our family get hurt." His smirk deepened. "Unless I'm the one doing it."

Reaver snorted. "Asshole."

Rev was about to throw down with some of the sibling rivalry they'd missed out on over the eons when Reseph approached, his eyes bloodshot, his expression shadowed with sorrow. And yet an aura of peace surrounded him, as if a shroud had lifted.

"How," Reseph croaked. "How did you do that?"

Rev shrugged. "I'm King Shit down here now."

"I don't know how to thank you."

The old Revenant would have demanded some sort of impossible payment. The new Rev...fuck it, he'd do the same thing. "You can, you know, not be a dick every time you see me."

Reseph winced. "Don't suppose you can come up with something else? I'm a dick to everyone."

That was pretty much what Rev had expected the Horseman to say.

"Yes, you are." He flashed them all to Reseph's place, where all of the Horsemen, their families, and several Underworld General staff members had gathered for the barbecue Reseph had been avoiding. "Let's just leave it at you owe me?"

"Cool." Reseph clapped his hand on Revenant's shoulder. "Thank you. I'm glad you aren't a big tool anymore." Grinning, Reseph headed for his mate, Jillian.

"Your son is a cocky son of a bitch, isn't he?" Rev looked over at his brother, amazed that they were actually standing next to each other at a family gathering. And no blood had been shed.

Reaver barked out a laugh. "Which son?" His gaze lit on each of his offspring before taking in every person milling around the tables of food. "Think our parents would be proud?"

"I think they'd be passed out with relief that all the cards fell into place and that we actually fulfilled some crazy prophecies. The odds of that happening must be astronomically out of whack."

"One in nine hundred trillion, according to Metatron."

Revenant spotted Blaspheme fetching a couple of ice-cold beers from the cooler and offering one to Eidolon's sister-in-law, Idess, but the female grinned broadly and refused, gesturing to her flat belly. Pregnant? Must be.

"Speaking of Metatron, how are things in Heaven?"

Reaver materialized himself a margarita, and one popped into Rev's hand as well. How considerate. "Everyone's still in shock that Raphael is gone, but funny, no one misses him." He smiled as he took a drink. "And Harvester is back to normal. Getting rid of Gethel and Lucifer did the trick. How's Sheoul treating you?"

"I'm King Shit, so, you know." He shrugged. "There are a handful of jackasses trying to sabotage me, but for the most part, life hasn't changed down there." He took a drink of his margarita, dropping bits of salt all over his boots. Didn't even bother him that his perfect brother hadn't displaced a single grain from the rim of his glass. Personal growth was a cool thing. "But I have a thousand years to prepare for the Apocalypse. Lots of time to make sure that when Satan returns, a lot of demons will defect, and those who are left to fight for Team Evil will be unprepared and ineffective. And I'm authorizing Azagoth to reincarnate only neutral and nonevil demon souls."

"Sounds like you've been busy."

Revenant shrugged. "It's a pretty good gig."

For a moment, Reaver was silent, and then he turned to Revenant, his brows drawn in a serious line. "You know you're welcome in Heaven. You and Blaspheme both. We can repair most of the damage you cause—"

Revenant held up his hand, cutting his brother off. "When Blaspheme chooses to make the trip over to Heaven, I'll be here to welcome her back. But I don't belong there."

"Rev—"

"No," Rev said, cutting Reaver off again. "We both know it. It's okay. I'm fucking *ruling* hell, and it's what I was meant to do. It's all cool." He held up his glass and clinked it against Reaver's. "To us. Dysfunctional family and all."

Reaver laughed, and in that moment, Revenant marveled at just how well everything turned out. Everyone at this get-together, plus countless others, had played roles in getting Reaver and Revenant where they were today. Revenant owed these people a huge thank-you. Not that he was going to get all mushy on them. But maybe he'd refrain from threatening to kill anyone for a day or so.

Blaspheme waved from where she was standing next to Limos's mate, Arik, as he flipped burgers and hot dogs on the grill.

"Looks like we'd better join the party," Reaver said.

Party. The word hit Revenant like a sucker punch. He'd attended several parties, but he'd never been invited to one, let alone been *welcome* at one. But here he was at a shindig thrown by his niece and nephews, and they had actually asked him to be here.

"You ready, Brother?" Reaver asked.

Reseph must have turned on the music, because suddenly Rodney Atkins was singing about going through hell and getting out before the devil knew you were there. Revenant looked over at the porch, where Reseph gave a crisp salute and cocky smile.

"Yeah," Rev said, "I'm ready." Ready, for the first time in his life, to be part of a family.

Thirty-Four

Three months later…

Blaspheme stood on the balcony of the home she and Revenant shared on the Italian coastline, her face to the warm morning breeze. She still couldn't believe she lived here with him, and that all her worries were gone.

And it definitely hadn't sunk in that she was an angel. A true, Heavenly angel.

She hadn't entered Heaven yet; to do so would activate *all* her angelic powers and instincts, but it would also render her unable to enter Underworld General. There was no way she could let that happen.

The False Angel enchantment had worn off, leaving her with a limited range of angelic powers and gorgeous violet-tipped white wings that were actually functional. Revenant had taught her to fly…and to make love while riding the thermals.

So for now, she was content with the way things were,

and hey, since Revenant wasn't exactly a traditional angel, either, they made a good pair.

She felt him approach, smiled when his chest pressed against her back as he slipped his arms beneath hers and wrapped them around her midsection.

"I missed you when I woke up." He pressed a kiss into her hair. "I was planning to wake you. With my tongue."

Her knees went weak. "Now *that* is an alarm clock I'd pay good money for."

He rested his chin on her head, tugging her even closer as they both looked out over the sparkling water. "There's always tomorrow."

"Tomorrow?" She placed her hands over his and relaxed against him. "I was thinking...shower? Ten minutes?" She felt the growing swell of his arousal press into her rear, and she casually rubbed against it.

"*One* minute." His husky morning voice deepened further, and she grew hot between her thighs.

"You're very impatient," she mused.

"And you're a tease."

She shrugged. "I guess some False Angel habits are hard to break."

"That's one I don't mind you keeping." He dropped a hand between them, and she felt a cool breeze hit her rump as he lifted the hem of her robe and positioned his erection at her core.

"I think you like my new habits better," she said as she opened herself to her newfound Heavenly powers and generated a low, pulsing vibration that buzzed through every cell. As Revenant entered her, he felt it, too, and he gasped.

"Fuck," he moaned, slamming home with an impatient thrust. "I like. Too much, I think."

Ditto, she thought, because she sure as hell couldn't speak. Already she was climbing the peak of ecstasy, and oh, yes, she *loved* exploring these new talents with Revenant. Last night she'd discovered that she could stimulate him without even touching him. She'd made him come in his leathers the moment he'd flashed into the house from work. He hadn't even gotten a hello out before he was shouting in pleasure.

He'd punished her for that by taking her to the floor and licking her until she begged him to let her climax. Then he'd dragged it out for another five torturous minutes and had used his own power to pummel her with sex, as if she were being caressed by a hundred tongues and being made love to by two thick shafts. A dozen climaxes later, she'd lain in a boneless puddle of bliss until Revenant carried her to the bedroom and held her, petting her and whispering beautiful things she'd never believed a stone-cold warrior would say.

The salt air caressed her face as her climax blasted through her, taking Revenant with her to the highest plane of existence. Their souls merged, tangling together in the way of angels so that their orgasms became one. It churned between them, suspending them in endless pleasure that lingered for an hour, until she realized she was on the verge of being late for work.

Again.

"We...have to stop...doing that," she said through panting breaths. Her arms trembled as she gripped the balcony railing, and it was a miracle they hadn't broken the thing with the intensity of their lovemaking.

"Never."

"Okay," she sighed. "But I really can't keep being late for work."

"We're newlyweds. Eidolon will understand."

No doubt he would. "I do have rules to follow."

"Rules." He snorted. "Sometimes there are work-arounds."

She loved that Revenant had loosened up about rules, even though he remained a stickler about most of them. Still, he was making progress, and she got a secret thrill every time he found a legitimate work-around to a stupid rule.

Smiling, she turned around and lifted her mouth to his. "I love you," she murmured against his lips.

"And I you." He kissed her so thoroughly she was dizzy when he pulled back. "There's not a rule I wouldn't break for you." He dipped his head and nipped her lip as he pushed her back against the railing, his hands burrowing under her robe again, and so much for work.

"I can't be *too* late today," she reminded him. "My mom is coming by the clinic for her second round of stem cell treatment. I really think she'll recover fully."

"Good." He pulled back, just a little, but his hands kept roaming. "Reaver and Harvester invited us to dinner tonight. Wanna go?"

Of course she did. It had taken months for Reaver and Revenant's fragile relationship to blossom, but now they were truly the brothers they should have been from the beginning. They'd even gone to a couple of football games together. Oh, Rev and Harvester still disliked each other, but for the most part, they kept the bloodshed to a minimum. The most shocking thing that had happened over the last three months was that Revenant and Thanatos had grown close. Hell, Revenant now got along with all of the Horsemen.

He did not, however, get along with the hellhounds. Some things never changed.

"Let's do dinner with them," she said, arching into his hand as it slipped between her legs. "And then you're all mine. We have a thousand years to enjoy each other. Let's not waste a minute of it."

A thousand years. Ten centuries of peace between the realms. And then after the Final Battle, when Satan was truly dead and gone, Metatron promised that with Satan's death, Rev's blood would be cleansed of all taint, and all of the heavens would become their sanctuary.

Basically, it would be one big celebration. And Metatron had promised something else.

There were butterflies in Heaven.

Not quite ready to say good-bye?

Go to: LarissaIone.com/blog/Not-The-End for
a special epilogue and a peek into what the
future holds for your favorite Demonica and
Lords of Deliverance characters.

Don't miss the novel that launched
the hot Demonica series!

Tayla is a demon-slayer who hungers
for sensual pleasure, but fears it will
always be denied her. Eidolon is her
avowed enemy—and the one man
who brings her to the brink
of ecstasy...

Please see the next page for
an excerpt from

Pleasure Unbound

One

> The demon is a prince of the air and can transform
> himself into several shapes, delude our senses for a
> time; but his power is determined, he may terrify
> us but not hurt.
>
> —Robert Burton, *Anatomy of Melancholy*

Had Eidolon been anywhere but the hospital, he would
have killed the guy pleading for his life before him.

As it was, he'd have to save the bastard.

"Sometimes, being a doctor blows," he muttered, and
jabbed the demon in a human suit with a syringe full of
hemoxacin.

The patient screamed as the needle passed through
mangled thigh tissue, releasing blood sterilization medi-
cation into the wound.

"You didn't numb him first?"

Eidolon snorted at his younger brother's words. "The

Haven spell keeps me from killing him. It doesn't prevent me from dispensing a little justice during treatment."

"Can't escape your old job, huh?" Shade pushed aside the curtain separating two of the three ER cubicles and stepped fully inside. "The son of a bitch eats babies. Let me wheel him outside and waste his sorry ass."

"Wraith already offered."

"Wraith offers to waste all the patients."

Eidolon grunted. "Probably a good thing our little brother didn't go the doctor route."

"Neither did I."

"You had different reasons."

Shade hadn't wanted to spend that much time in school, especially since his healing gift was better suited to his chosen field, paramedicine. He was all about scraping patients off the street and keeping them alive long enough for the Underworld General staff to fix them.

Blood dripped to the obsidian floor as Eidolon probed the patient's most serious wound. A female Umber demon, the same species as Shade's mother, had caught the patient sneaking into her nursery, and had somehow impaled him—several times—with a toilet brush.

Then again, Umber demons were remarkably strong for their petite size. The females were especially so. Eidolon had, on several occasions, enjoyed the application of that strength in bed. In fact, when he could no longer resist the final maturation cycle his body had entered, he planned to make an Umber female his first *infadre*. Umbers made good mothers, and only rarely did they kill the unwanted offspring of a Seminus demon.

Putting aside the thoughts that plagued him more frequently as The Change progressed, Eidolon glanced at the patient's face. The skin that should have been a deep reddish-brown was now pale with pain and blood loss. "What's your name?"

The patient groaned. "Derc."

"Listen, Derc. I'm going to repair this unsightly hole, but it's going to hurt. A lot. Try not to move. Or scream like a cowering little imp."

"Give me something for the pain, you fucking parasite," he snarled.

"*Doctor* parasite." Eidolon nodded at the equipment tray, and Paige, one of their few human nurses, handed him clamps.

"Derc, buddy, did you eat any of the Umber's young before she caught you?"

Hatred rolled off Shade's body as Derc shook his head, sharp teeth bared, eyes glowing orange.

"Today isn't your lucky day then. Didn't get a meal, and you aren't getting anything for the pain, either."

Allowing himself a grim smile, Eidolon clamped the damaged artery in two places as Derc screamed vile curses and struggled against the restraints that held him on the metal table.

"Scalpel."

Paige handed him the instrument, and he expertly sliced between the clamps. Shade crowded close, watching as he shaved away the shredded artery tissue and then held the newly clean ends together. A warm tingle wound its way down his right arm along his dermal markings to the tips of his gloved fingers, and the artery fused. The baby-eater would no longer have to worry about bleeding out. From the expression on Shade's face, however, he would have to worry about surviving more than two steps outside the hospital.

It wouldn't be the first time he'd saved a life only to have it taken once the patient had been released.

"BP's dropping." Shade's gaze focused on the bedside monitor. "Could be shock."

"There's another bleed somewhere. Bring up his pressure."

Reluctantly, Shade placed his large palm over the bony ridges in Derc's forehead. The numbers on the monitor dipped, raised, and then stabilized, but the change would be temporary. Shade's powers couldn't sustain life that wasn't there, and if Eidolon couldn't find the problem, nothing Shade did would make a difference.

A rapid assessment of the other wounds revealed nothing to explain the drop in vitals. Then, just below the patient's twelfth rib, a fresh scar. Beneath the razor-straight mark, something bubbled.

"Shade."

"Hell's fires," Shade breathed. His gaze snapped up as he raked his fingers through nearly black hair that, at shoulder-length, was longer than but identical in color to Eidolon's. "It might be nothing. It might not be Ghouls."

Ghouls. Not the cannibalistic monsters of human lore, but the term for those who carved up demons to sell their parts on the underworld black market.

Hoping his brother was right but not ripped from the womb yesterday, Eidolon pressed softly on the scar.

"Derc, what happened here?"

"Cut myself."

"This is a surgical scar."

UG was the only medical facility in the world that

performed surgery on their kind, and Derc hadn't been treated here before.

Eidolon caught the pungent stink of fear. "No. It was an accident." Derc clenched his fists, his lidless eyes wild. "You must believe me."

"Derc, calm down. Derc?"

Monitor alarms beeped, and the baby-eater convulsed.

"Paige, grab the crash cart. Shade, keep his vitals up."

An eerie wail seemed to leak from every pore in Derc's skin, and a stench like rotting bacon and licorice filled the small space. Paige lost her lunch in the garbage can.

The heart monitor flatlined. Shade removed his hand from the patient's forehead.

"I hate it when they do that." Wondering what had frightened Derc so badly he'd felt the need to stop his own bodily functions, Eidolon opened the scar with a smooth slash of a scalpel, knowing what he'd find, but needing to see for sure.

Shade dug through his uniform shirt pocket and pulled out his ever-present pack of bubble gum. "What's missing?"

"The Pan Tai sac. It processes digestive waste and returns it to the body so his species never has to urinate or defecate."

"Handy," Shade murmured. "What would someone want with it?"

Paige dabbed her mouth with a surgical sponge, her complexion still greenish, though the patient's death stench had largely dissipated. "The contents are used in some voodoo curses that affect bowel movements."

Shade shook his head and passed the nurse a stick of

gum. "Is nothing sacred anymore?" He turned to Eidolon. "Why didn't they kill him? They've killed the others."

"He was worth more alive. His species can grow another organ in a matter of weeks."

"Which they could harvest." Shade let out a string of curses that included some Eidolon hadn't heard in his hundred years of life. "It's gotta be The Aegis. Sick bastards."

Whoever the bastards were, they'd been busy. Medics had brought in twelve mutilated bodies over the last two weeks, and the violence had escalated. Some of the victims showed evidence of having been carved up while still alive—and awake.

Worse, demons as a whole couldn't care less, and those who did wouldn't cooperate with other species' Councils in order to organize an investigation. Eidolon cared, not only because someone with medical knowledge was involved, but because it was only a matter of time before the butchers nabbed someone he knew.

"Paige, have the morgue fetch the body and let them know I want a copy of the autopsy report. I'm going to find out who these assholes are."

"Doc E!" Eidolon hadn't taken more than a dozen steps when Nancy, a vampire who'd been a nurse since before she was turned thirty years ago, shouted from where she sat behind the triage desk. "Skulk called, said she's bringing in a Cruentus. ETA two minutes."

Eidolon nearly groaned. Cruenti lived to kill, their desire to slaughter so uncontrollable that even while mating they sometimes tore each other apart. Their

AN EXCERPT FROM PLEASURE UNBOUND 379

last Cruentus patient had broken free of his bonds and destroyed half the hospital before he could be sedated.

"Prepare ER two with the gold restraints, and page Dr. Yuri. He likes Cruenti."

"She also said she's bringing a surprise patient."

This time he did groan. Skulk's last surprise turned out to be a dog struck by a car. A dog he'd had to take home with him because releasing it outside the ER would have meant a fresh meal for any number of staff members. Now the damned mutt had eaten three pairs of shoes and taken over his apartment.

Shade seemed torn between wanting to be irritable with Skulk, his Umber sister, and wanting to flirt with Nancy, whom he'd already bedded twice that Eidolon knew about.

"I'm going to kill her." Clearly, irritability won out.

"Not if I get to her first."

"She's off-limits to you."

"You never said I can't kill her," Eidolon pointed out. "Just that I can't sleep with her."

"True." Shade shrugged. "You kill her, then. My mom would never forgive me."

Shade had that right. Though Eidolon, Wraith, and Shade were purebred Seminus demons with the same long-dead sire, their mothers were all of different species, and of them, Shade's was the most maternal and protective.

Red halogen beacons rotated in their ceiling mountings, signaling the ambulance's approach. The light splashed crimson around the room, bringing out the writing on the gray walls. The drab shade hadn't been Eidolon's first choice, but it held spells better than any other color, and in a hospital where everyone was someone's mortal enemy, every advantage was critical. Because of that, the symbols and incantations had been modified to increase their protective powers.

Instead of paint, they'd been written in blood.

The ambulance pulled into the subterranean facility's bay, and Eidolon's adrenaline shot hotly into his veins. He loved this job. Loved managing his own little piece of hell that was as close to heaven as he'd ever get.

The hospital, located beneath New York City's bustling streets and hidden by sorcery right under the clueless humans' noses, was his baby. More than that, it was his promise to demonkind—whether they lived in the bowels of the earth or aboveground with the humans—that they would be treated without discrimination, that their race was not forsaken by all.

The sliding ER doors whooshed open, and Skulk's paramedic partner, a werewolf who hated everyone and everything, wheeled in a bloodied Cruentus demon that had been securely strapped to the stretcher. Eidolon and Shade fell into step with Luc, and though they both topped six feet three, the were's extra three inches and thick build dwarfed them.

"Cruentus," Luc growled, because he never made any other noises even while in human form, as he was now. "Found unconscious. Open tib-fib fracture to the right leg. Crush wound to the back of the skull. Both injuries are sealing. Nonsealing deep lacerations to the abdomen and throat."

Eidolon raised an eyebrow at that last. Only gold or magically enhanced weapons could have caused nonsealing wounds. All other injuries closed up on their own as the Cruentus regenerated.

"Who summoned help?"

"Some vamp found them. The Cruentus and"—he cocked one long-nailed thumb back toward the ambulance, where Skulk had rolled out the secondary stretcher—"*that.*"

Eidolon halted in his tracks, Shade with him. For a moment, they both stared at the unconscious humanoid female. One of the medics had cut away her red leather clothes that lay like flayed flesh beneath her. She now wore only restraints, matching black panties and bra, and a variety of weapons sheaths around her ankles and forearms.

A chill went up his double-jointed spine, and fuck no, this would not happen. "You brought an Aegis slayer into my ER? What in all that's unholy were you thinking?"

Skulk huffed, looked up at him with flashing gunmetal eyes that matched her ashen skin and hair. "What else was I supposed to do with her? Her partner is rat chow."

"The Cruentus took out an Aegi?" Shade asked, and when his sister nodded, he raked his gaze over the injured human. Average humans posed little threat to demons, but those who belonged to The Aegis, a warrior guild sworn to slay them, weren't average. "Never thought I'd thank a Cruentus. You should have turned this one into rat chow too."

"Her injuries might do the job for us." Skulk rattled off the list of wounds, all of which were serious, but the worst, the punctured lung, had the potential to kill the fastest. Skulk had performed a needle decompression, and for now, the slayer was stable, her color good. "And," she added, "her aura is weak, thin. She hasn't been well for a long time."

Paige drifted toward them, her hazel eyes gleaming with something close to awe. "Never seen a Buffy before. Not a live one, anyway."

"I have. Several." Wraith's gravelly voice came from somewhere behind Eidolon. "But they didn't stay alive for long." Wraith, nearly identical to his brothers except for his blue eyes and shoulder-length bleached-blond hair, took control of the stretcher. "I'll take her outside and dispose of her."

Dispose of her. It was the right thing to do. After all, it was what The Aegis had done to their brother, Roag, a loss Eidolon still felt like a hole in the soul. "No," he said, grinding his teeth at his own decision. "Wait."

As tempting as it was to let Wraith have his way, only three types of beings could be turned away at UG, according to the charter he himself drafted, and Aegis butchers weren't among those listed, an oversight he intended to correct. Granted, as the equivalent to a human hospital's chief of staff, he had the final say, could send the woman to her death, but they'd just been handed a rare opportunity. His personal feelings about slayers would have to be put aside.

"Take her to ER one."

"E," Shade said in a voice that had gone low with disapproval, "catch and release in this case is a bad idea. What if it's a trap? What if she's wearing some sort of tracking device?"

Wraith looked around as though he expected Aegis slayers—"Guardians," they called themselves—to pop in from nowhere.

"We're protected by the Haven spell."

"Only if they attack from the inside. If they find out where we are, they could go Bin Laden on the building."

"We'll fix her and worry about the rest later." Eidolon wheeled the human into the prepared room, both paranoid brothers and Paige on his heels. "We have an opportunity to learn about them. The knowledge we could gain outweighs the dangers."

He removed the restraints and lifted her left hand. The silver-and-black ring on her pinky finger looked innocent enough, but when he removed it, the Aegis shield engraved on the inside of the band confirmed her identity and sent a chill through his heart. If the rumors were true, any jewelry bearing the shield was imbued with powers that bestowed slayers with night vision, resistance to certain spells, the ability to see through invisibility mantles, and gods knew what else.

"You'd better know what you're doing, E." Wraith whipped the curtain closed to shut out the gawking staff.

Judging by the number of onlookers, they'd probably been paged. *Come see the Buffy, the nightmare that lurks in our closets.*

"Not so scary now, are you, little killer?" Eidolon murmured as he gloved up.

Her upper lip curled as though she'd heard him, and he suddenly knew he wouldn't lose this patient. Death despised strength and stubbornness, qualities that radiated from her in waves. Unsure if her survival would be a good thing or a bad one, he cut away her bra and inspected the chest lacerations. Shade, who had been hanging around while waiting for his medic shift to start, managed her vitals, his gifted touch easing her labored, gurgling breaths.

"Paige, type her blood and get me some human O while we're waiting."

The nurse set to work, and Eidolon widened the slayer's most serious wound with a scalpel. Blood and air bubbled through damaged lung and chest wall tissue as he inserted his fingers and held the ragged edges together for fusion.

Wraith folded his thick arms over his chest, his biceps twitching as if they wanted to lead the charge to kill the slayer. "This is going to bite us in the ass, and you two are too stupid and arrogant to see it."

"Ironic, isn't it," Eidolon said flatly, "that *you* would lecture *us* on arrogance and stupidity."

Wraith flipped him the bird, and Shade laughed. "Someone got up on the wrong side of the crypt. You jonesing for a fix, bro? I saw a tasty-looking junkie topside. Why don't you go eat him?"

"Screw you."

"Shut up," Eidolon snapped. "Both of you. Something isn't right. Shade, look at this." He adjusted the overhead light. "I haven't been to med school in decades, but I've treated enough humans to know this isn't normal."

Shade peered at the woman's organs, at the tangled mass of veins and arteries, at the strange ropes of nerve tissue that wove in and out of muscle and spongy lung. "Looks like a bomb went off in there. What is all that?"

"No idea." He'd never seen anything like the mess that had scrambled the slayer's insides. "Check this out." He pointed to a blackened blob that resembled a blood clot. A pulsing, morphing blood clot that, as they watched, swallowed healthy tissue. "It's like it's taking over."

Eidolon peeled back the gelled mass. His breath caught, and he rocked back on his heels.

"Hell's rings," Shade breathed. "She's a fucking demon."

"*We're* fucking demons. She's some other species."

For the first time, Eidolon allowed himself a frank, unhurried look at the nearly naked woman, from her black-painted toes to matted hair the color of red wine. Smooth skin stretched over curves and lean muscle that even in unconsciousness conveyed coiled, deadly strength. Probably in her midtwenties, she was in her prime, and if she weren't a murderous fiend, she'd be hot. He fingered her ruined clothing. He'd always been a sucker for women in leather. Preferably, short leather skirts, but tight pants would do.

Wraith tipped the woman's chin back and inspected her face. "I thought Aegi were human. She looks human. Smells human." His fangs flashed as his tongue swiped at the bloody punctures in her throat. "Tastes human."

Eidolon probed a peculiar valve bisecting the transverse colon. "What did I say about tasting patients?"

"What?" Wraith asked innocently. "We had to know if she's human."

"She is. Aegi are human." Shade shook his head, making his stud earring glint in the light from the overhead. "Something's wrong here. It's like she's infected with a demon mutation. Maybe a virus."

"No, she was born this way. She's got a demon parent. Look." Eidolon showed his brother the genetic proof, the organs that had formed from a human-demon union, something that occurred more frequently than most knew, but that human doctors diagnosed as certain "syndromes." "Her physical abnormalities could be a birth defect. Or maybe these two species aren't compatible genetically. She was probably born with some unusual traits, ones she's been hiding or that haven't been blatantly noticeable. Like better-than-average eyesight. Or telepathy. But I'll bet my stethoscope this is causing problems now."

"Like what?"

"Could be anything. Maybe she's losing her hearing or pissing herself in public." Excited, because this kind of thing made his corner of hell interesting, he glanced up at Shade, who palmed her forehead and closed his eyes.

"I can feel it," he said, his voice rough with the effort he expended to go deep into her body at the cellular level. "Some of her DNA feels fragmented. We can fuse it. We could—"

Wraith let out a disgusted snort. "Don't even think about it. If you fix her, you could turn her into some sort of uber assassin. That's all we need hunting us."

"He's right," Shade agreed, the glossy black of his eyes going flat. "Depending on the species, it's possible that we could turn her damn near immortal."

Sedating and medicating could also prove difficult, given the unidentified demon DNA. Something as seemingly innocent as aspirin could kill her.

Eidolon studied her for a moment, thinking. "We'll take care of her immediate injuries, and deal with the rest later. She should have the choice about whether or not she wants the demon half to be integrated."

"Choice?" Wraith scoffed. "You think she gives her victims a choice? You think Roag had a choice?"

Though Eidolon often thought about their fallen brother, hearing his name out loud was a punch to the gut. "Do you give your victims a choice?" he asked softly.

"I have to feed."

"You need to drink blood. You don't need to kill."

Wraith pushed away from the wall. "You're an asshole." Lashing out with one arm, he sent a tray full of surgical instruments flying and swept out of the room.

Shade crouched to help Paige pick up the mess. "You shouldn't provoke him."

"You're the one who brought up the junkie."

"He knows I was yanking his chain. He's been clean for months."

Eidolon wished he could share Shade's certainty. Wraith liked to escape his life now and then, but since their species was immune to drug and alcohol highs unless the substances had been processed through human blood, eating a human druggie was Wraith's only path to blotto.

"I'm tired of coddling him," Eidolon said, pulling another tray of instruments to him. "Let alone constantly yanking his ass out of trouble."

"He needs time."

"Ninety-eight years isn't enough time? Shade, in two years he's going to go through his transition. He's not ready. He'll get us all killed."

Shade said nothing, probably because there was nothing to say. Their brother was out of control, and as the only Seminus demon in history to have been conceived by a vampire female, he was alone and had no idea how to handle his urges and instincts. As a male who had been tortured in the most heinous ways imaginable by the vampires who'd raised him, he had no idea how to live life at all.

Not that Eidolon had room to judge. He'd spent the last half-century concentrating on nothing but medicine, but unless he found a mate, in a few months his focus would shift and narrow until he became a mindless beast that functioned on instinct alone.

Maybe he should let the Buffy kill him now and get it over with.

He looked down at her, at the deceptively innocent face, and wondered just how easily and remorselessly she'd take him down.

Before she could do that, though, he'd have to fix her.

"Paige, scalpel."

Awareness came slowly, in a haze of black blotches punctuated by points of light. Warm, elastic darkness tugged at Tayla, luring her toward slumber, but pain prodded her into consciousness. Every inch of her body ached, and her head felt heavy, too large for her neck to support. Groaning, she opened her eyes.

Fuzzy, shadowy images swirled and pulsed in front of her. Gradually, her vision came into focus, and whoa... she must be in another realm, because the dark-haired man staring down at her was a god. His lips, glistening sensuously as if he'd just licked them, were moving, but the buzz in her ears drowned out his words.

She narrowed her eyes and concentrated on his mouth. Name. He wanted her name. She had to think about it for a second before she remembered. Great. She must have hit her head. Which, duh, explained the headache.

"Tayla," she croaked, and wondered why her throat hurt so much. "Tayla Mancuso. I think. Does that sound right to you?"

He smiled, and if she weren't dying on some type of table, she'd have appreciated the sexy curve of his mouth and the flash of very white teeth. The guy must have a fab dentist.

"Tayla? Can you hear me?"

She could, but the buzzing lingered. "Uh-huh."

"Good." He put a hand on her forehead, allowing her a glimpse of one muscular arm adorned by intricate, swirling tribal tattoos. "You're at a hospital. Is there anything I need to know? Allergies? Medical conditions? Parentage?"

She blinked. Had he said "parentage"? And could eyelashes hurt? Because hers did.

"This is a waste of time." The new speaker, an exotic-looking man, Middle Eastern, maybe, glared down at her.

"Go handle your own patients, Yuri." The hot doctor with the espresso eyes shoved Yuri aside. "Can you answer my question, Tayla?"

Right. Allergies, parentage, medical conditions. "Um, no. No allergies." No parents, either. And her medical condition wasn't something she could share.

"Okay then. I'm going to give you something to help you sleep, and if it doesn't kill you, when you wake up you'll feel better."

Better would be good. Because if she felt a little less like she'd been run over by a truck, she could jump on Dr. Hottie.

The very fact that she wanted to jump Dr. Hottie told her more about the state of her head trauma than anything else, but what the hell. The pretty nurse had just injected her with something that totally rocked, and if she wanted to think about boinking a bronzed, tattooed, impossibly handsome doctor who was so far out of her league she needed a telescope to see him, then screw it.

Screw him. Over and over.

"I'll bet you could make a woman throw out all her toys." Had she said that out loud? The cocky grin on his face told her that yes, she'd verbalized her runaway thoughts. "Drugs talking. Don't get excited."

"Paige, push another milligram," he said in his rich, smooth doctor voice.

A warm, burning sensation washed through her veins from the IV line in the back of her hand. "Mmm, trying to get rid of me, huh?"

"That's already been discussed."

Damn, this guy was saying some weird shit. Not that it mattered. Her eyes wouldn't open anymore, and her body wouldn't work. Only her ears still seemed to function, and as she drifted off, she heard one last thing.

"Wraith, I already told you. You can't kill her."

Aww. Her hot doctor was protecting her. She'd have smiled if her face hadn't frozen. And clearly, her hearing had gone, too, because he couldn't have tacked on what she thought he tacked on.

"Yet."

Two

Someone was having sex nearby. Eidolon could feel it. Smell it. The ability was part of his breed's gift; any Seminus demon within thirty yards would sense the same thing. As he walked, the scent of arousal grew stronger, making his body tighten and his balls throb. At any given time someone was screwing in the hospital—usually Wraith—but this time he scented only a female.

Normally, such arousal was a beacon for any incubus, but Eidolon had always fought the urge to seek out the horny female and take advantage of her lust. At least he had resisted the urge until a few months ago, when he'd entered his hundredth year and had begun The Change. Resistance had grown increasingly hard and painful. As his dick was at this moment.

Dammit, Wraith or Shade had better find the female and satisfy her cravings before they became too much of a distraction—or temptation—for him.

He moved swiftly through the dim corridors, nodding greetings to passing staff members, and as he approached the slayer's room, the scent of arousal became almost overwhelming. A low, drawn-out moan forced him to bite back his own sound of need.

Muttering obscenities, he brushed past the two imps stationed outside her chamber and armed with enough sedatives to bring down a Gargantua demon and entered.

Tayla lay on the hospital bed, fists clenched, her chest heaving with her panting breaths. His own breath froze as she cried out and tilted her hips as though taking some imaginary lover inside her.

Standing at the foot of the bed, his brother smirked. Eidolon should have known.

"Get out of her head, Wraith."

"You're just jealous because you don't have this power."

Eidolon inhaled deeply and prayed to the Two Gods for patience. Wraith's mercurial moods made it difficult to deal with him in any circumstance, but throw any of his primal instincts—sex, violence, blood-hunger—into the mix, and Wraith went from difficult to impossible.

"Wraith..."

"Chill, eldest male sibling. She kills our kind. I'm seeing how she feels about screwing us." He shot Eidolon a sideways glance. "Screwing you, anyway. I'm a little more selective about my partners than you are, so I'm feeding her your images."

Eidolon almost laughed. The words "Wraith" and "selective" canceled each other out. Both Shade and Eidolon preferred humanoid sex partners, though his preferences would soon change. But with the exception of humans and vampires, Wraith would nail anything that breathed. Though even that seemed to be optional.

Tayla's head thrashed back and forth, and suddenly he pictured her under him, doing the same as he pounded into her. He'd tangle his hands in fistfuls of her fiery hair and fuck her until she climaxed so hard she'd beg him to stop, and then he'd make her come again just to show her he could. His cock twitched, and he ground his teeth because this line of thinking was one that could only lead to No Way in Hell.

"Knock it off," he growled, knowing his brother would catch the scent of his own arousal if this didn't stop. "She'll tear her stitches."

The reasoning was weak; it had been twenty-four hours since Eidolon had patched her up, and in addition to his healing touch, she'd been bathed in regenerative waters and had received recuperative potions and spells from other, specialized staff members. She'd be up and running and killing demons as soon as the sedatives wore off. Which reminded him that they needed to fit her with restraints immediately. The Haven spell would prevent her from hurting anyone, but she could still tear the hospital apart.

"You know, I thought the *s'genesis* would loosen you up. It's only wedged that stick farther up your ass." Wraith elbowed Eidolon on the way to the door, and then halted with a knowing grin. "Or maybe not. E, man, you smell like a virgin male in a brothel who can't decide which whore to hump." He grimaced. "And eew. Dude, she's a Buffy. I'd sooner shove my dick into a month-dead corpse."

"You probably have."

Wraith snorted. "Eliminates the obligatory cuddling

afterward." He reached for the door handle, but drew up short. "Oh, Gemella called. Wants you to get in touch. Lucky bastard."

"It's not like that."

Gem, a demon masquerading as a human intern in a human hospital, regularly checked in with Eidolon, mainly to share intel on the types of demon activity that came through her hospital. He'd tried to talk her into working for him, but she felt her duty was to follow in her parents' footsteps, using her skills to intercept human-demon issues that would create questions if discovered by human physicians.

"Whatever. You ought to make it *like that*. She's hot."

Wraith sauntered out of the room, and Eidolon turned back to the slayer. Wraith had gone, but Tayla still squirmed. Her sheet had fallen to the floor, and the hospital gown had ridden up to her waist, revealing her silky black panties. He didn't need to touch to know they were soaked. Her scent, her sexual perfume, hung so thick and heavy in the air that it was only a matter of time before he became drunk with it.

"Damn you, Wraith," he muttered, and moved to Tayla's side.

Stay detached. Professional.

Yeah, because the erection popping a tent in the front of his scrubs was real fucking professional.

Willing his pulse to idle out, he lifted her gown and methodically checked her most serious injuries, which looked good, nearly healed. Only one of the wounds had required sutures, and her writhing hadn't disturbed the stitches.

"Yes," she whispered, and grasped his hand where it

rested on her rib cage. Her needs came to him in a rush of visions, a riot of tangled limbs and sweaty skin, and gods help him, a surge of excitement rocked his entire reproductive system.

Tamp it down, E.

He tried to pry her fingers loose with his other hand, but her iron grip tugged him upward to her breast. Beneath his palm, her flesh felt tight, hot, fevered in a way no thermometer would register. Her areola puckered at his touch, and his own body hardened in response. If he were made of stone he couldn't be any harder.

Eidolon exhaled slowly, reaching deep for control. He'd been born to the Judicia, demons known for cool, calm logic, something that didn't come naturally to him, but that he'd honed to perfection over the years both while growing up and later, when he'd served as all Judicium did, as a Justice Dealer.

But all those years fell away as he looked at Tayla. Even half-asleep, seductive, deadly power bled from her pores. She could crush him between her thighs and he'd beg her to make it hurt. *Idiot.* His brothers might like to mix it up with females like her, but Eidolon's tastes in bedmates ran more on the civilized side.

"Tayla." He struggled with her strength and his own desire as he drew his hand back. She was a killer of his people. A butcher. "*Slayer.* Wake up."

She shook her head and reached out blindly. He grasped her face between his palms and held her still. Using his thumbs, he lifted her eyelids. Pupils were equal and responsive when he turned her face toward the overhead light, though she didn't seem to see him.

Damn, she had beautiful eyes. Green rimmed with

gold, and so expressive that he doubted she could shield her thoughts from anyone. Pale freckles shimmered just beneath the surface of her creamy skin. High cheekbones added definition to her slightly rounded face, marred by the faintest tinge of a healing bruise. He let his gaze travel to her mouth, her pouty lips that parted slightly to let out the sounds of wanton desperation.

He wanted to take that mouth. Wanted to feel it take him.

Human medicine demanded ethics. Here, at Underworld General, if he, or any doctor, screwed every patient who came through the doors, few would care.

Eidolon happened to be one of the few.

Moral codes were not his concern; doctors didn't screw patients in his hospital not because it was "wrong," but because the hospital teetered in a precarious position. Demons weren't a trusting sort. Most held a distrust, even contempt, for those with power. Doctors with scalpels could kill. If word got out that the doctors were raping their patients, even fewer demons would trust the hospital's services.

As a result, most of the staff had agreed to keep their paws, claws, and teeth off the patients. Naturally, there had been exceptions and indiscretions.

Hell, he'd be willing to make an exception with the right woman, but an Aegi killer wasn't the right woman, no matter how much his throbbing cock argued that she was.

"Doc."

Tayla was looking at him, her eyes glittering with a combination of determination and lust so potent that he drew a startled breath. Her hand came up, grasped a handful of his hair near the nape, and pulled his head down with such force that he barely had time to brace his hands on either side of her head before his mouth came down hard on hers.

Her tongue pushed past his lips to tangle with his, and he growled at the taste of her. Her flavor was bold and wicked, like the scent of her lust, but beneath it all lurked a faint sweetness, as though innocence had been buried.

Buried under the corpses of his brethren she'd killed, most likely.

An icy blast speared his chest and he reared back, his control balancing on a scalpel's edge. This was his greatest fear, the loss of restraint as The Change took him— the *s'genesis* had to be the reason he was on the verge of mounting the enemy like a beast in rut.

But when her hand brushed his shaft, the beast suddenly didn't care who she was or what she'd done. He was a Seminus demon, after all, a breed of incubi that lived for sex, existed to deceive and cause misery through intimate means once the *s'genesis* was complete. Perhaps now wasn't the time to fight his nature. Perhaps his nature *was* his weapon against an age-old enemy.

Her fingers closed around his sex through his scrub pants, and fuck, he was tired of analyzing his body, his emotions, and his instincts. It was time to just feel.

He rocked his hips into her touch as desire rocked the rest of his body.

"Please," she begged against his lips, "please. Touch me."

Groaning, he dropped a hand down to one hip and lifted her so that his erection nudged her other hip.

So much for remaining professional.

Do you love fiction with a supernatural twist?

Want the chance to hear news about your favourite authors (and the chance to win free books)?

Keri Arthur
Kristen Callihan
P.C. Cast
Christine Feehan
Jacquelyn Frank
Larissa Ione
Darynda Jones
Sherrilyn Kenyon
Jayne Ann Krentz and Jayne Castle
Lucy March
Martin Millar
Tim O'Rourke
Lindsey Piper
Christopher Rice
J.R. Ward
Laura Wright

Then visit the Piatkus website and blog
www.piatkus.co.uk | www.piatkusbooks.net

And follow us on Facebook and Twitter
www.facebook.com/piatkusfiction | www.twitter.com/piatkusbooks

piatkus